A SKY UNBROKEN

A Sky Unbroken

Book 3 of the Earth & Sky trilogy

Megan Crewe

SKYSCAPE

SKYSCAPE

Text copyright © 2015 Megan Crewe

Published by Skyscape, New York
www.apub.com

Amazon, the Amazon logo, and Skyscape are trademarks of Amazon.com, Inc., or its affiliates.

ISBN-13: 9781503946576
ISBN-10: 1503946576

Cover design by Krista Vossen
Interior design by Girl Friday Productions

Printed in the United States of America

To Chris, with every sort of love

1.

Skylar

I wake up in a darkened room stiff and aching, and alone.

When I open my eyes, there's nothing to see. Not a speck of light. The floor I'm slumped on is cool and hard. A familiar mineral smell laces the air. I grope out with my hands and feet and find walls on all sides. The space isn't much bigger than my bedroom closet at home.

Home.

A wave of fire rushing through Earth's atmosphere, searing across the planet's surface as I watch from above. Flaming red-and-violet clouds roiling in its wake. Every particle of living blue and green burnt away.

My stomach heaves. I tilt my head, gagging on acid-soured spit. Then I push myself away, off the floor, until my back smacks the wall behind me. Sitting there, I wipe my mouth. My legs tremble. I don't think I could stand up if I wanted to.

My home is gone. My house, my street, my school, the park where I ran cross-country practice, Michlin Street with its cafes and the pie shop and Angela's favorite thrift store and—

Angela. Mom and Dad. Lisa. Evan. My grandparents. Every classmate and teacher. Every one of my neighbors. Everyone . . .

The horror of it swells inside me, suffocating me. My eyes burn. Gone. They're all gone.

My mind balks—twists away from the thought and skitters around the fringes like a mouse trapped in a cage with an elephant. There's no room for the full truth of it inside me. But there's nothing else. Just me, alone in the dark. I lower my head and rock.

I don't realize I'm crying until the sobs start hitching out of me, tears dripping off my cheeks, salt on my lips. A strange, low sound rips up from my chest, as if my body is trying to drown out the truth. As if, if I drown it out, it will stop being true. I squeeze my arms around my knees, still rocking.

No. No. No. I refuse to accept it.

• • •

I'm not sure how long it's been when I come back to myself. I'm suddenly aware of the rawness in my throat and on my face where I've rubbed it against my jeans, of the dampness seeped down the collar of my shirt, and of the multiplying threes spinning out like an echo in the back of my head: *3 times 19,683 is 59,049. 3 times 59,049 is 177,147. 3 times 177,147 is . . .*

The knowledge of what's happened is still there, looming like a distant mountainside behind my consciousness. I hold off from looking closer. As long as it's over there, tangible but separate from the rest of my thoughts, I feel more like myself. I can't deal with the enormity of this catastrophe right now. I'd get further trying to factor infinity.

Instead, I drag in breaths slow and even, and press my palms against the cool floor. There's a hint of a tremor in the surface beneath me. I'm still on a ship, I think. A ship that's moving rather quickly, even by Kemyate standards, for that tremor to be perceptible.

I was on a ship when it happened. Tabzi's brother's pleasure jetter. In the navigation room, staring through the view screen at those churning clouds . . .

Win said the bomb used the same technology that led to the accidental destruction of his planet and forced the Kemyate survivors onto the space station orbiting above it millennia ago. I traveled down to their former planet as part of a mining expedition. There wasn't the slightest sign of life, just dull brown land, dull gray water. That's what Earth must look like now.

My gut lurches, and I shy away from the image. Not going there. I have to deal with what's happening right now first.

My impressions of what followed the detonation are fragmented. A squad of Kemyate police burst in with Thlo in their midst. The six of us stared at them, and at her, the woman who'd led our group of rebels to that point. At her impenetrable eyes as she flicked her hand toward the Enforcers. I remember the out-of-tune twang of a blaster and Isis's body crumpling, black-and-red curls scattering; Britta leaping up and shot too. Thlo gesturing to me. "*Take care of that one.*"

Win threw himself in front of me and caught that blast, but it didn't matter. As I reached for him where he was sprawled and gasping, another crackle hit the back of my head.

Nothing after that but blackness.

I have no sense of how long I was out. Obviously I was moved from the navigation room—but how far? Am I even on the same ship?

And where are the others? The Enforcers shot to numb, not to kill . . . While I was watching, at least. They could all be gone too. Tabzi and Emmer, who I hardly knew, but who came through when we needed them most. Isis, who took charge in Thlo's absence in her usual mellow but focused way. Britta, who risked her life with me, distracting the ships that came to stop us, smiling all the way. And Win. The one person I've been able to count on all along, who was protecting me right until the end.

I hug myself, feeling the echo of his embrace. The last time I held him, I knew it was supposed to be the last. I was supposed to leave and never see him again. But at least I was going to know he was okay, working toward the future he'd dreamed of.

Maybe he, and the rest of them, *are* still okay. I'm alive, after all, despite being an Earthling brought into Kemya illegally, allowed to witness every aspect of their lives and tech. "Standard protocol" would dictate I should have been killed immediately.

Unless the Enforcers wanted to interrogate me first.

Thlo wouldn't like that, if she's sticking to her cover story, pretending to be loyal to Kemya's Council of leaders. So many things I could tell the Enforcers about who's been behind the rebel activities all these years.

I brace my feet against the floor and my back against the wall. I don't know what I'm going to do when someone does show up, but I'm not giving up without a fight. Even if my world, and all the people I was fighting for, are . . .

Not thinking about it. Not thinking about it. Not thinking about it.

Time passes, and the darkness doesn't waver. The slight tremor in the floor never ebbs. No sound penetrates the walls.

No one comes.

My stomach is too unsettled for hunger, but my mouth has gone dry and ashy. The back of my head aches where the Enforcer's blast hit it, though the skin itself doesn't feel bruised. I could rest my forehead on my knees and shut my eyes, just for a moment—but I'm worried I'm so worn out it won't be just a moment.

My eyelids are starting to droop of their own accord when a rectangle of light whispers open in front of me. I barely have time to register a silhouetted figure before the blaster twangs.

· · ·

The second time I wake up, it's to a spread of thin, interlocking lines glowing across a low ceiling. I'm lying down, with a pressure around my neck, forearms, and calves that prevents me from making any movement larger than a twitch. A stinging pain shoots up my arm when I test the restraints at my left, as if I've been stung on the inside of my wrist.

"*It isn't active yet,*" a man says in Kemyate, beyond my view. "*Ask her what you want, and tell me when to . . . it.*"

What isn't active? A figure moves into my line of sight. A woman, dark-skinned and muscular, with a blaster attached to the silvery belt around her waist. She's an Enforcer.

I stiffen as her eyes meet mine. She cocks her head, the corners of her lips curled down.

"I have a few questions for you," she says in English, her intonation flat. "You came from Earth, how long ago?"

Two months. Two months since Win and I chased Jeanant, the rebels' former leader, around my planet and through its history, collecting the pieces of the weapon he'd hidden there when his mission to free Earth had failed. Two months since Win invited me come to Kemya with him, to see that mission finally carried through. I don't know how much of that the Enforcers have already figured out. So I say nothing.

The woman doesn't press, just moves on. "You aided your Kemyate 'friends' in planning to disable Earth's time field generator?"

We didn't just plan—we succeeded. For maybe ten glorious minutes, Earth was free of the Kemyate scientists and Travelers who'd been tweaking our past across thousands of years of experiments.

Ten glorious minutes before Emmer spotted the bomb dropping into the atmosphere.

"Yes," I say. No point in denying the obvious.

"Did you intend to return to Kemya after this?"

"No," I say. "I wanted to go home and forget you all even exist."

I've choked up. The Enforcer's mouth curls again, this time into what looks like a smirk. Am I amusing her?

"You dislike Kemya so much?" she asks.

"Kemya is fine," I say roughly. "I just prefer Earth. I wanted us to be free, and to go back to my life the way it was. That's all."

"And now?"

Now all that is gone. It takes me a moment to find my voice again. I am not going to cry in front of her.

"I don't know."

"You wanted to free Earth," she goes on without pausing. "Why do you think your 'friends' did this?"

Partly for the same reason as me, but I don't think mentioning that will help. "Because they care about Kemya," I say. "They wanted the experiments to stop so you would start looking for a new planet to settle on—a real home."

"What did they have planned next?"

"Nothing. We were done. That was all we wanted." Fear prickles through me. I can't help adding, "Where are they? My friends?"

The Enforcer ignores me. She raises a hand to her ear, and then steps away. After a moment, she murmurs something I can't make out. Talking to someone through a communicator?

"*Finished,*" she says after a minute to someone else in the room. "*Start it.*"

Finished? She hasn't asked about the others who might have been helping us six, or who was leading us, or anything else I would have expected. Who interrupted the interrogation, and what did they say to her?

There's a mechanical click near my head. My wrist stings again, but only for an instant.

"*How long does it take to . . . ?*" a new voice asks, nasal sharp. My chest clenches.

"*The effect begins immediately,*" the man from before answers. "*It will take a short time to adapt to her . . . reactions.*"

A different woman appears by my feet. A slim woman with sleek, white-blond hair and milky skin.

Kurra. The Enforcer who tracked Win and me on Earth, who almost caught me on Kemya. Who I watched turn a little Earthling boy's face into a blackened crisp outside a cave in Vietnam. My pulse skitters as her ice-gray eyes peer down at me. She's going to— I have to—

The rush of panic has barely hit me before it retreats, as if my body is a sponge and the feeling has been absorbed back into it.

My throat prickles with a vaguely yeasty taste. I stare up at Kurra. Someone else is talking. Not my language. But I should be able to—

A few phrases penetrate my scattered thoughts. " . . . *orders were to . . . with the others . . . not a problem of . . .*"

"You know me," Kurra says. My attention snaps back to her. Another jolt of terror lurches up, and just as quickly is sucked away.

I can't think. What was—

She's looking at me. She asked a question. "Yes," I say.

"I have you now," she says. "Are you frightened?"

The next jab of panic is little more than a flicker, there and gone. I blink at her. I should be. The blaster at her hip. The boy . . .

But her figure fills my vision and everything is placid.

"I don't know," I say.

She smiles thinly and says something over her shoulder that I don't catch. When she steps closer, the first woman returns, touches her arm. They exchange words, too quickly for me to follow. My mind swims in and out of focus. They've *done* something. They've—

The sense of urgency dulls as quickly as my earlier panic.

The other woman is reaching for my elbow. I flinch and my arm moves. The restraints are gone. A flash of relief is sucked back into the placid pool that's filled me. A man grasps my other arm. They haul me to my feet. I teeter on the floor before catching my balance. Sleek beige and steel-like structures stand around me in the small room, glowing green displays with foreign characters floating among them. I'm tugged out the door. My legs move, left, right, following my captors.

We walk out into a narrow hall, pale gray walls and floor, low lights. Not where I was before.

Before when?

The impression is hazy. As we turn a corner, I grapple with the jumbled images in my head: a soft, spongy floor; a broad navigation room with gleaming consoles and a screen stretching across the wall. My planet. Blue and green and white and rippling red and violet—

My breath catches.

Placid.

I'm reaching for the pieces again when one Enforcer waves open a door, and I hear several voices falling into a hush.

She shoves me in. The lighting in this room is even dimmer than the hall. A couple dozen shadowy people stand and sit along the walls in small clusters. There's a chill in the air. The door sighs shut behind me. Then a figure with long, black hair throws herself at me, arms wrapping tight:

"Skylar! Oh my God, I thought—"

I'm hugging her back before my mind has caught up. The smooth face pressing close to mine, the voice sunny even in her shock, the hint of jasmine-scented shampoo in that hair. Joy bursts inside me.

Placid.

I'm already squeezing her closer. "Angela?"

When she pulls back, I gape at her. Angela's here. Angela. Here. She should have been—

A pinch of pain.

Placid.

"Skylar? Oh, honey . . ."

I'm wrapped in an embrace from both sides. Shaking arms, a kiss pressed to the top of my head, teary eyes. *My* eyes widen. For a second I can't breathe.

"Mom? Dad?"

The pool inside me swallows everything up, leaving only calm. It's a dream. It has to be a dream. The atmosphere even has that dreamlike flavor, flimsy and vague. The way people keep saying things I don't totally understand. The slipping of my attention no matter how hard I try to focus.

This is what I'd want to dream. My parents. Angela. Before, in the dark, I was—

Placid.

My gaze wanders through the room as more words wash over me. There's Evan, stepping toward us, and—Ms. Cavoy from physics? A few kids I recognize from that class. Over there—Daniel? And a couple of his friends. A dark-complexioned man I think teaches chemistry, and a ruddy-cheeked woman from the English department. There's the Sinclairs from across the street, and Ruth and Liora from a few doors down . . .

It doesn't make sense. I saw Earth catch fire. Everyone here, they should all have—

My emotions shift and settle so smoothly I lose the thread of that thought completely. Mom is still talking.

"—you've been. When you didn't come home—no one had seen you—we're just so happy you're all right."

"I didn't come home," I repeat. Getting the words from my brain to my tongue is like pushing them through mud.

"Yesterday night," Dad says, and pauses. "If that is yesterday, still. That's not important, Sky. What's important is you're here now, wherever here is."

"We'll find out what's going on," Mom says, her voice fierce. "I don't know who's responsible for this, but they can't lock us up with no explanation—this is ridiculous!"

They don't know. They don't know this is a spaceship, they don't know our captors don't follow Earth rules, they don't know that Earth—

Placid.

My whole head has become murky, thoughts and memories and feelings like slippery minnows that dart in and out of view just below that still surface. I shake myself, but the water won't clear.

"Skylar," Angela says, clutching my forearm. I look down at her brown fingers against my paler skin and a glimpse of memory flickers by. A young woman, *Yenee*, vague and robotic. Tabzi, tapping her wrist, right there. *The implant, it keeps her . . . relaxed.* In a small room, with a—

What was I remembering? I fumble after the images and come up empty.

"*Are* you okay?" Angela's asking me. "Did they do something to you?"

They did. Yes. Interlocking lights on the ceiling. A stinging in my wrist.

If I could pull those ideas together, maybe I could answer properly. But Angela's peering at me with those wide, dark eyes, wider with each second I'm silent.

"I'll be fine," I hear myself say. I touch her arm. Grasp Mom's sleeve. They *are* here. My fingers tighten, keeping them near. A single definite question drifts up. "How did you all get here?"

"Three young men," Mom says. "We'd just gotten home from work—they must have broken in— They walked right into the living room and—" She glances at Dad. "What was it they used, to knock us out?"

"They must have had Tasers," Dad says, but he's frowning. *Blasters*, I think.

"I was at home with Mom," Angela says, nodding to a short figure I hadn't noticed earlier—her mother, crouched in a corner of the room—"and Evan, helping him with this photo thing . . . But Dad was upstairs. We haven't seen him. You don't think they'd have hurt him?"

Mom has started digging through her pockets. "I almost forgot. The one, right before he . . . zapped me, he made me take this. He said I should give it to you. Do you know what it means?"

She hands me a scrap of paper. I gaze at it dumbly. A line of alien characters is scrawled across it. My vision blurs and steadies as their meaning comes to me.

I did what I could. J.

That's all. *J.* Dark eyes, warm lips, a low teasing voice. *Jule.* I gulp as pain slices through me. Those eyes anguished, a rawness in my voice. *You put all our lives on the line for—*

Placid. Deep, deep, deep, all the way down.

My hand has closed around the paper, crumpling it. Why are my teeth clenched? That's gone too, the ripples on the water stilled. Jule did what he could. Then he is why my parents, Angela, everyone else is here—how?

I'm too muddled to stitch it together. My legs wobble, and Mom pulls me to her. I let myself sink into the comfort of her arms.

"It's okay," she says. "We can talk about it later."

They're here, somehow. On a ship. Heading to a space station like a shard of ice hovering above a barren planet.

The people there, they don't like us. I know that much. And now my parents, my friends—they're just as captive as I am.

2.

Win

A stun shot to the head from an Enforcer-issue gun will knock out a person for fifty-five minutes. Residual pain may continue for an hour longer. No permanent nerve damage should result, other than in rare cases involving underage targets or preexisting sensitivities. We Kemyates make our weapons as we make everything: efficient, reliable, and quantifiable.

When I first joined Thlo's group and dedicated myself to a mission that broke several of our laws, being shot by an Enforcer became a real possibility, so it seemed prudent to do some research to prepare myself. Waking in what looks like a storage room converted into a holding cell with all those facts, I don't feel remotely prepared. I should have realized it would be impossible. Even as I was fighting our Kemyate insistence on certainty and security, my own mind was following those same assumptions. I might find that amusing if not for the terrifying weight of the things I *don't* know right now.

Without intending to, I imagine telling Skylar, seeing her laugh with that teasing glint in her light brown eyes. The image makes my stomach knot, because I can't see her in the actual room before me. Hers was the first face I looked for when I opened my eyes. There are five of us spaced out along the dun walls in the otherwise empty space, far enough apart to prevent physical contact, each with one wrist and one ankle fixed to the floor with temporary binding-strands: Isis, Britta, Emmer, Tabzi, and me.

The best-case scenario is they've confined Skylar elsewhere. The worst— The worst is that the Enforcers saw her as just one more disposable Earthling.

I jerk at my wrist binding. Reliably, it doesn't budge. Across from me, Tabzi is slumped with her head listing to the side. Emmer, beside her, hasn't woken either. They must have been shot at least a few minutes later than me. Isis, who went down first, is resting her free hand on her knee as her heavy-lidded eyes take in the room. Britta, beside me, presses her thin fingers to her forehead where the tendrils of her wand-tattoo creep into her hairline. When we headed for Earth, she hadn't yet recovered from her Travel jump injury. I don't know if the stun shot will have harmed her more because of that.

I don't know who gave the order to detonate that bomb in Earth's atmosphere, or why. I don't know if Thlo always meant to turn on us or if our unexpected departure without her forced this outcome. I don't know what will happen to us next.

I don't know where Skylar is.

Tabzi stirs. She lifts her head and moves as if to stand up. Her slender arm jars against the binding. She stares at it as if she can't believe what she's seeing. *She* might not have considered the possible consequences if our mission failed. Unlike the rest of us, she has the luxury of her parents' money and her mother's political influence to buffer them.

Her pointed chin trembles, and then her whole face crumples. Annoyance prickles over me.

"Earth," she says after a moment. "Did they really . . ."

Her voice falters, but she's said enough. The flaring scarlet-and-purple clouds are etched in my memory.

"Yes," I try to say. What comes out of my mouth is a croak. I clear my throat, but a lump has lodged in it.

I was supposed to go down to the planet one last time. It would have been only a minute, bringing Skylar to the nearest Travel point so she could make her way home, but it would have been a minute to draw a few more breaths of moist air and feel the rays of a sun unfiltered by screens. I don't need data in front of me to know that air is toxic now. The whirling clouds drown out that sun. The cities, forests, jungles, and marshlands I Traveled to with Skylar, and all the people living in and around them, are burnt to oblivion.

She might be too. The Enforcers could have seen that as a reasonable solution: return the Earthling to the planet she was never authorized to leave. Let her burn alive in the chemical sear . . .

My hands clench, tendons flexing against the wrist binding. If that's what they've done— If they acted so—

Then I'm going to what? By all evidence, I'm completely under the Enforcers' control. They could walk in here, stun me again, and toss *me* down into those clouds, and I'd have as much say as the atoms in this ship's reactor.

Emmer wakes with a grunt, his gangly limbs twitching. He rubs his face. Then Isis, who's acted as our leader since we left Thlo behind, finally speaks.

"Is everyone all right?"

"As much as I can be," I say. Emmer nods, and Tabzi whispers, "Yes," in a tone that makes me glance at her again. She's started to cry, silently, tear tracks shining down her tan cheeks. Her earlier words suggest it's not her own predicament that's upset her. She's crying for Earth.

During the few months she's been a part of this group, I took her to be frivolous. She seemed excited about the trappings of planet life and the thrill of seeing herself as a rebel without much deeper concern. Now she's the only one of us openly grieving.

"Britta?" Isis says, her voice gentling as she looks to her girlfriend. Britta brushes back a wisp of chestnut hair that has escaped her ponytail and gives Isis a shaky smile.

"Headache," she says. "I'm sure it won't be my last. It'll pass."

"Did anyone see—" I start to ask, and catch the question. What Tabzi or Emmer might have seen after I was shot will tell me nothing about what has gone on in the hour since they were shot too.

Isis's gaze settles on me. I suspect she knows what I was going to ask—whom I was going to ask after. She welcomed Skylar, and I think she and Britta came to consider her a friend. I'd guess they're worried too.

I just want to know she's alive.

"I think we should all rest. Recuperate," Isis says. She flicks her eyes toward the ceiling. If this is an Enforcers' ship—and whichever ship we're on, it will be theirs now—there's a high chance they're monitoring us. Thlo could have told them anything, but the most solid evidence is admission of crimes from the perpetrator's own mouth.

Would it make any difference if we spoke of her involvement, using her real name rather than the code name that comes to all our tongues automatically? It seems unlikely she wouldn't have planned for that.

So we sit in silence. With each passing minute, the weight of my uncertainties grows. I haven't bitten my fingernails since I was five years old and a teacher shamed me enough about the *dirty rotter habit* that I balked even in private, but I have the urge to gnaw on my fingernail until I reach the quick.

Then the door opens, and Thlo walks in.

Though none of us was speaking, her presence casts a hush over the room, as if we've stopped even breathing. She folds her arms over her chest as the door closes behind her. Her short, sturdy frame looks even more imposing when viewed from the floor—and Thlo is plenty imposing even when you're looking down at her.

"It's just us," she says in the same calm, measured tone she used when making plans to evade the Enforcers, steal supplies, and destroy everything our Council stands for. "No surveillance. This conversation remains between us."

"And we're supposed to trust you on that?" Britta says in a pained rasp. She's stopped holding her head, but her delicate features are pinched. We all look at Thlo, waiting for the answer to that very reasonable question.

"What I say could incriminate me as much as you," Thlo says. She tucks the curve of her white-speckled black hair behind her ear. "It's not my intent to abandon you. This has simply been a necessary step toward getting you safely home. I apologize for the lack of warning. I'm sure you recognize that it was impossible for me to consult with you once you left the station."

She says that last bit with a dryness that's her mildest form of criticism. She's peeved that we left without her, before she's even asked us why.

"The station was going into full lockdown," I say. "Isis couldn't contact you. She tried. We knew if we waited any longer we might not get the chance at all."

We finished the mission without needing her help. Who knows how many more days, weeks, or months it might have taken if we'd waited for her to respond?

Thlo waves my explanation off. "That's no longer of importance."

"You'd call this 'safely' home?" Isis asks, wiggling her leg against its binding.

"You *are* criminals," Thlo says. "You can't expect Security to escort you in comfort. But as long as you follow my instructions, you'll be free enough once we reach Kemya."

She steps farther into the room, swiveling to look into each of our faces in turn. "This is the story you will give when asked: You're a small group who believed Kemya had become too obsessed with Earth, to the point of distraction. You disabled the time field generator to release Kemya from that obsession and to allow us to progress as we ought to. You do not care about Earth; you do not care what happened to it. All that matters to you is that Kemya can move forward and grow."

"But . . ." Tabzi murmurs, trailing off at Thlo's glower.

"It doesn't matter what your true feelings are," Thlo goes on. "I have encouraged the Council to see you as extreme nationalists, putting your concern for Kemya above all else. They're already inclined to believe it's in everyone's best interest if you return to regular life with a minimum of publicity. We want Kemya talking about our future, not your actions. You will only have been gone for six days. Anyone who's inquired has been notified that you were exposed to an unpredictable substance and are quarantined in a health center. When you return, you will be monitored closely and expected to stay away from each other, but you will keep your jobs, your living situations, and your minds. And you will continue to do so as long as you act completely loyal to Kemya. If the Council sees reason to suspect you value Earth over your own people, however—that, they won't tolerate."

"And you'd prefer we didn't mention you, I assume," I say.

"You will not involve *anyone* else," Thlo says. "There's no benefit to drawing Mako, Pavel, or Odgan into this."

"My brother knows we left the station," Tabzi says. "It was his ship."

"Your brother knows he's better off not sharing that information widely," Thlo replies. She eases toward the door. "Are we understood?"

She can't leave it at that. "What about Skylar?" I blurt out.

Thlo's eyebrows arch, and her tone turns even drier than before. "You will no longer be associating with her either, but she's safe enough at the moment."

"Where?" Britta says, leaning forward. "What have you done with her?"

"She's not your concern," Thlo says, and my heart sinks. That's all she's going to give us: a vague reassurance—and a veiled threat. If Skylar's only safe *at the moment*, then at some future moment she might not be.

"And Earth?" I have to ask. "The detonation? Aren't *you* concerned about that?"

She stares at me with a directness she hadn't quite shown before, looking . . . surprised? Her expression stirs my memory. Days ago, Skylar and I listened in on a meeting in the Earth Travel offices, between the division head, Thlo, and several others. Thlo was making a proposal we couldn't understand, having missed the initial explanation. *An extreme measure*, the others called it, while she talked about setting Kemya on the right course, away from Earth.

"What happened to Earth should have been done a long time ago," Thlo says now. "We made a mess there, and it needed to be cleaned up. You all know we were too tied to that planet. Now those ties are severed. Jeanant's vision, our vision, will be seen through."

A chill penetrates me from the inside out. Of course she isn't concerned. It was *her* idea. She planned to have Earth turned into the same unlivable wasteland as our own planet. Those billions of Earthlings didn't get even the brief warning our ancestors had that allowed some to flee to the space station before the chain reaction became critical. The Earthlings didn't have anywhere to flee to. She erased them as if they were nothing more than an extraneous report.

"Are you sure the Council will see it that way?" Britta says.

Thlo offers a thin smile. "The Council has already approved. I'm here on their orders to oversee the measures they agreed needed to be taken."

My shock cycles back to anger. She used us. Because of her we risked everything for a mission that's turned our people into the vilest possible murderers.

I want to hit her. I'd swing at her like an Earthling would, not a pitiful Kemyate swat. Just let her step closer.

She doesn't give me the chance, just turns on her heel and stalks out.

Silence settles over us again. The surge of anger fades, leaving me feeling ill.

From one perspective, Earth *was* our "mess." Every Earthling was a descendent of the original Kemyate colonists, and every aspect of the world they lived in had been reshaped a million times by our interventions in their history. That perspective, though, depends on seeing the Earthlings as nothing more than an extension of those original colonists rather than full human beings with their own rights. Jeanant's goal was to give Earth the freedom it deserved as much as it was to free Kemya from our "obsession." You can't watch a single one of his speeches without recognizing that. I knew some of the others in our group held on to the old prejudices, and Skylar showed me I'm hardly without my own biases, but I thought Thlo, who worked so closely with Jeanant and so clearly admired him, must have agreed with him on every point.

When Britta was injured I suggested leaving the station even earlier than we did. I thought Thlo dismissed the idea because she believed we'd risk failing to see Jeanant's *true* vision through. She must actually have been protecting this secret proposal she hadn't yet gotten approved.

The story she just gave us may be her real story. It was all for Kemya, all along. Freeing Earth was merely a coincidental aftereffect, one she had no qualms about negating. That is what we Kemyates have become: a people so hardheaded and hardhearted we'll end billions of lives without a pang of conscience.

No. I know we're more than that. Thlo may have perverted Jeanant's cause, and our Council may have supported her plan, but the five of us in this room are proof that we're not all so narrow-minded. We have to keep proving that.

I will go back to my old life. I will regurgitate the words Thlo's given us. I will tell more lies to my family and friends, until I find out where Skylar is and how to reach her.

After that, I *will* move forward—in my way, not Thlo's.

3.

Skylar

In the first instant when I open my eyes to a stark blue sky, I forget everything that's happened. All I know is I'm back on Earth. Relief swells in my chest so fast it brings tears.

An instant later it's swallowed by the now-familiar placid pool inside me. I blink. Strange that my eyes feel wet.

My gaze snags on a tuft of cloud. A tuft of cloud that sends a tiny shiver of *wrong*ness through the muddle in my head. I can't identify what's struck me about it, only that its drift across the sky feels off in some indescribable way.

"Where are we?" Angela says beside me. I sit up, bracing my hands against pavement. A sidewalk. The twenty-three of us are sprawled in front of a row of brick townhomes, bright red with white trim around the windows. Each has a short square lawn and a post with a streetlamp out front, though the lamps have a globe-like shape that seems somehow . . . outdated.

I twist around to take in the rest of the space. On the other side of the narrow asphalt street is a squat concrete building with a single-wide window and a sign that says "General Store." Next to it lies a stretch of grass holding what looks like the frame of a swing set without its swings, a volleyball net, and an empty circle of cement. And a bicycle rack? Though no bikes. Beyond that is an area that's totally empty: no grass, no concrete, nothing except a long, seamless beige surface that ends abruptly at a stack of equally seamless peach-toned boxes.

They weren't finished unpacking, I think. *They weren't . . . ready?* I don't have a clear sense of who *they* would be or why they should have been *ready.*

The street extends on past the end of the block, but the impressions of the buildings beyond send another vague twinge of *wrongness* through me.

Most of my companions are standing up. Mom walks down the sidewalk. She stops just past the first row of houses, reaches out her hand, and then jerks it back, her fingers clenching.

"I don't think we should go any farther that way," she says, her eyebrows drawing together. "It isn't safe . . ." She edges back, one step, and then another, before turning and hurrying to rejoin us. As I get up, she grips my shoulder protectively.

The chemistry teacher—Mr. Patterson, I've gathered—and Ruth have reached the other end of the block. "It'd be too dangerous to head this way too," Mr. Patterson says with a frown.

There's a twinge in my gut, and that yeasty flavor in the back of my throat. In that moment, I notice another familiar taste. The air. That hint of minerals in it. Like on the ship, like on the Kemyate space station.

This isn't Earth. Of course it's not. Because Earth—

Whatever was rising inside me is sucked away with a snap so sharp it leaves me dizzy. I struggle to gather my scattered thoughts. If this isn't Earth—if this is Kemya—but it looks like Earth—

Slivers of images float through my mind. A family clustered in a cave projected on a screen. A man in a robe walking toward a grove of fruit trees. A zoo of sorts. An Earthling zoo that I stumbled into on the space station.

That's where we are. Are they watching—

I am placid.

Angela grasps my arm. "This is so crazy," she says. "Why did they put us here? *Who's* doing this? What did they do to you, Skylar?"

Yes. She's asked that question before. I open my mouth, wanting to express the fragments I've put together—a people who see us as shadows instead of fellow human beings, a city orbiting a ruined planet, a hall of exhibits for their Earth "studies"—but the words tangle in the murk inside me.

"We're stuck here," I come out with. "They don't want us to leave." I know that.

Dad has approached the end of the block where Mom went before. He walks across the road as if along an invisible wall. "At least this area is secure," he says. "Out there . . . We need a better idea of what we're dealing with."

Out there. Walls. Yes. Walls, and a window looking in. I squint at the distant buildings.

"Well, we'll just have to stick together until we figure this out," Angela declares. "Let's see what we have." Her chin trembles even as she juts it out, but she marches up to one of the houses.

I amble after her. During all the time Angela's been my friend, and with all the things I've appreciated about her, I don't remember thinking of her as brave. But she is. I want to smile, but I can't summon the feeling.

• • •

The insides of the houses give the same unfinished impression as our "outside" surroundings. No panes in the windows. Gaping spaces around the kitchen counters where a fridge and an oven would normally stand. No furnishings in any of the rooms except for a big stack of thin, plastic-y-feeling blankets in one of the three bedrooms. Touching one brings a flicker of memory—panicked voices around a slim figure lying on an apartment floor, *Britta*—that's quickly sucked away.

"We should divide ourselves between the houses," Mom says, and everyone agrees. She and Dad immediately offer to share with Angela and her mom.

"And Evan should stay with us too," Angela says, tugging our friend closer to the group. Evan gazes at us with a blankness that I know I don't like even if the discomfort of it escapes me. I find myself remembering his awkward smile when Angela dragged him over to have lunch with her and Lisa and me, halfway through seventh grade. Where was it they'd gotten talking? She told me . . . Gym class? Neither of them was very good at . . . whatever sport they were learning. After a few minutes in the cafeteria he was chatting with us as if there'd been an empty spot just waiting for him.

"Do you think there's any chance . . ." Evan says, and shakes his head, hard. "No. I wouldn't want Lisa, or my parents and Emma, or anyone else ending up here."

"We'll get back to them," Angela says, squeezing his hand.

No. No, we—

A jab, and then nothing but placid. I swallow the yeasty taste. There's a pattern to it. A consistency. If I could think . . .

. . . *act as if your feelings are numbed* . . .

I grope after that voice, the instructions given, but it slips away from me, so I cling to the fraction I got. Whatever they've done, it's taking my feelings. If I can just . . .

"Let's take a look at the store," someone says, and I lose the thread.

The whole bunch of us troops into the building across the street. The shelves hold food—ration bars of a few different types that I look at with immediate if hazy distaste—and cubes of what appear to be soap, and that's it. No one to buy them from. So we just grab what we need. We eat our first meal sitting in clusters on the sidewalk. The ration bars leave a familiar chemical aftertaste in my mouth.

The taps in the houses run water, but we have no toothpaste or toothbrushes. That night, Mom gets us rubbing our teeth with our fingers. Looking at the ration bar wrappers after, it occurs to me that maybe we don't need to worry, because, after all, it'd be very efficient to have food that cleaned your teeth for you.

I laugh out loud, and everyone stares at me.

Wait, what was funny?

We create makeshift beds out of the blankets, the adults taking one bedroom, Angela and I another, and Evan the third. In the hall, before we turn in, Mom grabs me, pulling me close. She hugs me a long time, and then Dad does too. I hug them back. I don't want to lose—

I catch it coming, the gathering emotion, and divert all my attention to the hard surface of the buttons on Dad's shirt. The feeling eases back, but I still have the edges of it, a cool tinge of sadness. It hasn't been wiped out.

I have to keep doing that. I have to keep myself. They need me.

The next day, several of us set out to explore the boundaries of our new world. I catch a glimpse at the corner of my eye of a boy emerging from a house—black hair, golden-brown face, *Win!*—but when I whirl toward him, breath catching just before that prickle fills my throat, it's one of Daniel's friends I'm staring at. Not quite right. Who . . .

Win. Out there, somewhere. Or . . . maybe not? I reach toward that uncertainty, and the yeasty flavor crawls right onto my tongue. I swallow thickly.

Everyone has a definite sense of how far it's okay to wander, where we'd be crossing a line into dangerous territory. It hits even me, for an instant, before the placid inside me leeches it away: a gut punch of dread that makes my legs lock.

Stay away. We're not to go there.

But we keep looking. Over the next few days, we examine the houses and store from top to bottom. We notice that the store closes up in the middle of each night for an hour, window shuttering and door locking, with a new stock of rations on the shelves afterward. One evening Mr. Sinclair and Ms. Cavoy decide to see who's delivering them by keeping watch in the store, but it simply never closes up, and the next day everyone's hungry by lunchtime.

"Just leave it alone," Angela's mom says to them. "We're not getting anywhere if we starve to death." People are still talking like that: about "escape," about "getting home."

There is no home. But even if I knew how to tell them that, even if there weren't all this mud between my mind and my mouth, I'm not sure I'd want to. The only time anyone around me sounds happy is when they're talking about getting out of here. Going back to their real homes. Their missing loved ones.

Burnt up. Burnt up by red-and-purple clouds.

I'm getting better at remembering without losing everything. When the emotion starts to hit, I push my focus away, but let the fragments of information continue to collect behind my thoughts. As they gather, as I resist the urge to try to set them in order, they form hints of a bigger picture. One I have to be content looking at sideways, not completely understanding. It's more than I had before.

The most compelling fragments involve a young woman in stereotypical tribal dress, her eyes vacant. An implant. A girl with a heart-shaped face touching her wrist. *Numbed,* someone said. *To help them relax.*

It's important. Angela said, *What did they do to you?* With each sliver of meaning I gather, I'm more sure that's the answer. Numb. Drugs. Wrist.

Other fragments: staying silent in a hallway, figures moving along a screen. *Surveillance.* I look up at the sky that's always blue with just a few sparse clouds, and wonder.

We're watched. Maybe even inside the houses. I could do more if I could get away from them—those alien eyes.

On the seventh day—I know, not because I can keep track in my head, but because Angela and I decided to scratch them on the tiled floor in our bedroom with her old house key—the light from the streetlamp outside the window starts niggling at me as I try to sleep. I grab another blanket. Curled up beneath the layers, I find myself in total darkness. My breath slips in and out. And my body relaxes in a way it hasn't quite since . . . since before . . .

A blaze of red-and-violet clouds on a wide screen. An out-of-tune twang. Bodies falling.

I hold those pieces apart, inhaling, exhaling, avoiding the crash of emotion and the sudden retraction that used to come so often.

Drugs. Wrist.

My fingers slide along the sleeve of my sweater to my left wrist. Where the girl—*Tabzi*—tapped hers. Smooth skin, two delicate lines of bone. I trace up and down, over and over, not entirely sure what I'm searching for until my hand stills over it.

There. A minute impression, a slender lump about a quarter of an inch long, softer than the bone but fractionally harder than the natural tissue beside it. *Wrong.*

· · ·

In the morning, I listen to my parents and Angela and Angela's mom hash out our situation, the possibilities, our options—so far from the truth. I feel their eyes on me. Murmurs between Mom and Dad: *Does she seem any more alert today? I don't know what else to try . . .* I eat the ration bars they hand me, offer the brief comments I can drag from my clouded head, and join Mom on our morning jog up and down the street, which I know she hopes might clear my mind. I need something. I'll know it when I see it.

Two days later, while the adults are downstairs, I wander into their bedroom and my gaze falls on Dad's watch sitting next to his makeshift blanket bed. His watch with the stainless-steel links and the overlarge glass face Mom's always teased him about. *Are you sure that's not a wall clock they just soldered a strap onto?* He must have taken it off to shower.

I scratch the back of my neck, thinking of eyes, cameras, video screens. Ambling over to the blankets, I sit down and set my hand carefully on the floor. As I gaze at the off-white wall, I nudge the watch into my sleeve. Stand up and meander off again, fingers curled inside the cuff, steel cold against my wrist. A tickle of guilt about the theft, but if I could explain it to him, he'd understand.

I wash my socks with the weird cube soap that doesn't lather, until the water in the sink runs perfectly clear, and then hang them to dry. The "weather" here is always warm, and the ground clean enough to go barefoot. In the afternoon, I head inside for a "nap," curling up by the wall. Under the blankets, I set the watch against the floor, angle my body to hide the movement as much as I can, and smack the glass face with my elbow. At first tentatively, and then with more strength. The shock of the impact radiates through my arm with an ache that almost immediately drains away.

So it's not just emotions but physical sensations that are muted. Good to know.

I've been at it a few minutes, tendrils of worry starting to creep around the edges of my consciousness, when the glass finally cracks. I pry at a shard that's about a third of the circular pane. With a creaking sound, it snaps out of the frame.

When I go back outside, I sit apart from the others on the sidewalk. With the shard tucked against my palm, I run the edge against the hard, not-quite-cement corner. Again and again. Until it pricks my finger when I test it.

I stuff the socks in my jeans pocket that evening. Lie down in my makeshift bed with the blankets pulled high, waiting until Angela's breathing slows. I lay one of the socks under my forearm. Holding the shard of glass between forefinger and thumb, I prod with my other fingers until they locate that tiny lump in my wrist. Then I grit my teeth, set the sharp edge of the glass against my skin, and press down.

4.

Win

When the Enforcers release me from custody, I head down the hall outside the Security offices feeling as if I'm wearing a uniform that fits too tight. My awareness of the surveillance cameras prickles down my back. They'll be purposely tracking me now, rather than simply glimpsing me here and there in their standard scans.

Just before I reach the inner-shuttle stop, Shakam Nakalya's russet-brown, square-jawed face appears on a public screen. My rush of anger makes me stumble, even though he's merely giving his standard ten-day address.

The Enforcers showed me some of his broadcasts during the interrogations, to gauge my response to our mayor's account of Earth's destruction. The bare fact of it is, he's lying. Thlo said the Council had approved of her plan to obliterate Earth if the time field generator were disabled. I saw her sharing that plan with some of the Council members with my own eyes. It's impossible Nakalya is unaware the official story he's presenting, that Earth was devastated not by a purposeful detonation but an accidental atomic shift caused by the shattering of the time field, is rot.

"It is a tragedy, but we will remain united and move on," he said. How convenient for the Council that this version of events makes everything the fault of the unnamed rebels.

I hear my fellow citizens "moving on" as the inner-shuttle carries me to my sector. "Just gone," one passenger murmurs to another. "The whole planet."

The other nods. "The poor, pitiful things."

"Well, it's all over now. Did you see the Science division's new mining presentation?"

My jaw clenches. I hold my tongue.

We elect our leaders based on reason and reliability, so we assume they will guide us with rationality and facts. Some part of *me* still assumed that, despite having seen firsthand how much divisions like Earth Travel have come to prioritize their own power over what the data shows. I know the Council would gain nothing from admitting the truth. Yet my first reaction, when I heard Nakalya's lies, wasn't anger. It was shock.

If Kemya accepts the loss of Earth so easily, what will that mean for Skylar, wherever Thlo is keeping her?

I walk into my family's apartment with excellent timing: just after Dad, Mom, and Wyeth will have returned from their cafeteria dinner, Dad recently finished with his shift in the waste-processing plant and Mom preparing to leave for hers in residential maintenance. Dad is standing with a tiny canvas perched on his easel—a hobbyist-constructed canvas that's more synthetic polymers than fabric, but still difficult for him to afford. Sitting next to Wyeth on the floor as my brother points to something on his tablet, Mom is dressed in the standard Kemyate clothes her boss insists on, with the lump of a gauzy scarf showing under the neckline as a small, concealed rebellion. This, at least, feels normal.

Then they look up, and it isn't normal anymore. Wyeth grins, but Dad and Mom just stare.

They didn't expect me to come home. However solid Thlo's cover story was, they saw through it.

I suppose I haven't been completely circumspect in the comments I've made around them in recent times. I can admit it was a soft-brained desire for them to notice I was waging a much bigger, much more meaningful rebellion. My mysterious disappearance, the supposed quarantine, and a catastrophe on Earth that precisely coincided would be easy pieces to connect.

"Win!" my brother says. "So you're not contaminated after all. Or did they just clean you up well?" He gives me an amused once-over. "Did you hear—you must have even in the health center—about Earth? Can you believe it? The last batch of feeds just arrived. There won't be any more."

His voice drops off at the end, as if he's torn between excitement over the magnitude of the news and sadness at the loss. I'm not sure he comprehends just how immense it was. His favorite TV programs are gone, yes, but also billions of people he's never known as more than images on a screen, the many-flavored air he's never tasted, and the warmth of a sun he's never felt.

My parents have recovered themselves. "It's about time they released you," Dad says gruffly. "They never tell us enough."

"Was it bad?" Mom asks, getting up. It's an unusually vague question from her. She peers at my face.

For a second, I want to answer the question she's really asking. It was bad; it was awful; it still is. I fought for Kemya and Earth and lost the second half of that battle, hopelessly. I've lost the girl who helped me understand how much it mattered. Everyone around me is repeating lies they don't know are lies. It was in our power to save all those people, and instead we exterminated them.

They would care. As much as the name they gave me and the artistic interests they encouraged made me feel embarrassingly different when I was younger, I appreciate that difference now. It's evidence they'd stand behind me if I told them what I've been doing.

I shouldn't have let them suspect in the first place, though. This isn't taunts from classmates or rolled eyes in the fitness room or sneers when I ventured into the higher levels of the station. I'm no longer a child. It's my turn to shield them, as well as I can. I can at least avoid making them complicit in my actions, as I've managed to up until now.

"It was fine," I say, a brief lie that feels enormous falling from my mouth. Their gazes weigh on me, and I'm suddenly aware of how exhausted I am. There wasn't much sleep allowed during the interrogations. "I'm just tired. Do you mind . . . ?"

"Of course," Mom says. "Go ahead."

"Wait!" Wyeth says. "You *have* to see this glider recording some ninth-level kids put up. It's wild what they can do."

I drag in a breath. "All right," I say, crouching beside him.

He flicks the recording back to the beginning. I rest my hand on his shoulder as the kids careen back and forth and up the walls in a residential hallway—brighter and with sleeker fixtures than ours—balanced on bars that hover a foot above the nearest surface. Wyeth makes a crowing sound as one of the boys pulls off a full forward flip.

"Mom says even if she and Dad saved up every extra credit they'd usually spend for me, it'd take five years before I could get one of those," he says as the recording ends.

"You can play with antigrav equipment in the fitness room," I say. "You don't need one of those fritterer toys."

"It's not frittering," Wyeth protests. "You exercise and practice balance."

"You impress the girl in class who was talking about how 'cool' gliders are," Dad remarks with a teasing tsk of his tongue.

Wyeth dips his head. "It's not just that," he mutters.

When did my little brother start getting crushes? I haven't been gone even a week.

"You know a better way to impress someone?" I say, nudging him. "Take those classes more seriously so you can get a good upper placement."

"Sure, sure," he says, but he nudges me back.

I rub my face, and notice my parents studying me again, Dad more curious, Mom more concerned. Beyond them, Dad's paintings cover the walls with so many tiny representations of Earth: a landscape, a building, a figure from a recording. Each one sends a jab through my chest.

"I'm going to bed," I say, and escape into my room.

· · ·

The next day in the cafeteria, I tense when Markhal sets his broad frame down in the spot across from me, even though technically there's nothing suspicious about it. We grew up together, sectormates and classmates; talked about everything, including Earth-related interests and sympathies, during the first few years of upper school; experimented a little before deciding we got on better as just friends. Then, a year and a half ago, he started bringing the boyfriend he'd met in training at the Health division to social gatherings in our sector. The boyfriend sputtered a laugh at my name when Markhal introduced me and pulled faces whenever anyone mentioned Earth. Once, when someone started playing an Earthling film, he glanced at the screen and called the people on it "those *things.*"

"How are you?" Markhal asks.

"The same," I say.

He raises an eyebrow. "It can't be that much the same when the place you've trained to work on has been wiped out."

"Well, no," I fumble. "We're still processing data, though. No one's talking about reassignments yet."

"Is it true, what the Council is saying about the time field?" he asks, leaning over his plate. "That it was the only thing stabilizing the planet, and losing it triggered the flare in the atmosphere?"

"I don't know much about that side of things," I say, willing my fingers to stay relaxed around my eating stick.

"There wasn't any indication that this problem might arise?"

"It's not something I can talk about," I say, too loud to blend into the normal cafeteria chatter. Markhal blinks at me, and turns to his food.

That went well.

In the Earth Travel offices, the workrooms feel even closer than they used to. As we sift through the last batches of experimental results, the guy at my left rambles on to his other neighbor about how it was only a matter of time before Earth imploded, and someone behind me remarks that the planet served its purpose. My jaw is starting to ache from holding my mouth shut.

Thlo—no, Ibtep, I need to start thinking of her by her real name now that she's not part of our rebel movement—passes through the room partway through the day, checking on everyone's progress. I suspect I'm the only one who's resisting a cringe the entire time she's nearby. She ignores me, but her face accompanies me home, along-side the Council members on the news reports my parents turn on. Even though Silmeru is still Earth Travel's division head, it's Thlo—Ibtep—whom Nakalya asks to offer her opinion about whether it's time to leave our former planet. She does so in a measured tone that does as much of the convincing as her actual words. Her efforts to push us toward her ideal future are already succeeding. The next day my colleagues speculate that Silmeru may step down from the Council and let Ibtep officially take her place.

On the fourth day after our return, I pass her in the hall in hushed conference with the one person I enjoy seeing less. Neither she nor Jule looks up as I hurry past them. I go back to my workroom and sit at my terminal, but I don't trust my hands to reach for the screen.

He played with Skylar's emotions and broke her heart, and now he's colluding with the woman responsible for destroying Skylar's entire planet? I suppose I shouldn't be surprised. Why would he care, as long as he gets the standing he wants?

I still don't know where Skylar *is*. Jule is working his way into the Council's inner circle, and the rest of us have been back four days without having accomplished anything.

My thoughts halt there. I look down at my hands, uncurling my fingers from my palms. *The rest of us.*

I haven't accomplished anything because I haven't tried to. I don't know where to start; I've never had to work alone. Even when I set off with Skylar on Earth against my orders, I had the group's mission to guide me and Jeanant's messages to follow.

I'm not so deluded to think I'm capable of tracking down Skylar on my own without Security catching on. Yet by all evidence I am so deluded that I let myself believe I just had to wait and new orders would arrive.

I'm the one the others always accused of impatience and lack of caution. If I've been too nervous to reach out, how can I expect anyone else to?

It's up to me. I remember the looks exchanged in the holding room. There are at least a few people who'd still fight for Skylar and for Earth. I have to find a way to contact them—a way Security can't track.

After two days of grappling with that problem, an assignment sends me past the doorway to Earth Travel's equipment refurbishment area. I glance at it, and then glance again. The shelves within are stacked with time cloths and recorders and a range of other devices in need of repair. It's unlikely anyone is working on them now, considering our experiments are finished.

At the end of my lunch period, I duck inside. I look at the inventory display quickly and amble between two high shelving units toward a cluster of distractor spheres. Sliding my hand along the edge of the shelf, I catch one between my fingers and palm it. Then I continue on toward a stack of data drives.

Before I've emerged from the aisles, a tall figure walks through the doorway. "Traveler Pirios," he says immediately. "What are you doing in here?"

It's Pital, one of the supervisors. He knew who he was looking for before he saw me. They *are* watching me closely.

"One of the reports I was inspecting mentioned some recorded footage confined to a malfunctioning drive," I say, holding up the pyramid-shaped data unit. "I thought I'd see if Tonda could extract the footage. She's good at that sort of thing."

It will all check out. Tonda's even working in the same room as me today. Pital frowns. "Next time ask permission first," he says, but he motions me out without another word.

My apologies for taking initiative, I reply silently.

I walk straight to my assigned room, sweat cooling on my neck. The little sphere I tucked into the carry-pouch at my waist will have to be enough. I don't think any excuse would allow me to wander into the storage area again now that they've caught me there once.

I don't touch the sphere until I'm in the relative privacy of my bedroom. Bent over the bunk-side desk, I mark a tiny *D* on the side of the distractor with a bit of Dad's precious paint. The device has a camouflaging function, but, according to the inventory, that's only working intermittently. I *want* Isis and Britta to notice it in their apartment.

I bring up the tiny data display, enter the coordinates I want it to follow, and send it off. Then I wait.

After a few days with no word, I begin to suspect this is a refusal. They wouldn't turn me in, but now that Ibtep's betrayal is no longer fresh, they could have decided they've taken enough risks. I'm pondering whether I should reach out to Tabzi, or Emmer, while trying to go to sleep that night when something drops onto the bunk beside my head. I reach up and my fingers close around my distractor.

It doesn't feel quite right. I prod it in the darkness, and it splits open. A smoother, more pliable ball rolls into my palm. A smile tickles across my face. It's an earpiece communicator. Isis will know how to set up a private link. I press it into my ear.

The opening of the distractor must have sent a signal to her, because a moment later, her low voice carries out.

"You with me?"

"I'm here," I murmur, listening for any sign of Wyeth waking on the bunk below. "Not a safe time to talk."

"Understood," she says. "What hour works for you tomorrow?"

If I grab breakfast early I'll have the room to myself while Wyeth's in the cafeteria. "Eighth," I say.

"I can do that."

I tuck the communicator between my clothes on my shelf of the closet, and then lie back down. For the first time since I woke up in those bindings, there's a quiver of hope running through me.

5.

Skylar

The blare of a horn wakes me. Angela is already moving to the bedroom window. I get up to join her, careful not to move too quickly.

It's been two days since I cut the implant out of my arm. The bloody sock is hidden in my blankets, my sweater sleeve pulled low over the bandage I made with the other. But I haven't said anything to Angela or my parents yet, even though it's been killing me staying silent. As the medication's effects faded and my thoughts have come back into clarity, I've only become more sure we're in the Earthling zoo I saw from the outside before—which means any move I make could be seen. I don't want to find out what will happen if someone discovers I have my mind back. So I've stayed quiet and vague, the drugged act I first practiced when I was pretending to be Jule's "pet" Earthling to justify my presence on the station.

"That's weird," Angela says. Across the street, in that blank area near the storage containers, a small group of people is standing around a metal platform with a glass-like tube arcing over it and a couple of tables lined with gleaming instruments. I stiffen. What are they going to do to us now?

A short man with wavy black hair raises his hand to his mouth. "Please come out and take part in the health clinic," he says, his voice artificially amplified. "Everyone will receive a free examination."

His English barely hints at a Kemyate accent. He and his colleagues are all dressed in Earth-like styles, not the usual seamless Kemyate clothes. They're keeping up the pretense that we're still on Earth.

When no one emerges from the houses, two of the other Kemyates, a man and a woman, stalk to the first house's doorway. The athletic grace of their movements sends a nervous flicker of recognition through me. *Kurra*. Neither of them has her pale coloring, but they could be Enforcers. As the man raps on the door, the woman rests her hand on a lump beneath her fitted jacket. A blaster?

"Let's go," the man says. "Everyone needs to be checked."

Checked for what? If they were concerned about our health, wouldn't they have "examined" us on the ship?

Angela reaches toward me, and I grip her hand, giving it a tighter squeeze than I've dared to before. She peeks at me sideways.

"Do you know those people, Skylar?"

I'm not sure how much I can get away with saying. "Dangerous," I murmur.

Mr. and Mrs. Sinclair, their little son, Toby, and Ruth and her daughter, Liora, slip out of the house. "What's this about?" Mr. Sinclair demands, his face flushed, as the Enforcers motion them toward the tables.

"A simple practical procedure," the woman replies. "It's for your benefit."

"I don't want any procedures," Mr. Sinclair says. "You people need to let us out of here. The way we've been treated is—"

He grasps at the woman's arm as he rants, and in the same instant the other Enforcer sidles closer. I flinch as a twang hums through the air. Mr. Sinclair's legs crumple. He collapses, wheeling his arms to keep his torso upright.

"Daddy!" Toby cries, leaping between him and the woman Enforcer, and there's another twang. Toby topples, unconscious. Mrs. Sinclair yelps.

"What did you do to him?" Mr. Sinclair snaps, struggling to move his legs.

I can't just watch any longer. We're in no position to fight back right now, and whatever the Kemyates are trying to do to us, they'll clearly do worse if we don't agree.

I give Angela's hand a tug, my heart thumping. "We should go get our examinations," I say in a distant voice.

She considers me. "You think so?"

"We have to," I say. I need to set a model of compliant behavior.

Angela comes with me when I head down the stairs. "Skylar!" Mom shouts as we reach the front door.

"We have to go," Angela tells her for me. "Look what they're doing to people who won't."

A sudden swell of affection fills me—that she understood what I was trying to communicate, that she's attuned to me enough to trust what I'm saying despite my act.

We walk across the street together. "They'll be able to move again soon enough," the man Enforcer is telling Mrs. Sinclair, who has knelt on the ground to cradle her son. "If you behave aggressively, we have to respond."

"He's *five years old*," Mrs. Sinclair says. Ruth and Liora are stand-ing a few feet away, wide-eyed, Ruth's arm around her daughter's shoulders. I stop and direct my vague gaze toward the three Kemyates waiting by the tables. A twinge runs up my left arm, and it occurs to me belatedly that I'm facing another risk here. If they make me pull up my sleeves, it'll be obvious I've cut out the implant. I don't know what this "examination" involves.

"We're ready to be checked out," Angela says before I have time to speak. Her hand trembles in mine.

I'm not making her go first. Maybe I can control the procedure more if I give the impression I'm trying to help. "Yes," I say, letting go of Angela and meandering toward the tables. "Examinations are good."

The short man with the amplifier and the lanky woman next to him exchange a look. She's holding one of those thin, rollable tablets I used a few times with the rebels. The Kemyate character imprinted on the edge means "health." So they are from the Health division, at least.

"*That's the one with the . . .*" the amplifier man murmurs to the tablet woman. "*We can't use her. Her data will be . . . by the time.*" He's using too many words I don't know, but I assume it's something to do with my being drugged.

"*We won't record,*" the tablet woman says. "*She can show the oth-ers to not be afraid.*"

As she waves me to the first table, I keep my fingers curled around the cuff of my sleeve, poised to offer my other arm if asked for one. To my relief, she doesn't seem interested in either. She picks up one tool off the table, and another, and another, holding each in front of my face in turn. "Blink two times. Swallow. Cough. Stick out your tongue." She guides a flat, circular device with a distorted mirror surface around my entire head and then down my front to my toes. Then she presses an indented yellow cube to the base of my throat. There's a slight itch before she removes it.

"Here," she says, directing me to the metal platform. Light flashes through the tube as I stop under it. A humming tingles through my bones. I inhale, exhale, trying to stay relaxed.

The man motions me out again. The tablet woman has already started on Angela, this time consulting her unfurled tablet as she goes. Angela stands stiffly. When she steps onto the platform after me, the man has her stretch her arms out to the sides and then down to her toes, lift one leg, and then the other, all while gesturing at a tablet of his own. It seems they didn't bother taking me through the entire process.

What are they recording? I ease closer to the man, peeking at his tablet's screen. Some of the characters are too small for me to make out from a distance, and most of those I read must be medical terminology I'm not familiar with, but I catch a word and the two-syllable characters of a name at the top of the screen. *Project Nuwa.*

Nuwa. I haven't heard of that before.

The rest of my fellow Earthlings are straggling out of the houses. The woman at the table has started on Dad. Angela's mother hustles over to Angela when she's released from the platform.

"What were you thinking, rushing over here like that?" Mrs. Tinapay whispers, her gaze flicking between her daughter and the scientists. "I was terrified."

"Sorry," Angela says. "I didn't mean— I'm okay. It wasn't that bad."

My mom is looking over the instruments on the table. When the woman finishes with Dad and motions to her, Mom sucks in a breath. I tense.

"I want to know what you've done to my daughter," Mom says before the scientist can start her examination. She points to me. "*She* deserves proper medical treatment."

Oh no.

"She is unharmed," the woman says. "Blink twice."

Mom ignores her instruction. "Bull," she says, louder. "She hardly talks, she can't answer most of the questions we ask her, her attention's all over the place—"

"Patricia," Dad says, and she waves him off.

"It's not all right," she goes on. "She's not all right. And she was just fine before you took us."

One of the Enforcers steps toward her, and my pulse hiccups. "Mom!" I say. I control my expression as well as I can, faking placid. "Why are you upset? The examination's okay."

I catch her eyes for an instant and then let mine drift. Both she and the scientist are staring at me. Please don't let them see that my heart's about to jump out of my chest.

Then Mom glances to the side and notices the Enforcer. Her gaze travels from him to the Sinclairs still huddled on the ground, and back to me.

"Let's just get through this," Dad says. Mom's jaw tightens, but she nods. As the woman starts her examination, the man tugs Dad off the platform. Dad comes over to me, hugging me as we wait for them to finish with Mom.

He wants the same answers she does, of course. He just realizes we have no leverage with which to get them.

Before all this, I meant to get back from Kemya before they knew I was gone, with the magic of Win's time cloth. I knew how scared they'd be if I didn't come home—because of the time twelve years ago when my brother, Noam, didn't come home ever.

I messed that up. I'm still here with them, but, from the looks on their faces, they feel they've lost me too.

There has to be a way *I* can give them the answers they need, before they get themselves hurt trying to help me.

• • •

Mr. Sinclair and his son have their examinations last, after their numbness has worn off. It's only in the afternoon that we notice Toby may not have completely recovered. He lies down for a nap and won't rouse no matter what anyone does. When he finally wakes up, he looks paler than usual and stumbles when he walks. Mr. Sinclair keeps him close and mutters about what he'd like to do to "those people," but a gloom has settled over us. We all know there's nothing we *could* do.

I'm watching Toby roam around the unfinished playground a couple days later—almost as steady as he was before—when something flickers in the sky beyond him. I squint, but it's gone. Then the sky flickers again, right in my line of sight. A short string of Kemyate characters, flashing white against the blue. *Store. After nightfall.*

My breath stops in my throat. The message has to be directed at me. No one else here could read it.

The characters blink two more times in the next ten minutes, and not again. There are hours to go before our artificial nightfall arrives. I amble along the street, around the storage containers, and back to my house, reining in my rising anticipation.

If it's some sort of trick to test my awareness, I'm pretty sure I could have read those characters and remembered them even in my drugged state. If I go, that won't prove anything to our captors. I just have to keep up my act the whole time.

If it's not a trick . . . then someone out there has found a way to reach me.

As the sky dims, I gulp down the ration bar dinner and head upstairs to wash up with the others. The sky darkens to full black, speckled with stars only I know are fake. After we've turned in to our rooms, I murmur to Angela something about still being hungry, and wander downstairs as if to get a snack.

I slip past the door and through the glow of the streetlamps into the thicker darkness around the store. The door is unlocked, a few hours left before the usual restocking. I nudge it open.

In the thin light that streams through the large front window, the store's interior looks the same as always: the shelves on one wall empty except for the few remaining ration bars, the bare counter that seems to beg for a cash register, the equally bare clothes racks built into the opposite wall. I wonder how it was intended to work, if we'd been the planned inhabitants brought to a finished exhibit. Would a Kemyate have played shopkeeper, or would one of us have been set up in that job somehow?

I walk to the clothes rack and back again. And then the shutter drops on the window. An electric light gleams on overhead as a low hum sounds from behind the counter. I spin around.

For a second I can only stare at the figure ducking through the space that's opened in the wall, my heart thumping. Win draws himself upright, brushing his jagged black hair from his deep blue eyes, which soften in relief when they meet mine. His mouth curves into that wondrously familiar crooked smile.

"You got our message," he says with his usual British lilt, and my vision goes watery. He's alive and unharmed and *here*.

I don't think about moving, it just happens. I'm standing there staring, and then as he skirts the edge of the counter I'm rushing to meet him. His arms pull me in as I wrap mine around him. I press my head against his shoulder, absorbing the warm realness of his body against mine. My throat's choked up. I didn't realize how alone I felt even with my parents and Angela, until this moment when I don't anymore.

I'd wonder if I should be embarrassed by the way I'm clinging to him, but he's holding on to me just as tightly. He swallows audibly. "I'm sorry it took me so long," he says, and I almost laugh. It's a miracle he's here at all. His breath tingles over my skin, and my heart thumps again, hard. I make myself ease back, just far enough that I can look into his eyes.

"Are you all right? And everyone else? How long do we have to talk?"

He peers at me, his forehead furrowing, as if he hadn't expected me to be desperate for information. "You're not—" he starts. "Isis thought, based on the records Britta was able to dig up, that you'd been given an implant to medicate you calm."

"Oh. I was. I took it out." I do laugh then, but it comes out strained.

"You—" Win's gaze drops. I pull back my left sleeve. The cut is scabbed over but still sore, the skin around it dark pink. He makes a pained sound. "By yourself?"

"I couldn't ask anyone to help," I say. "And I had to get it out. I didn't even totally understand what it was, I was so muddled, but . . . I knew that."

Win's mouth has twisted. "I brought the tools to remove it for you, but of course you couldn't know I was coming. I can at least put one of the heal patches on."

"Please," I say. I've been worried about infection, with the wound being so difficult to wash while keeping it hidden. Win produces a beige patch from the pouch at his waist and smooths it over the skin, so gently I barely feel the pressure. Like the one he gave me on Earth when I sprained my ankle, it blends into my arm as if there's nothing there. A cool twinge washes away the remaining sting.

I grasp his hand before he lowers it, still wanting that contact. He curls his golden-brown fingers around mine, his thumb tracing a slow loop over the back of my hand, and smiles at me again. There's something different in his face. A firmness to his gaze and the set of his mouth, as if he's aged since I last saw him, though it's been less than three weeks.

Three weeks and a lifetime's worth of horror. Maybe he sees the same in me.

"It's good that you're already aware," he says. "We can really talk. Isis wants us to keep this under half an hour. She's okay—Britta too. Ibtep—Thlo—arranged things so we went mostly unpunished. Other than you. Are *you* all right?"

"I think so," I say. "I've been trying to be careful. Are we on display out there?"

"Not exactly. This part of Earth Studies is still closed off to the public, but Security must be monitoring the feeds. We didn't know where you were until Britta found them. There are about twenty Earthlings with you? Do you know why they were taken?"

I hadn't realized he'd be as confused as I am. "Yes and no," I say. "It's my parents, a couple of my friends, some people from my neighborhood and school. I don't know the whole story, but apparently Jule and a couple other Kemyates grabbed them from my present time right before the bomb dropped."

"Jule," Win repeats with an edge in his voice.

"He left a bit of a note," I say. "I don't know how, or why . . ." Remembering his betrayal is a sliver of pain amid the constant ache of grief for my planet, but it's still a pain I'd rather avoid. "He hasn't said anything to you?"

"No. He's too busy—" He cuts himself off, shaking his head. "That's not important. I'm also supposed to ask you—did something happen in here two days ago? Isis found a loop in the recordings, for more than an hour. It was subtle, but she could tell someone had repeated earlier footage instead of showing what was really happening—it gave her the idea to do the same so we could talk now."

"A few Kemyates from the Health division came in," I say, and tell him about the examinations. "So they were hiding that from Security?"

Win is frowning. "Yes. There weren't any records of medical scans either. It's bad enough that the Council is keeping your presence here a secret, but to be running tests on you as well?"

"It wasn't really . . . invasive, as far as I could tell," I say. "If you look up 'Project Nuwa,' maybe you can find out what they were after."

"I'll tell Isis and Britta," he says. "This isn't right. I think we'll have to move faster."

"Move faster doing what? Have you figured out a way to get us out?"

"Yes and no," Win says, repeating my earlier answer with a flicker of a grin. His thumb resumes its soft circling of my skin where our hands are still clasped. "We know the first step is letting everyone on the station know what really happened to Earth, and that you're here. The Council is claiming the detonation was an accident. If we reveal that they destroyed your planet purposefully, and then show there are Earthlings who survived and deserve our sympathy . . . it'll make it much harder for anyone to hurt you without fallout, while we work out what to do next."

"Then *everyone* will be watching us," I say, remembering the Kemyate kids peering at the people in the other Earth Studies exhibits as if they really were animals in a zoo.

"More people watching means more witnesses if they try . . . tests that are more 'invasive,' or worse," Win points out. "You have a little privacy. They'll never put surveillance in the bathrooms, mainly to avoid encouraging 'degenerate' interests in the audience." He grimaces. "There's also a space behind the storage units that Isis says doesn't have an active feed right now. Whoever's monitoring the exhibit will probably notice if you start going over there a lot, though, so I'd only use that if you have to."

"But you really think they'll eventually let us out?"

"We're going to work out something," Win says. "It'll just take time. We have to wait and see what the public reaction is before we can decide on the best strategy. I'm not letting them keep you in here, Skylar. You can add that to my promise to you."

His promise—to bring me home safely. The tears that sprang to into my eyes when I first saw him well up again.

"It's all gone," I say. "Everything we were trying to save. My home. It's all gone, Win."

He tugs me closer, back into his arms. "I know," he says, his voice raw. "I'm so sorry. That's why I'm going to keep fighting until you have a real home here."

"How can that happen when everyone out there thinks we're just . . . shadows? We're as human as any of them—why can't they *see* that?"

Win pauses. "If we could make them realize you *are* just as valid, just as strong . . ."

"We can start showing them," I say, straightening up at that flare of hope. "They're used to seeing us in edited bits of entertainment and news footage, or drugged numb. I can get the others to show off just how smart and strong we can be."

"That could help," Win says. "Whatever you can manage."

My mind drifts back to his earlier words. The Council is making claims—the Council is keeping us secret. "So it was the Council who arranged it?" I say. "The bomb? Do you know why?"

His expression hardens. "It was Ibtep," he says. "She told us, afterward . . . She thought it was the only way to be certain people here would forget about Earth and move on."

Thlo. No, Ibtep, that's her real name. I'm not that surprised, given the way she looked at me, spoke to me. *Expendable*, she called me once. "Because Kemya brought human life to Earth in the first place, she figured she had the right to take it away," I say. I've heard echoes of that attitude around me since I first set foot on the station.

"And she convinced the Council to agree with her. Do you remember that meeting we saw—the plan she was sharing with Silmeru and the others?"

The images trickle back to me. "An extreme measure, in case the rebels succeeded . . ." My body goes rigid. "Then if we'd left the time field in place, let them keep their experiments—"

"Don't think that," Win breaks in. "Ibtep wanted to cut us off from Earth. She'd have seen it through one way or another. She's the one responsible."

But I am thinking it. If we hadn't succeeded in our mission, if I hadn't helped, everyone on Earth might have lived at least a little longer.

• • •

When I get back to the house, everything is quiet, the windows dark except Angela's. I can't think of any excuse to wake up my parents and drag them and Angela into the bathroom that wouldn't look incredibly odd to whoever's watching. So I force myself to offer nothing but a vague nod when Angela says, "You got your snack?" I curl up in my nest of blankets, the lump of the bloodstained sock under my head.

Maybe I should try to smuggle that out to Win the next time he comes. Whenever that happens. *If* it happens; if he and the others aren't caught . . .

I close my eyes against the swell of fear and run my thumb over the back of my hand the way he did. The echo of his touch conjures the reassurance I felt in his presence. We can do this. We have to.

At least I'm not completely alone in here. I reach out across the floor toward Angela. She curls her fingers around mine.

"Skylar?" she whispers.

"Tomorrow," I murmur, as if half asleep.

The next morning during breakfast, Angela eyes me more intently than usual. After I've choked down my ration bar, I remark, "I need to wash my clothes."

"Yeah," she says without missing a beat. "Me too."

Because the Kemyates haven't supplied us with clothing, every few days we've been washing the outfits we arrived in using the sudsless soap and the bath water, wringing them out as well as we can and wearing them damp afterward. But I don't even switch on the water after we go in. As soon as the door's closed, I turn and grab Angela in a hug.

I haven't hugged her like this since before our imprisonment. Her breath catches in her throat with a rasp.

"Skylar," she says wonderingly, and then, "are you okay?"

I nod against her shoulder. For the second time in as many days, my eyes are filling with tears. I blink them back. "I can talk to you now," I say. "My parents need to hear this too. Can you get them in here? Make up some excuse—tell them I got a little dizzy and you're worried about me."

"Of course," Angela says. She hesitates when she steps back from me, looking into my face. I can meet her gaze steadily for the first time in days. She smiles, her own eyes watery. "I was so worried. I didn't know how I was going to keep doing this with you so . . . I'll go—I'll get them."

In no time at all she's back with Mom and Dad, who gather me into a joint embrace. For a minute I let myself just hang there in the warmth between them. But I need to get talking before it starts to look suspicious that we've been in here so long.

"Let's sit down," I say. "This is going to take some explaining."

6.

Win

I'm standing at the edge of a forest of spiky-leaved trees, a field of fluffy yellow grass before me, a sun beaming overhead. The imagery is so well constructed I could forget it's all projections if it weren't for the hovering glowing squares that extoll the virtues of K2-8, the planet Ibtep is campaigning we set a course for. The Council set up this virtual reality room so the public can "experience" the planet and get used to the idea. I drag in the air they've made taste moist and loamy, and a knot in my chest releases, the way it did every time I went down to Earth. Some part of my body knew this is the sort of world we're supposed to be living on from the very first time I left the station.

Unfortunately, not everyone has the same instinctive reaction. Wyeth has walked close to me along the paths, gripping my arm as he stared at the spiraling trunks and the sticky blue-brown dirt. Several of my sectormates showed up at the same time as us—people I once considered friends, though I faded from their social gatherings to avoid the discomfort of the lies I'd have to tell after I joined Ibtep's rebel group—and they've been chattering nervously the entire way.

Dev, the humorist who's ended up in the Education division, hugs himself as an animal call echoes behind us. "Will it always be this noisy?"

Ilone, the target of my first—unrequited but thankfully brief—infatuation, pokes at one of the informative squares. "It says the area where we'll land is 'prone to light rainfalls, with larger storms being much more rare.'" She shudders. "I don't want any storms, thank you."

"They're not so bad," I say. One downpour in Vietnam sticks in my mind with particular clarity: the shock of cool water from above, Skylar's rain-damp eyelashes so dark against her skin in the shelter of the time cloth, just before I proved myself a soft-brain by letting a twinge of attraction mingle with curiosity and kissing her just to see how it would feel with an Earthling.

Suddenly I'm thinking of three nights ago, of the urgency in her embrace and the salty-sweet smell of her hair.

Celette interrupts. "You've hardly been down-planet more than, what, a day? Different when you can't leave."

Weeks, actually. I can't say that, though, and she's the last person I want to argue with. Celette, with her voice as loud as her blue-dripped braids, started a petition in our first year of upper school to send the Earthling pets home, and convinced a bunch of us to stage a protest outside the Earth Studies hall the year after that. Those efforts have gotten her assigned to scrounger duty: she spends 90 percent of the year cruising the nearest solar systems gathering raw materials, too far away to even talk with anyone back home. All *my* work on Earth's behalf has been in secret, sparing me the penalties she's faced.

Now, she looks across the field and says, "I don't know if I could ever get used to this." If even she's balking, how must the *average* Kemyate feel?

All the misinformation Earth Travel put out over the centuries to make people afraid to stop the experiments on Earth—so the division wouldn't have to give up its influence and the Travelers their freedom on a planet totally under their control—is holding us back now. This should be a time of excitement and celebration. We're going to have a real home.

"Do you think they'd let some of us stay behind on the station if we wanted to?" Dev says.

"I heard once we get there we'll need to start disassembling it for materials," Markhal puts in. He's ignored me so far, likely put off by my previous abruptness. "It's possible they can leave a little of the space livable."

Wyeth stops by a span of cleared soil, where a square informs us that we'll plant crops to supplement and gradually replace what our synthesizers can produce. "Do you think we can get things to grow with the tech we already have?" my brother asks. "Or will we have to invent new equipment?"

"It shouldn't be too hard," I say. "Earthlings managed to grow things without any tools except their hands, sometimes."

Some of the inhabitants of the Earth Studies hall still do that. They could teach us a lot once we're down-planet, couldn't they? We have thousands of years of research to guide us, but it's research no Kemyate has put into practice. The Earthlings could make the transition so much easier for us . . . if we let them.

Leaving Skylar in that exhibit—looking at her cut-up wrist and the loss etched on her face, and walking away—was one of the hardest things I've ever done. I *have* to have better news for her the next time I see her.

Wyeth lingers, crouching down by the garden plot. His eyes have lit up with what looks more like interest than anxiety now.

"It's kind of amazing, isn't it?" he says.

"Better than gliders?" I say with a grin.

He makes a scoffing sound, but he also grins back at me. It could be there's hope here too.

"I think I'd like to see how a real plant would grow," he says, running his fingers through the simulation soil.

The Enforcers usher us through a door up ahead, into a regular room with a raised platform at one end. Nakalya is standing there, flanked by a few other Council members, along with Ibtep and people I recognize from Earth Travel. Jule is leaning against the wall by the far edge of the platform, as if it means little to him to be included. I yank my gaze away from him as the rest of this group of fifty squeezes in around us.

"We'll be taking questions about K2-8 for the next thirty minutes," Nakalya says over the murmuring of the crowd. "Step to the speaker point if you wish to be heard."

A man goes up and asks about living arrangements, and Ilone inquires about the exact frequency of these "larger" storms. Nakalya responds to the former and steps back to give Ibtep, the acknowledged expert on K2-8, the latter. As she discusses weather patterns and rainfall measurements, I study Nakalya. It's the first time I've seen our mayor in the flesh since I returned to the station.

He towers over Ibtep's stocky frame, with an unusual serenity in his square face. In the two years he's been mayor, and the decade he was head of the Health division before then, people have always commented on how hard he's working, mainly I suspect because he's constantly looked rather harried, as if he's about to rush off to solve one problem or another. Now his expression appears almost relaxed, lines vanished from his russet skin like smoothed clay. It's not what I'd expect from someone trying to prepare our people for the biggest move we've ever made.

The evidence suggests genocide agrees with him.

When Ilone leaves the speaker point, it's taken by a guy I know but hadn't noticed during our "tour": Vishnu. We were in the same half year in school, and the same group of friends, until everyone got tired of his complaining about his name, about his parents' insistence that he wear a sarong to class, and about how much everyone hassled him over it. In third year, word went around that he'd had a tantrum and set all of his sarongs on fire. We had a laugh about that, but we also, when he started showing up proudly in Kemyate clothes, gave him a wider berth.

"You're talking as if the decision has already been made," Vishnu says now, speaking louder than the amplification requires. He jabs his scrawny, freckled arm in the air. "We demand a choice. The only planet Kemya belongs with is right here. You can't force us to give up our real home!"

He outright yells the last sentence, and the people next to him cringe. Someone in the back, though, whoops in support. "Now, listen," Nakalya says. Vishnu kicks at the speaker point and stomps out of the room without waiting to hear his answer.

"Do you think he's going scatterbrained, like Ilone's great-aunt?" Dev murmurs beside me. A few years ago Ilone told us her great-aunt had started talking to people who weren't in the room and misidentifying people who were, and the medical clinic hadn't been able to do much other than give her medication to quiet her mood.

Celette shakes her head. "Whether he is or not, he won't accomplish anything like that."

I'm not as certain. Vishnu said *we*. How many people are already standing by him?

. . .

I've just left Earth Travel when Jule hustles out behind me. He strides past to tap a code into the inner-shuttle stop's panel. He's summoning a private shuttle, no doubt—with a code he bought using credits he obtained by selling our group's secrets. I slow, and to my relief the shuttle arrives almost immediately, sparing me a wait in his presence. I move to summon a public one as he steps inside.

"Get on," Jule says quietly.

When I look at him, he makes a sweeping gesture with his arm, keeping it within the shuttle where, thanks to the privacy code, there'll be no surveillance.

I have no desire to talk to Jule in public or otherwise, but Skylar did say he's the one who took the other Earthlings. He could know something about these tests the Health division was running. When I last spoke to Isis, all she and Britta had been able to find regarding Project Nuwa was a vague reference in a requisitions document from sixty-two years ago. Either there've been two Project Nuwas, or it has to do with more than just the most recent Earthling arrivals.

I square my shoulders and step in beside Jule. As soon as the door shuts, he sets the shuttle on a winding course.

"Sorry about the subterfuge; I'm sure you realize the situation's a little delicate," he says, with a politeness I've seen him offer our superiors from time to time, but never me. It grates more than his usual disdain. Once my annoyance might have risen up, loosening my tongue. Today I find it settles into a slow simmer that sharpens my thoughts and flattens my voice.

"What do you want, Jule?"

He pauses, and crosses his arms. "You've been talking to her. Skylar. You've seen her."

He thinks I'd admit that to him? "I don't even know where she is," I say.

"I *know* you have," he says. "I know *her*. Ibtep thinks she's medicated, but you've found a way to see her, to take the implant out or turn it off."

"That's a very interesting story you've come up with," I inform him. It's possibly a little gratifying watching his jaw clench.

"I've seen her do her 'pet' act," he goes on. "I know what it looks like, *Dar*win. The actual pet she observed, Tabzi's friend's—there's a thing Skylar does with her mouth that isn't the drug, it's just something she saw that woman do. No one else is going to notice, because no one else was there when she learned it. But I know. Until a few days ago she wasn't doing it and now she is."

He isn't bluffing, but I'm still not inclined to admit anything. I have questions of my own. "Ibtep lets you watch the feeds?"

"It's part of our deal," Jule says. "*She* wanted Skylar dead. The rest of the Earthlings I got out of there too. But I convinced her to convince the Council it was better to hold on to them. I check in twice a day to make sure she hasn't gone back on her word."

"So she takes your orders now?"

Jule grimaces. "I wasn't sure we could trust her to protect us after we finished Jeanant's mission. So I . . . recorded a few of our conversations, where she said things she wouldn't be able to explain away now. If something happens to Skylar, the Council will get them. If something happens to me, the Council gets them."

That sounds like a Jule sort of plan, though that doesn't guarantee it's true.

"Look," he says before I can respond, "I know I made a hash of things before. I'm *trying* to help—you and whomever else is still involved."

He expects to march right into the middle of this after everything he's done? "Well, *I'm* telling you," I say, "I don't know anything about this."

"You think I'd believe that in a million years?" he demands. When I gaze back at him silently, he bangs his hand against the shuttle's floating grip-pole. "Stop being a soft-brain for once in your life and let's talk. Or are you enjoying having her to yourself too much?"

In that instant, my annoyance boils over into anger. I draw in a breath, and see Jule ready himself, anticipating an insult thrown back. He looks almost eager to work this into a fight. The anger washes out of me.

It's pathetic. Even he has to know how ridiculous that accusation was—that I'd be protecting Skylar out of possessiveness and not because he nearly got her killed more than once.

"If you give me a reason to trust you, I will," I say evenly. "Maybe you should take a look at yourself if you've started to believe everyone around you is going to be that petty."

"Just answer the rotting question, Win," he snaps, looming over me. Unfortunately for him, it isn't much of a loom when I refuse to cower. He's only a couple of inches taller. All I see in him now is desperation. It isn't gratifying at all.

I reach for the control panel, instructing the shuttle to take the next stop.

"I don't know why I ever cared whether you thought I was a soft-brain or anything else," I say as the shuttle slows. Jule's mouth opens as the doors do, but I don't give him a chance to speak before I stride out.

He doesn't follow.

• • •

Halfway through our family dinner the next day, the benches packed around us, Wyeth is sulking over an argument with one of his friends, Mom is trying to cajole him into better spirits, and Dad is studying the texture of the protein-medium on his plate as if considering using it in a painting. The buzz of the usual dinnertime chatter fills the room. Then the lights blink dimmer.

The chatter fades. Heads turn as the cafeteria crowd listens for an official announcement. The large public screen opposite the meal distribution area flickers on, and an electronic voice carries through the speakers.

"What you've been told about Earth's destruction is not true. Please watch, so you can see the facts for yourselves."

My heart starts to thud. Isis and Britta did it. Isis told me they were almost ready, that they'd dug up the necessary recordings and were just finishing making arrangements to muddle any trace on the transmission, but I hadn't expected it this soon.

Wyeth straightens up, his earlier complaints forgotten. Dad and Mom exchange a puzzled glance, and then Dad's gaze slides to me. I try to look as startled as everyone around us.

Footage from just before the detonation plays on the screen. Real voices fill the cafeteria with the command sequence to launch the bomb. The view shows a lumpy power condenser descending from one of the research station's apertures toward Earth as strings of data flit across the bottom of the screen. The pattern imprinted on the corner of the recording will confirm to anyone who checks that this is real footage, not something conjured in a vision well.

I've seen this before, but I'm bracing myself. I know better than anyone else in the room what comes next.

The power condenser crumples in on itself in a shower of sparks. They whirl into a miniature cyclone, darkening from yellow-white to red. The air around them erupts with tongues of ruddy cloud. The cafeteria is completely silent as the swirling clouds surge together. Then they burst forth, flooding the atmosphere in the recorder's view and drowning out all sight of the land below in an instant. Wyeth drops his eating stick.

"Detonation successful," one of the recorded voices says. "Five hundred degrees at the surface. All oxygen consumed."

Wyeth grabs Dad's arm. "It isn't real, is it?" he says, his voice quavering. "Someone's making that up. The people on the research station didn't really—"

"I don't know," Dad says. He looks queasy.

The clouds blaze across the screen for several seconds longer before the feed cuts out. "One more truth you ought to know," the electronic voice says. "Twenty-three Earthlings were saved that day. Our Council purposefully destroyed their planet, and this is the new home we've given them."

They've lifted footage from the exhibit surveillance feed: shots of Skylar's companions staring at the bare rooms of their houses and testing the invisible boundaries outside, their faces drawn with fear. One of the men yells out, "You can't just leave us in here!" A little girl huddles on her front step, sobbing.

"You have the facts. Decide what to do with them."

The screen goes dark. Voices rise around us. Several people are already heading out the door, their meals unfinished, presumably to seek out people they believe can offer answers.

If I know Isis and Britta, this scene is playing out all across the station, in every cafeteria, every workroom, and every fitness center.

Dad has glanced at me again, with that hint of curiosity I saw when I first got home—and something else. He looks pleased, in a particular way that reminds me of the day a much younger me announced that I was going to be as good at creating songs as he was at creating pictures.

I set aside my musical interests years ago, when yet another snarky remark finally made it seem like a lax-act endeavor. No one wanted to listen, so why was I wasting my time? Dad never criticized me for it, but I haven't seen that pleased look since.

In the breath when I could have offered a hint of a smile to say, *Yes, I'm part of this, still fighting for Earth*, white-blond hair glints at the edge of my vision.

Even at a distance, it's easy to recognize Kurra's striking near-albino coloring, almost certainty a result of parentally purchased genetic customization. She and two other Enforcers have just marched in. Kurra's gaze slides across the room and catches mine.

My stomach flips. As menacing as she was when chasing Skylar and me on Earth, she never struck me as quite so dangerous as now. She knows who I am.

I drag my eyes away, back to Dad. "Do you think we should go?" I say evenly, offering nothing.

"Yes," Mom says. "It's too tense here."

As we stand up, Celette charges past our table toward the hall, exclaiming to the group she's in the midst of. Kurra spins on her heel, saying something sharply to them. Any triumph I felt drains away.

I'm part of this? What have I contributed other than pretending I'm not even glad to see that presentation?

That's what I've spent most of my time doing all along. I've pretended to lose interest in my friends. I've pretended my coworkers' dismissals of Earth don't sting. I've pretended to my parents I don't mind the name they gave me, while pretending to everyone else it's something else.

I pretended I didn't want to kiss Skylar the entire time we stood together in that false store. I pretended it didn't kill me to leave her there.

I could jump up on the table right now, stand and shout out a call for justice or a confirmation that the footage was real. I imagine doing it—and my heart seizes up.

The fact is, it'd be impractical to make a scene now. In ten seconds Kurra will have arrested me. Drawing attention to myself would hurt the whole group and our efforts help Skylar. My parents and Wyeth could end up arrested too.

Those are facts, but I know they're not the only reason I let the moment pass as we hurry to the door. It's impractical for any Kemyate to declare public opinions that don't follow the majority, or to make a stand for change where Security can target you. There can always be unfortunate consequences. Ibtep knew it when she was still Thlo; Isis and Britta know it; I know it.

No matter how many things I hate about this place, I'm still one of them.

. . .

I'm at work the next day when a message flashes on my console. Ibtep requests my presence in her office. I look at the words, my skin tightening. Isis and Britta will have been careful. She can't have proof we were responsible for last night's presentation.

The entire station is buzzing about it. The Council released a statement in the early hours of the morning, but all they said about Earth's destruction was that they were investigating the claims. Ha. They also acknowledged that twenty-three Earthlings were now residing in a closed-off portion of the Earth Studies hall "perfectly well provided for." Several feeds from inside their exhibit were made available on the public network as evidence of this. It's our first victory.

I weave through the increasingly constrictive grid of narrow halls to the innermost rooms where the Earth Travel division councilors work. When I tap my thumb to the panel with Ibtep's name over it, she makes me wait a margin longer than feels comfortable before the door opens.

Her small office space holds a private console and a small fold-down desk, with a hover stool between them. She has to get up so I can come in. The room feels crowded the moment the door closes. Normally meetings would be held in the somewhat larger rooms for that purpose. I suppose Ibtep wanted to avoid any chance this conversation would be overheard. There are things I know about her that she'd rather keep secret.

Her impenetrable gaze skewers me. I'm at least half a foot taller than her and yet somehow she takes up most of the space.

"You wanted to see me, Respected Ibtep?" I say.

"You were told to stand down," she says.

"I have."

"I'm supposed to believe you had no hand in that network broadcast?" she says. "That you weren't even aware it was going to happen?"

She is just guessing, then. The tension inside me ebbs. "I can't control what you believe," I reply. "I didn't make that presentation. I wasn't expecting to see it." *At that particular moment*, I add silently.

"You've been talking to Earth sympathizers."

I haven't— Oh. She could be counting Celette, in the VR room.

It could be the Enforcers who were monitoring the room reported me . . . or it could have been someone else. I thought I was being paranoid about Markhal before, but maybe I shouldn't put it past Ibtep to have tapped someone in my social circle to keep an eye on me.

"We happened to be in the same place at the same time," I say. "I offered nothing but support for your plans. Am I expected to completely shun my neighbors?"

"I don't know how you're managing it," Ibtep goes on as if I haven't denied it. "But you should realize you're jeopardizing everything that is important to you. If we find a single piece of evidence that shows you've acted against me or the Council, you will be reassigned once we reach K2-8. A small crew will be required to stay behind on the station to help with the gradual dismantling and to maintain the remaining systems until the process is finished. Our best estimates indicate this will take thirty, perhaps forty, years. Any permission to visit the planet before your term is up can be revoked."

A chill washes over me. Adding together the twelve years to the planet and then thirty or more after, I could be as old as my grandparents are now before I start my real life on the new world I've helped direct us toward.

"You won't find any evidence," I say, managing to keep my voice steady, "because I haven't done anything." I pause, remembering Jule's claims. "Why did you allow the Earthlings to stay alive at all if it bothers you so much for people to be concerned about them?"

Ibtep lets out a humorless chuckle. "'Allowed.' We all make the compromises we need to. It seems more and more I should rethink mine." She turns. "Dismissed, Traveler Pirios."

I walk back to my workroom with her threat gnawing at me. All it will take is one tiny misstep for me to end up watching my family and friends leave the station without me. That manufactured environment in the VR room could be the closest I get to the world I've wanted for so long.

Well, I've been risking that since the beginning, haven't I? I dedicated myself to Jeanant's mission for all those other people too— for everyone on Kemya. I couldn't take my freedom in exchange for knowing Skylar and the other Earthlings will be imprisoned for the rest of their lives, or worse.

Still, I'm distracted enough that I don't notice Jule approaching in the hall until his shoulder has bumped mine.

"Watch where you're going, Darwin," he snaps, his wrist hitting my side as I glance around. My carry-pouch falls to the floor. "Lax-act," Jule mutters, bending to pick it up. He shoves the pouch into my hand, and surprise softens my retort.

"Better a lax-act than a coaster."

"*I'm* getting my work done," he says, already moving on.

My fingers curl around the pouch and the solid weight inside it that wasn't there before.

7.

Skylar

I know this is hard to believe," I finish. "*I* wouldn't believe it if I hadn't been there. But it's true. There's nowhere to go back to. Earth is . . . gone."

Mom, Dad, and Angela are staring at me. I shift on my awkward perch on the edge of the bathtub. Dad rubs his forehead as if he has a headache. Mom shakes her head, but she doesn't seem capable of speech. It's Angela who breaks the silence.

"That's crazy," she says. "How could you have been off in space for weeks? You were only missing for a day!" But there's more fear than denial in her eyes.

"Time travel," I remind her. "The people who took you, they didn't know the exact day Win met me, so they didn't line things up perfectly. But if they hadn't come and taken you, you would have lived seventeen more years and I'd never have come back, and then . . ."

A wave of fiery clouds swallowing the planet.

"Skylar, this obviously seems very real to you," Dad says in his quiet, methodical way. "But—you said you've been drugged—are you sure some of it hasn't been hallucinations, or impressions these people induced somehow? We could still be *on* Earth."

I wish I could believe that. "I've only been drugged since after I saw the detonation over Earth," I say. "Everything before then, I was completely myself."

"That doesn't mean—" Mom starts. She swipes her hair back with a hand at either temple. Her mouth is tight.

"I know how it sounds," I say. "But you can see, can't you, *something's* going on that's . . . unearthly? The materials they used to construct this place. The borders we can't see or touch, that just make us feel we can't keep going. Why would anyone grab all of us and stick us in a place like this and just leave us? Maybe this is crazy, but what explanation could there be that *isn't*? And if it isn't true, if this is a story someone brainwashed me into believing, why would they have drugged me and tried to stop me from telling you?"

Another silence settles over us. Angela's expression cracks. "Then my dad . . . Lisa . . ."

"Yeah," I say, my eyes tearing up. "I'm sorry. I wish it weren't true."

"They were— You said you knew one of the boys who took us," Mom says with a rough gesture of her arm. "Where is he now?"

Her description of the guy who gave her that note confirmed that it was Jule. I swallow hard. I don't know how he found out what Thlo was planning, how he managed to get there before us—maybe using one of his rich friends' "fun ships"—but it doesn't matter now.

"I don't know," I say. "He . . . He was informing on our group. He isn't someone we can trust."

I believed he cared about me. He even told me he—

I wince away from that memory. He was passing on information about our plans to the Enforcers in exchange for credits to help his father and grandfather maintain their extravagant lifestyle. He risked the entire mission, he set Britta up to be injured, he let me stick my neck into danger so many times while he hid his secret. Even when I confronted him, he still talked about it as if his decisions had been perfectly *reasonable*.

"If all this started happening before you . . . left, why didn't you come to us?" Mom goes on. "You should have told me. Maybe we could have helped."

"You hardly believe me now," I say. "You never would have believed me then. And telling you would have put all of us in danger."

"I would have *tried*," Mom says, and the pain in her voice makes my stomach twist. Dad reaches past me to squeeze her hand.

"Patricia," he says, "it doesn't make a difference now, does it? We're here. From what Skylar's said, her telling us wouldn't have changed the outcome. If it is all true."

I can tell there isn't any point in pushing the idea further, not right now. They need time for it to sink in.

"We're going to get through this," I say. "Win and some of the others, they're doing everything they can, and there are things we can do too. But first—if you want to talk about what I just told you, with me or each other, *please* make sure you're in here. Everywhere else, they're monitoring us. It's dangerous if they find out I'm aware enough to have told you this, which means we all have to keep pretending I'm drugged, too. And you have to be careful what you do out there. The more they see us making a fuss or acting aggressive, no matter how much you want answers, they'll take that as a sign that we're as unstable as they think. To write us off. If we're going to survive, we need to show them they can respect us, and what they respect is reason, practicality, and patience."

I look at Mom while I'm saying the last part without really meaning to, thinking about the way she demanded answers from the Kemyates during the Health examinations. Her shoulders go up.

"We can't stand by and let these people—whoever they are—do whatever they want," she says. "If they try to hurt you again—"

"Then I need you to back down and let me handle it," I interrupt. "If you try to get in their way too obviously, they'll just hurt *you*. You saw what they did to Mr. Sinclair and Toby."

"Skylar—" Mom protests, but Angela breaks in.

"So what can we do?" she asks. Her chin is trembling and she has to swipe at her eyes, but she holds my gaze. "How can we get them to stop treating us like this?"

I want to hug her. "I guess . . . the first thing is deciding what to tell everyone else."

"What do you mean?" Dad says.

"It seems wrong, letting them keep hoping we can get home when that's not true," I say. "And they don't know just how careful they need to be if people from outside come in again."

"But you already said we have to pretend we don't know," Angela says. "You really think we can trust everyone else to keep quiet about it? What will these . . . Kemyate people do to you if they figure out you've been talking?"

"I don't know," I admit.

Angela pulls herself straighter, her jaw setting. "You tell everyone else that everyone they knew, everything back home, it's all gone—my *mom* isn't going to be able to hold it together," she says. "Or Evan—you remember how shaken up he was when his grandfather had that stroke and died overnight? He's not going to be able to act like everything's the same. It sounds like it'd be way safer for all of us if we don't say anything about . . . aliens, or Earth being destroyed, to anyone."

Mom's frowning, but Dad sighs and says, "That's a good point."

I think of watching our neighbors talk about returning home to the people they miss, and my skin crawls. But I've already seen how quickly even a well-laid plan can end in tragedy. I can't put everyone at risk just to clear my conscience.

"Okay," I say. "Then . . . if you want to help, I think the best we can do from now on is show off the ways we *are* strong and capable. Mom, you could encourage people to keep their fitness up. One of you could suggest that Ms. Cavoy and Mr. Patterson apply their science backgrounds to building things we can use, or testing the boundaries more systematically. You can all start conversations with people about things they know a lot about, so the Kemyates can hear about it. Get into intellectual debates. Question what's going on and the most likely possibilities and outcomes—show we can get thoughtful and logical. And avoid anything that'll make us look weak. Stay calm, and help anyone else who gets upset calm down. That sort of thing."

Mom stands up abruptly before I've finished speaking. She shakes her head again. "I don't know. I can't wrap my head around this."

Dad gets up, touching her shoulder. "Let's give ourselves some time to think it through," he says. "We can talk more later if we need to."

He glances at me. I nod. "As long as we're in here. Just make an excuse, and I'll come."

"We have to—" Mom mutters, and cuts herself off with an exasperated noise. She lets Dad direct her out.

I slide closer to Angela, and she leans against me. "I guess we should start washing these clothes," she says, but she doesn't make a move to start. She draws in a breath, and screws her eyes shut.

"Ang," I say, my voice breaking. She turns toward me as I wrap my arms around her, a sob bursting from her throat.

I've been released from the burden of being the only one here who knows the truth by shifting that weight onto the people I care about most.

• • •

I go back to my drugged act the second I step out of the bathroom. It's harder now. Throughout the day I catch myself on the verge of giving too thoughtful a response, too alert a look. My skin crawls at the sense of those distant watching eyes.

I don't know if Win and the others have managed to spread word through the station yet. Tens of thousands of Kemyates could be staring into the exhibit now.

"You know," Angela says to Mr. Patterson that first afternoon, almost brittle in her chipperness, "you and Ms. Cavoy and Mrs. Green should start teaching us again. I don't want to end up way behind everyone else when we get out."

I stifle a wince at the lie, but Mr. Patterson nods and says, "It would be good for all of us to keep our minds active." I guess everyone was getting pretty bored, because all the kids from the high school and even Ruth and Liora come over when he starts demonstrating a few ways to compare the composition of different types of ration bars, using our tap water and the soap cubes.

"I should be able to come up with a physics experiment for us to try in the morning," says Ms. Cavoy, looking so keen I wonder how bored *she's* been. And after dinner everyone gathers by the playground to listen to Mrs. Green from the English department begin an annotated telling of her favorite novel, *A Tale of Two Cities*, abridged by her memory. I'm not sure how much appreciation the Kemyates will have for that, given their feelings on art, but it does seem thematically appropriate.

The next morning, Mom goes into personal-trainer mode, leading everyone willing through an hour-long routine of stretches, crunches, push-ups, laps, and aerobics. "We're not letting ourselves get soft in here," she announces. Dad puts his accounting skills to use by offering math lessons, though we're reduced to scratching figures in the dirt where we pull up some of the grass.

I can't tell how much he and Mom believe my story, versus accepting it as a possibility they'll play along with because staying physically and mentally engaged is good for us either way. Every now and then Mom will turn to Dad, or Dad to Mom, for a hug or a touch or just a few murmured words, more often than I remember them doing before. At least they have each other to share the burden if they're starting to accept it.

Dad seems to pick up on the moments I need reassurance most, giving a subtle pat to my back or a squeeze of my shoulder when one of the others starts talking about home. For the first couple days, Mom hardly talks to me at all in my fake zoned-out state and jerks her gaze away awkwardly when I catch her watching me—but when we're brushing our teeth the second night she leans over to give the back of my head a peck and says, "If you need anything, anything at all, I want you to *tell* me. I'll make it happen."

"Of course," I say, even though the things I need most, she can't possibly arrange. "I will." And she relaxes a little.

Operation "show off our strengths" has been going on for five days when Angela comes rushing back from the store and says, "There's more stuff!"

All six of us from our house troop over, meeting with a bunch of the others as we go. Inside the store, my eyes widen for a second before I control my reaction. Fresh shirts and pants in a variety of sizes and colors—and Kemyate-style fabric—hang on the racks. A few new types of ration bars sit on the shelves, alongside a selection of canned beverages. A stack of metallic rectangles that prove to be solid, tablet-size screens waits on the counter. Dad picks one up and wakes it with a tap of the display, which I notice is designed to look like the tablets we had back on Earth.

"Games," he says, sounding puzzled. "And some videos and music."

It's done. Kemya must be watching now, and the Council has provided us with additional supplies to try to pretend we aren't so badly off.

I hope Win and the others made it through the reveal safely.

The tablets provide enough distraction that for a while no one does much other than play the loaded Earth media, as if we can reach home through those screens. I act as if I'm interested too, but I have to tune out inside. It's too painful seeing fragments of the world I know is ashes. Too painful watching everyone else wrapped up in them, not knowing.

After a full day of that, I escape outside, though it's not much of an escape with all those Kemyate gazes weighing on me. I sit down on the sidewalk and lean against one of the lampposts, gazing up at the sky as I will a message to come. The same false blue stares back at me.

I let my eyes drift shut. My mind slips back to that night in the store. To Win's arms around me, warm and steady. His breath on my cheek. *I'm going to keep fighting until you have a real home here.*

"Are you all right, Skylar?"

My eyes pop open. Mr. Patterson is standing over me, his face shadowed with concern. My back stiffens. For him to ask, after the daze I've been in since we arrived here, I must have looked even more out of it than usual. Or maybe just more upset. I'm supposed to be numb.

"Sure," I say in my practiced hazy way. "Just enjoying the sun."

He peers at me for a moment longer before walking on. I realize I've clasped my hands in front of me, running my thumb over the back of one. I drop my arms to my sides. Pulling myself to my feet, I head back inside.

Over the next couple days, we gradually pick up the lectures and experiments and workouts again. Wandering the exhibit, I try to see my fellow Earthlings through Kemyate eyes. What would they make of Mr. Patterson managing to light a flame with bits from a pencil Cintia had in her pocket when she was taken? Of Mom cheering a group through a scrambled climb of the tower of storage boxes?

Nearly everyone is rising to the challenge wholeheartedly, without even understanding why it's important. But we're only capable of so much with the limited resources we've been given. I somehow doubt the Kemyates will take that into consideration. They'll just see how basic most of our efforts still are.

I'm smothering my impatience to talk it through further with Angela, to see if she has any ideas of what else we could try, while I sit on the dining room floor with her and Evan that night, only half engaging in their conversation. Evan's face is sallow, his shoulders hunched as he flicks at the wrappers of our meal.

"I wish there was some way we could let them know we're still alive, and okay," he says without looking at either of us. "I keep thinking about how frantic my parents must be."

Angela catches my eyes for a second before reaching over to grasp his hand. Of course Evan would be worrying not about himself, but how other people are being affected by his disappearance.

They're not frantic, I think. *They're not feeling or doing anything at all.* The secret, the knowledge we're keeping from him, coils in my gut. I don't know what I can say that won't stick in my throat.

"We're going to get through this," Angela says, like I said to her and my parents that first morning. He smiles at her weakly. She smiles back for just an instant before her jaw twitches.

"I need to— I'll be right back," she says abruptly. We stare after her as she scrambles up and bolts for the stairs. My stomach knots.

"I wonder what's going on," I say carefully, getting to my feet.

"I didn't mean to make her upset," Evan says, looking even more sick than before. "I— I'll just clean this up."

He gathers the wrappers as I head upstairs after Angela. The bathroom door is closed. I knock.

"Ang?"

"You can come in."

She has her back to me when I open the door. As soon as I close it, she turns around, her hands over her face.

"I'm sorry," she says between teary gulps. "I know I can't let them see— I know. I know."

I pull her to me and she drops her head to my shoulder. A lump rises in my throat as she shivers against me.

What if it's too much for her, for my parents, to go on like this? Maybe I shouldn't have told even them.

8.

Win

There are nine doors between the inner-shuttle stop and my apartment. One of those belongs to Celette's family. Unfortunately, she's stepping out just as I get off the shuttle on my way home from work.

Her gaze latches onto me immediately. "Win!" she says as she bounds over, with a grimace I know is because she thinks I should go by my full name. "I'm glad I caught you. A bunch of us are going to the Council rooms tomorrow at twelfth hour. We have to *insist* that they give us more information. You'll come, won't you?"

I'm abruptly twice as aware of the watching eyes on the other end of the hall's surveillance feeds. I offer Celette a careful smile.

It's been four days now since the Council's initial statement. Their "investigations" have produced no conclusions they've shared so far. People are getting restless.

This is what I wanted. I wanted everyone pressing the Council for the truth and thinking about what we can do for the Earthlings.

I hate how uncomfortable Celette's question makes me, and how I have to answer.

"I'll see," I say, and she pushes my shoulder.

"It matters to you, doesn't it, that they must have lied to us?" she says. "You used to care about this stuff. Did all that Traveler training rot your conscience?"

No, I think. *It's made me care too much for it to be safe to show it.* I give her another awkward smile and say, "It's nothing to do with that. I just— I'm not certain the best thing is . . ."

Her mouth flattens. "Never mind then," she says before I can decide how to finish that sentence. She strides off down the hall.

Very smooth, Darwin.

Inside my apartment, Wyeth has one of the exhibit feeds up on the main screen. He's leaning against the wall, holding a can of sizzle-water, as he watches the group of Skylar's schoolmates and the chemistry teacher drink similar beverages and eat their ration-bar dinner.

"Are they going to stay in there forever?" he asks me when I join him. "What about when we get to K2-8?"

"Good question," I say. "I suppose the Council is still deciding, though I hope they'll let the rest of us have a say." I pause. There's no surveillance in here. "What do *you* think should happen to them?"

Wyeth frowns at the screen. "I'm not sure. They don't seem very happy. It's because they weren't taken properly, right? The other Earth Studies Earthlings don't act as if they mind."

Mom must have caught at least some of our conversation, because she comes out of her bedroom saying, "The Council should let people go in to set up the rest of the exhibit the way it was meant to be. That would help the new Earthlings settle better."

I stare at her. "Is that your position? They should just learn to like the life we're giving them in there?" I'm not certain how I expected her to see the situation, but I was hoping for better than that.

Her gaze darts to me, her dispassionate expression faltering. "It seems to me," she says hesitantly, "that they would be more comfortable in a familiar setting . . ."

Before she can finish that thought, Dad bursts in from the hall. "There's a public announcement starting," he says.

The screen has already blinked from the exhibit feed to an image of Nakalya in the Council chambers, the other Council members surrounding his tall form. He steeples his muscular hands in front of him. I step closer. Possibly Celette won't need to stage her protest after all.

"My fellow Kemyates," our mayor says. "We have heard many of your concerns over the past few days. It is our goal, as always, to find solutions that all Kemyates can take confidence in. On the matter of the assault of Earth, we are still gathering data."

An exasperated sigh escapes me. Dad glances over. "You think they already know the details of what happened."

I *know* they know. "I think it would have been impossible for someone to carry out an operation that large without the Council being aware," I say carefully.

"Hush," Mom says. "We'll know nothing if we don't hear him."

"On the matter of the Earthlings recovered shortly before the assault," Nakalya is continuing, "we have arrived at a plan we believe will result in maximum comfort and security for all. As they are unlikely to adjust to their current quarters, we would instead provide them with a greater freedom. Several families have approached the Council with offers of sanctuary. Once appropriate preparations have been made, we will equip the Earthlings with implants to help them relax into their new surroundings and place them with host families with whom they can access a greater area of the station."

He says it so smoothly my spirits lift for just an instant before the one vital phrase sinks in. *Equip them with implants.*

"That sounds generous of them," Mom says.

"They're going to give them *implants*," I say sharply, "like the pets. They'll be medicated out of their minds."

To my relief, a look of horror crosses her face. "Oh," she says. "I didn't— You're right. The way he said it, it sounded . . . different."

Nakalya makes a finishing gesture. "We hope you find this solution satisfactory and welcome your response so we can ensure it is so."

A sickly cold pools in my stomach as the screen flicks back to the feed Wyeth was watching. That's their solution. After everything, somehow I still expected better of *them.* The Council cannot have made it more clear: they will never willingly accept the Earthlings as our equals.

Wyeth is looking at me and Mom now. "Do you think they'll really do it?" he says.

"It'd be a tragedy!" Dad says. "That drug, it dulls all the creativity out of them."

"The innovation," Mom says, nodding. "You can see how much it means to them even now to be able to problem solve in their environment."

My voice chokes before I manage to speak. "How about how much it means to them to make the most basic decisions for themselves? How about simply being able to feel happy or sad about what's happening to them, around them . . ." I throw my hands in the air. "They don't exist just to represent the parts of Earth that interest you. They're *people.*"

"I think Win's right," Wyeth says quietly into the stunned silence that follows, which would probably please me more if my parents weren't gaping at me as if I'd just declared I was signing up for scrounger duty. I probably would find myself signed up for scrounger duty if I said half of that in public. My body's gone rigid, but inside I'm shaking.

All the ways they love Earth and all the things they appreciate, it's still not enough for them to see Earthlings as fellow human beings.

"Win," Mom says. "Of course it's awful too. But there isn't any—"

I don't want to hear it. "Stand there, watch, and really *look* and *listen*," I say, pointing at the feed on the screen. "Imagine those boys were me and Wyeth, and then tell me what we can't do for them."

I swivel, longing to stalk out of the apartment to put more space between us. Instead, I march into my bedroom and throw myself on my bunk. I drop my head into my hands.

The fact is, it's not them I'm really angry at. I'm disappointed that they think that way, but the anger, that's for Nakalya—Nakalya and his Council and probably Ibtep too, for their unconscionable plan.

It sounded good even to Dad and Mom, who at least respect *some* Earthling qualities. That means it'll have sounded good to almost everyone.

• • •

I browse the network well into the night, and, as I expected, only find a few notes protesting the Council's pet plan. Most of the discussions accept the idea as a solution and merely focus on the logistics: how soon, which families should take them.

In the morning, after Wyeth and my parents have gone for breakfast and I'm waiting for a scheduled talk with Isis, I pull out the palm-size tablet Jule tucked into my carry-pouch the other day. It contains only one file, two video clips edited together. Both are of Ibtep and Jule talking in his apartment. In one, the two of them discuss details of Jeanant's original mission, with Ibtep explicitly mentioning her intention to disable the time field generator. In the other, she offers suggestions of how to undermine the Earth Travel authorities she's pretending to support.

It's undeniably incriminating—and not just of Ibtep but of Jule. I told him in the shuttle I'd trust him if he gave me a reason to. He must be hoping this is reason enough. Protecting Skylar and the other Earthlings matters enough to him that he was willing to put the evidence in my hands, so I could choose to expose both him and Ibtep if I wanted.

I'm not sure how much sway Ibtep might have over the Council, but maybe there's some way we can use this to halt their plan—if it's real.

The communicator in my ear crackles. "You there?" Isis says.

"Of course," I say. "You saw the announcement, I assume?"

"Yes."

"We have to do something," I say. "We can't let the Council hand them out like bonus credits. No one else cares!"

"I know," Isis says. "We've been monitoring the network. I hate to say it, but I think Skylar's efforts may have worked against us. She's kept the Earthlings from showing much weakness, but that seems to have convinced people that drugging them won't make them lose much. What does it matter if their emotions are numbed if they don't seem very emotional to begin with?"

"That's ridiculous," I say. "They're obviously—" I stop. It's obvious to me, because I'm willing to see it. For someone who wants an excuse not to think about the problem anymore, it may not be. "So I tell her to get them acting more emotional now. Show how much it means to them to stay together."

"That seems like the best approach for them to take," Isis says. "Maybe they could emphasize how important it is for them to remember Earth and be able to talk about it too."

Yes. "We can make it sound as if erasing the planet from their minds would be like destroying it all over again," I say with a flicker of inspiration. "Have you found anything that indicates how much time we have?"

"Nothing solid, but from what I've seen I'd guess the Council is aiming to finish this within the week."

"A week," I repeat.

"We have more time than that," Isis reminds me. "Even after they have the implants, we can still—"

"No," I say. "You know how pets get treated even by the more considerate families. If any of them ends up with a bad one . . ." We're all aware there are those who take advantage of their pet's drugged state behind closed doors, illegal though it is in theory.

"I know," Isis says. "But we're asking all Kemya to completely alter their attitudes about Earth. This sort of thing takes time. You can't let your impatience lead the way."

It's a familiar criticism, but this time, after watching Nakalya's calm pronouncement, after hearing my mother reason out what Skylar and her companions deserve, I feel myself hardening against it.

"I can," I say sharply, "because it's not impatience. It's recognizing what any decent person would see as a necessity. Whatever we have to do, whatever we have to risk, we need to fix this *now*. The fact is, if we'd all been a little more 'impatient,' we'd have left Kemya right after Britta was injured and this entire catastrophe might have been avoided. I'm not watching those people turned into pets. Whether you keep helping is up to you."

There's a moment of silence, filled only by the thudding of my heart. I don't know what I'll do if she pulls out now, but I don't regret a word I just said.

"I agree with Win," a chirpy voice speaks up.

I hadn't realized Britta was listening. Despite the tension inside me, I smile. When I asked before, Isis said Britta was still recovering, but she sounds like her usual energetic self.

Isis clears her throat. "I do too," she says. "We'll get through to them, one way or another. I'll signal Skylar so you can meet with her tonight. And we've been compiling footage from the exhibit feeds as well, to put together another presentation emphasizing how human the Earthlings are. We should be able to use that too."

"I might have other footage that'll be useful," I say, and tell Isis about Jule's tablet. "Would you be able to confirm whether it's authentic?"

"If you can get it to me," Isis says. "This is interesting. I looked into Jule's activities—I'd wondered if he'd been working with Ibtep before, creating those delays in our work so she'd have more time to convince the Council of her plan for Earth, but it appears he did stop passing on information after Britta's injury, as he told Skylar. And that was before Ibtep even presented her proposal, wasn't it?"

"It was," I say. "So he's a horrible person but not completely appalling? Do you think he could honestly want to help us?" I'm certain I don't *feel* good about involving him, but my feelings don't matter if he can extend our reach.

"Let me look at his recording first," Isis says dryly.

"Win can drop it on his way to the Earth Studies hall," Britta says. "I'm assigned to collect the tech disposal bins on the eighth level tomorrow. There's one just a few sectors from the entrance."

Isis's voice goes quiet as they talk to each other in their apartment. "I don't know. If you were caught with it . . ."

"It won't be hard to hide when I'm carting a whole bunch of devices around."

"When we agreed—"

"Blast the agreement," Britta says. "Unless you can think of a different ploy that isn't at least ten times more risky? This is nothing, Ice."

I don't know what agreement they're talking about, so I just wait. Isis sighs. "All right."

"I had another idea," I say before they sign off, and share the thought I had in the VR room about the Earthlings helping us adapt to K2-8. "You could compile some footage that supports that idea as well," I finish. "There's little we Kemyates like less than wasting something we could have put to good use, is there?"

Isis laughs. "That's one way of looking at it. We'll pull something together."

Any humor in me fades as I take out the earpiece. In a few days, we have to convince the Kemyate public to completely change how they think about Earth and the people who lived there.

．　．　．

My nerves are jumpy as I stroll down the hall one level below the Earth Studies exhibits, even though no one should be watching me now. Britta will have hacked into the surveillance feeds, and Isis will be dropping in loops that don't include me, covering me as I walk through the station. The two of them can't account for everything, though. An off-duty Enforcer or a rescheduled patrol could pass by, or someone from Earth Travel who'd recognize me.

I insert Jule's tablet into the receptacle Britta indicated and hurry on to the narrow door that leads into the exhibits' maintenance passages. Inside, I hesitate, breathing as quietly as I can, listening for movement in the dimness ahead.

The thin gray walkway is empty. When I reach the main crosspath I turn left, toward the newer exhibits.

The lift-pad to Skylar's exhibit is the last in the line. I hover Isis's doctored scan-key over the lift's control panel and its display lights up. When I gesture at it, the air solidifies beneath my feet, pushing me upward.

The lift deposits me in a small, dark alcove with its own set of controls. I instruct the panel in front of me to open, and duck out behind the store's counter.

Skylar's leaning against that counter. She straightens up as I do, with the smile that makes my pulse skip no matter how many times I see it.

"You're still okay," she says, and hugs me. For a long moment nothing in the universe exists except the press of her arms around me and the softness of her skin where her temple brushes my cheek.

She eases back, still smiling. The toll captivity is taking on her shows in the paling of her skin, the thinning of her face, but her brown eyes are just as steady as when I met her. She isn't beaten.

The thinning reminds me. I pull the packet I spent a few extra credits on out of my carry-pouch and hand it to her, grinning as her face lights up.

"I can't believe I'm excited to get Kemyate food," she says, twisting the corner to set the pseudo sausage-and-toast meal heating. "But thank you, so much."

"Even Kemyates know our ration bars are wretched," I say. "That's one of the types you particularly liked, isn't it?"

"Yes," she says. "It's perfect."

She gulps it down, and I hold out my hand for the empty wrapper, to remove all evidence. A little more color has come into her face. I wish I could bring her a month's worth of meals, but at least I could offer this much before the bad news I have to deliver.

"The Council's announced a new plan," I say. "They've decided since you're not 'happy' in here, you'll all be better off placed as pets."

Skylar stiffens. "They would really— And everyone's okay with that?"

"Not *everyone*," I say. "But enough. You know how most Kemyates think."

"I do," she says. She pushes her hair away from her face, a gesture I now recognize she picked up from her mother. The feeling of having been a spectator to her life through the feeds sits uneasily in me.

"Once we're out of here, and drugged," Skylar goes on, "the Council would be able to keep doing those examinations, or other tests, without anyone really knowing, wouldn't they? Did you find out what Project Nuwa is?"

I hadn't thought the situation that far through. She's right. The Council could easily ask that the Earthlings' "owners" bring them by for regular medical checks and do whatever they want then. Is that why they chose this solution?

"Britta and Isis couldn't find out very much," I say. "It does look as though the project has existed for a long time—decades."

"Decades?" Skylar says. "Why would they be keeping some project about Earthlings secret— Oh." Her eyes widen.

"What?"

"What's the one thing that 'justifies' the way you all treat us?" she says with a sudden fervor. "What supposedly makes us less than the rest of you?"

"The experiments on Earth," I say, not quite following. "The way the time shifts degraded the atomic bonds of everything there, including the people."

"Exactly," she says. "What if they've found out we aren't as 'degraded' as they assumed—or that there's some way to reverse it? Maybe being off Earth, we've started to recover. It would explain the secrecy, wouldn't it?"

The suggestion conflicts with every fact I know about the effects of time manipulation, but that doesn't make it impossible. There are a lot of "facts" I've learned I shouldn't have taken for granted.

"If that's true," I say, "and we could show that, then it'd be undeniable that we should accept you as equals. I'll see if Isis and Britta have any more tricks they can use to pry into the records."

The eagerness in Skylar's expression dims. "I guess we don't have much time. Is the Council putting this 'pet' plan into motion soon?"

"We might have a way to stop it altogether," I tell her, and repeat the ideas Isis and I discussed about emotion and memory. "I know it'll be a hard balance, still showing you should be respected while also revealing more sensitivity. We'll push on the public's sympathies from our end as hard as we can. We won't let this happen to you. And maybe we'll find out something about this Project Nuwa in time for it to help."

"All right," Skylar says. "I can get my parents and Angela to work on the others." She drags in a breath, and I see how scared she is. I don't realize the fear might be for more than herself and her Earthling companions until she adds, "What will the Council do to you, if they find out you're still going against them?"

"Don't worry about that," I say. She has enough hanging over her.

"Is it still just the three of you—you and Isis and Britta?"

"Odgan helped relay the transmission revealing what happened on Earth through Kemhar to obscure the source," I say. "Tabzi reached out to Isis a little while ago, quietly, to offer support if we need it. Emmer's kept his head down, and I don't know what Mako and Pavel think, since we left them out in the end. The only member of the group Ibtep's still associating with is Jule."

At the pained crooking of Skylar's mouth, I wish I hadn't mentioned that last bit. She inclines her head. "Of course," she says. "I guess it's no surprise that *he'd* take advantage of her influence, no matter what she's done. I can't believe I was so blind."

I'm not certain knowing Jule's real reasons for associating with Ibtep would reassure her, and I don't yet know if the proof he shared is valid. I do know: "Skylar, you weren't—"

"I was. I should have seen what he was really like. I know you thought so."

A signal buzzes, the warning I programmed into my armlet to let me know to wrap things up. I have only a few more minutes in the window Isis thinks it's safe to keep looping the feed, but I can't leave Skylar like this.

There's just one thing I can think of that might convince her—a thing I've tried to forget myself. I've wanted to speak the truth a little more, though, haven't I?

"I really didn't," I say, propping myself against the counter next to her, her arm just an inch from mine. "I— When I started Traveler training, Jule was already through the first half year, but they mix students across the curriculum so you get to know your future colleagues. We had a few classes together; I'd see him in the common areas: this brash guy who could get everyone laughing and never seemed fazed by anything." I pause, my face warming at a particularly clear recollection: standing at the back of one class or another, that first week when I knew no one in the room at all, watching Jule tip back his head with a guffaw at the instructor's response to a challenge he'd made. The smooth, dark curve of his throat, the flash of his teeth. "He makes people feel it's good to be around him, as if his attention is a special commodity. I *know*. It's easy to be attracted to that. It's only if something else gets in the way, like if there happens to be something about you that means when you go over to try to talk to him, he'd rather laugh at you than with you . . . You saw enough of that. Then he doesn't seem so great. That doesn't mean I don't understand why other people see him differently."

It occurs to me then that Skylar may not read between the lines, not just because it's Jule I'm talking about but because he's a guy. From what I recall, her community on Earth was stricter about limiting attraction along gender lines than Kemyates tend to. Although, from the startled look she's giving me, I suspect she's absorbed enough Kemyate culture to figure it out. Then the corner of her mouth curls up.

"So who were you jealous of: him for being with me, or me for being with him? Or both?"

I shoot her a sideways glance. "Who says I was jealous of anyone?" I say, matching her light tone, and she nudges my shoulder with hers. It's not as if I didn't confess a small portion of my feelings for her on the way back to Earth.

She has no idea of the full measure, though. I didn't want her to. She could easily think it was a fleeting desire that's now gone.

I'm acting as if it were only that by making it a joke, aren't I?

My chest tightens. It's time for me to leave, but I can't stand to keep pretending. If I could tell her about Jule, I should be able to tell her about *her*.

I step away from the counter, finding her hand as I turn to face her, twining my fingers with hers.

"It's been a long time since I was interested in anything from Jule other than an end to his hassling," I say. "And I might have been jealous of him, but in a way, I was glad it happened. Because you being with him, it showed me . . . I heard my mother say, when I was younger, that you only know you care about someone to the center of your being when you want to see them happy more than you want to see them with you. I didn't completely understand what she meant, until then."

Skylar's not just looking but staring at me now, her lips parted. "I . . ." she starts, and as she hesitates, my armlet buzzes again. I'll be caught if I stay. There's no time left.

"I have to go," I say. "I'll try to come back in a few days to let you know what progress we've made. Stay safe."

I squeeze her hand and let go. Then I duck back through the opening, the panel sliding shut behind me.

9.

Skylar

I leave the store in a daze I don't have to fake. I wade through the streaks of lamplight and climb the front steps of my house, but in my head I'm still standing by the counter, held by Win's low voice and the untempered affection in his eyes. *You only know you care about someone to the center of your being when you want to see them happy more than you want to see them with you.*

When he talked to me after he caught Jule and me kissing, he didn't try to convince me that Jule was a bad guy. He didn't criticize my judgment. It bothered him, I could tell, but he accepted it.

At the time I assumed he accepted it because it was only my friendship he really wanted, and I'd shown him he hadn't lost that. But it was obviously more. He could see that Jule was making me happy right then. I mattered enough to Win that he wouldn't take that away from me, no matter how much he wished things were different.

I should have said something—he laid it out, and I gave him *nothing.* I stop in the front hall of the house, my hand rising to my mouth. Remembering the one time we kissed, an age and three months ago. The conversation afterward, when he admitted it'd been more an experiment than anything else, soured the moment, but we've come a long way, both of us, since then. *I* almost kissed him on that first trip to Kemya—if I hadn't gotten the impression he was rebuffing me, it might have been Win and me instead of Jule and me from the beginning.

Maybe the problem was I tried to *say* something. If I'd simply touched his cheek, drawn him closer . . .

Is that all *he* was looking for, though? *To the center of your being.* When I reach down to the center of me, beneath the tingling racing over my skin, all I feel is the sharp little fragments of my heart, cracked by Jule's betrayal and then shattered by the loss of my entire world. They dig into my chest as I inhale the still, dry air. I don't know if I could assemble them into anything close to the devotion Win expressed. Just thinking about it makes the ache spread deeper.

There are still things I could have told him. Like that, other than a few particles of happiness here and there, the only real joy I've found in the last few weeks is in those brief interludes with him, when I could forget about where we were, joke like we might have before, make our plans toward a better future.

I will tell him that, when he comes back. Which he has to. The news he brought creeps to the fore of my mind with a trickle of nausea. The Council would have us all numbed insensible, handed out to be used and abused. I suppress a shudder at the memory of Jule's friends poking me, ordering me about, talking about passing me around like a living sex doll.

This time it would be everyone except me. If they come for us, they'll probably check my implant and discover I've been faking. And then . . .

We can't let it come to that.

When I reach the top of the stairs and find Mom standing out-side her doorway, I startle. She looks as if she's been waiting for me.

"Why don't we brush our teeth?" she says with an odd edge in her voice. I nod and shuffle into the bathroom.

"Where were you?" Mom says as soon as she's shut the door. "You were meeting with that . . . alien boy again?"

"Yeah," I say, torn between relief at her almost acceptance of the "alien" idea and confusion. "He had some news he needed to tell me. I was going to talk with you and Dad and Angela about it tomorrow."

"Why didn't you tell us you were going?" she says. "How many times have you snuck off like that before?"

"This is only the second time I've seen him," I say. "And I didn't—It's not like it's *easy* for me to tell you things. If I'm dragging you into the bathroom nine times a day, the people watching us are going to realize something's up. It wasn't like you needed to know."

"I think I'm the best judge of what I 'need' to know," Mom snaps, and presses her hand to her forehead. "I just don't like you wander-ing off into the night without a word."

"I was fine, Mom," I say. "I mean, as much as I am any other time, right now. The people Win's working with, they have it set up so no one knows we're meeting."

"Well, maybe your father and I should be meeting with him too. I have plenty of questions about this situation."

That wouldn't be awkward at all. I can already imagine Mom—bluntly—and Dad—more delicately—prying Win for proof that the world he grew up on actually exists. And then Isis would have three people whose absence from the house she'd have to cover up. "We never have much time," I say truthfully. "It's more effective if I work things out with him and then talk with you after. If there's something you want me to ask him—"

"That's not the point," Mom interrupts. "The point is you're *seventeen*, and I'm your mother. If anyone's taking a risk negotiating with these people, it should be me. I'm supposed to be watching out for you, but I can't be here for you if I don't even know where you *are*."

Her voice breaks as she looks away, and I realize she's tearing up. "Mom," I say, my own throat tight, but I don't know how to fix this. I'm the only one who has anything close to a full understanding of what we're dealing with; I'm the one who has to take the lead.

"We'll never know what happened to your brother," she goes on, gripping the edge of the sink. "If what you said about Earth is true, then he's just . . ."

Oh. This isn't about just me.

I didn't tell them what I know about Noam when I was explaining about Win and our initial Travels around Earth before. I thought I was giving them enough to grapple with already. I didn't realize how much my brother's disappearance might still be eating at Mom.

"Noam was already gone, Mom," I say. "He— When I was Traveling with Win, at the start, I wanted to find out what had happened to him. We went back to the day he disappeared. He didn't run away. He was just trying to help a friend who'd gotten into trouble, and one of the guys the friend was in trouble with brought a gun to intimidate them, and he . . . shot Noam accidentally." It still chokes me up, remembering watching that scene from the confines of the time cloth. I bow my head. "They were afraid of what would happen to them if people found out, so they hid his body and decided not to tell anyone. It was awful. I was going to see if we could do something, get some kind of justice for him, before— It wasn't your fault. And if something happens to me, that won't be your fault either. You're doing everything you can to watch out for me. I know that. But there are things I have to do by myself. That's just how it's turned out."

Mom's eyes have widened. "Noam was dead? This other boy—"

"Yeah," I say softly.

"Oh, Noam," she murmurs. "I still hoped . . ." A noise escapes her throat that's somewhere between a laugh and a sob. She shakes her head. "And you saw it. You saw him."

A quaver creeps into my voice. "I wanted to tell you before. There's just been so *much* . . ."

"Oh, honey," she says, and pulls me into her arms. I hug her back, tears leaking down my face as I press it against her shoulder. Maybe I haven't been letting her watch out for me quite as much as she could.

"I didn't mean to push you away," I say. "Okay?"

"I know," she says with a shaky inhalation. "I've been trying not to let it bother me so much. I . . . I knew you were going to grow up, Sky. I just wanted to see it. It seems it's all happened while I wasn't around."

"I don't think I'm all the way there yet," I say.

"Well, good," she says. She eases back, smooths a stray strand of hair behind my ear, and manages a wobbly smile. "But you're growing up well, you know?"

. . .

Mom seems more relaxed with me during breakfast the next day, but remembering her distress the night before, I decide to skip over the details of exactly *why* we're changing our approach during our clothes-washing conference afterward.

"We want them to feel guilty, like they need to make up for what we've lost," I tell her, Dad, and Angela as we take turns rinsing our new Kemyate-manufactured clothes. "I was thinking we could do a sort of memorial . . . Get together and take turns talking about the people we're worried about, the things we want to go back to. I'll need you to organize it, since I can't. Say it's to help us express our fears and the things we miss, to try to catch the sympathies of the people who've taken us."

Angela lingers when my parents go out. "Are you sure this is safe for you?" she asks, her forehead crinkling the way it always does when she's worried. "That it isn't going to look strange, the three of us closest to you coming up with this idea, even if we don't mention Earth being ruined? They did give us extra stuff in the store less than a week ago. We're getting by. We don't have to try to push things faster."

"We're all in more danger if we don't try something like this," I say.

She frowns. "Something happened, didn't it? Out there on the station. Win told you about it. What we're already doing isn't working?"

I can't lie to my best friend again. "Yeah," I say, and tell her the Council's plan and the ways Win and I are trying to counteract it. Angela bites her lip as I finish.

"So we'd all be like you were before. You could hardly have a conversation! And they'd take me away from Mom . . ."

"That's why we're going to stop them from going through with it," I say. "We have to risk this. As long as we keep acting like we think we're still on Earth, they shouldn't get too suspicious."

"I just don't want them to hurt you," she says. "It was scary enough when you were zoned out like that."

"If we don't stop them, I'll end up hurt anyway," I say. "And everyone else too."

Her mouth twists. "I know this is a kindergarten thing to say, but I can't help it. It's not *fair*!"

I laugh, and after a moment she does to, but neither of us can put much energy into it. "No," I agree. "It's really, really not."

• • •

The unfairness of our situation hits me even harder that evening when all twenty-three of us gather in the vacant lot where a couple weeks ago the Health officers conducted their examinations. Mom sets down a glowing light panel that she removed from our living room wall, and we form a loose circle around it.

I let my gaze drift around the ring. Daniel is holding hands with Cintia, her head tipped against his shoulder. That's a new development. I prod the fractured pieces of my heart for a reaction. A few weeks ago by their time, a few months by mine, I'd have been prickling with jealousy. Now he's just another surviving Earthling, of no special importance other than that. I crushed on him for a year . . . more? And it's just gone.

Ms. Cavoy talks about her husband, how she can't wait to see him again, about her best friend, the kids she should be teaching, the school she loves working at. When she finishes, Angela steps up, mentioning her dad, Lisa, her favorite places in our city. Then one of Daniel's friends takes a turn. Then Mrs. Sinclair. They go one by one, as if feeding their longing to the light. The glow reflects off each yearning face that approaches, and fades away as they retreat. Their words wash through me, leaving only that same dull ache of grief.

Without the Kemyate drug, I'm not numb, but I can't pretend I'm the same girl I was before. In that moment in the growing darkness, as people talk about the world that no longer exists, I feel like nothing more than a collection of rough-edged pieces jarring against each other into only the vaguest semblance of a person.

They still hold so much hope for the people and things we've lost forever. *I'm* letting them keep that hope. Guilt swells around the ache.

I'd intended to stay quiet, but suddenly there's no one left, and Dad is motioning me forward. I draw in a breath. No one expects me to be eloquent in my supposed stupor. No one needs to know I'm expressing not just what I miss, but what I'm mourning.

"Lisa. Jasmin. Marie. Ms. Vincent. Everyone at school. Cannon Heights High. The park. Running cross-country. Michlin Street. Pie Of Your Dreams. Vintage Fleas. All the shops. All the people . . . Grandma and Grandpa. My house. I want it *back.*"

The last comes out more fiercely than I intended. A murmur ripples around me. Dad rests his hands on my shoulders. I lean back against him, closing my eyes. When I open them, I notice Evan watching me, his eyebrows drawn together.

• • •

I'm washing up the next morning when someone knocks on the bathroom door. "Can I come in?" Angela asks. "Are you decent?"

"Yeah," I say, dabbing at my face with a blanket we're using as a towel. When I raise my head, it's not just her hustling in but Evan too. My heart sinks.

"I'm sorry," Angela says before I have to decide whether to keep up my drugged act. "I didn't know what else to do. Evan has questions I didn't think we wanted anyone overhearing."

She glances at him, and he grimaces at her before turning to me. "You're okay," he says.

I set aside the blanket. "I am. I'm sorry—I had to keep pretending—it's complicated. The people who put us in here, if they knew I was better, they'd do something even worse."

His face twitches as if his expression is caught between relief and pain. "You told Angela but not me. Did you really think I couldn't keep a secret for you?"

"There's more to it than that," I say. "What we've had to keep secret, it's a lot."

"I got that impression," he says, his posture still tensed, defensive. "The way you talked about home yesterday night . . . It made me wonder. And what you said just now—you know who's put us here? How? What's going on, Sky?"

When Angela dissuaded me from telling him, she mentioned his grandfather's sudden death. It's true, that shook Evan up. But the way he's talking right now reminds me more of the time he stood up and quietly but firmly asked our ninth-grade science teacher if he wanted to rethink his statement, when the guy had made a scoffing remark about girls and academics after I'd asked a question he'd found hard to answer.

He might be quiet, and sensitive, but I shouldn't have let myself start thinking he's weak. The two of us are the only people in this place he knows well, and instead of letting him in, making him a part of our plans and mutual support, we left him wandering blindly.

"It's going to be hard to hear," I warn him.

"That's fine," he says. "I want to know everything."

So I tell him the condensed version as Angela shifts her weight anxiously beside him. When I get to the part about the detonation, my throat still closing up despite how many times I've confronted the truth, Evan's intent expression quivers.

"You really believe . . ." he says, and can't seem to finish.

"I *know*," I say quietly. "I was there."

He sits down on the floor and tips his head forward into his hands. I exchange a glance with Angela. She kneels next to him, setting her hand gently on his back. I'm not sure he'd want anything from me right now.

After a few minutes, he exhales roughly. "So my parents, my sister, Lisa, they're all . . ."

"Yeah," I murmur.

"If I'd brought her with me . . . The last thing I said to Lisa, I *lied* to her—I told her I had an essay I had to get done, so she wouldn't know—"

"So we could pick out photos for a one-year anniversary present she was going to love!" Angela protests. "How could you have brought her along for that?"

I crouch down across from him. "You had no idea. There's no way you could have known it was going to happen."

"Why did they take us?" he asks. "Why *not* Lisa, or anyone else?"

"I don't know," I admit. "I think they were probably just grabbing people they thought I knew, whoever they could find fast enough." *I did what I could.*

If Evan hadn't happened to be at Angela's house, he would have been burned up too.

"And everyone else . . ." Evan shakes his head. "My dad used to say, when there was some kind of catastrophe, 'Heaven just grew a whole lot bigger.' But that . . . Seven *billion* people . . ."

"That's why we didn't tell you," Angela says. "It's hard enough being stuck in here, but to have to think about that too . . ."

He looks up at her then, before turning his reddened eyes toward me. "Whose idea was it? To keep me in the dark?"

Angela opens her mouth, but I get there first. "Mine," I say. "I'm so sorry."

"I was going to have to know eventually," he says. "At least, if you'd told me before, I could have spent the last two weeks figuring out how to feel about it, and *helping* you."

"You understand you can't tell anyone else, right?" I say. "You can't talk about knowing any of this. It wasn't just how you'd feel, it was—"

"Whether I could keep my head together enough not to screw everything up," he says. "I understand. You don't have to worry. But I—I need to be somewhere else right now."

He pushes past the bathroom door without meeting my or Angela's eyes again. I hear the door to his bedroom thud a moment later.

"You could have told him it was me," Angela says. "I said we shouldn't tell him."

"No," I say around the lump in my throat. "It was my decision in the end. I kept quiet. I'm the one responsible."

"He won't stay angry," Angela says. "He never does." But that crease on her forehead has come back.

I've taken responsibility for everyone. Every person in this place except Mom, Dad, and Angela—I made the choice to keep them in the dark, as Evan put it.

If we don't survive this, it'll be all my fault.

10.

Win

We've made progress," I comment to Isis in another eighth-hour conversation. "Those video posts Odgan was able to route through Kemhar have gotten some people talking."

"They have," she says with a tentativeness that's less than reassuring. "It's good to see people suggesting the Earthlings deserve more respect. But the Council hasn't even commented on the situation so far."

I'd noticed that too. When Nakalya broadcast a message last night, it was to address a problem Vishnu and his little group of anti-move advocates created, holding up Earth Travel employees outside the division offices until Enforcers broke up the protest. "Our greatest strength has been our unity, coming together toward a common goal," Nakalya said. "No Kemyate should treat another as an enemy."

I can no longer summon any surprise that he won't extend that generosity to all *humans*.

"They might think they can go ahead with the plan and any dissent will blow over quickly," Isis adds.

"At this point, it probably would," I acknowledge, grimacing. "Have you or Britta uncovered anything more about Project Nuwa?"

"No," she says. "I'm sorry. There's no information on any of the areas of the network we've been able to reach. Wherever the data's kept, it must be sectioned off the way the financial records are."

"There must be somewhere we could get to it."

"If I could go around testing terminals in divisions I don't even work for, I would," Britta pipes up. "Believe me, I've tried everything available to me."

"Then we need to get the people who agree with us to take action," I say, thinking of Vishnu's display. "We could . . . have them gather around the Council offices and refuse to move until the Council addresses their concerns. Nakalya can't ignore *that*."

"If we have enough supporters," Isis says. "It's easy to throw around ideas on the network. We don't know how many of those people will actually stand up and say, 'This is wrong,' in a way they can't back down from. Too small a group, and they'll just be rounded up in a few hours like the anti-movers were. And if anyone who was uncertain sees that, they'll be even less likely to speak up with us."

That's true. "And we lose the people who *were* willing to."

"If we have enough support, there's a better target," Britta says. "I saw the work order come through last night—Tech staff have been assigned to begin servicing the station engines tomorrow. We block that, and the Council will have to pay attention. The move is the last thing they want delayed."

"We don't want to get in the way of it either," Isis points out.

"What's a few more days if it helps Skylar and the others?"

"You know it'll be more complicated than that. You shouldn't be—"

"I'm not one of the people assigned there," Britta interrupts her, sounding faintly exasperated. "You don't have to worry about that."

I don't like the idea of delaying the move either—but we're running out of time. "We should block the engines," I say. "We still need the numbers, though. How many do you think would have to show up for it to work, Isis?"

"Those maintenance area halls are pretty tight. I think . . . If we had at least a hundred, they could hold that ground long enough to shake things up."

"A hundred," I repeat. It's only a tiny segment of Kemya's citizenry, but it seems huge. For the last year our group has consisted of no more than ten.

If Vishnu can gather a few dozen people to his cause, we should be able to find a hundred who'll fight for the Earthlings' rights, shouldn't we?

• • •

It's my day off, but I hardly feel like relaxing. I head to the fitness center, hoping exercise will clear my thoughts and bring fresh inspiration. Instead, the pedantic tones of the warm-up/cool-down "music" leave my teeth on edge. The people around me, from my sector and those nearby, are some of the most Earth-enthusiastic on the station, but glancing around as we go through the motions I get no sense of how deep their commitment might run.

Markhal's coming into the center as I'm leaving. "Win," he says, drawing me to a halt. He hesitates, his gaze unusually intense. "It's been a while since we got together," he says. "Stop by my apartment at twelfth hour?"

I'm not in much mood for socializing, especially with someone whose loyalty I'm so uncertain of. Then again, if Markhal is involved with Ibtep's scheming, he might let useful information slip.

"I have a lot going on," I say carefully. "But I can drop by."

I head down the hall to his family's apartment a couple of hours later, as promised. He offers me a can of sizzle-water, and we sit at opposite ends of the wall bench. It's strange to think I used to come here every other afternoon—and the alternate afternoons, he was usually in my apartment. The place looks the same with its blue-and-lilac color scheme and the rough tapestries his mom spends years weaving hanging on the walls, but any sense of comfort is gone.

"Have you been watching the feeds from the new Earth Studies exhibit?" Markhal asks.

"Isn't everyone?" I say.

"I guess so," he says, and chuckles. "It's been . . . enlightening, don't you think?"

Is he trying to prod an incriminating comment out of me? "What do you mean?"

"It's just . . ." He looks away, taking a sip from his can. "It's different from watching their entertainment, or the clips of recorder footage. They're more . . . real. Like real human beings."

"Like Kemyates are, you're saying?" I say, keeping my tone neutral.

"Maybe. That shouldn't be so controversial, should it? They *were* Kemyates, a long time ago."

He drags in a breath, and I suddenly register his body language. His broad shoulders are slightly hunched, his forefinger tapping the side of the can. He's nervous—nervous of me.

This isn't a trick to draw me out. He's putting himself out there, trying to figure out how far he can trust me. He knows where I work and how I've distanced myself from people like Celette.

A bark of a laugh catches in my throat. I've done such a good job keeping *my* loyalties quiet that I'm being tentatively recruited to the cause I'm leading.

I'm one of those people who won't stand up and say, "This is wrong."

My hand tightens around my drink. I can reveal a little in the relative privacy here.

"They were," I acknowledge, and Markhal's shoulders relax incrementally, which makes me feel even more a rot-head for how standoffish I was being a moment ago. Still, I can't help asking, "Have you talked with Ovni about that?"

Markhal frowns at the mention of his boyfriend. "We haven't been talking very much at all lately," he mutters.

I suppose he ignored the anti-Earth comments, until he couldn't. "I'm sorry," I say, "but he was kind of a blusterer."

"You know, he really was," Markhal says, and we both laugh. This is a chance, I realize. Markhal is an opening to the people we want to reach.

"It seems as though there's a lot of talk about the Earthlings on the network now," I say. "Good to see."

He nods. "I wasn't sure if you—"

I wave off his concern. "It's tricky, working where I do."

If he knows others who feel the same way, how can we confirm their commitment? Perhaps I should be asking myself what line *I'd* be afraid to cross. My thoughts slip to a smaller pro-Earth effort I declined to join: my parents' petitions. Dad and some of his artist friends have tried to drum up support for Kemyate artistic expression every couple of years with a list of names. They never accomplished anything, but that doesn't mean the basic strategy is unsound.

"I heard something," I say. "The people who put together the footage of the assault on Earth, they're planning something new, and they want to know who's completely with them. There's going to be a list on the network that anyone who'll publicly declare their support for the Earthlings can add their name to. Though I suppose it's possible no one will even start it, if people aren't committed enough."

Markhal doesn't ask where I heard this from. His expression has already turned thoughtful. "We *should* have something like that," he murmurs as he lifts his can again.

. . .

It doesn't take long. I wake up the next day to the network buzzing about a "registration" for any Kemyate who will officially put their name behind their concern for the homeless Earthlings. When I call it up, the list is already over a thousand names long. I inhale sharply.

We needed a hundred, and we have a thousand.

I'm smiling when I walk out of the bedroom to find my parents standing in front of the common screen.

"These are severe measures," Mom is saying. "Is it really fair to the Council?"

"They *still* haven't reported on who ordered that bomb dropped on Earth," Dad points out, flicking through the information on the display. "They decided how to deal with the Earthlings without getting public feedback on the idea first. I think it's time for some insubordination."

"What's happening?" I ask.

"There's a group of Earth allies that's been forming," Mom says, eyeing me. "Someone's sent around a call for them to assemble outside the station engine rooms to block the maintenance staff until the Council reconsiders its plan to place the Earthlings as pets."

Isis and Britta moved fast. I catch myself before my smile widens.

"At least a few hundred people are headed there already," Dad says eagerly.

"What?" Wyeth says. He's emerged from the bedroom behind me, rubbing sleep from his eyes. "Do you think it'll work?"

"Earthlings managed to make a lot of changes through public protest," Dad says. "Maybe it shouldn't have taken an entire planet being destroyed before it occurred to us to do the same." He turns to Mom. "We should go. I want to see what's happening firsthand."

"You're going to protest for the Earthlings?" Wyeth says.

My stomach lurches as Dad says, "Yes, I think we should."

Mom's brow has furrowed. "Are you sure that's wise? The Council won't be pleased."

Despite my uneasiness, the comment rankles. Then Dad says exactly what I want to: "If we care about Earth, we should be willing to risk a little 'displeasure' to protect the only Earthlings left."

He glances at me as if seeking my approval—or my forgiveness. We've barely spoken since I blew up at them the other day. I recover my smile, trying to show the appreciation I honestly feel beneath the rush of guilt.

This is my fault. I pushed them to rethink their position. I wanted to see them standing up for Earth not just because it fit their own interests but because they realized the Earthlings deserve their support. I hadn't considered that might mean watching them rush into danger. We don't know how the Enforcers will handle the blockade.

"*I* want to go!" Wyeth declares. "It's more important than going to class, that's for sure."

"No," I say immediately.

"Definitely not," Mom says as Wyeth stares at me. "You're not missing class, and I don't want you receiving a Security note in your file before you've even applied for your first work placement."

"But—" Wyeth starts, and I grasp his shoulder.

"She's right," I tell him. "You'll be able to see it on the news feeds."

"And hear about it from us," Mom says. "Your father's right too. An ideal means nothing if we're not willing to fight for it."

Another no rises in my throat. I don't want them in the midst of this.

What message am I sending if I encourage them to back down, though? Whatever progress I've made with them in seeing Earthlings as people, it's shaky. I could undo it so easily.

As Dad slips on his shoes, Mom looks to me, expectant. Of course they assume I'm coming. Am I going to say getting to work on time matters more to me than fighting for *my* ideals?

That's what I will be saying, if I bow out. I won't just be saying it to my family either, but to Markhal if he looks for me in the crowd, to Celette and Ilone and any of our other friends who might join in, to everyone who sees me at work. That will be my official statement: it wasn't worthwhile to me to protest on Earth's behalf. I'll be pretending so thoroughly it might as well be true.

I gave Isis and Britta the idea of staging a protest. I nudged Markhal on this course. If anyone's going to face consequences, it *should* be me, not my parents, my friends, or the strangers who've thrown in their support without even knowing who's behind this.

"Let's get down there," I hear myself saying before I'm completely aware of having made the decision.

My pulse is hammering as we head out the door. If Ibtep or anyone else questions me, I can say I went to try to talk my parents out of it. She might not believe that, but, well, nothing she threatened is as awful as what Skylar and the others are facing.

That sense of conviction doesn't stop me from fidgeting as the shuttle carries us down into the belly of the station. Dad's eyes are lit with anticipation, but Mom is standing stiffly, her expression fretful. Just by being here, they're proving themselves so much braver than I believed.

"I'm sorry I got angry at you earlier," I say.

"Nothing to apologize for," Dad says gruffly. "You should be able to speak your mind with us."

Then the shuttle stops. The swell of voices in the hall beyond seeps through the shell before the doors have even opened. As soon as we step out, we can see bodies packed from a couple doors down to as far down as I can make out. There's barely room for two people to stand abreast between the dingy gray walls. In the dim illumination of lights set to half brightness, heads dip and bob like the current of the rivers I saw on Earth, before they were scorched dry.

Two maintenance workers stand at the edge of the crowd. "Don't you have your own jobs to do?" one of them shouts, his face red with frustration.

No one answers him directly. The protesters are chanting, "When the Earthlings are free, then we'll fly! When the Earthlings are free, then we'll fly!" A few people are starting to clamber onto each other's shoulders, leaning against the walls for balance. I spot Vishnu's freckled face farther down the hall, hoisted above the others. "They can't make us leave our home," he hollers into an amplifier. "They can't make us fly!"

I grit my teeth. This wasn't meant to be a platform for *his* resistance.

Dad's already brushing past the workers to join the crowd. I follow, Mom trailing after me more hesitantly. A few more people have reached our end of the crowd when four Enforcers emerge from the shuttle alcove, hands resting on their belts by their guns.

"Go home," one tells the maintenance workers. "You'll be pinged when access is clear."

"This is a disruption to scheduled work," another of the Enforcers bellows at the crowd through an amplifier. "If you leave now, there will be no penalties. Move toward us, and we will help you onto the inner-shuttles."

There might be people in the crush who'd take that offer, but only those near the edges have any hope of moving, and we're sticking fast. "When the Earthlings are free, then we'll fly!" the chorus goes up, Dad adding his voice to it now. I see a twitch of the Enforcer's arm, and the young woman between them and me crumples.

The Enforcer shoots the man next to her, and the boy behind him, with numbing blasts to the head. I brace myself to shield my parents if I need to. A surge ripples through the crowd, panicked voices mingling with the chant.

Yet the Enforcer has stepped back. He leans together with his colleagues in discussion, and I see their problem. They can't knock everyone out. There's barely room to step around the bodies already fallen. The crowd seems to realize the same thing, and a cheer overwhelms the faint protests.

The cry sweeps through the crowd again, all of these hundreds of Kemyates rallying for what remains of Earth, and suddenly I don't care what the surveillance feeds pick up. "When the Earthlings are free, then we'll fly!" I yell with them.

• • •

When Isis reaches out to me the next day, the blockade is still in place.

"You were taken into custody?" she says. "Britta saw the record."

The Enforcers switched from shooting people to hauling them off before too long yesterday, and, at the edges of the group, I was among the first. "I think it went all right," I tell her. "All they did was have me sit on a stool and ask me why I was there. I told them I was worried about my parents' safety. Then they let me go." The surveillance footage will have shown I didn't resist arrest, and technically it isn't illegal to stand in a hall. They must have believed my story.

"The Enforcers have stopped the removals," she says. "New people have been showing up as soon as others are taken away, or get tired or hungry. Security must have decided it isn't worth the effort, better to wait it out. While they do that, I'm going to make use of this list of yours to see if anyone out there can access information on Project Nuwa through their own channels."

With that knowledge, I'm in good spirits when I arrive at work. I sit down at my scheduled terminal and wave up the display. My hand jerks back at the sight of the message that appears with it. "Traveler Darwin Nikola-Audrey Pirios, position reassessment: ten years on station disassembly crew commencing on arrival at K2-8."

My heart sinks as I read it again. I knew Ibtep meant her threat. I knew joining the blockade could result in this. I still wasn't prepared.

She gave me ten years, when she said the process is expected to take at least thirty. The cleverness of that sickens me. She's holding on to leverage. If I step out of line again, she'll add more years.

The display prompts me to start my work. I shut my eyes, breathe, and open them again. Then I reach toward the files I need.

I've managed to push my punishment to the back of my mind when a request pops up just before lunch, summoning me to one of the meeting rooms. Is Ibtep coming to gloat? I drag myself off my stool and down the hall.

It's not Ibtep who's waiting for me in the four-person room but Jule. I stop just inside the doorway, my body stiffening.

"You checked what I gave you?" he asks.

"I did." Isis confirmed his recordings were authentic.

He props a shoulder against the wall. "I handled our earlier conversation badly," he says.

"That would be an understatement," I remark. I'm not in the mood to navigate the tangle of his intentions right now. "Why are we talking? You're aware Ibtep has me monitored, aren't you? She'll know you called me in here." The meeting rooms are private, but clearly all that matters is what Ibtep *thinks* is going on.

"She knew before I called you," Jule says with a faint smirk. "I told her I was having concerns about the move being put off and that I thought I could regain your trust enough to find out how much you were involved in the blockade."

"And she believed that?"

He shrugs. "She believed I'd try. I'm not sure she believed you'd ever actually trust me."

"Well, I'm not testing how much I can by telling you anything, if that's what you were hoping for," I say.

"No," he says. "I meant what I said before. *I* want to help. This isn't what I wanted—for the Earthlings, for Skylar."

I believe that. He may have placed his own interests over hers, and ours, but that's far from hoping she'd be harmed. "And if I happened to be able to use your help, what kind are you offering?"

"The Council's discussing options for countering the blockade," Jule says. "I've overheard Ibtep talking about it with them. I might be able to find out what they decide in time for you to prepare."

"Might" doesn't get us very far. It occurs to me, though, that there's other information Ibtep must have access to that we want very much. I find it hard to believe she isn't involved with this Project Nuwa.

"Do you think you could get an opportunity to use her office terminal?" I ask.

Jule tilts his head. "She's pretty careful around me, but I'd imagine I could find a way. If I'm going to stick my neck out that much, though, there's something I'll need first."

11.

Skylar

The next signal from Isis comes five days after the last. I've been watching for it, not sure whether to expect it so soon, despite what Win said. No one's carted us off as pets yet. Does that mean our strategy worked? Or is Win coming to warn me it's about to happen, to arrange some last-ditch effort?

Sitting on the store's counter, I curl and uncurl my fingers around the edge. I'm still not sure what I'm going to say to him about the feelings he confessed last time. I'm hoping that when I see him, I'll figure it out.

I've been waiting maybe five minutes when the wall splits. The gap widens as the panel whispers to the side, and I start to smile.

My body reacts first. I'm pushing myself off the counter, my chest clenching up, when I consciously register that the figure ducking through the opening has hair far too short and wiry, shoulders too wide, skin too dark. I've backed three steps away before Jule straightens up.

He looks at me, and I look at him. Seeing him brings all the memories roaring back. I can't breathe. The ghost of the sensation of those hands, those lips, moves over my skin. I'd thought time had muted that pain but apparently not. Apparently it's just been buried under the larger tragedy until right now.

I want to scrub my skin right off. He doesn't deserve any space in my memory after the way he betrayed all of us.

What is he doing here at all? I take another step back.

"I had to see you," he says in that familiar low voice, and then Win clambers out behind him.

"You . . ." Win says roughly. His gaze slides past Jule to me and his mouth twists. He steps around Jule, planting a hand on his shoulder as if to shove him back. But he doesn't shove him, just holds him there.

"You were supposed to let me come in first and make sure she was okay with it," he says in a tone I've never heard from him before, his stance rigid. I blink, startled out of my haze. I thought I saw a change in Win when he first met me here, but this isn't a little extra firmness. There's steel in him.

Jule must hear it too. For the first time, his gaze jerks away from me. "She would have said no," he says. "I just need a chance—"

"No," Win interrupts, as cool and even as before. "You stick to the deal, or you leave completely."

I can't see Win's face, but whatever's there makes Jule's expression stutter. "Fine," he bites out, and spins on his heel.

"Wait," I say. "What's going on? What deal?" From what Win told me, Jule has been working with Ibtep. Has *she* found out what's going on here?

Win's eyes have softened when he turns toward me. "I'm sorry," he says. "It wasn't supposed to go like this. Jule figured out you weren't drugged anymore. He's decided he's going to help us—he provided proof. And he managed to enter a code that's given Britta access to Ibtep's private computer, so she can check for information on . . . you know."

Nuwa, I guess. So they haven't been able to dig up anything on their own.

"We agreed if he got us access, I'd ask if you'd *consider* seeing him." He cuts his gaze back toward Jule.

Jule hesitates by the panel, looking at Win and then me. The contrast hits me, comparing this moment to all the times I've seen the two of them argue before. Jule used to be the one coolly needling Win until he provoked a retort. Faced with the same confidence thrown back at him, he looks more uncertain than Win ever did.

Why wouldn't he? Win has always had the principles, the conviction. Jule just put up a good front to cover the allegiances he was jumping between.

The pain inside me starts to dull. The guy I laughed with and made out with and started to think I might love, this isn't him. He was just a figment of my imagination. *This* guy, the real Jule, I hardly know.

We might as well get this over with. I can handle it, and then we'll be done for good.

"He's here now," I say, and to Jule, "If you want to talk, talk."

Win moves to the side, crossing his arms as he watches Jule, who eases toward me.

"Your mother gave you my note, didn't she?" Jule says. "I wanted you to know— I wish I could have gotten to more people, and I wish I'd had a better idea who mattered to you, but there wasn't much time. I did my best. Ibtep found me after you'd left. She wiped the drug out of my system, and she said something about what the Council was planning. I couldn't just let it happen, not after you tried so hard to save them. You were supposed to. So I did."

"Thank you," I say, with honest gratitude. "I'm glad you did." I *am* incredibly grateful to have my parents, and Angela and Evan, and the others. It's just hard to feel that fully when I'm also a little sick, imagining Jule thinking about my entire planet being destroyed and only caring because of how *I'd* feel about it. Racing out there to rescue a few people he thought I knew instead of trying to stop the bomb altogether and save everyone.

He's studying me, as if he were expecting more. "Is there something else you wanted?" I add.

His next words come out in a rush. "I didn't get to say, the last time we spoke—what I was doing, passing on the group's plans, that was before I knew how much you were going to mean to me. And I had no idea what Ibtep was planning, the rest of it, until after. I had nothing to do with that."

Oh no? My voice goes so tight it sounds unfamiliar to my ears. "You don't think maybe Win and Isis and everyone else deserved some loyalty before I showed up? You don't think maybe we could have finished the mission and Earth would have been left alone if the delays you made hadn't given Ibtep time to convince the Council?"

A flicker of discomfort crosses his face. He lowers his gaze, and then raises it again.

"She would have convinced them soon enough anyway," he insists. "And if things had happened differently, I might have been on that ship with all of you instead of in a place where I could find out what was going to happen and do something about it."

Is he seriously trying to spin his betrayal into some sort of blessing? "You can't know that," I say. "Maybe if we'd gotten the time field down and she hadn't had the bomb ready, she'd have given up that part. She'd have had the new planet to focus on."

"You wouldn't think that if you'd heard her talk," Jule says. "Besides, I couldn't have known what she was planning. None of us had a clue."

No, we hadn't. Even Win and I, listening in on her meeting with her coconspirators, couldn't put the pieces together. Wouldn't have believed her capable of it.

"I hate what's happened," Jule goes on, more assured after my lack of argument. "I hate that I couldn't save more people. I hate how they're treating you right now. I've done everything I could to protect you."

"*What?*" I say.

"He blackmailed Ibtep so she'd keep you and the others alive," Win says quietly. "I would have told you before, but we hadn't confirmed it. He has recordings—that's the proof he showed us. 'Everything' might be an exaggeration."

Jule scowls at him. Then he takes another step toward me. I waver but hold my ground. Win tenses by the counter.

"I've tried," Jule says to me. "I never would have done anything I thought would hurt you. I meant it, Skylar, when I said I love you."

That's the last thing I want to remember. I close my eyes with a cringe he must see, because he stops talking.

"It doesn't matter," I say, gathering myself. "Whatever we had, you're not the person I thought I had it with." I force myself to meet his gaze again. "And the problem isn't really what you did, is it, Jule? It's what you *didn't* do. You know how long I've had to think about every moment when you *could* have told me you were the one who'd leaked our plans? You arranged for me to go to that function, where Kurra almost saw me. You knew I was going out investigating around the station, in the clubs, risking getting caught—getting killed, because that's what would have happened if I was. We talked about it, you kept telling me you were worried about me, to be careful, but you could have stopped me from taking any of those risks just by admitting it was you, problem solved. But you didn't. You were willing to let me *die* so you could keep everyone's good opinion of you. Maybe that fits the Kemyate definition of love, but on Earth our standards are a little higher."

There's a rasp in my throat by the time my tirade runs out of steam. Jule is staring at me, Win eyeing the floor. The silence hangs heavy. And I'm still so angry.

"You know what's even worse," I say, with more control. "You came here acting like you expected the one good thing you did to just erase everything else—the way you risked my life, the way you risked everyone else's and nearly did get Britta killed, selling us out to save your family a little *embarrassment*. To erase how that might have contributed to my whole *world* being destroyed. I really am glad you got the people here off Earth alive. I am. But I already knew you can be generous, and . . . valiant, when you want to be. The problem is now I also know you can be the opposite."

Jule looks as though he might say something, but then his mouth presses into a flat line. He turns away, jerkily, and climbs through the opening in the wall. Just like that, he's gone.

He didn't even apologize, I realize. He gave me explanations and excuses but not a hint of taking actual responsibility.

My vision blurs. As I bring my hands to my face, my legs feel suddenly insubstantial. I sink down, head bowed, until I'm crouched by the floor. Tears stream out.

I don't even know what I'm crying about. I accepted that what I had with Jule was a lie ages ago. Maybe it's the thought of how all this

could have been different. I might still have my city, my planet, all
the people and all the things we talked about missing the other day,
if only he'd acted better.

Hands brush over my hair. Win has knelt in front of me. I lean
against his shoulder, one sob slipping out, and he wraps his arms
around me. He smells like warm sand, like places that no longer
exist, as if his skin still holds a fraction of the sunlight he absorbed
back on Earth.

As my tears slow, I notice the thump of his heartbeat where my
face, the backs of my hands, are pressed against him. The last time he
saw me, he was telling me he cared about me to the core of his being,
and here I am crying on his shoulder over, in essence, another guy.

"I'm sorry," I say.

"Jule's the one who should be sorry," Win says, rubbing my back.
The steel I saw earlier has given way so quickly to tenderness.

I completely believe it then, what he said before. He doesn't
blame me, not at all, for falling for Jule. He just wants me to be happy.

I still haven't answered him.

I need to see his face. I ease back, turning my hands, wondering
if I'll be able to feel the interplay of hard and soft, strength and gen-
tleness, as I rest my palms against his chest. He starts to pull away. It's
been months since the kiss that ended with me ordering him never
to touch me again, but I know that moment has lingered in his mind.
I was trying to be careful, he said on the trip to Earth, *after the way I
screwed everything up before.*

Before he can get very far, I curl my fingers into his shirt, raising
my other hand to touch his cheek. He gazes back at me, his eyes the
blue of the deep ocean, of the sky back home at the edge of evening.

And I might not know what shape my heart will form when I manage to stitch the pieces back together, but I know what I want right now.

I tug him toward me, meeting his lips with mine. A soft noise escapes his throat, and then he's kissing me back, tilting his head so our mouths slide together at an even more perfect angle. His fingers tangle in my hair, sending sparks over my skin. Mine trace along his jaw and around his neck. *Yes, this.* I can't rewrite the past anymore, but I can write over the memories I'd rather lose. It should have been him, before. I wanted him first.

As we kiss, the heat kindling between us forms a cocoon, shutting out the rest of the world. The worries, the regrets. It's good. Good and *real* amid the false wood and artificial food and unnaturally still air.

Win's mouth leaves mine for just a second, his hands slipping forward to cup my face. "Skylar," he says, low and solemn. I'm a little dizzy, in the most enjoyable way, and his tone strikes me as amusing.

"Darwin," I reply in a teasing echo. His grip tightens and all at once he's kissing me again, harder, which is just fine with me.

Both of us are breathless when he draws back again, a fraction farther this time. "I've never liked my name quite as much as when you're saying it," he says with a chuckle.

"Oh, really?" I say, smiling. "Maybe I should say it more."

"Skylar," he says before I can put that to practice, his determined expression fighting the desire in his eyes, "I just need to know. You were upset. I need to know this is you coming to *me*, not you running away from Jule."

The guilt I felt as I cried on him jabs at me again, because I can't answer automatically. I have to think about it. He deserves the truth—he deserves me being sure.

"What if it's both?" I ask. "I *was* upset. Seeing Jule, it hurt. But *you* make me happy. You're the one I want here with me. If you weren't, I wouldn't be kissing any of the boys out there instead." I motion toward the door.

Win's face relaxes with a small smile of his own. "I suppose that's acceptable," he says dryly.

I'd like to go back to kissing, but his question has dug deeper inside me. *I'm* happy—what about him? Maybe he needs this to mean more than I can say it does. I drag in a breath, trying to steady my whirling head.

"What you said, last time," I say, "I can't give you that back. My feelings are a mess right now. Sometimes it feels like I'm *never* going to be okay enough to . . . to feel that strongly . . . about anybody. If you don't want to— If that makes it too hard— I'm sorry. I should have said something before." I bite my lip, looking at his, and he smiles more completely.

"It's all right," he says.

"Are you sure? Maybe I—"

"Skylar," he says, "your being honest with me is all I need. Trust me to look after my own feelings? If this, right now, is all this ends up being, I'll still be happy to have had it."

He grazes the tip of his thumb over my mouth, and then we're kissing again. I let the happiness it is carry me away.

• • •

The next morning, I drift through the exhibit in a circuit I've established to surreptitiously check for any change along the borders. I can't say my attention is all there—my mind keeps flitting back to last night with a warmth that still courses over my skin.

And not just because of the kissing. After that, Win said the Council has announced under pressure that they'll hold a public forum in a few days to debate their plans for us, which should mean we're safe until then. We're getting through to people. This might actually work.

Then I come around the hill of storage containers, into the space Win told me has no surveillance, and my legs lock.

Ibtep is standing in the shadow of the containers, an Enforcer-style blaster held loosely in one of her wide hands.

I've been gaping at her for a few seconds before I remember my act. But even drugged I'd be startled to see her, wouldn't I?

"Hello," I say in my dulled voice. "What are you doing here?" *How* is she here? Someone would have seen her if she'd come through the store.

"Come closer," Ibtep says.

I amble over until we're just a few feet apart, resisting the urge to cross my arms as if to shield myself.

"You don't have to continue this pretense," Ibtep says with a gesture to my slack posture. "I don't believe it anyway. I'm not certain how you or they managed it, but, conveniently, it works to my advantage at this moment. We might as well speak frankly."

Jule, I think. He could have gone running to her after our conversation yesterday. Or she could just be hoping I'll reveal what she only suspects. I look at her hazily. "Frankly?"

She sighs. "If you must. What's important is what you do afterward. The rest of them, they'll listen to you, won't they? You know what we're capable of. You'll convince them."

I let some of my honest bewilderment show. "Convince people what? I don't understand."

She ignores that. "This little . . . game has gone too far," she says. "Your needs are met. You have enough. We are never going to allow you to live alongside the rest of us. You have to accept that, and you have to make your fellow Earthlings accept it too."

She doesn't know Win's told me about the pet plan, then—or she recognizes that's hardly "living." "But we'd like to leave here," I say, which seems safe.

"I'm certain you would," she replies. "But that's no longer an option in any form. You can imagine the various ways we could dispose of every Earthling here. We'd rather wipe you out and accept the disapproval of those who'll suspect it was no accident than continue drawing this situation out. That is your first option. Your second is that we see all of you showing how grateful you are for what we've provided and how content you are to stay within these walls, before two days are done. There is no third option."

I think I've managed to keep my eyes vague, my expression befuddled, but my spine has stiffened. I *can* imagine. A toxin in the food or drinks they could say was simply some Earthling disease. A sudden tech malfunction. Ibtep could probably think up a dozen ways to "dispose" of us without straining a brain cell.

"Consider it," Ibtep says. "Don't make us wait long."

She motions past her. Her words have hit me so hard I'm not faking the moment it takes me to realize she's indicating I should continue my walk. "I don't understand," I try again, and she gives a sharp little laugh.

"Then I suppose it'll be option one," she says. "Off you go."

I let her stride past me, and take a few wobbly steps away. Then I stop. No. I can't just let her—

I whirl around, but Ibtep is already gone.

She was here, wasn't she? My mind hasn't broken—I'm not hallucinating?

No. She wouldn't want me to think that. There's a mark imprinted on the ground, near where she was standing. Two Kemyate characters. *Your choice.*

12.

Win

"There's nothing," Isis says.

"Nothing?" I say. "Are you sure?"

"Britta went through all Ibtep's private files. No mentions of Nuwa, and nothing about Earthling examinations or even that lines up with the date the Health department went into the exhibit. We didn't find anything about a response to the blockade either, although she has a meeting booked with Nakalya and the head of Security today that isn't on the public schedule."

I'd woken up to my nerves humming with memories of last night: Skylar's lips against mine, her hands on my skin. The warm buzz dulls when I think of what came before it. I put Skylar through that confrontation with Jule for *nothing*?

"Could Jule have tipped Ibtep off so she could remove anything incriminating?" I ask. "Is he using us again?"

"I don't think so," Isis says. "If he was, there'd be no reason for her to hesitate in having us arrested. And . . . we caught a transmission from his apartment a few hours ago. He's put in a transfer request to be moved to one of the lower-level apartments, with an assigned roommate."

He's giving up his deluxe apartment, along with the luxury of having a space all to himself? "Why?" I say.

"I was hoping you might have some idea. How did his conversation with Skylar go?"

I grimace. "Not well. She was pretty angry."

"Good on her," Isis says. She has plenty of reason to be angry with Jule herself. "Maybe he's rethinking his priorities."

I remember the way his expression stiffened as Skylar laid out every reason she has not to trust him. I thought it was defiance or frustration, but it could have been regret.

"Maybe," I agree hesitantly. "So this means Ibtep *isn't* working on Nuwa?"

"Possibly. Or it could be she—wisely, if the files are that sensitive—kept them completely out of her work areas. It'd be much harder to access her home terminals. The records could even be restricted to a single unnetworked server somewhere in the Council offices, or the Health department, that the involved parties load data to and from directly. I put out word to our supporters yesterday. None of them have posted any progress so far, but it hasn't been even a full day yet."

"We need all the leverage we can get," I say. Nakalya may have agreed to a public discussion, but at this point I suspect he'll do nothing more than offer a prettier-sounding solution that still treats the Earthlings as subjugates.

When I go out to leave for work, Dad's the only one in the common room. It's his day off, and he's dressed in one of his favorite Victorian Britain–facsimile shirts, the one with the expansive sleeves that make it impractical at his job. He's fiddling with the cuffs while watching a network report on the blockade. For the last two days, the Enforcers have merely been supervising. Seeing the footage of them poised there, watching, makes me tense. We still don't know how the Council will decide to respond.

"It's impressive," Dad says. "Four days, and the protesters haven't backed down."

"Are you going to join them again today?" I ask.

"I'm not sure." He pauses. "I was thinking it's not enough. I'd like to contribute something bigger than being one in the crowd."

I stop by the door. He's got that dreamy tone usually reserved for grand artistic visions. "Something bigger? What are you thinking of?"

He raises his eyebrows with a conspiratorial arch that I don't like. If he takes independent action, the Council may conclude I've put him up to it or that he's been part of the rebel group all along. I doubt Security will let that go with a simple questioning.

"If you want to support the cause, helping the blockade is the best way," I add.

"It seems to me, in Earth's history of protests, increasing the pressure has often led to more success," he says.

"That's dependent on it being the right sort of pressure. There are actions that can harm a cause."

Dad frowns. "I think I know how to make a peaceful statement."

His gaze slips from me to the little paintings crowding our apartment's walls. He's made so many peaceful statements that most of the people out there have never wanted to see.

I can't say I don't wish he could get the recognition he longs for, but this isn't the right way.

"That's not what I meant," I say. "It's not— If you act on your own, you'll become a target."

"There are worse things," Dad says. "Weren't you the one saying we shouldn't always put our own interests first?"

"It's more complicated than that." I realize even as I speak how weak the words sound. Anything specific I tell him could be used as proof of his complicity in my "crimes" if the Enforcers interrogate him. It's an impossible position. I draw in a breath. "I do think people should stand up for the Earthlings. But if you draw attention to yourself . . . It won't be just you they're considering when they're choosing a punishment. It'll be about me, and things I've done before."

There, it's out, in as clear a form as I can offer.

Dad studies me. "What things, exactly?" he says quietly.

"Things that would mean even a small gesture from you could be viewed as a major infraction," I say. "Things I *can't* tell you about, because knowing about them would only incriminate you more."

"There wasn't really any quarantine," he says. It's not a question. "Dad . . ."

"Why shouldn't I be implicated?" he demands, his sleeve billowing as he waves a hand. "I raised you to think the way you do, didn't I? To appreciate what Earth can . . . could . . . show us. Why did you think I wouldn't want to be a part of it?"

Because it wasn't my choice, before, and because now the consequences of any action he takes will far outweigh the benefits. It seems unlikely he'll accept that explanation, though.

He thinks he's serious, but he's really only playing at it. I know, because I was the same way. I felt so clever and important, sneaking off to clandestine meetings and carrying out the small tasks Ibtep gave me at first. It wasn't until they left me on Earth in the second decade of the twenty-first century, alone with my time cloth, several bundles of currency, and nothing else, that I realized how far I'd fallen in. I was over my head in what seemed like a blink.

It won't be real for Dad until an Enforcer is applying interrogation "encouragement" to his pain receptors. I don't want it to come to that.

"It's complicated," I repeat. "If there's a time I can tell you about it, I will, I promise. Right now I need to know you'll be careful. Go to the blockade if you want. Just don't stand out. Please."

"You're going to be late for work," he says.

"Dad?"

"I'll keep what you've said in mind."

I open my mouth, and his flattens. I can see that's the best I'm going to get.

• • •

I'm in the midst of putting together a series of clips that demonstrate rope-weaving techniques, occupied enough to forget to worry about Dad for a few minutes, when a murmuring rises up at the other end of the room.

"Look at that."

"Security will have it off in an hour."

"The culprits were fast, not to get caught before they finished it."

I glance over. A few of my colleagues have brought up a news feed in the corner of their displays. I squint at it, and then do a quick network search on mine. An image pops up of the hall outside the Council offices.

A grin flickers across my face before I can suppress it. Someone has painted the Earth on the wall opposite the doors, the first thing any Councilor coming out would see. "Give them a home here," say the words scrawled around it. The planet's circle looks nearly as tall as I am, rippled with blended hues of blue, green, brown, and pale streaks of cloud. The forms aren't perfectly accurate, but there's a care and an affection in the brushstrokes that no photo could create.

Someone has *painted*.

My awe falls away with a lurch of my stomach. Oh, Dad. It's lovely, but my coworkers are right—it won't last the day. The Council members may never even see it other than on news feeds like this. I have the urge to leave, to take a shuttle up there so I can see in person the largest work he's ever done, but that would likely get us into even more trouble.

All the Enforcers will have to do to identify him is check the surveillance footage. They might already have apprehended him. I was careful enough with what I said to him, wasn't I? If they blame him for *my* offenses . . .

My stomach is outright churning by the time I head home. I brace myself before I open the apartment door.

Dad looks up from the bench where he's watching the news reports on the common screen, and smiles a little sheepishly.

"If I'd had better paint, they'd have had a harder job of it," he says, motioning to the footage of a maintenance crew who's already wiped clean most of the wall. For a second, seeing his work destroyed as thoughtlessly as the Council's order destroyed Earth overwhelms my anxiety.

"I wouldn't have thought you had that much paint at all," I say lightly. "Should I be worried you'll be charged for theft as well as vandalism?"

He flushes. "I had to borrow some. And Daudi helped. It'll be a long time before I can afford a new canvas to work on. But it was—"

The door chime blares, and the door snaps open before either of us can do more than flinch. Three Enforcers stride into the apartment, a man leading the charge. Kurra flanks him. She narrows her eyes at me as the other two circle Dad and me, checking us over.

My mouth has gone dry. They planned it this way. They wanted me to be here for the arrest, so they waited until I got home.

Likely they intend to find an excuse to arrest me too, even if they have to manufacture it. If they conduct a full interrogation, not a moderated one as Ibtep arranged before, the things they could wrench out of me now . . . It would ruin the lives of all my allies. It would ruin *everything* we've worked for.

"Nikola Carroll-Eliza Pirios," the man says, flashing a palm display, "you are being secured for seven violations of law."

"*Seven?*" Dad says, his body rigid. "I only—" His voice breaks off as Kurra raises her gun. The leader twitches his hand, and she hesitates. It's odd seeing her in a subordinate position.

"The details of your violations will be available on detainment," the leader says to Dad. "You can see our permission to search your quarters." He gestures to his colleagues. "Be thorough."

The other woman grins. "Look at all this rot," she says, grabbing a painting of an old Earth mansion off the wall with a squelch of detaching suction. "We have to ensure it's not concealing evidence."

Dad yelps when she cracks the frame against her knee. The fake canvas stretches, mangling the image, as the Enforcer twists it to peer along the inner edges of the frame. My fingers clench against the urge to snatch it away from her. They're trying to provoke us.

She repeats the process with another painting, and another. Kurra stalks over to the wall cabinets, flicking open the doors and knocking a row of beverage cans to the floor.

My breath catches. Isis's communicator is in my closet. I can't think of a way they could track it back to Isis, but that doesn't mean there isn't one. My simply having tech I can't show I bought or had assigned to me would give them exactly the excuse they're looking for.

The communicator should have a self-destruct function built into it, as with all tech Travelers use on Earth. If I can get my hands on it, I've rehearsed the pattern enough times in training to release it in an instant.

I take a step toward my bedroom. None of the Enforcers pays much mind, Kurra and the other woman continuing their carnage of the walls, the man prying around our screen. Dad notices, though. Some of my concern must show on my face, because his eyes widen.

"You can check them without ruining them," he says abruptly, hustling over to Kurra and the other woman, who are both wrenching apart paintings now. "Let me—"

"Back down!" the woman says, but he's succeeded in distracting them. As he gestures to the painting Kurra is holding, I amble toward my bedroom as quickly as I feel I can move without looking suspicious. My hand has touched the door when the man's voice rings out behind me.

"Stay where we can see you!"

He strides over, grabbing my arm and yanking me into the middle of the room. "Watch *both* of them," he orders the women. "You should know your jobs."

Kurra glares at him when he's turned away, and then turns that glare on me. She shoves Dad over beside me. "Stay there," she snaps. Dad gives me an apologetic glance, and I dip my head. It isn't his fault.

"You won't get away this time," Kurra goes on, still glowering at me. She cracks another frame without even bothering to check for anything inside. "You've run too far."

"I what?" I say. She sounds almost addled.

"I won't be embarrassed again," she says, almost a hiss. "I'll show them what we were dealing with. I can address the issue at its root. They'll have to tell her—"

"Enforcer Ettar," the leader says, frowning as he joins us. "What did he say to you?"

He assumes I've angered her on purpose. I hold up my hands. "I was only standing here."

"He's—" Kurra begins, and halts. For an instant, she looks far too bewildered to be frightening. Then her usual cool expression falls back into place. "It isn't relevant."

I eye her as she turns to yank another painting off the wall. Dad winces.

When only a few paintings remain, near Kurra, the other Enforcers turn toward the bedrooms. My body tenses. I could get a chance after all.

The leader nods to the other woman and ducks into Dad and Mom's room. The woman opens up mine and Wyeth's. As she steps over the threshold, I rush after her.

"Whatever you need to look at," I say in my most helpful tone. I wave down the desks, flick on the terminal's display, and slide open the closet before she's had a chance to answer. My fingers grope after the communicator amid the stack of clothes as I swivel to hide the gesture. For an endless moment, they find only fabric. Then they close around that small, smooth sphere.

"Hey!" the Enforcer says. I'm already tracing the destruction command with my thumb as I pull my arm back.

Kurra has followed us into the tight space. She jerks my hands in front of me, peering so close I feel her breath on them, and flips them over. The communicator is gone, disintegrated into a dust so fine it's invisible.

"Out," Kurra barks, and I come obediently. She motions for Dad and me to sit on the floor. There's a soft thump from my bedroom, clothes tumbling.

The woman comes out of the bedroom holding a rectangular object that fills both of her hands. "What's this?" she demands, shoving it toward my face.

Oh. It's the mbira Dad and Mom gave me for my sixth birthday. The keys are made from Kemyate polymers, but the base is real Earth wood. I can still taste my shock when they brought it out, at the thought of the credits it must have cost to have it made.

Years after that, I shoved it in the back of my closet in a fit of shame. A frittering thing, I called it when Wyeth asked. *When you really grow up, you have to stop playing around.* I'd thought I'd been really grown up before I'd even finished upper school. That's a laugh.

"It's a musical instrument," I tell the Enforcer. "A thumb piano. I can show you."

She hesitates, and then hands it over. With the looming sense that this might be the last music I ever create, I tuck my fingers under the mbira's base and stroke my thumbs over the keys. They're still pliable, sensitive to my touch. After a few experimental movements, I find the rhythm I first picked up all that time ago. A tinkling melody glides from the keys. Despite everything going on around me, it sends a tickle of pleasure through me.

I missed this.

My fingers jar as the Enforcer kicks the instrument from my hands. It hits the floor a few feet away with a clunk. She sniffs. "More rot," she says.

The leader has emerged from Dad and Mom's room empty-handed and scowling.

"You two," he says to Kurra and her colleague, "wait here with them. I need to call in."

He steps outside to make his call where we can't hear. I rub my palm against my pant leg as if some of the communicator's dust might be clinging to it. They have no legal reason to bring me in, but I no longer believe that will stop them.

Dad leans his shoulder against mine. "I wasn't sure you still had that," he murmurs, looking at the mbira.

He thought I'd sold it? I suppose some might have, for the credits it'd bring just for the materials. I hadn't even considered that. Some part of me must have realized I wasn't really giving the music up.

"Of course not," I say. "It's the best present anyone's ever given me."

"Quiet," Kurra says, and we fall silent. I peek at Dad from the corner of my eye, and see him smiling. He's about to be hauled off to interrogation, he must know that, but he's smiling because I still like his present.

I tip toward him, returning the pressure. It was a soft-brained thing he did today, especially after I'd warned him. That doesn't mean it wasn't also a marvelous thing. He did it for Earth—for Skylar and everyone with her.

Dear Kemya, I think, *let us outlast this catastrophe too.*

13.

Skylar

I finish my slow circuit of the exhibit, keeping up my drugged act automatically as I wrestle with Ibtep's threat. My skin is crawling. I keep thinking of how easily she spoke about murdering us.

I need to talk to Win, but he was here just yesterday. If there's no surveillance in that area, Isis won't have seen the confrontation, won't know there's any reason for concern. Which is no doubt exactly why Ibtep arranged to speak to me there, however she got in and out.

My hands have balled into fists. I force them to relax.

I could shout it out to the sky. Announce that we were all just threatened with extermination on the Council's behalf, that we've been asked to deceive the Kemyate public. Except I don't know which feeds are available to the public, where I'd need to be to make sure I'm heard. I can't even be sure that Security doesn't have the footage on a slight delay, like live broadcasts were often set up on Earth, so they can interrupt the transmission if they need to. And as soon as I show I'm willing to go that far, what reason would the Council have to trust me to keep my mouth shut in the future? I'd be killing all of us.

At the end of my circuit, I wander up and down the street a few times. My fingers itch with an old desire for the bracelet I lost during my race through Earth's history with Win. The beads my brother, Noam, bought for me so long ago, that I used to spin along with my mental multiplication to calm me when a shift in time sent me into a panic attack.

I pause.

To calm me when something was *wrong*.

Win knows about that. He'd remember.

I amble over to Ms. Cavoy and ask in a languid voice if I can have one of the bits of Kemyate brick she and Mr. Patterson have chipped off and found work like chalk on the road. She looks at me curiously as she nods. I drift away and sit on the pavement outside my house.

At first I scrawl random lines, as if I'm bored and doodling. Then I write, in big jagged numbers:

$3 \times 3 = 9$

$3 \times 9 = 27$

$3 \times 27 = 81$

For the benefit of our observers, I stop there, frowning as if I can't calculate any further. Pretending it was just a random impulse that came over me, I shake my head, turn to the side, and write my name. I draw a few more doodles to deflect attention, and then I drop the chalk and leave, praying Win will see my secret SOS.

. . .

I let the day pass as usual, fighting a cringe every time someone makes a remark about wishing they knew what was happening back home, about how creepy this strange prison is. No one could mistake us for content, let alone grateful, right now. And I encouraged this.

It was working. We must have been making real progress, for the Council to think this threat was necessary. If I can tell Win and the others, maybe there'll be some way we can still fight this.

But no answering signal from Isis has come by the time "evening" falls. I'm on my own. *Two days*, Ibtep said. Even if Win notices my message tomorrow and can arrange to meet with me that night, it could be too late.

My parents, Angela, and I gather in the bathroom to talk while we wash up, as we've been doing regularly the last several days. "There's a problem," I say, and explain about Ibtep's visit.

When I'm finished, the three of them are standing very still.

"They could kill us that easily?" Angela says. "They would?"

"They destroyed our entire planet," I say.

"Then we have to do what she said," Dad says, his voice not quite careful enough to hide the strain.

"And then we live in here forever?" Mom says.

"Maybe not," I say. "The people working to help us on the outside, they might be able to figure something out." Even if I can't imagine what.

Angela frowns. "Can we even trust *them*? They're 'Kemyates' too, right? If this is the way most of them think about people from Earth . . ."

"Win's risked his *life* protecting me," I tell her, with more heat than I intended. I take a breath. "They'll do whatever they can. I just . . . don't know how much they *can* do if the Council is willing to kill us just to cut the conflict short."

Mom rubs her chin, her gaze distant. "I don't know how easy it'll be to convince everyone to pretend to be happy, now that we've been pushing them in the opposite direction. We have to give them a good reason."

"Do we have to *all* be completely happy *all* the time?" Angela asks.

"That's what it sounded like," I say.

And Mom's right. No one will take this seriously—seriously enough to avoid any mistakes—when they don't know just how serious this situation is. My chest tightens.

"I have to tell them," I say.

"Tell them what?" Angela says.

"Everything."

• • •

"I-I'm really sorry I've kept this a secret all this time," I say an hour later to the audience gathered in the area behind the storage containers, where we're out of surveillance range, at least for now. "It seemed like the safest thing for all of us. But you can see we're not safe at all now."

The glow square Mom brought lights a pallor on all the stunned faces before me that's not entirely artificial. "You believe this?" Angela's mother says to mine.

"It's hard to, completely," Mom says. "But I haven't seen any indication that Skylar's mistaken or deluded."

"This is ridiculous," Mr. Sinclair says, standing up. "Aliens? Space stations? Earth hasn't been destroyed. I doubt we've left it for a second."

"Rod," his wife says, reaching for him, but a murmur is passing through the group.

"I believe Skylar," Evan speaks up. "I've known her for years. She's smart. I don't think anyone could trick her into believing something like this."

I smile at him, but he hasn't looked at me despite the show of support. The ache inside me deepens. The first couple days after I told him the truth, he hardly left his room, and he hasn't spoken to me since then. I know he's got to be hurting over what he now knows, but I also know he's shutting me out not because of that but because I didn't trust him to begin with.

"I have to admit some of the substances I've worked with here don't match anything from Earth," Mr. Paterson says slowly.

"Does that prove anything?" Mrs. Green asks.

"Look," I say. "You don't have to believe me. The only thing we need to agree on is that the people who took us have total control over what happens to us here, and if we don't start acting as if we're happy, they *will* murder us. Can you accept that?"

"Acting happy," Daniel says. "What does that mean, exactly?"

"No more complaining about being stuck here," I say, "or about anything or anyone you miss. No more looking for ways to get out. We can keep up the exercise and the lessons and all that, but we talk about those things as if we're doing them just because we enjoy them. Compliment the food, the houses, the—I don't know—temperature. If you're sad or scared and you don't think you can hide it, go in one of the bathrooms and let it out there."

"For how long?" Cintia asks.

"I don't know," I admit.

"There's a lot you don't know for someone who says she has all the answers," Mr. Sinclair says.

"I'm sorry," I say. "I'm trapped in here just like the rest of you."

"But you've been involved with these people, the ones who put us in here," he accuses.

"Not the same ones. The people I know are trying to help us. Can we please just play along for now? I don't want anyone to get hurt."

My voice breaks on the last few words. It's my fault. I got them involved in this resistance without asking them, without them having any idea what it meant.

"We might as well try it for now," Ms. Cavoy says. "We'll see if anything changes, and then we can reevaluate."

The murmur that follows sounds like agreement. Mr. Sinclair lets out a huff. "I still say it's ridiculous. Come on."

He tugs his wife to her feet and ushers her and Toby away. I watch them go, my skin chilling. We should have one more day. One day to convince him.

"You knew this all along?" Angela's mom is saying to her in a low voice. "You were helping go against these . . . 'aliens'?"

"Not the whole time," Angela says. "And what I did wasn't that big a deal. I just talked to people."

"You didn't know they wouldn't attack you for that," her mom says. "You should have left it alone."

"I'm *fine*," Angela protests. But she's not. None of us are, not as long as the Council can reach us.

• • •

The first thing I hear the next morning is Mr. Sinclair coming out of the store.

"Same flavors as always," he says, loud enough for his voice to carry to my bedroom window. "Whoever's leaving these should really consider giving us some *real* food for once."

Angela sits up beside me. "The idiot," she mutters, rubbing her face. "Doesn't he remember how they *shot* him?"

He must think if they didn't really hurt him then, they won't now. Maybe Dad can talk to him.

And if that doesn't work?

Mr. Sinclair isn't the only one who's decided on defiance. After Mom's morning workout, I overhear Daniel's friend Jeffrey making a comment about how our captors are trying to kill us with boredom. Daniel and Cintia try to shush him, but he waves them off.

"It's true," he says. "We should be able to say what's true."

One more day, I remind myself, but I can feel the minutes slipping away. Even those who are going along with our new approach aren't acting content so much as subdued.

Worry knots my stomach. I've been carrying an ache inside for so long that I don't realize something more is wrong until, shortly after we've choked down a ration bar lunch, my gut outright rolls, and I find myself doubling over our lawn.

"Skylar?" Angela says from behind me. I sway, flush with a sudden fever.

"I think—" I manage. Then I vomit my lunch into the too-green grass.

My legs give. I fall.

Someone carries me into the house. I think it must be Dad, because I catch a glimpse of Mom huddled by the toilet before I end up in my room. He lays me on my makeshift bed.

The blankets are too hot and the floor too hard and the ache that was in my stomach is bleeding out into my bones. I squirm and gasp. *Two days*, I'm able to think. *We were supposed to have—*

Then my head starts to throb and I can't form any coherent thoughts at all.

I'm aware of moments. I'm shivering on top of the blankets, Angela curled into a ball across from me. Dad is saying something to Evan about "eleven of us." A glass of water is set in front of me; my hand shakes so much I knock it over trying to grasp it.

Between those moments I'm lost in a haze of nausea and pain. I don't know how much time has passed when a shout carries from downstairs.

A slim bronze-skinned man strides into the room. He holds a shiny disc to my forehead and chest, and nods. Then he takes a pear-shaped device out of the pouch on his belt and presses the narrow end to my throat. A tingle like a static shock jolts through me. He rises and moves to Angela.

"Are they going to be all right?" Dad is saying. I miss the answer. But the fever is already retreating. By the time the man has left Angela and is heading out of the room, my head's clearing enough that I register he must be Kemyate. Come from outside. Dad rushes over as I push myself upright.

"He said you need to rest to recover completely," he says, nudging me back down.

"Mom?" I ask, my voice rasping.

"He's looking after her now," Dad says. "He said it was an allergic reaction."

He keeps his voice even, but his expression shows his skepticism—and his fear. I'm aware enough now to share both. I lie back, staring at the ceiling, echoes of pain still rippling through me.

The Council is making a point. Next time, whatever they use will hit us all, too quickly for any medic to save us.

. . .

By the late evening I'm walking around, only mildly dizzy. When we gather behind the storage containers again, I lean against Dad while he holds Mom's hand at his other side. She wasn't hit as hard as me, but her face still has a yellowish cast. Neither of us could stomach dinner.

"We're going to do what they've asked," Mom says to the others. "We're going to be grateful to have our lives and some sort of home here, and that is going to be all we could want. I am *not* losing my daughter because a few of you can't keep your opinions to yourselves."

She glances toward Mr. Sinclair with that last comment, but he already looks broken, sitting slumped with his arms around Toby. Dad told me that Mr. Sinclair didn't get sick, but his son and wife both did. Jeffrey, who looks a little wobbly after his own bout with "allergies," nods, his eyes downcast.

Whether they believe the rest of my story or not, they're convinced our captors' threat is real. I should be thankful, but all I feel is the suffocating sense of those invisible walls pressing closer in on us.

Evan, who was spared, is standing near Angela. "You think this is the right thing to do, Skylar?" he says, addressing me directly for the first time in days. "This is the only choice we have?"

I inhale slowly. I've been in a position like this once before. The moment I realized I couldn't go back in time to save Noam, not without putting the lives of everyone I knew in the Enforcers' sights. I gave my brother up to avoid a greater tragedy. I have to give up our fight for freedom for the same.

"Nothing matters if we're dead," I say. "So let's do what we have to do to stay alive."

14.

Win

It's past the twenty-fourth hour, long after I should be asleep, but I'm still crouched on my bunk rewatching clips from the exhibit feeds on a tablet. The tension inside me is wound too tight for me to rest.

I've wanted to speak with Skylar since I first heard about the sudden illness that struck several of the Earthlings, but I haven't gotten word from Isis yet, and it'd be all but suicide to try to sneak into the exhibit without her tweaking the feeds. I could hardly believe the Enforcers didn't haul me off with Dad two days ago. If I'd had any faith in our leaders left, I might have been reassured that Security was still unwilling to break their own laws, or the Council unwilling to cover it up if they did. Instead, I was just confused, until I saw how the Earthlings were behaving today.

The Council didn't order me arrested because they saw no point in bothering. They had another plan to crush our rebellion already in motion.

In the footage from hours earlier, Skylar's parents stroll along the street commenting on how comfortable they now are in their new home. A few of Skylar's former schoolmates talk loudly about what a relief it is not to have to worry about essays or exams. At one point the girl who looks a couple of years younger than Wyeth complains to her mother that she wants to go "somewhere *not* here," but her mother quiets her, telling her to be grateful they have all they need.

Even Skylar, still with her medicated pretense, offers the occasional vague remark: how nice it is that it doesn't ever rain, how she likes it being just the small group of them.

Nakalya made a public statement while I was taking dinner. "In light of the concerns raised by our fellow Kemyates, we have revised our proposal," our mayor said with the stoic expression that now sets my teeth on edge. "It seems our assistance in their time of need has prompted our new Earthling guests to feel more comfortable in their exhibit. Given their expressed enjoyment of it, we are pleased to allow them to stay there. Let us support their preferences, not force other ideals onto them."

I went down to the engine-room sector a couple of hours afterward and found most of the blockade had already dispersed. "It doesn't make sense to push for their freedom if they don't want it," a man Dad's age explained to me on the shuttle ride home.

I can't believe the Skylar I saw just a few days ago, who told off Jule in no uncertain terms and was asking about our progress even after that and other . . . distractions, would have told her companions to stand down unless she knew the "illness" was a purposeful threat.

Finally, I set aside the tablet and lie down, but I sleep very little amid the blaring of my thoughts. I posted a message on the network with the code word we agreed upon to indicate trouble, but I couldn't tell Isis what exactly the trouble was. How long will it take her and Britta to find another secure method of communicating with me?

When the lights come back on, I drag myself to breakfast with my family. Dad looks almost as worn out as he did when Security released him yesterday. Ultimately his punishment has been a docking of credits and a warning on his file; he also informed us, with a slightly longer look at me, that the Enforcers have blanket permission to search our apartment at any sign of further misconduct. He didn't say much about the interrogations, even when Wyeth asked, but he didn't need to. Along with his weariness, there's a twitch in his eyelid whenever someone moves past him quickly and a tremble in his hand holding his eating stick. I hope those effects are temporary.

Back at the apartment, I check the network one last time while Dad and Wyeth head to work and school. There's nothing. I fidget with my carry-pouch as I wait for the next shuttle to pull up.

Then I glimpse a head of familiar red-streaked curls on the other side of the shuttle door.

My heart skips a beat. If someone realizes we've met— Well, they won't know if I don't give it away. I step onto the shuttle as if there's nothing unusual about it. My pulse trips again when I see it's not just Isis and me. Britta and Tabzi stand at the far end of the car. This is the first time any of us has been in the same space since the return trip from Earth.

Isis inclines her head to me, lowering her heavy-lidded eyes, as the door slides shut. "Tabzi's provided us with a private shuttle," she says. "After we couldn't reach you over the communicator, and with the message Jule sent—I thought we needed to discuss this all together, so we can hear what everyone has to say and ask whatever questions we need to before we make a final decision."

"I had to destroy the communicator—Security was searching my apartment," I say. "Does Jule know what the Council's done to the Earthlings?"

"I'm assuming so," she says. "He indicated his information was especially urgent."

"We think Skylar was trying to leave us a message too," Britta says. She looks well, with a healthy flush to her cheeks that I haven't seen since before her injury, which I'd be more relieved by if not for the worried light in her eyes. "It's hard to make out on any of the public feeds, but we caught it on one of the others."

She holds out the tablet to me. The screen is paused on an image of Skylar sitting on the sidewalk. Her name and childish drawings—a sun, clouds, a rainbow—cover most of the surface around her. Then, to her left, she's written out a series of multiplication equations: times three, times three, times three. My fingers tense around the tablet.

I heard her murmuring those figures to herself once or twice in the worst of her attacks. Three was her special number, she said, that helped her calm down when she started to panic.

"When did she do this?" I ask.

"The day before they got sick," Isis says. "I only caught it last night as I was going through the earlier footage."

Three days ago she tried to tell us something was wrong, and we never answered. I push the tablet back toward Britta, my throat tight.

"What does it mean?" Tabzi ventures.

"She knew they were in trouble already," I say. "She must have been hoping I'd come so she could tell us about it, so we could help." I should have been there. "Can you get me in tonight?"

"That's another concern," Isis says.

"I was visiting a friend who lives on the eighth level, and noticed there's an Enforcer stationed outside the maintenance passage now," Tabzi says. "That's why I contacted Isis."

"They've had someone there on a strict rotation since sixth hour yesterday," Isis says.

"Then how do we get to Skylar?" I demand.

"Maybe we shouldn't," Isis says. "She could have been warning us away. It's possible what's best is for us *all* to pretend everything's wonderful for a while, until the Council backs off again."

Leave Skylar and the others to the Council's mercy? "No," I say. "Not without knowing what's happening."

"We're hoping we will know in a minute," Britta says. "We're picking up Jule next."

"You're letting Jule get on here with all of us?" I say, staring at her and then Isis. "You're *that* certain he isn't going to turn us in? So he's giving up his apartment—that doesn't mean—"

"There's more than that," Isis interrupts, and nods to Tabzi.

"Many of the upper-level families are gossiping about it," Tabzi says quietly. "Jule visited his father yesterday, and afterward his father drank . . . too much of the wrong sort of thing, and was ranting about ungrateful children and how he deserves to have the support he's given returned. People are saying he's only been able to keep his situation because Jule's been covering his expenses, which we knew from Skylar—and they're saying Jule cut him off."

Jule has severed ties with his father without caring who knows it? It was to protect his family's image that he sold us out in the first place. I'm almost impressed, but I can't help thinking that if he'd taken this stand a little earlier, he might have saved us from most of our current troubles.

"I believe he's made his intentions clear," Isis says. "Enough that we should hear what he has to say."

She motions us to the far end of the shuttle as it slows. The door opens, and Jule strides on without hesitation. He doesn't seem fazed by Isis, but halts abruptly at the sight of the rest of us.

"This isn't exactly what I expect when I call a private shuttle," he remarks with half a smile. His shoulders have drawn up, making him look uncharacteristically awkward, as I suppose he should feel when faced with four of the people he betrayed all at once.

"You needed to tell us something?" Isis says curtly.

"I found out what the Council decided," he says. "Ibtep told me outright yesterday—she *wanted* me to pass it on to Win. She spoke to Skylar. Told her they'd see to it that all the Earthlings were 'accidentally' killed if they didn't start singing praises. The 'illness' was to prove how easily they could follow through. And they *are* ready to follow through, and deal with the consequences after, if they feel they have to. Not just if one of the Earthlings acts out—if you make any further moves toward freeing them too."

"They can't just . . ." I start, but I know they can. They proved it to us as well as to Skylar.

"We should be glad they didn't go straight to that solution," Jule says. "Ibtep is no longer concerned about whether I reveal those recordings—she said she'd rather be dismissed from her position than see the move to K2-8 disrupted by infighting."

"Then we have nothing to bargain with," Isis says.

Tabzi's face has fallen. "What *can* we do?"

"We have to figure something out," I say. "Skylar came all the way here to help us, she did more than we ever should have asked, and then we *incinerated* her entire home and most of the people she cared about. The Earthlings aren't happy; they must be petrified.

We can't leave them like that. Even if the exhibit was an acceptable place for them to live, which it's not, how do we know the Council won't decide to 'accidentally' get rid of them anyway once everyone's calmed down and stopped paying so much attention?"

"We may not have a choice," Isis begins, but Britta's already shaking her head.

"We can't think like that," she tells her girlfriend. "Win's right. We owe it to Skylar, to all of them. We can't just give up."

"I agree," Tabzi says. "But how can we help them now?"

My mind spins with the facts we do know. "They control the Earth Studies hall," I say. "The life-support systems, the resources—that's what allows them to make that kind of threat. We stopped them from reaching the engines, at least for a while. Can we blockade Earth Studies and give the Earthlings a chance to tell the real story without retribution?"

"Not likely," Jule says with a grimace. "They installed a Travel point inside one of the storage units in the exhibit. They have instant access from any Travel bay on the station."

I open my mouth, and then pause, eyeing him. "We shouldn't discuss this any further with him here," I say to Isis.

"I could have turned you in weeks ago if that's what I wanted to do," Jule says.

Isis presses her lips together as she considers. "No, we shouldn't," she says, and reaches for the control panel.

Jule's jaw clenches, but he seems to catch himself. "Fine," he says. "But don't leave me out of this if you can use my help. I know what you all think of me, but I *do* want the same things as you."

He steps off at the next stop without a backward glance.

"Is there any way we could disable the Travel point, or get Skylar to?" I ask as soon as he's gone.

"Without being caught?" Isis says. "It's doubtful. And even if we could, to cover all the possible areas that affect the exhibit one way or another, we'd essentially need to take over the entire eighth and ninth floors."

She says that as if it's impossible, but the idea lights a flame inside me. "That's the answer," I say. "If we take over the upper levels, we can let Skylar and the others out of the exhibit, block it off, and protect them that way."

"Win—" Isis says, sounding tired, but I break in before she can argue.

"We could do it, couldn't we?" I glance from her to Britta to Tabzi, gaining momentum as the idea crystalizes in my mind. "If we organize people quickly enough, if we tell them about the Council's threat to the Earthlings—we have enough supporters to pull it off. Some of them must have skills they could contribute. We wouldn't have to hold the levels forever—just long enough to convince the Council to give way."

"You know, I think it could work," Britta says slowly. "The station's designed so that any level can be sealed off from the others in case of breach, after all. And we have enough tech-head friends to keep the Council from shutting the other systems down, don't we?"

Isis sighs, her mouth caught somewhere between a smile and a cringe. "We might be able to manage it. We'd want to take the tenth level too, so we wouldn't be facing attacks from both ends . . . But if we're going to do this, we have to be sure it's really worth it. There won't be any going back from this. We'll need to *be* there, leading the way. If we fail, we won't have Ibtep telling stories for us. The Council won't be kind."

A chill settles over me, but I've been ready to stop pretending for weeks. We've been so very careful, and it's gotten us nowhere. "Then that's the risk we have to take," I say. "We know we can't trust the Council. We can't protect Skylar and the others without doing something this big. The longer we wait, the more support we lose. If we're going to make up for what we've done to the Earthlings, we need to get them out *now*. If we don't, then we may as well accept that we're forever going to be a people who could have atoned for the horrible thing we did to an enormous number of fellow human beings, and instead gave up our last chance out of concern for our own security."

Tabzi and Britta nod. Isis rubs her mouth, and adds, "We'd be setting back the moving plans too. We won't be getting the station out of orbit in the middle of a civil war."

War. That's what it has come to, hasn't it? I cross my arms. Getting to K2-8 with this Council still in control and the Earthlings still captive—or dead—would be as awful as staying here.

"It is what it is," I say. "The Council has pushed it this far, not us. It's time Ibtep sees just how right Jeanant was. If we're going to set off on a new course, it needs to be all of us, Kemyates *and* Earthlings."

15.

Skylar

On the third day of our playacting at Ibtep's command, the signal I've been waiting for finally flashes in the sky. I don't say anything to anyone else, but a flutter of relief passes through me. Maybe it's Win or one of the others coming to say that we're finished, there's nothing more they can do. But at least it means they're still out there, and they've seen we need them.

Before dinner, Angela and I slip into the bathroom to wash clothes and talk. She slumps against the wall.

"I don't know how you've managed to keep up the whole drugged act so long," she says. "It was hard enough pretending not to know you were all right, before. Pretending to *like* it here, constantly—ugh."

"I know," I say. "I'm sorry."

"Sorry?" She pushes herself upright. "It's because of you we're okay. And we *are* okay. I was just venting."

I suppose we are okay, but it's "okay" by a definition we'd never have found remotely acceptable back home: "not dead." And even that could change with one little screwup.

Or without. Clearly our getting sick the other day didn't provoke any protest so massive the Council couldn't ignore it. Why should they bother keeping their end of the deal? I can picture them making a big show of how sad they are that the medics couldn't treat some new Earthling disease in time, and then shunting our bodies off into space and wiping their hands of us.

"We'll get through this," Angela says firmly, giving me a sideways hug. As she's pulling away, her mom opens the door.

"You're washing?" she says with a raised eyebrow.

"That's the plan," Angela says more brightly, and starts the water running. Mrs. Tinapay steps in, a bundle of folded clothes in her arms. She fixes her gaze on me. I turn over the pair of pants I'm holding. I've never gotten along with Angela's parents as well as she does with mine. Partly because we've never spent much time around them—her mom had a tendency to hover when we were kids, which meant Angela usually suggested hanging out at the park or at my house—and partly, I suspect, because her dad witnessed one of my panic attacks early on and must have told her mom about it, and since then they've always seemed a little wary of me beneath their politeness.

"I hope you're not drawing Angela into any more secret plans," she says to me now.

"Mom," Angela says, reaching for the soap.

Mrs. Tinapay shakes her head. "You knew she'd try to help you because you're friends," she goes on. "You took advantage. You shouldn't have put her in that position. When you needed help, you should have turned to the adults first."

"I didn't mean—" I start, my stomach twisting, and Angela spins around.

"*Mom*," she says, "it was my decision. I'm glad Skylar told me. Being eighteen and officially an 'adult' wouldn't have made me suddenly so much better at dealing with this."

"You saw what they did," her mom says. "You think it was a coincidence *you* were one who got sick."

"I don't care!" Angela says. "Skylar didn't make me do anything. I should be allowed to decide how much danger I put myself in, not you. If there was another chance to get us out of here, I'd go for it, because *that's* what's really important."

I blink at her, startled. I've never heard her sound that angry at anyone, let alone her parents. Mrs. Tinapay's chin wobbles. She bunches the clothing in her hands, and then turns and hustles out.

"I get why she's upset with me," I say. "It's all right."

"No," Angela says, slapping a wet shirt down on the side of the tub, "it's not. We're not kids anymore. I'm tired of trying to figure out how to do what I think I have to without making her worried about it. It's not like we've been stupid. She should be able to see we're *all* in danger *all* the time anyway."

She scrubs soap over the shirt, scowling. I touch her shoulder.

"I'm so glad you're here. You know that, right?"

Her face relaxes enough to give me a small smile. "Same to you, Sky."

• • •

A few hours later, I creep across the road to the store. I don't realize how scared I am that it won't be Win who emerges from behind the panel, that it'll be one of the others come to tell me he's been caught or Ibtep herself arriving to gloat, until he's ducking out. I catch him in my arms before he's quite straightened up.

"Hey," he says, returning the hug and pressing a kiss to my temple. "I'm sorry I wasn't here sooner. We only just worked out what's going on."

"You know?"

"Ibtep told Jule, so he'd tell us—about the Council's threat, the deal they've made with you. It extends to us too. If we organize any more protests . . ."

"They'll kill us for that," I say. As I suspected. So we're going to have to keep up this charade for the rest of our lives, however brief they may be? I squeeze my eyes shut, willing back tears.

Win brushes his thumb over my cheek, and I need to feel something, anything, other than this hopelessness. I ease back just enough to raise my lips toward his, and he meets me halfway with a kiss that sends a shiver all the way to my toes.

I haven't lost him. I haven't lost this. No one can erase this moment.

When the kiss ends, Win stays close enough that our noses could touch, our breaths mingling. It's only then I notice he's got a lump of familiar silky fabric tucked under his arm.

"You brought a time cloth?"

"Oh." He sets it on the counter. "Not for Traveling, of course. Security has stationed a guard outside the maintenance passage I use to get here. Isis had this stashed from a bunch she was refurbishing before our first trip to Earth. I just used it for its cloaking properties so I could get close. She and Britta created a distraction long enough for me to get through the door."

"But if they'd caught you—"

"We made certain they wouldn't," he says before I can express the whole of my fear. "I had to talk to you. We have one last move we can make."

A thread of hope tickles up inside me. "Really? What?"

"It's big," he says, his voice speeding up. "It's going to be danger-ous, but I think it's far more dangerous to leave all of you like this, in the Council's reach. I just needed to make sure you want to try."

"What?" I repeat.

"We're going to take over the top three levels of the station," he says. "The area around the Earth Studies hall and above. We'll hold those levels until we're certain we've come to an agreement in which we can trust the Council to let you go free. It has to be done quickly, though. If we're going through with it, we act tomorrow, midmorn-ing by your day cycle in here."

"You're going to take over a third of the station?" I say, staring at him. "The Council—they'll have *you* killed."

"Not if they can't get to us either," Win says grimly. "The station is designed so that any level, sector, or ward can be sealed off from the others in case of external damage. Britta's familiar with the sys-tems because they're similar to the ones on our ships. We just have to make it up there . . . It could all go wrong before we've really started, and we won't be able to protect you then. But it's the only real chance we have."

I try to imagine the chaos the station will be thrown into. From my readings into Kemyate history, I'm not sure anyone has ever bucked the order here on a tenth as large a scale. The Council will be desperate. Win didn't deny what I said earlier—maybe they will have the rebels outright killed if they regain the upper hand. At the very least, I doubt Win or the others would ever have their own freedom again.

"Are you sure *you* want to try?" I say quietly.

Win holds my gaze, resting his hand on my side. The gentle warmth of his touch clashes with the fierceness in his eyes. "I don't make promises lightly," he says. "And I couldn't live with myself knowing we had the chance and I gave it up to protect myself. You're the ones in the most danger. Are you ready to really fight?"

My mouth's gone dry. If this goes wrong, we're all dead. I don't want to make another decision for everyone. But there isn't time for me to consult the others.

Angela's voice comes back to me, telling her mother she'd risk anything to get us out. I think of my mom and her longing to take action, of Evan, hurt that I underestimated his strength, his courage.

Not one person here wants to keep going like this. I know that. I believe in Win, and Isis and Britta, and whoever stands with them. We can do this. We *have* to. Two options, Ibtep gave me, neither of them truly livable. *There is no third.* Well, now there is.

"What would we need to do?" I ask.

He exhales in a rush and gives me a tense smile. "Hold on to this key. It'll open the panel for you." He takes a metal token about the size of a stick of gum from the pouch at his waist and presses it into my palm. "The sky will flash three times when you need to move. You get everyone out of here, and down the air lift. Then place this on the outer side of the panel." He unwraps a metallic device that looks like a small, ridged Frisbee from the time cloth. "It's a . . . construction tool—it'll solder the panel to the wall, and stay hot for several hours as long as it's left there. They have another entrance into the exhibit, and we don't want them using it to come after you. Then you go down the hall and turn to the right, and the door there will let you out onto the eighth floor. You can join in with the rest of us, whatever we need then, which will depend on how it's going."

Depending on how it goes, we could emerge to find ourselves faced with a squad of Enforcers. I glance toward the shuttered store window, and find myself remembering looking into the Earth Studies exhibits from the other side, weeks ago.

"We're not the only people in here," I say. "The Earthlings in the other exhibits—what will happen to them?"

Win closes his eyes for a second, his hand tensing against me as he mutters a curse. "I hadn't thought of that. I should have. We were going to seal off the entire hall to ensure the Council can't get at us, but they could order all the other inhabitants killed, to punish us."

"Then we have to get them out too," I say. "They don't deserve to stay locked up in here any more than we do, even if they're used to it."

He nods. "I think all of the exhibits use the same key. There are nine others, but only five or six people in each. They won't understand what's going on, though. I can try to send someone to help you, who'll speak some of the languages . . . We don't know yet how many people we'll have on our side."

"We'll just do our best, then."

I slip the key into my jeans pocket. My heart is thumping as if we're breaking out right now, not tomorrow morning. Win opens the cabinet under the counter and slides the soldering tool inside.

"I'd better get going," he says. "I have to time it right so I can get past the guard. And we have a lot to set in motion in the next twelve hours."

No. Not yet. In twelve hours he'll be putting himself directly in the Enforcers' sights. If something goes wrong, I'll never see him again. That's been a possibility every other time he's left here, but it's never felt so real before.

"Win," I say, but I have no words to express the swell of feeling inside me. Instead, I pull him to me, kissing him hard. As if, if I can make this moment real enough, it'll last beyond now and carry both of us through all those dangers ahead.

His breath is ragged when we part, his eyes bright. My fingers are clutching his shirt. I don't want to let go.

"I want you out there waiting for me tomorrow," I tell him. "I'm not done kissing you yet."

A little chuckle escapes him. "I'll be there."

16.

Win

When Ilone opens the door to her apartment, the rolling melody of Earth music—Brazilian, I think—greets me with her. The room behind her is crowded with more than a dozen of the people I grew up with. Some of them are holding cans of giddy-drink, and I feel abruptly awkward that I haven't brought any refreshments to contribute, especially since technically this party was my idea. I sent Ilone a quick message last evening commenting on how long it's been since the bunch of us former classmates got together and hinting that tonight would be a good time, and Ilone's never been one to pass up an opportunity to socialize. The fact is, though, *I'm* not here to socialize.

If she notices my empty hands, Ilone doesn't comment. She grins, gives me a quick hug, and nudges me toward the nearest group. I suppose these days it's unexpected that I'd turn up for one of these get-togethers at all.

To my relief, I spot Markhal's broad form and Celette's blue hair near each other in a cluster of conversation on the other side of the room. I squeeze my way over, nodding greetings, until I can bump Markhal's elbow with mine. When he turns toward me, I lean in to speak under the music.

"I need to talk to just you and Celette—quickly. Can you tell her and follow?"

He gives me a curious glance before he scoots around Dev to speak to Celette. When she looks at me, I motion with my shoulder toward the secondary bedroom. I'm grateful to find no one has yet claimed it for other activities.

"What's going on?" Celette asks as the door shuts, filtering out most of the music and chatter. In that moment, the loudest sound is the rush of my pulse.

The bedroom is so small I can't look at both of them when we're all standing. I sit down on the edge of the bunk, gathering my words. Seeing them here should be safe. Ilone has never been actively involved in any protests.

Markhal sits beside me, and Celette props herself against the wall next to him, her fingers tapping her arms where she's crossed them over her chest. I clasp my hands together on my lap, recognizing as I do that it's a gesture I've picked up from Ibtep. I almost unfold them, but I could use her air of authority right now.

"I'm talking to you because you're the only two people I trust completely," I say. "If you're on board with what I tell you, I want you to pass it on only to people *you're* certain you can trust—face-to-face, like this, not over the network where Security could see—as many of those people as you can between now and tenth hour tomorrow. We need all the help we can get."

"Who's 'we'?" Markhal asks, his dark eyebrows drawing together, at the same time as Celette leans forward and says, "Help with what?"

I look down at my hands, and back at them. "'We' is me and most of the other people who were on the ship that disabled Earth's time field generator," I say. "Who arranged for everyone to see what really happened there. Who organized the blockade by the engine rooms."

Markhal's jaw goes slack.

"*You* . . ." Celette says, her eyes widening, and can't seem to finish.

"I'm so sorry," I continue hastily. "I lied, I pretended I didn't care—I had to keep my involvement secret when it was just the small group of us, and since we made it back we've been under strict surveillance."

Markhal is still staring at me. "The other day," he says. "You suggested—you said you'd heard—the registry was actually *your* idea."

I incline my head.

"You could have told me," Celette says. "You should have known you could tell me."

"I was reprimanded just for making conversation with you in the VR room," I say. "Why do you think we're talking here instead of me calling you over to my apartment? I'm telling you now. We're organizing something big, and we need it to come together fast. Do you want to hear it?"

"Of course," Markhal says. Celette is frowning, but she nods.

Her frown fades into a dawning eagerness as I explain about the threat to the Earthlings and how we intend to fight back.

"That's insane," Markhal says when I'm done, but his expression is thoughtful.

"Brilliantly insane," Celette says with a breathless laugh. "The Council would never expect us to go that far. It wouldn't even occur to them. You know how much I've tried to advocate for Earth, and it wouldn't have occurred to *me*. They probably won't believe it when it's actually happening, not at first. That's why it'll work."

"We could get into a lot of trouble," I say, and Markhal makes a dismissive gesture.

"We're already in a lot of trouble if we let this pass. I don't want to spend the rest of my life ruled by people who think wiping out civilizations for their convenience is right."

Their certainty strengthens mine. "You know people who'll join in?"

"At least a few," Markhal says. "Maybe more—I spoke with a lot of people during the blockade."

"A dozen or so, I hope," Celette says. "Some of my 'troops' are off-Kemya right now, but . . . I can round up whoever's here."

"Good," I say. "You'll all need to be wearing plain clothes tomorrow, nothing Earth-like. Watch the Earth supporter registration. Tomorrow around tenth hour a post will go up saying we need to put aside our previous tactics. That's your signal to move."

• • •

The buzz of my nerves makes my sleep restless. I get up early, leaving Wyeth still sleeping, and catch my parents right after Mom's gotten home from work. Dad's only just woken, but the bleariness vanishes from his eyes when I say I need to talk to them.

It's going to be a fine line giving them a choice without taking it away in the telling. I drag in a breath.

"Something is happening," I say. "Something that means I . . . will have to leave for a while. You don't need to know anything more than that. It has nothing to do with you. I think you'll be better off here. But it's possible there will be consequences that extend to you."

"Win," Mom says, "*what's* going to happen?"

Dad grasps her hand, still holding my gaze. His mouth has tightened. He's the one I talked to about taking action and the dangers that could come with it. He's the one the Enforcers interrogated. I think he'll understand they'll only be safe from punishment if they don't know enough that Security could claim they conspired with me. If I tell them too much, they and Wyeth will have to come with me—and that's hardly safe either.

"It has nothing to do with us," he says softly, repeating my words. "Unless you need our support . . . ?"

Until he offers, I didn't realize I wouldn't have expected him to. It is a note of comfort amid the tension building inside me.

"No," I say. "I can handle it. I just— You haven't had the best experiences lately. I don't know for certain what will happen." I don't want to believe the Council would outright hurt them or Wyeth to get at me—I don't *think* they'd take the risk that such an action would turn more people against them—but I don't know. "If you don't think you could handle staying here . . ."

"But if we don't know—" Mom starts, and stops herself. "We don't need to know. Are you sure *you* have to do this?"

"I am," I say. I've never meant anything more.

They look at each other in silent conference. For an instant, I want them to ask to hear everything and come along. I'll be completely cut off from them once the upper levels are sealed. Then I imagine Wyeth dodging Enforcer fire, and my stomach lurches.

Dad must have had a similar thought. "I'd be more curious if it weren't for your brother," he says carefully. "It sounds as though this shouldn't involve us."

"Yes," Mom says. "If nothing else, for Wyeth."

"For me what?" demands Wyeth, stepping out of the bedroom rubbing his eyes. We all stiffen.

"For you I'm going to bed early, so I can be up for you to show me your antigrav flips in the fitness center as you asked," Mom covers.

Wyeth pauses, not looking entirely convinced. Then he grins. "All right," he says, and ducks into the bathroom.

Dad grips my shoulder and then pulls me into a hug. "Look after yourself," he says.

. . .

It's five minutes to the tenth hour when Isis pings me, just a blip on my terminal's display. The tension in my gut melds into a heavy lump. I grab my carry-sack.

In less than an hour, Ibtep and the Council will have definitive proof that I've broken our agreement. There is no escaping their notice today, no keeping my head down and pretending not to be involved. I may never return to this apartment. I may never see my parents or my brother again. If I do, it's likely to be through a medicated haze so thick I'll hardly be there at all.

I pause by the front door, taking a long look at the main room. Dad managed to rehang the few paintings that took minimal damage, but the yellow walls look far too open now. His easel stands empty in the corner. One of Mom's filmy scarves is lying on the bench, next to a sizzle-water can Wyeth didn't bother to toss out. My lungs clench, as if the air has become too thick.

I'm doing this.

I feel strange walking down the hall, giving the usual polite nod to the neighbor I pass and the people already on the public inner-shuttle I summon, as if I'm seeing them from a distance. Our world is changing—I'm about to change it—and they have no idea.

I'm the last person left on the shuttle when it reaches sector 84-6. The hall there is empty. A few doors down, I find the equipment Britta contrived to leave in the service stairwell. These stairs are one of the emergency access points that will remain partly operational after the rest of the passages between this level and the one above are sealed.

As I step out with my carry-sack heavy at my side, Markhal arrives with five others. He's introducing them when Celette emerges from the next shuttle with eight—"and six more should be showing up any time now," she tells me, face flushed and eyes bright.

We're crowding the hall. Isis planned to leave the surveillance feeds on a hacked-in loop while we marshaled our collaborators, but there's no telling how long that will last before someone in Security notices.

"Have everyone put on something from in here," I say to Celette and Markhal. The packages I hand them contain Enforcer-style belts and guns that will numb but not kill—obtained on the black market at no small expense by Tabzi—as well as maintenance-worker patches Isis constructed. "I'll keep a few of your people, Celette. When the others get here, you take them to sector 2-87-3. Markhal, bring yours to sector 1-85-8. When you're in 'uniform' and in position, wait by the service stairs there. As soon as the alarm sounds, everyone on the upper levels will start coming out. Hurry them down to the seventh level. We want as many people as possible out before the real Enforcers can interfere. If anyone comes by with an Earthling pet, tell them the pets are being temporarily quarantined and keep the Earthlings with you. We don't want to leave them where the Council can get to them. All right?"

"What if someone argues with us?" Markhal says.

"Once they see your Enforcer attire, that Kemyate discipline we've perfected should kick in," I say with a crooked smile. "If anyone *does* stall, say Security will discuss the matter in more detail shortly. Tell them whatever you need to that'll keep them moving. Just get them out."

"And when the real Enforcers show up?" Celette asks.

"There's a code in the package I gave you. As soon as you see an Enforcer, enter it into the data panel by the entrance. That will start the final manual seal. If you need to, you can shoot them unconscious with the guns. If any citizens are left in your area when that happens, send them into their apartments or workrooms, or numb them if you have to. We want to avoid hurting anyone—that'll only harm our cause. Now go!"

I usher the four I'm taking with me—a couple women I've seen around at Celette's past protests, a guy who's one of her scrounger colleagues, and an older man who often sits with her group in the cafeteria—back to the maintenance door. There, I put on one of the Enforcer belts before passing the other to one of the women, Solma, and giving the maintenance patches to the other three. Then I press the communicator Britta left me into my ear, though Isis cautioned us not to use them until the seal is complete. Around the station, our allies should be in place at each of the twelve emergency access points.

Even though I'm expecting it, I flinch when the siren blares on overhead. The translucent ceiling flashes red. "Breach detected," an electronic voice announces, booming through the hall. "All inhabitants must descend to level seven or below. Emergency seal will complete in fifteen minutes."

My heart pounds nearly as loud as the siren's wail. All through the sector, apartment doors are sliding open automatically. I send the others to fan out and escort anyone who's dawdling. "This way!" I holler. "Quickly and calmly!"

Britta determined the time when the fewest number of citizens would be working or at leisure on the upper levels, but no area of the station is ever empty. People hurry past us in a steady stream, faces tense under the flashing lights, this sector's residents giving way to people from farther down the halls.

"Quickly and calmly," I keep saying between the bursts of the breach announcement, waving people to the stairs. Most of them hustle past without a word, only a glance at my belt. I pull aside a medicated Earthling girl who wanders over alone, telling her to wait in one of the vacated apartments. My companions detach a few other pets from their owners to join her.

"Where's the breach?" a woman demands of me, pushing close as the rush of figures continues past us. "How could this have happened?"

How do you think? I want to ask her. "More information will be available shortly," I tell her. "Please keep moving. Evacuation is our first priority."

She huffs, but she goes.

"Breach detected. Emergency seal will complete in six minutes."

I'm facing the stairwell doorway when someone taps on my shoulder. "You," a harsh voice says. A stout, gray-haired man with a real Enforcer belt is eyeing me. "I don't know you. What's your number?"

At the sight of the gun in his hand, my stomach flips and my mind goes blank. I'd forgotten Isis's warning that there'd be a few Enforcers stationed on the upper levels. As I clamp down on my panic, calling up the number that should give me a temporary pass, his eyes narrow further.

"439," I snap out, but he's reaching for his communicator. I can't let him speak to anyone at the Security offices—they have to know this is a false alarm by now. My hand twitches to my own gun, but if I stun him, then I'll have to explain that to all these witnesses.

Instead, I reach for the restless impatience Ibtep and the others so often chided me for. "Why are you standing around up here?" I say, motioning to the door. "We've been expecting someone to handle the lower exit since five minutes ago. Get on with it!"

The Enforcer pauses, staring at me. "Can't you hear it's a breach, you rot-head?" I charge on. "We're running out of time!"

His eyes flicker at the insult, but I think that's what convinces him. "Right," he says. He's reaching toward his communicator again as he joins the stream of figures down the stairs, but now we have a door we can put between him and us. I take out my gun, bracing myself.

The countdown has reached three minutes. The people still arriving hurry even faster. "Quickly and calmly," I shout again, my voice hoarse. I glance down the stairwell every few seconds, watching for the first sign of movement heading toward me. "Solma, with me," I call, and my fellow "Enforcer" comes to the other side of the door.

An angry yell echoes from below, ordering people to make room. My palm is suddenly damp against the warm polymetal of the gun. Footsteps clatter up the stairs.

"Seal completing," the electronic voice says. I step to the control panel to close this entrance, catching a glimpse of three Enforcers, including the man I sent down before, racing to the top of the stairs.

Even as they dodge the last stragglers heading down, two of the Enforcers draw their guns—guns that, unlike mine, can kill. I shoot at them as I jab at the panel, and miss. Their shots twang out. Solma staggers, clutching her hip, but still manages to fire. The man I talked to before slumps, hand pressed to his chest. My fingers trip over the code. I swipe it in and jerk out of the stairwell just as the other Enforcer aims a shot my way.

A sliver of fire darts past the closing door and hits my elbow. I wince at the prickling shock—and the door clicks shut. We've done it.

We've done it for now. As the seal bolts hiss into their sockets, all four of my companions gather around. I can hear the Enforcers working at the door from the other side.

"Can they get through?" Solma asks, balancing herself on her good leg.

"They won't be able to after this," I say. I drop the gun and drag a final item out of my carry-sack: a long coil of sealant tape the width of my palm and as thin as Earth paper. My numbed arm dangles at my side as I step closer to the door. "A little help?"

The three still uninjured rush to my side. We tear off strips of the slick, shiny material and smooth them around the edges where the door meets the wall. With a few hard taps, it heats up, melding with the surface beneath it. *They'll have to go back for laser cutters to go right through the door*, Britta said when we discussed this strategy. *And by then we'll be ready to deflect them.* I hope she was right.

A voice breaks from my communicator. "Need some assistance in sector 86-9," a voice I don't recognize shouts. "Blast. Quick, please!"

My body tenses. "Hold this spot," I tell Solma and the older man. "It should be secure for now, but keep the post until you're told otherwise. You two, come with me."

Snatching up my gun, I take off running.

17.

Skylar

We're sitting on our front lawns, waiting, when the call comes: three flashes of white across the endless fake blue sky. I scramble to my feet, and everyone follows me to the store.

I press the key Win gave me to the wall behind the counter, and the panel there opens. Someone behind me sucks in a startled breath. The space on the other side is dark and silent.

"Is this really the best idea?" Jeffrey says suddenly. "I mean, we're basically *asking* them to kill us, right?"

I turn. Several of the faces before me look equally uncertain. Mom, Dad, Angela, and Evan passed on word of what we needed to do today, and they reported back that everyone seemed relieved by the thought of leaving. Obviously stepping through this doorway will make it more real than just a thought.

"You never wanted to give in to them in the first place," I can't help saying. *He* almost got us killed, out of stubbornness. "We're basically asking them to kill us as long as we stay in here, where they control the air, the food, everything. We're a problem to them no matter how 'happy' we act. This is our only chance to make sure we stay alive for more than a few weeks."

"We don't know that for sure, do we?" Mrs. Green says. "Would they really hurt us, even if we're following their rules?"

"Haven't you been paying attention?" Mom says with a jerk of her arm. "How many of us got sick for doing nothing at all, before we even hit the deadline they gave us? They'd rather shoot us or poison us than reason with us. I'm not waiting around to see what they do next."

"I'm not forcing anyone to come," I say. "If you'd rather take whatever mercy the Kemyates will offer, you can stay here and surrender when they come. Maybe they won't hurt you. But after everything I've seen, I doubt they have any mercy at all for people from Earth." I raise my voice. "Everyone who wants to come, let's go. We've got to get moving."

In the end, no one decides to stay behind. I take the lift down with the last group after smacking the soldering tool to the outer side of the closed panel. A faint orange glow seeps from it into the wall.

"Head that way," I say when I reach the others in the dim, narrow hall below, pointing in the direction Win said would lead to the exit. "Turn right and then wait by the door."

Mom, Dad, and Angela stay with me. We have nine exhibits with fellow Earthlings—who can hardly have imagined what sort of world they've been kidnapped into, who are unlikely to understand a word of English—ahead of us. We'll just have to do the best we can to get them out. Once we join up with the Kemyate rebels, I'll let *them* explain.

I don't know what to expect as Dad and I head up on the next lift over. I only saw two of the exhibits, the ones at the front end of the hall, when I came as a visitor before.

The panel that opens for us lets us out into a cool wood-paneled room with bulging sacks stacked against one wall and bundles of straw against the other. A partly raised flap across the door lets in hazy sunlight and a damp breeze. We descend a ramp that's half ladder, half staircase into a packed dirt clearing. The building we've left and the cluster of straw-roofed houses surrounding it stand on stilts. A narrow gush of a stream flows by at our left.

The whole exhibit feels so much more . . . complete than our own, from the moisture in the air to the wild tangles of plant life that fill the spaces around the buildings. No vacant stretches of land, no inexplicable boxes. The people brought here must still have known something was wrong, but I can imagine them over time accepting life in this one "safe" space enforced by the invisible boundaries.

A man in wide-legged pants and a loose shirt emerges into a garden area between two of the houses, gaping at us. He calls out an alarm, and a woman and a boy in his early teens hurry to a nearby doorway. With a rustling amid the trees beyond the houses, another man and woman rush out, the woman with a toddler in a sling on her back. They look Asian, with smooth dark hair and tan skin. I'm not sure of their exact nationality, but it wouldn't help if I did—the only languages I know other than English are Spanish and Kemyate.

"We've come to help," I say in the friendliest tone I can manage, hoping that will convey my meaning. I spread my arms in an attempt to indicate I mean no harm. "It isn't safe here anymore. Please come with us." I gesture toward the building we exited.

The villagers draw together, talking among themselves as they shoot suspicious looks our way.

"Let us show you," Dad says, moving toward the doorway. The man and the woman with the child hesitate, and then approach.

They peer through the doorway as we pass through it and I key open the panel. The man makes a sharp exclamation.

"It's safer this way," I tell them, wishing I knew that for sure. "Please come with us."

Dad steps through the opening and back into the room to show where we want them to go. The couple seems to be arguing. How long do we have before the Council notices what's going on, if they haven't already? How long before they send Enforcers in?

"Danger is coming," I say, letting my urgency color my voice. "Please come with us. It'll be safe out there."

The other villagers enter the building. The couple gestures to the opening. The second woman walks up to it and pokes her head through. She jerks back, but stays next to it, frowning.

"*Please,*" I say again, and something about my tone or my expression must convince her. She eases out onto the platform and calls to the others. After a little more muttering, they join her. There isn't room for us too. I send down the lift, hearing a yelp as it starts to descend and Mom and Angela's reassuring comments as they help the villagers off. Then Dad and I follow.

"Can you bring them to the exit hall?" I say to Dad, who nods. He ushers the anxious villagers down the passage. They huddle together, staring at the walls wide-eyed, but they move.

Mom, Angela, and I have just reached the third lift when Dad returns with an unfamiliar figure in tow. Dad's face is tense. "This young man says he's come to assist us," he says, nodding to the guy, whose pale green outfit contrasts sharply with his blue-black skin even in the dim light.

"Skylar?" the guy says in Kemyate-accented English. "I'm Jai. Tabzi said you would need help in here."

"Yes," I say with a flood of relief. "We have to get everyone out of the exhibits—I don't know any of the languages."

He hands me a small tablet and holds up one of his own. "I speak two, and the others these can translate for us. Will someone come with me? I can speak to the Inuit."

"You know him?" Mom asks me.

"No," I say, "but I know Tabzi. She's with us."

"All right," Mom says to Jai. "Let's get going."

"The next over are Polish," Jai informs me as he steps onto the lift. The squeal of an alarm penetrates the hall from outside as I rush to the next exhibit with Dad and Angela close behind.

The Polish townspeople don't come easily, but at least I'm able to express my desire to help and the need for haste in a somewhat mangled version of their native language. After a few minutes, they descend with me into the hall—stepping into the unknown, prepared to face whatever will come, just as the villagers were earlier. I wish the Kemyate public could see *this* side of Earthlings.

Then Dad and I find ourselves faced with an agricultural settlement of people Jai called the "Tiwanaku." We convince the bewildered farmers to come into the rough stone building that holds the exit opening, and then they balk. The alarm is pealing through the darkness beyond.

"*Please come,*" I beg them. "*We're helping. There's danger.*" But they obviously don't trust us. I fumble with the tablet's translation program, searching for the right words.

"*You'll die,*" I tell them, which could very well be true. Unfortunately, the Tiwanaku seem to take the comment as a threat. One of them pulls a knife from his belt, and Dad tugs me behind him.

"*We will help you*," I say. The man snaps out a few words, motioning us toward the lift.

"*Please*," I say one more time. Dad squeezes my arm.

"If they won't come, we can't fight with them," he says. "It's their choice."

He's right. But my stomach knots as we descend to Angela alone.

Jai catches up with us and finds the next language on the tablet for me. "They're from a community in what's now—what was—Algeria," he shouts over the alarm before jogging on.

By the time we've urged those five into the lift, Jai and Mom have finished the rest of the exhibits, returning from the end of the hall with the family of cave dwellers I saw in the first one months ago. The young couple hurries along their son and daughter as we all hustle toward the exit hall that will take us into the station proper. Even Jai can't know for sure what's waiting for us out there now.

"Out," he says nonetheless. "Quickly. We need to get out of this sector so I can signal the others to seal it off."

"I couldn't get the Tiwanaku to leave," I tell him, and he grimaces.

"I'll give them a try. You get the rest to the next sector. If we don't close off this area soon, you're all at risk."

As Jai darts off, I squeeze past the waiting figures to the door and unlock it. We spill out into a wider hall with light gray walls, splashed with red as the lights blink above us. An electronic voice is saying something in Kemyate about a breach. A couple of guys in Kemyate clothing run past me, sparing only a surprised glance my way. One of them taps his ear and says something I'm too far away to hear. They don't try to stop us, so I assume they're on our side.

"What's going on?" Angela says. The mass of us—some seventy Earthlings now—has stayed bunched close to one wall. I gesture for everyone to follow me.

"I'm not sure," I say to Angela, my pulse stuttering with a fresh blast of the alarm. I can't tell if the situation is going well or badly.

Jai reaches us as we pass the sector archway. He's alone. "Wait here," he tells me. "We'll sort you out when everything's secure."

As we wait, our voices in their multitude of languages echo through the hall beneath the alarm. Tablet in hand, I walk the length of the group, checking that the people I know are hanging in there, managing to calm one of the Inuit children who's weeping, telling the other restless groups with the help of the translator that the danger is almost past.

I've just come back to the head of our shifting line when a young woman with braided blue hair and coppery skin bursts out of a cross hallway up ahead. Her steps skitter when she catches sight of us, recognition crossing her face. She opens her mouth, and then closes it as if realizing she doesn't know what to tell us. "Stay there," she says, and runs off down the hall.

She's not acting as if these levels are secure. I can do more than stand around, waiting for rescue.

"I'm going to see what's happening," I tell the people closest to me. "But some of you need to stay and keep everyone together and calm."

"Let me take that," Mr. Patterson says, pointing to the tablet he's been watching me use. "In case we need to talk to the others."

"I'm coming with you," Angela says.

"Angela," her mother starts, and Angela shakes her head.

"I'm doing this, Mom."

"Not a chance I'm letting you out of my sight," my mom says to me.

"Fine," I say. "Just . . . follow my lead."

My parents, Angela, her mom, Evan, and Ms. Cavoy trail behind me as I lope down the hall after the blue-haired girl. Most of the doors along the walls are open, showing glimpses of the apartments beyond, but no one's going in or out. We've crossed a few sectors when my ears catch a cry in Kemyate:

"*Help! Whoever can come—help!*"

I push myself into a sprint. Past the next archway, the two guys I saw before and the blue-haired girl are crouched around a doorway, along with a few other men and women. Three bodies are sprawled, unconscious, on the floor nearby. The door is only slightly ajar. A sliver of light crackles through the gap, and I understand why they're all hunched down. Trying to avoid Enforcer fire.

I press myself against the wall as I edge closer, motioning for my companions to do the same. The door shudders as someone on the other side heaves at it. The blue-haired girl and a couple of the others are leaning their weight against it, but there's a small object the size of a textbook on the floor at the foot of the door, holding it open. The two guys are trying to jam it back through, but they can't quite twist its hook-like protrusions around while staying out of blaster range.

"*Stop and stand down,*" a sharp voice calls from the other side, and I freeze. Kurra. I can't see her, but that voice immediately conjures an image of her pale form just beyond the door.

It shudders again, and the girl's feet slip. As she scrambles up, another shot twangs, catching one of the boys in the forehead. A hoarse chuckle rings out as he crumples, and my body comes back to life. I throw myself forward, joining the other boy in scrabbling at the wedge.

"*You can't save them,*" Kurra is rasping. "*I'll see to it. The Earthlings can never be permitted—*"

Angela jumps in with us. The three of us yank together, and the hooks turn. I shove the wedge away and the door snaps shut.

"Thanks," the blue-haired girl says, breathless, as she grabs a roll of metallic sort-of-fabric from the floor. Her gaze lingers on us a fraction longer than feels normal. She knows us from the feeds, of course.

She and the other Kemyates tear off pieces of the fabric-ish stuff and paste them around the door. I swivel, scanning the hall, but no one I recognize is around. *I want you out there waiting to meet me*, I told Win. He'd be here if he could. Maybe he's dealing with a problem like this wherever he's stationed.

Maybe the Enforcers have broken right through there. He could be lying somewhere stunned . . . or dead.

Throat tight, I head farther down the hall, listening for more shouts. The flashing lights are starting to make me dizzy. I pause to steady myself against the wall at the next archway, and just then Win comes into sight up ahead.

I straighten up, a smile stretching my mouth as I step toward him, and he speeds to a run. He catches me in an embrace, spinning me halfway around. A laugh jolts out of me.

"We did it," he says, still holding me close. "This part of the station is ours now."

It's not the victory we were supposed to have, weeks ago, but after all that time trapped in the exhibit, elation rushes through me. I ease back just enough to bring my lips to his.

I'd probably kiss him a lot longer if it weren't for the clearing of Dad's throat. I forgot we had company. I pull back, my face flushing, and turn toward the others.

"Mom, Dad, everyone," I say, my hand on Win's arm, "this is Win. It's because of him we're free."

For the moment. But not even that addendum can dull my joy. It may be only the first battle, but we fought it and won.

18.

Win

"So far, no injuries the equipment here can't heal," Markhal tells me at the doorway to the tenth-level medical center we've taken over. The normally stark lights of the round, ivory-walled room are glowing at half brightness to conserve energy. In their illumination, one of Markhal's medic friends is holding a health monitor disc over a man's chest where he reclines on a cot. Skylar's mother, who offered to help with her Earth-based knowledge of first aid, is applying bandages to the arms of a girl who just walked in laced with bleeding scratches. Enforcer fire burst a tech panel next to her.

"Security was aiming to stun, not kill, which was lucky for us," Markhal goes on. "I don't think they considered we might seriously pull this off."

"*I* still have trouble believing we did," I admit with a tired chuckle. "How are the pets and the people from the Earth Studies hall doing?"

"We're tapering off the medication from the pets' implants in preparation for removing them. I've only seen a few of the Earth

Studies people—minor issues like a sprained ankle, bruising. I gather confusion is a larger concern for them than physical difficulties."

That's one way of putting it. Skylar's group is getting the other Earth Studies inhabitants settled in a nearby sector. When I checked in a few hours ago, there was enough shouting and crying to paint a picture of general distress. Even the members of Skylar's group were looking rather stunned. Skylar has only asked for help from the few Kemyates among us who are familiar with one or more of the necessary languages, though. *I don't want anyone getting superior with them,* she told me. *We can handle things ourselves.*

"They're getting by," I say to Markhal. "Keep up the good work here."

He gives me a mock Earth military salute. "Aye, aye, captain."

Skylar's mother walks over to us. "She's saying she has a bad headache as well," she says, nodding to the girl she was treating. "I thought you'd want to make sure there isn't a more serious head injury?"

"Thank you," Markhal replies in English. "I'll see to her."

Skylar's mother lingers after he moves away. She crosses her arms as she scrutinizes me, a wary stance I've seen Skylar take more than once. They have a similar build and coloring, though her mother's cinnamon-brown hair is flecked with gray. It's odd seeing a representation of how Skylar might look in thirty years' time.

"So," her mother says, "from what I've heard, you're the one who kidnapped my daughter and dragged her all around history and across the galaxy."

I can't help tensing. Yesterday there wasn't time for more than brief introductions after Skylar kissed me. From what I know of her era's cultural standards, seeing that may not have given the best first impression.

"I think Skylar would object to the term 'kidnapping,'" I say cautiously. "She's been quite adamant about making her own decisions about where she goes and what she does there."

The corner of her mother's mouth twitches. I'm not certain if it's amusement or irritation until she acknowledges, "She can be pretty stubborn, I'll give you that." She sighs. "I don't understand enough about what's going on to have much of a say, but can you keep in mind that there are other people who care very much what happens to her?"

The worry in her voice—not about me, but for Skylar—eases my nerves. "I'm one of them," I tell her. "And Skylar's proven at least as capable of looking after herself as I am." Better, I suspect, if we were to add up all the danger each of us has put ourselves in and gotten each other out of.

Skylar's mother draws in a breath as if to say more, but the communicator in my ear chirps the two-note code meant to summon me to our headquarters. "Sorry, I have to go," I say, and she waves me off.

Outside, I step onto my glider. One of Britta's friends discovered a set of them in a ninth-level shop, and we've borrowed them for faster travel since disabling the inner-shuttles. Isis feels we're better off drawing little of the station's power. We're also talking face-to-face as much as possible, to avoid any chance our opponents could pick up communicator signals. I've spent most of the last fifteen hours making the rounds between our various pockets of people, checking in and dealing with any concerns before they warrant an emergency call.

Touching my heel to the bar-like contraption's controls, I set off at a half-a-foot hover, the training function enabled so if I wobble too far, a field will shoot up to grab me. *My* head is starting to ache through the hum of adrenalin that's kept me going since yesterday morning. I've only grabbed fragments of sleep, fifteen or twenty minutes here and there when I've had to wait for others to report back to me, since our takeover began.

Wyeth would likely laugh seeing me on this rich-kid toy. As I glide through the halls, I try to picture him asleep in our bedroom, even though I doubt he's there. One of Isis's crew was able to determine that my parents were both taken into Security's custody shortly after the eighth level was sealed off. Wyeth is too young for a full interrogation. It's most likely Mom's brother, our Uncle Kenn, has taken him in for the night.

Dad and Mom didn't know anything concrete. They should be fine. I have to remind myself of that at least once an hour.

As I turn the last bend before the headquarters room, I catch sight of the other person whose safety I can take comfort in. Skylar's heading the same way.

"Sky," I say, hopping off the glider as I catch up with her. She turns, and although her smile is as weary as I feel, it lights me up inside. "Is everything all right?"

"Yeah," she says. "Well, we're still trying to get everyone comfortable. But most people have calmed down, at least. Isis called me in, I'm not sure what about. You?"

"The same. I was just at the medical clinic. Your mother's been a real help."

"Great." She smiles more freely then, with a mischievous glint in her eyes. Her voice drops. "It's good to see you, *Darwin*."

It's impossible to quantify the effect of her saying my full name that way: the tingle of heat over my skin, the giddy rush inside. I have to kiss her. It still feels miraculous that I can, just like that—and even more miraculous that she kisses me back, her fingers uncurling against my cheek. She tugs me closer, the press of her body sending a flood of thoughts through my mind, of all the things we could be doing as well as kissing if we weren't standing in the middle of—

A guffaw carries down the hall, and I pull back. Britta's ambling toward us, smirking. "What is it Earthlings say—'Get a room'?" she remarks in her usual cheery tone, despite the shadows under her eyes that suggest she hasn't gotten any more sleep than the rest of us.

My face flushes, though Skylar just laughs, resting her chin against my shoulder.

I don't think there was any judgment in the raise of Britta's eyebrows at Skylar's and my joined hands when we first met up with the others yesterday. She took Skylar's relationship with Jule in stride. Still, it's one thing when a guy from a respected Kemyate family finds an Earthling girl attractive, and another when it's someone who's always been considered *too* keen on Earth. The comments tossed my way when Skylar first met the rebel group echo through my mind: Emmer's jokes about the extent of my "Earth love," Pavel's insinuations that I was indulging some sort of *perversion* . . .

I force myself to exhale, releasing those memories. I know my regard for Skylar has nothing to do with what planet she's from.

The three of us walk into the workroom we're using as headquarters and find Isis and Tabzi already inside. Isis looks up from her display and gives us a quick smile. She turns on her stool as we gather around her. Her clothes are rumpled, her face worn—I don't think *she's* slept even a fragment. Her and Britta's tech-head friends are crammed into the rows of consoles beyond her, but she hasn't wanted to hand over responsibility for our safety yet. They've already fended off several attempts by Security to shut these levels down over the network, while putting up deflection fields to repel the Enforcers' ongoing efforts to physically break through to the eighth level. The screens on the walls glow with a station's worth of data feeds.

"A few of Celette's people have gotten one of the cafeterias running," I report. "They have enough pre-prepared foodstuffs on hand to keep us going at least one ten-day, they estimate. Most of the injuries have been dealt with, and the pets are adjusting without much difficulty."

"Excellent," Isis says. She pushes her hand through her thick curls and looks as if she's suppressing a yawn. Britta scoots over to press a kiss to the top of her girlfriend's head.

"You were supposed to rest," Isis says, studying her.

"I tried," Britta says with a shrug. "I got a little. I'm fine, Ice."

Isis frowns, but she turns back to the rest of us. "I thought it was time to discuss our next steps."

"How has the Council reacted so far?" Skylar asks.

"Nakalya sent around an official statement about an hour ago," Isis says. "They're presenting us as a few poor Kemyates who've been caught up in overconcern, because no one could possibly have agreed to disrupt the station like this unless they misunderstood what Earthlings really are or need. They're implying that freeing the Earthlings like this is *more* cruel than keeping them on display."

"Anyone who doesn't agree is going to be hesitant to speak up, of course," Britta puts in, "but from what I've seen on the network, even the people who were sympathetic are taken aback by the lengths we went to."

"So naturally the Council will play to that as much as they can," I say, trying to ignore the sinking feeling inside me. Keeping Skylar and the others safe for now and for the rest of our lives depends on the public coming around to our side. I squeeze Skylar's hand. "We have to show them the truth as we did before, about the Council's threats and about how capable the Earthlings *really* are. Now we can do it openly."

"What if we made video recordings to really *show* everyone what we're doing and why?" Tabzi says. "We could send those over the network, couldn't we?"

I remember how much impact our reveal of Earth's destruction had. "That sounds great."

"You want to be in charge of making them, Tabzi?" Isis says.

Tabzi lowers her eyes shyly. "I do have a little . . . practice. My friends and I, we made some—very short, not very good— recordings trying to be like Earth movies."

"My friend Angela could probably help," Skylar says. "She's mostly into still photography, but she's done video work too."

"Along with that—" Isis says, and pauses. "Yes, Zanet?"

A young man has poked his head through the doorway. "There's someone who wants to speak with you," he says. "He's claiming he knows you, but he didn't know where you would be, which I thought was strange . . . His name is Jule Hele-Rennad Adka?"

Skylar's fingers tense around mine. Isis stands. "He's with you?"

Zanet nods. "I had him wait in the room across the hall."

"We don't want him seeing our setup in here," I say.

Isis nods. "Let's go find out what he wants—and how he got here."

Skylar keeps gripping my hand as we cross the hall to the smaller, unused workroom. Jule is leaning casually against a console, but his fingers are drumming its side nervously. He straightens up when we all come in. His gaze slides to Skylar first.

"What are you doing here?" I demand, and his gaze snaps to me.

"I thought it would be obvious," he says. "I've told you I want to be involved in your plans. So here I am."

"Maybe you could explain how you managed the 'here' part?" Britta says with eyebrows arched.

"I *live* on the eighth level, remember?" Jule says with a slanted grin. "I was home when the breach alarm went off, and, after the way you all were talking the other day, I figured it was you and not a real emergency. So I stayed in my apartment until most of the evacuation was finished, and then I helped seal the exit near me. I'd have come looking for you sooner, but I thought you'd have a lot of other things to deal with early on that were more important than me."

Jule the humble. He's not wrong, but that doesn't mean he's telling the whole truth either. "I don't think this is a good idea," I say.

"I agree," Tabzi says softly.

"If you do actually want to help," I go on with a flicker of inspiration, "you'd be more useful to us down there with Ibtep. Isis, you could set up a way for him to communicate with us, couldn't you?"

"I could," Isis says, studying Jule. "And I'd rather he was down there too."

"It won't do you much good," Jule says. "Ibtep's never really trusted me, and I can't hold those recordings over her head to keep me in the loop if she isn't afraid of being exposed anymore."

"Who said anything about blackmail?" Isis replies with a thin smile. "Beg. Show up saying you'll do anything to get into her good graces, that you've already managed to reach out to us and gotten information for the Council. It might not work, it might be you'll only pick up a few scraps, but better than you wandering around up here."

"If you don't like that idea," I offer, "we could seal you up in your apartment like the other upper levelers who didn't make it out in time."

Jule pauses, as if hoping one of the others will speak up on his behalf. Then he makes a dismissive gesture. "Fine. If that's what I need to do, I'll go back. I just want you to know I'm going to keep supporting the cause the way I should have before, until you let me do everything I can."

He's looking at Skylar again, but she's ducked her head toward me, ignoring him. "Come here," Isis says. "We'll set up a communication protocol, and then Zanet will get you down to the seventh level."

The rest of us drift into the hall after them. "I should get back to our Earthling 'neighborhood,'" Skylar says.

"Is there anything you need?" I ask.

"Short of magic, no. I think we have all the supplies we can use." She brings her hand to my face and gives me a quick peck before heading down the hall in the opposite direction. When I turn back, Jule is watching me over Isis's shoulder. His jaw works, but he glances away to reply to whatever Isis is saying to him.

I retrieve my glider from outside the headquarters room. My next goal was to arrange for the cafeteria crew to start bringing food to our main work areas, since everyone's been too busy to leave for a meal. I suspect most of us are as short on nutrition as we are on sleep.

"Zanet," Isis calls. "Please take Mr. Adka to the shuttle stop at sector 2-83-2. I'll confirm when it's clear to escort him down through it."

Jule glances toward me again. "Darwin," he says without his usual mocking lilt, "walk with us a minute?"

I'd rather be back exchanging fire with the Enforcers than have the conversation he likely wants, but he asked instead of insisting. I can always walk away if he switches to insults.

I join them, matching Jule's strolling pace as Zanet leads the way. Jule trains his gaze straight ahead.

"This was *your* idea, wasn't it?" he says finally. "Taking over a third of the station? No one else would have come up with a plan that crazy."

I'm too tired to bristle. Besides, he sounds almost impressed under his skepticism. "Extreme times call for extreme measures," I say, and then wish I hadn't, because it reminds me of Ibtep's "extreme" solution for Earth.

"I suppose they do, and, as crazy as it was, you made it work. That's something. And you got her."

He doesn't need to say who "her" is. "She's not a thing to be gotten, Jule," I say. "And I didn't orchestrate a civil war in order to date her."

"You know I didn't meant it that way," he says, and I find that, actually, I do. "She accused me, back at the beginning, of agreeing to host her just to annoy you," he goes on. "And she was right. From the moment I caught up with you two in that safe house on Earth, it was obvious you were hooked. And you are far too easy to mess with." His mouth twists. "But then she became more than that. I'm not surrendering. If I can make up for what happened, if she can see—"

I've heard enough. "Please tell me that *you're* not aiding a civil war just to have another chance with her," I say, and he lets out a bark of a laugh.

"No," he says. "I don't want to stay under this Council any more than you do." He's quiet for a moment. Then he adds, "She was also right about the things she said the last time we talked. And the worst thing is, if I could do it over, knowing how it would turn out, I might still have kept my mouth shut. If I'd told her sooner, she'd have hated me *then*, and I wouldn't have even had . . . what we did have. I never thought putting my interests above everyone else's was something to be ashamed of before. But here I am, and I'm trying to do this right. I just thought fair warning was the more gentlemanly approach."

There's a candor in his voice I've never heard from him before. I glance at him, but he's eyeing the floor now.

Ahead of us, Zanet has stopped at a maintenance stairwell. Jule pauses, and turns to face me for the first time.

"Also," he says, "I may be in no position to draw lines, but if *you* hurt her, you should know I will happily feed you in small pieces down a fission chute."

That sounds more like the Jule I thought I knew. He strides on toward Zanet with an air that makes it clear I'm not expected to follow. A distant part of me suggests I should be annoyed by that last comment, but all I can summon is wry amusement. The fact is, it'd be difficult for me to break Skylar's heart when she's made it clear she can't offer it right now. I have to say I'm fine with Jule's misperception on that particular subject.

· · ·

A few hours later, Tabzi is centering me on her portable recorder while I stand in front of a screen displaying an image of Earth—what the planet looked like before Ibtep condemned it, at least. I peer back at it as I swipe at my hair.

"Are you sure that's not overdoing things?" I ask in English for Angela's benefit.

"Providing the . . . visual is important," Tabzi says. "We're reminding them of what was lost."

"Exactly," Angela says beside her. "Hey, Win, can you turn a little more to the left? There. The blue's reflecting on your face. People associate blue with honesty . . . if it's the same here."

"There's a science to that," Tabzi tells her, beaming. "It is the same for all humans."

"Well, perfect then," Angela says, grinning back. They seem to have hit it off quickly.

Then Tabzi finishes fiddling with the recorder and gives me a tilted thumbs-up. "Go ahead. Just talk. If you want to start over anywhere, that's okay. I'll edit afterward."

I'm going to be honest—it should be easy. Yet when I open my mouth, the words bunch in my throat.

We're going to broadcast these "films" across the network. *Everyone* will see me. Everyone will be making judgments about me and what I say.

I switch back to Kemyate. "My name is Win Ni—" I start, and catch myself. How can I tell anyone else to appreciate Earth while I'm denying the name I was given? I begin again, more firmly. "My name is Darwin Nikola-Audrey Pirios. I stand with those who believe the Earthlings should be integrated into our world as equals."

I ramble on about how my parents raised me—after making it clear they weren't involved in the takeover—and about Traveler training, my first visits to Earth, seeing how much we were missing living on the space station, and becoming increasingly uncomfortable with our scientists' disregard for the effects of their experiments on the people whose history we were altering. Tabzi records it all patiently, but I suspect she's going to have a lot of editing to do. I leave out all mention of Ibtep when explaining Jeanant's mission, since we don't want her involvement to distract from our core message.

The last thing I have to say I knew would be the hardest. I draw in a breath.

"I didn't truly understand, even when I arrived on Earth to try to free it," I say to the recorder. "Even those of us here who believe we respect the planet and the people who were there . . . We still have that sense that they're less than us because of the way the shifts have deteriorated their physical composition. *I* still had that sense, until I started talking with them and working with them—really seeing and listening to them. Earthling, Kemyate, those are just words. We're all *human*. Whatever our scientific readings and atomic measurements might indicate, there's nothing about the way they think or feel that's any different from how we do. They're capable of everything we are. Sometimes they're capable of more. We're going to try to show you that, so you can see and hear for yourselves how badly we've been misled. Even if you think I'm simply confused, if you can't believe Earthlings could be more than a shadow of us—if you're right, then that's what you'll see. Only a soft-brain would avoid looking clearly out of fear you might be wrong. It's not so awful, being wrong. Once you realize you are, you can start being right."

I step to the side. "I think that's all I've got," I say in English.

Tabzi puts down the recorder and claps. "That was perfect, Win. You express it so well."

"I just hope they listen," I say. "Where are you going next?"

"We're going to take some footage of the Earthlings working together," Angela says. "All the different cultures learning to cooperate."

"And Skylar said she would talk about how Ibtep . . . threatened her," Tabzi adds.

"That might have to wait a bit," Celette says, coming into the room. "There's been a tussle among our 'hostages,' Tabzi. We were hoping you could calm them down."

"Oh dear," Tabzi says with a roll of her eyes. She's been keeping relative order among the ordinary Kemyates who didn't get out, since as an upper-level resident she commands a little more respect than the rest of us.

She hands the recorder to Angela. "See if you can take some . . . shots. I'll come when I can." Then she rests her hand on my arm. "Thank you again, Win."

Celette grins at me as the two of them hurry out. "Look at you turning into a ladies' man."

"Tabzi wasn't—" I protest automatically, and then stop. Tabzi has always been *nice* to me, smiling and complimentary. I'd thought that was just the way she is. Suddenly I remember occasional blushes I couldn't explain, and how eagerly she hustled over to me when she spotted me at the Joining Day ceremony a few months ago, despite her friends' frowns. "She never said anything," I amend.

"Sometimes a person doesn't, when they realize the other person's wrapped up in someone else," Celette says.

I press my palm to my forehead. Have I been *that* oblivious? Does Tabzi think I've known? I'm suddenly aware of at least a dozen things I've said or done since Skylar joined us that could have seemed incredibly callous.

I think through Celette's words again, and peer at her around my hand. "Just to be completely certain, please reassure me you're not speaking from your own experience."

She laughs. "Don't worry, Win. I'm pleased to call you my friend, and pleased to have it stop there."

I've been oblivious to other things too, though, haven't I? "You're with someone. Cormac. I haven't seen him . . ." I never even asked before.

Her face falls. "He's off-Kemya," she says quietly. "His scrounger left a week ago. I was supposed to trade shifts, to get on the same one, but when I saw what was building here . . ." She shakes her head. "He'll be far enough out he won't even know it's happened until it's already over, most likely. It's my parents who'll be losing their heads."

"I'm sorry," I say. I've been so absorbed with my own reasons for doing this, I didn't think through all the sacrifices I was asking of her, and Markhal, and the people they brought with them.

"It'll work out," Celette says. "What we're doing, it needed to happen. I'm glad I got to be a part of it."

She ducks out, leaving me alone in the room. *It'll work out.* Dear Kemya, let that be true. Every one of us here has far too much to lose.

19.

Skylar

The Thai villagers hardly touched their lunches," Angela says when I come out of the Inuit family's apartment. Because most of our fellow zoo escapees are still shell-shocked, we've been bringing their meals to them. "I don't know what they were eating in their exhibit, but I don't think they like this stuff."

"Who can blame them?" I say, thinking of the goopy Kemyate stew I just served. But it's no joke if they let themselves starve. "See if you can find that guy—the one with the neck tattoo?—to talk to them. He has some Thai."

"He was around a while ago, said he'd check if there are other options." Angela stretches her arms in front of her with a yawn. "Funny how none of the . . . Kemyates seems to have any idea how these people were actually taken care of."

"They're encouraged not to worry about it," I say. "I'm impressed so many helped with the takeover in the first place."

Celette, the blue-haired girl I met earlier, comes over to join us. "The Polish folks are getting restless," she says in her throaty

Kemyate-accented English. "They want to know when they can go home. They won't even sleep on the bunks—they've been huddling in the corner of the main room."

"They probably just need more time," I say, hoping that's true.

"The Japanese group had a few questions, but there wasn't any trouble," Celette goes on. "The Assyrians didn't want to talk at all, but they seemed happy to get the food. Is there anything else that needs doing?"

I look up and down the hall, trying to sort out my thoughts through the haze of fatigue. "Ms. Cavoy and Mr. Patterson wanted some learning material," Angela reminds me.

"Right." I turn to Celette. "They're in Apartments 8 and 11. Could you walk them through the network interface and show them the most basic science tutorials? Their specializations are physics and chemistry, and they'd like to find out enough about your tech to help out more."

"No problem," Celette says, smiling. "I'm sure headquarters could use more able minds."

"She seems nice," Angela comments as the other girl hurries off.

"They're just people, like us," I say. "The trouble is getting more of them to remember that. You and Tabzi seemed to get along well."

"She's very . . . enthusiastic," Angela says with a laugh. "She wanted to know everything I could tell her about visual composition, framing . . . I don't know how much of it she could use for the videos, but it was kind of fun, working on them. It feels really good just to be *doing* things, like that and bringing around the meals here. You know, maybe that would help some of the other Earthlings. There are ways they could pitch in without understanding the tech, right?"

I think of the older Inuit couple, who refuse to even look me in the eye, and the Algerian parents cuddling their wailing children when I spoke to them an hour ago. "I don't want to put any more pressure on them," I say. "We've already forced them to deal with so much." None of them were even slightly prepared to be dragged into a totally alien world in the midst of a civil war. I insisted on bringing them out here to protect them. I owe it to them to keep protecting them.

"We could just ask," Angela says.

"I guess. Let's let them adjust a bit more first." I nudge her. "Is your Mom still on your case about how involved you've gotten?"

Angela grimaces. "A little. I think she'll understand, once she's had more time to adapt too. This isn't about grades or making a good impression—it's about staying *alive*. Your parents are doing okay, right?"

"As far as I can tell." I've hardly had a chance to exchange more than a few words with them since we broke out. I opted to share an apartment with Angela rather than them, because she needed space from her mom and I didn't feel good about leaving her alone, but I'm not sure it'd have made much difference the other way. While I've been constantly on the move, Mom has spent most of the last day and a half helping the medics, and Dad has been racing through Language Learner lessons so he can communicate with some of the other groups.

"How about you?" I say to Angela. "You're holding up?" She's known the truth longer than almost everyone else, but she was there when I brought up the footage of Earth's destruction yesterday for those who were still demanding proof, and the horror on their faces as our situation became completely real is etched in my memory.

"Yeah," Angela says. "Getting to work is good for keeping me distracted too."

When we bring the empty containers back to the floating cart the cafeteria crew will come to collect, some of the others are gathered in the hall nearby, eating their own dinners. Daniel and Cintia and a couple of their friends, Mrs. Green and Ruth and Liora, but also a couple of our Kemyate helpers: Jai and a petite but muscular girl named Solma. The two of them are sitting at one end of the cluster, mostly talking to each other.

My stomach grumbles. "We should eat something too. Do you want to see if Evan will come out?"

"Definitely," Angela says. "I don't think it's good, him staying on his own so much."

When Evan answers our knock, I'm relieved to see he looks less pained than earlier, when he simply told me he wasn't up to talking and turned away. The footage of Earth hit him harder than most. His face is still sallow, his eyes red. But he manages a weak smile.

"Come have dinner with us," Angela says.

"I don't know—" he starts.

"Come on," I say. "We just want ten minutes. After that you can hole up in here again all you want."

He grumbles a little, but his smile warms. We join the others, sitting near Jai and Solma, and for the first couple minutes all I can do is gulp down the stew. The solid bits are oddly spongelike and have the usual artificial aftertaste, but it's warm and creamy and so much better than ration bars. I can't remember if I ate lunch.

"Has Tabzi finished her recordings?" Jai asks Angela.

She nods. "They're sending them out tonight."

"It is good that the rest of Kemya will see how brave you are," Solma says quietly. "My older sister, we lost her because of the Council, and that was . . . very hard. I cannot think what it would be like to lose so much more."

Evan, who's been eating in silence, swivels toward her. "What happened to your sister?"

There's an edge in his voice that sounds almost aggressive. I watch him as Solma looks down at her hands.

"She was a medic," she says, "and she was assigned to a ninth-level clinic, so she had Earthling pets come in as well as Kemyates. The things she saw . . ." She shudders. "She reported a couple of the owners for . . . treating their pets illegally, but the owners denied it, and she was told to be quiet. Instead, she went to talk to the Council. They would not let her into their offices. Enforcers came when she refused to leave. They gave her an implant and put her on a mining labor detail. A month later there was an accident . . ."

Angela has lowered her bowl. "Oh no."

"We believe it truly was an accident," Solma says. "But she would not have had the accident if the implant was not blurring her thinking. She did not deserve that punishment."

"Of course not," I say.

Evan's expression has softened. "Do Kemyates believe in an afterlife?" he asks.

"After life?" Solma repeats, frowning.

"It's a religious thing," I say, not sure what the closest Kemyate words would be. "The idea that after you die, part of you, your . . . spirit, moves on to another place."

"Oh! Yes, I know of— For us, it is not exactly like that. When Kemyates die, they return to Kemya. And so they are still with us."

"The bodies go through a fission chute," Jai explains, "like anything else no longer functioning. The atoms are redistributed and become something new."

The atoms are redistributed . . . I glance down at my empty bowl, my stomach flipping. It wouldn't actually be eating a *person*. A carbon atom that was once in a human being isn't any different from a carbon atom that was once in an apple or a rock. But the thought that my dinner might have contained tiny pieces of someone's dead relatives still makes me queasy.

Kemyates: efficient and practical, even in death.

Angela is making a face I imagine reflects my own, but Evan looks thoughtful. "Kind of like being an organ donor," he says. "Giving your body to help other people. That's actually . . . pretty generous."

Solma shrugs. "It is how we do things."

"My parents, and my sister, and everyone else—they didn't get that chance."

For a second, I'm afraid Solma or Jai will ruin the moment with a comment about how "wasteful" Earth's destruction was. But Solma simply dips her head, and Jai says, "Our Council—all of us—failed the Earthlings when we should have been generous to them. I apologize for those who won't."

Solma offers Evan her hand, tentatively. He takes it. "You believe in an 'afterlife' for them?" she asks. "Your family?"

He hesitates. "I think so. It's hard to imagine, after seeing . . . I *want* to think so. We're more than just atoms."

"That is true," she says. "An atom cannot be cruel or generous."

He smiles at her then, like a light coming on, faint but present.

• • •

Some hours later—I keep losing track of time—Isis summons us for another meeting. It feels like ages since I saw Win, though we've crossed paths a few times. Once, when he looked a little less hurried than usual, I couldn't help leaning close and murmuring his name in his ear like an appeal. He tugged me into the closest empty room with a haste that made me giddy, and for a few careless minutes his touch, his lips, drew me away from all the uncertainties outside.

Angela was right. Distraction is good.

When I walk into the headquarters room, the smile that slips across his face, just for me, makes me want to steal a few more minutes. I have to settle for looping my arm with his. His thumb traces a line on my palm.

"We have all of Tabzi's recordings on the network now," Isis says to the group of us, and dips her head to Tabzi. "They look good. We're monitoring the responses."

Tabzi brightens. "I can make more if they're helpful."

"Have you taken any breaks, Isis?" Win asks. "It won't do us any good if you burn out."

I'd thought she was looking a bit fresher than last time, but as Win speaks she shifts on her stool, and I notice the stiffness of her posture, as if she has to hold herself tightly to make sure she doesn't fall over. Suddenly I'm not sure if the grayish tint to her dusky skin is only a result of the dim lighting. She closes her eyes and opens them again.

"I'm fine," she says. She turns toward me. "The main point I wanted to bring up is, I think we've located your Project Nuwa."

My heart leaps. "What? What did you find?"

"We were wondering why Ibtep threatened you when she did," Britta steps in. "The blockade had already been going for a few days then. But we *had* just put out word that we wanted information related to the name 'Nuwa.' I'm guessing that made the Council nervous. So I analyzed the activity across the station on that day to see if anything unusual came up. I IDed a small group of rooms on the first level that's assigned to the Health division, which drew a greater amount of power then, as well as on the day of your 'examinations.' When I dug into the records for those rooms, I came across one reference to 'Nuwa.' Only one, and no specifics otherwise, but it's enough to convince me. I can't access anything inside, though. I'd bet all the files about the project are isolated on a private network in there."

"So we'd have to physically break in to get to them?" I say.

"If what Britta suspects is true, yes," Isis says. "And it'd be difficult for us to send anyone down there safely."

I can already see her, in her weariness, sinking back into that usual Kemyate restraint. No. We're so close to reaching whatever the Council is guarding so closely.

"We have to investigate it," I say. "I'm sure Tabzi's videos will help, I'm sure we'll find other ways to reach out, but if the Council knows something about Earth that would change everything they've been telling people—prove that we're not as degraded as they thought, or that we can be 'fixed'—that could make the difference between whether we win or lose here."

"I agree with Skylar," Win says, with that new firmness I'm only just becoming used to. "If you're right that the Council stepped in because they knew we were searching for the project, it's even more certain they knew we could use it against them."

Isis draws in a slow breath, her gaze lingering on him. Before the catastrophe on Earth, she'd taken on the role of the rebels' secondary leader. Primary leader, when we had to leave Ibtep behind. I'm not sure what happened within the group while I was stuck in the Earth Studies hall, but since we've regrouped, I've noticed her—and Britta and Tabzi too—looking to Win in the midst of discussions, waiting to hear what he'll say before making any official decisions.

I guess they've finally realized his risk-taking, rule-breaking approach has gotten us a heck of a lot further than the old Kemyate caution.

"All right," Isis says. "It's going to take some complex maneuvering, but we'll come up with something."

"Could we ask—" Tabzi starts.

"Isis!" one of her colleagues calls out from the console he's stationed at. "*There's a transmission incoming from the Council offices. A recorded message.*"

The corner of Isis's mouth curls up. "About time they came to us directly. Let's see what they have to say."

She spins to face her own console, bringing up the transmission with a few flicks of her fingers. A square image swims into clarity on the translucent display. The seven Council members—the heads of the divisions of Technology, Earth Travel, Industry, Health, Treasury, Education, and Security—sit in a circle around the man Britta identified to me the first time I saw him as Kemya's "mayor," Shakam Nakalya.

"*To those holding the upper levels,*" Nakalya says in a stately voice, "*I and the Council wish to inform you that this . . . will not be tolerated. We will restore unity and order to the station. We would prefer to do so peacefully. If you leave off this . . . endeavor at once, we promise leniency to you and the Kemyates who've joined you.*"

Britta snorts. "Sure they do. And what about the Earthlings?"

I study the Council members in turn, my gaze catching on a slim woman with bronze skin and a looping braid around her head, who averts her eyes for an instant. The gray-haired, freckled man beside her can't seem to restrain a twitch of his knob-like chin, a motion like a swallowed sigh. Maybe the Council isn't united on this matter after all.

"*If you continue to resist,*" Nakalya goes on, "*we would remind you that not all the Earthlings on the station are within your reach. Things may not go pleasantly for them.*"

The pets on the lower levels. The Tiwanaku tribe who refused to leave the Earth Studies hall. My jaw clenches.

"*We await your response, and your surrender,*" Nakalya finishes. The video blinks away.

"Do you think they mean it?" I ask in the silence that follows. "They'll hurt the Earthlings we couldn't get out?"

"I don't know," Win says. "It could be a bluff. It wouldn't help them, if we've already shown we aren't cowed by the threat."

"We can make that part of the recording public," Isis says. "They can deny that they meant it as a threat, but it'll still prompt people to watch what happens next. Say what you will about the rest of us, most Kemyates wouldn't approve of attacking Earthlings for someone else's crime. The Council won't risk the disapproval."

The reassurance isn't enough to dislodge the dull weight that's settled in my gut. The pets, I couldn't do anything for them in the first place. But that farming community we left behind . . . The sectors around Earth Studies are sealed off now; the Council disabled all the surveillance inside after we escaped; they might already have taken the Tiwanaku into custody. We can't go back for them now.

It was their choice, to face the danger their own way, I remind myself. That's all any of us in there had.

But the sooner we win this war, the sooner they'll be safe too.

20.

Win

Jeanant wrote a poem in which he described the inner passages of Kemya as having "a dark that stays so deep no matter how brightly the sun is shining." I read it more than a year ago; I quoted it to Skylar from one of his messages a few months ago. Now, balanced on a glider in a vacant inner-shuttle tunnel, I fully understand his meaning for the first time. Except during the brief flashes of Celette's light to check our location, I can't see any of the four hovering beside me. I can't see my own body when I look down at myself.

At a flash, I brake the glider with my heel. I'm sitting astride the bar in a position Skylar likened to "a witch on a broomstick," grasping the bar in front of me with my feet tucked behind. She's the one who pointed out we'd be more secure sitting rather than standing. With the training function off so we can go at full speed, a loss of balance at the wrong moment could mean falling the entire height of the station.

"1-104-8," Celette murmurs, so quietly I only hear the words through my communicator, even though she's just a short distance away. We're practicing the same caution here that we'll need once Isis lets us through the breach seal into the levels below. "Proceed?"

"Everyone ready?" I say. "Let's see how these do."

I pull up beside Celette as she sets her light to hold at its faintest setting, so we'll be able to see when we reach the ninth-level tunnels. The plan is to stop there and let the gliders recharge. The modifications one of Isis's colleagues made to them allow them to hover at a much greater height than normal, but he warned it would strain their power capacity. Once we see how they perform and how long the recharging takes, we'll make the final decision about whether to proceed past the seal toward the rooms we believe hold the answer to Project Nuwa.

The glider trembles under me as we ease over the tunnel opening and begin our descent. We stay close to the wall, ready to grab the maintenance grips if the gliders fail. My palm is sweating against the bar. A hum rises from it as the tunnel crossing below comes into sight. I steer the glider into it and drop down to the channeled floor.

"Any problems?" I say to the group as they land around me.

"I could feel mine working harder, but it seemed to handle the height all right," Skylar says.

"Same here," Markhal says, and Solma nods.

We were only two levels above the seal. The real test will come when we drop below it and face an initial height four times that. I check the power reading on my glider's display.

"Mine's already halfway back to full charge. That's a good sign."

I take the lead as we hover down to the eighth level, where we check the readings again. "It felt fine," Skylar says beside me. "Let's do this."

I gesture to my communicator. "Isis, we're at sector 1-84-8. Gliders are performing well. Are we safe to go down?"

"The sensors are still showing all clear below," Isis says over the link. "No reports of Enforcers assigned near that area. You're prepared for me to unlock the seal?"

"Yes."

"Here we go."

The smooth mechanical spiral covering the downward passage sighs. My heart beats faster as it starts to rotate, a hole appearing at its center. I glide toward it, holding still above the open space below. The bar's trembling increases, the hum more of a whine now, but the glider doesn't so much as dip.

We *can* do this, Council and Security be rotted.

"We're heading down," I say.

We drop through the opening in a column, breaking apart to hug the walls once we're through. As we reach the seventh level, a shudder runs through my glider. I veer into the tunnel just before the power shorts out. I pushed my glider too far with that initial test.

The others settle beside me without a hitch, Celette shutting off her light. "Next time I'm letting someone else go first," I murmur, and she chuckles in the dark.

Clearly we're going to have to pause at every level on the way down. We could return and see if the gliders can be improved before making another attempt.

I resist the urge to shuffle my feet as I watch my glider recharge. "Win?" Skylar whispers.

We're here now. Security isn't expecting us—and slow and careful is the Kemyate way, isn't it? My mouth forms a crooked smile no one can see.

"Onward."

The word has barely left my mouth when a patter carries from down the tunnel. As I spin around, a brilliant light blasts our faces.

I step back, swinging onto my glider, and a pale figure with an Enforcer's glinting belt charges past the glow square she's dropped.

"Halt!" Kurra yells, as I shout, "Abort!" I catch a glimpse of her as she raises her gun—face pinched, stray hair flying from her normally sleek braid—and then I'm hurtling out of the tunnel after the others. Markhal's already soaring up through the seal opening. Solma darts after him, Skylar just below. Only Celette is behind me.

The gun twangs. I flinch as a bolt of light shatters against the tunnel wall to my left. "Start closing the seal!" I call to Isis. The spiral sighs again and rotates inward. My glider trembles. I glance down at Celette and see Kurra stepping to the tunnel's mouth, gun aimed. There's no time for me to get out more than a strangled noise of warning before the next sizzling bolt streaks upward. It catches Celette's elbow.

She cries out, a choked, painful sound. Her glider dips. I don't think; my heel presses the control automatically, jerking me down just far enough to grab her other wrist.

"I've got it, I've got it," she says, but there's a whimper in her voice. In the portion of glow light that flows from the tunnel, I catch sight of her injured arm.

Her sleeve and the skin beneath are crackled and blackened from hand to shoulder.

I swerve, my stomach rolling, as another bolt streaks past us. Then I yank us both upward. The opening is halfway closed already. My glider is outright shaking now. I kick out one final surge of acceleration, and we burst into the darkness above.

I tumble with a clatter onto the outer edge of the seal, my hip jarring against the rim. The glow disappears as the opening whispers shut. Then the only sound is the teary rasp of Celette's breath.

I haul myself to my feet. "Markhal," I say, my own voice rough, "we have to get Celette to the medical center—fast."

• • •

I used to long for a deluxe apartment—to have a common area with nearly twice as much breathing room, a slightly bigger bedroom and bathroom, a proper table, a private exercise chamber, and all the other benefits. The entire tenth-level residential ring is made up of those. I don't even have to share this one. It's brand new, too, because Isis's crew switched over the power from a few of the previously inhabited sectors to the spare ones awaiting continuing population growth, so we couldn't be accused of ransacking people's homes.

I'm not taking any pleasure from the place, though. All I can do is stare dazedly at the overlarge wall screen as I sit on one of the three cushioned benches. My mind is still in the shuttle tunnel.

It could have been Celette's life, not just her arm, that she lost. It could have been all of us lying blasted. The fact is, though, we were overconfident. We assumed Isis's monitoring would protect us from the Enforcers. Kurra proved us wrong. She was carrying no tech other than her gun, nothing Isis could pick up. Based on Security's records, she was assigned to a shift in the surveillance monitoring station.

We couldn't have predicted she'd be walking the tunnels of her own accord—that her vendetta against the rebels would send her stalking around the seventh level in defiance of her superiors. Still, we should have been watching and listening more carefully. We should have known there's always an unpredictable human factor. It's how we dodged Security in the past, using their reliance on technology to hide our activities.

I didn't need to ask Markhal to know Celette's arm can't be saved. We Kemyates make our weapons as reliable as we make everything. Flesh that's been struck with a killing shot can't be returned to life.

Isis ordered the rest of us to take the night off. She held out her hand for my communicator and informed me that she didn't want to hear about me trying to do any work at all for at least nine hours. I might not have agreed if I weren't worried I should have taken this step earlier. It's possible if I'd had more than five fragmented hours of sleep in the last few days, I would have gotten us out of there faster.

My body doesn't follow orders, though. I lay down on the bed formed by the two lowered bunks in the main bedroom, but my eyes wouldn't stay closed and my mind wouldn't settle. After a while I got up and came out here. I thought bringing up the music composition program I used to work in might distract me enough for exhaustion to get a foothold. So far all I have is a derivative melody and an ache at the bridge of my nose.

I stand up, wave at the screen, and adjust a few of the notes. I'm staring at them again without quite seeing them when the doorbell sounds. My pulse skips. No one should be contacting me unless it's urgent.

When I motion open the door, Skylar's standing on the other side. She looks at me, and the clenching inside me eases its grip. When I stopped by the Earthling sector after speaking with Isis, Jai told me she was taking dinner with her parents. It seemed rude to interrupt, no matter how much I wanted her with me.

"Come in," I say, stepping to the side.

"I'm sorry," she says. "I know you're supposed to be resting too. I just— I couldn't sleep."

"Me neither."

"Solma said the medics will probably have to remove Celette's arm. Don't you Kemyates have some, like, super high-tech prosthetics or something?"

"The way the guns damage the nerves, the usual tech for loss of a limb . . . It doesn't work well," I say.

"Oh." The discomfort of that knowledge leaves us silent for a moment. "Well, I hope she's an exception," Skylar says. "I like her." She gives me a faint, slanted smile. Her gaze travels past me to the screen.

"That looks like work. Isn't that against the rules?"

"It's just— I was fiddling around with a song," I say. "If you can even call it that."

"Win the composer," she says. "I didn't realize. You should have sent me some of your stuff, before."

"I haven't created any music in a while," I admit. "I got . . . out of the habit, you could say. I think it's something I should return to, when this is over." That is, assuming it ends well.

"You should," Skylar says. She tilts her head forward, her cinnamon hair drifting to obscure her face. There's something odd about the way she's holding herself, as if she's being particularly careful about the space she takes up. I've seen her tired before, and this doesn't look like that.

I turn to her, and it hits me. She's holding herself apart from me. She hasn't touched me, or stepped closer to me, but kept the same distance as when she stood outside my doorway.

I swallow hard, abruptly certain what this must mean. She's come to say that now that she's had time to think, perhaps jarred by that close call, she's realized she doesn't care for me *that* way after all. She thinks it's best if we go back to the friendship we had before.

When she said she couldn't return my feelings completely, I told her I didn't mind. I didn't; I wouldn't give up the little time we've had for anything. I just hadn't thought through how difficult it was going to be to lose that intimacy with her after having it. I'm not prepared.

She's looking at me again, through the stray strands of hair that have fallen across her eyes. I want to brush them aside. I'm afraid she'll stop me.

"Are you all right?" she says.

"Other than the usual?" I say wryly. No, this isn't the time to joke. We should get it out there. "You look as though something's bothering you."

"Not really," she says, and bites her lip. I find I do still have the capacity to tease her.

"You'd never let me get away with saying that, looking like that," I say, and a hint of her smile comes back.

"No," she agrees. She rests her hands on my chest then, two points of heat. Her gaze dips from my eyes to my lips, in the way I've come to recognize means she's about to kiss me . . . and possibly I was wrong.

"You would tell me?" she says. "If I ever asked for too much from you, you'd tell me, wouldn't you?"

Is that all she has on her mind? "Of course," I say with a rush of relief. "I have trouble imagining how that could even be possible, though."

She kisses me before I can say anything else. The words I always want to say, but haven't, stay locked in my throat.

I love you.

She knows; she has to. I've said it using so many other words. The trouble with those three, the most accurate ones, is they're not mine alone. She cringed when Jule said them. He's tainted them, and that's the last thing I want to remind her of.

So I kiss her back. I don't need words. I have the tremor of her breath and the shape of her body fitting against mine as we connect and create something more than when we were apart. An urgency I haven't felt before passes from her to me and back again. She pulls me even closer, her hand sliding under my shirt and up my back, skin to skin. Her mouth slips to the edge of my jaw and then the side of my neck. I'm set alight.

She presses another kiss to the base of my throat, leaning into me, and says, "Take me away from here?"

The question takes a moment to sink in, and even then I'm not certain I understand until she eases half a step toward the bedroom.

Yes. A thousand yeses.

I follow, drawing her to me. Everything is warmth and breath and skin from here to the bunks, and if this invitation is what she thought might be too much to ask, she's obviously never had a glimpse inside my head.

As we sink onto the bed, intertwining, it's just us, her and me. The rest—the apartment, the station, the cold depths of the universe outside—falls away behind the world we're creating between us. A world no one else can touch, let alone destroy, for as long as we're together.

21.

Skylar

The lights haven't lifted from the nighttime phase of their cycle when I wake up in Win's arms, but it's the first time in days that I feel close to refreshed. I lie there a minute, taking in the slow rise and fall of his chest against my back, the quiet that surrounds us. The quiet inside my head, as if the rush of our coming here has swept away all the clutter that was there before.

Almost all the clutter. One niggle of uncertainty I managed to drown out last night has crept back in. It nibbles around my thoughts, and I know that, even though I'm still tired, I'm not going to get any more sleep here.

As I sit up, Win's arm slips from around my waist. All the stress that has tightened his face in the last few days has relaxed. I look down at his sleep-rumpled hair, his thin lips curled with a soft smile, the lean angles of his shoulders. *Mine.* In a couple hours he'll be back out in the halls, hurrying this way and that after his multiplying responsibilities, but this moment of him, right now, belongs to me alone. I just wish I didn't feel selfish taking it.

Before I can decide whether it'd be worse to rouse him from the sleep he needs so badly or to let him wake up to find me gone, his eyelids flutter and open. He gazes up at me, his smile widening.

"Good"—he pauses to squint at the dim light panel—"very early morning."

My mouth twitches with a smile of my own. "I can't stay," I say. "Angela's probably wondering where I am. I don't want her to worry." It's true enough. She saw me heading into our shared apartment after I mentioned Isis's order to rest, and she must have noticed by now that I'm no longer there.

Win dips his head. "Maybe another time," he says, lightly enough to strip the comment of any pressure or expectation. It's exactly the way I needed him to respond, and somehow that makes me feel more selfish.

He touches my face, tracing his thumb down my cheek. I lean down to kiss him one last time—only it blurs into another, and another, his fingers trailing heat down my side, and "another time" almost happens now. Reminding myself how much *he* needs rest gets me off the bed. His eyelids are already drooping when I head out the door.

As I reach my apartment, I'm struck by an overwhelming gladness that I'm rooming with Angela and not my parents. Me ducking inside in the early hours of the artificial morning would lead to an awkward familial conversation to top all others.

The main room is empty. I take a breath as the door shuts behind me. The space feels less claustrophobic than it did last night, which was really the first time I'd spent more than a few minutes awake in here. The first time it sank in how identical it is to Jule's apartment in every detail except the color scheme. It stirred up memories I didn't want crowding my head, not just of all the words and gestures I let myself believe meant more than they did, but of the mockery of his friends, of living with the constant awareness of Enforcers patrolling outside. Reminders of how far most Kemyates have to come before they'll see someone like me as human. I couldn't stand hanging around in here. I wanted to write over those memories with something totally separate, something better.

It worked. I run my hand down my arm, pleasant shivers following the echo of Win's touch. And then that niggling guilt.

It worked, but not perfectly.

I'm heading for the second bedroom to see if I can sleep a little more when Angela's door opens. She peers out, her forehead crinkling up even as she yawns.

"There you are," she says. "Cintia said she saw you leaving hours ago. I thought you were off duty for the night. Did something go wrong?"

"No, everything's fine," I say. Too quickly, obviously, because Angela's eyebrows rise and I feel myself blush. So much for being discrete.

"So where were you?" she asks with a teasing note in her voice.

"With Win," I admit.

Her eyebrows leap higher, and she steps out of the bedroom. "Like, *with* with?" she says, and my face flares hotter. Angela shakes her head, grinning. "I guess I've got some catching up to do."

"Don't say that," I plead, with a jab of a different sort of guilt. Angela's never even had a boyfriend, never kissed anyone except a guy she met at camp right before we started high school—once, on their last day. I told her, in bits and pieces, about what happened with Jule and about the fledgling *something* that was forming between Win and me, but only what I felt I needed to. I hid too much from her back on Earth, and I want to be honest with her now. But going into detail on this particular topic would have seemed like rubbing her situation in her face.

Angela has cocked her head. "You don't look happy about it."

"It's not that, it's just— It's stupid, isn't it, to be worried about boys when . . ." I gesture vaguely toward the walls, meaning to indicate the tenuous, dangerous situation we're *all* in.

"As far as I've seen, you've been doing lots of worrying about everything else," Angela says. "If there's a quota you need to reach before boy worries are okay, I'm pretty sure you've gone over. Spill."

"It's really not a big deal—"

"Nope." Angela cuts me off, dragging me to the folding benches. "You are sitting down with me and getting this out, because if we don't talk now, tomorrow you're going to be running around like crazy again. I *want* to hear about it, Sky."

I let myself sit. "So," she prods. "You went to see Win . . ."

I exhale and drop my forehead into my palms. "I don't know what I'm doing," I say. "It isn't fair to him."

I wanted to be with him. He wanted to be with me. It shouldn't be complicated. It probably isn't for him, at least not the way I'm thinking. Britta explained to me weeks and weeks ago, when we found time to chat amid official rebel business, the Kemyate view of romance. You feel attracted, you act on it, and as long as you're up front about what you're offering, it's good. Win even told me that all he needed was for me to be honest and trust him. I'm just not used to the idea that it could be so simple.

"How wasn't it fair?" Angela says with a nudge of her elbow. "Was he complaining?"

I can't help laughing at that. "No," I say. "There are just things he's said . . . This means more to him. I care about him, I do, a lot." The image of his sleeping form, the moment that belonged to me, floats into my mind, and a lump rises in my throat. "But I don't know if it's ever going to be as much as he'd want." I can't shake the fear that I'm going to disappoint him, hurt him, sooner or later.

"Why wouldn't it be enough?" Angela asks. "You like him, you *like* him. You've only known him, what, a few months?"

"True," I say. "But if he's already feeling more than that . . . I can't tell if I'm going to keep wanting this in a year, or a month, or even tomorrow. *That* isn't fair to him."

Angela shrugs. "Why should you be able to predict the future? You do have kind of a lot going on right now. If he's cool with it, you're not doing anything wrong."

I thought I could call what I had with Jule "love" in less time, before I found out everything. Of course, when I think about it, that exhilarating sense of challenge between us—who could distract the other more, make the other want more, feel the most—left a separation between me and him despite the intensity. A space that held all the talking we hadn't done, the many things I didn't know. Maybe I'm not quite as head over heels for Win, but what we do have is *real*.

And as Angela said, a lot has been going on since that time with Jule.

"I don't know, Ang," I say. "Sometimes, after everything, after seeing Earth . . . Just thinking about all those people . . . It's been weeks, and I still feel broken. Like there are pieces missing, forever, and I'm never going to be able to fit the ones that are left back together. Maybe I'm never going to be able to more than *like* someone, ever again."

Angela lets out a huff of breath and slings her arm around my shoulders. "You know we're going to be best friends forever, right?"

A smile creeps across my face. "Yeah, I'm pretty sure about that."

"So maybe some part of you is broken," she says. "But if that's true, then it's probably true for all of us. We'll just keep . . . carrying on with what we have."

"I'm sorry," I say, hugging her back. "I've been making this all about me. I'm so glad you're here, Ang. I know *that* one hundred percent."

"I couldn't have gotten through this without you either," she says. As she pulls back, mischief glints in her eyes. "You know, if you want to contribute to that catching up business, I did notice a couple of the Kemyate boys Tabzi brought around who I wouldn't mind getting to know a little better. When all this is over, maybe you two can help set me up."

I elbow her, and she elbows me back, and then we're both laughing. Angela stops to yawn.

"I should let you get back to sleep," I say.

"You too," she says, waggling her finger at me. "You need it more than anyone."

When I crawl into bed a minute later, I find the conversation seems to have given me the last release I needed. I'm asleep just a few seconds after I lay down my head.

• • •

Heading out later that morning, I happen on Solma standing outside a door two down from mine. She lowers her dark eyes when she sees me.

"I thought I would ask Evan if he'd join me for another meal," she says.

Before I can respond, Evan's door opens. He blinks at Solma, looking as though he hasn't been awake very long, but a smile touches his face that's similarly shy. Interesting. I leave her to make her suggestion uninterrupted, with a grin of my own.

The thought that even Evan is finding a place among the people here steadies me as I walk to the one place in our domain that I've hesitated to face. I slip down the service stairs to the eighth level and stop outside Jule's apartment.

The door still opens when I press my thumb to the panel. I square my shoulders and step inside.

The main room looks the same as always, with its mix of red-and-yellow hues, no other personalization. No sign I was ever here before. Jule left the table up when he came to talk to us. I have the urge to tap it down. I inhale and exhale, registering the air that tastes exactly like the air upstairs.

Just normal Kemyate air. Just a normal Kemyate room. Its only significance is what I give it. Suddenly my trepidation seems silly.

Absently, I open the cupboards. At the third, my hand halts in midair. There's a note folded in front of one of the square orange packets I liked, printed in English: *Help yourself.*

He couldn't have known I'd come here. It's a gesture made just in case. Clearly he at least suspected, when he left here that day, that he wouldn't be back any time soon. He's arranged the packet foods that were my favorites on that shelf: square orange, triangular blue, circular white.

Something pinches in my gut. Would taking them indicate a sort of acceptance I'm not yet willing to offer him?

No, I decide. The whole point of coming here was to look the past in the face until it lost some of its meaning. I'll keep a few for Angela and me, and bring the rest to the cafeteria for everyone to share.

I grab a shirt out of the closet in the second bedroom—my bedroom—not anymore—and knot it to create a bag before tossing in all the packets. I pause at the fourth cupboard, considering the three bags of coffee stashed there. My fingers clench, and then reach to tip two into my makeshift sack. I can already imagine Win's face lighting up when I present him with a cup. Jule should be glad I'm leaving him any.

Then, with a lighter heart, I go.

• • •

"Even with time cloths, there's still the problem of the patrolling Enforcers," Isis says. "We can't hide the seal, and I won't be able to guarantee more than a few minutes of a safe window to open and close it. That isn't enough."

We've been hashing out our second attempt to reach Project Nuwa for nearly an hour. It seems every time we've thought of a solution, a new problem arises. I rub my forehead, and Win touches the small of my back, sending a spark tingling up my spine. It felt a little odd, seeing him for the first time since I left his apartment this morning; my skin started to buzz with the sense that the others would know what we've been up to just by looking at us. But not even Britta has made any comment, and Win has seemed so relaxed that I've relaxed too.

"Then we need to give some of those Enforcers a reason to be somewhere else, so we have a larger window," I say.

"We can use Jule," Tabzi says. "Isn't that why we made him go back? So he could help us down there?"

Isis shakes his head. "He said Ibtep doesn't trust him. If he creates a disturbance, she'll assume it's a ploy."

"So we need someone they won't expect to be associated with us," Win says slowly. "Ibtep knows the five of us still want to reach K2-8. She wouldn't think we were involved if something happened because of the anti-move group—Vishnu and the others." He pauses, his mouth twisting. "As long as we can find something for them to disrupt that doesn't actually hurt anyone."

"We could use Jule for that," Britta says, nodding. "He can send a message to them using that fancy rerouting code he used to screw us over before. What would appeal to the anti-movers, do you think, and catch Security's attention fast?"

"If we don't want them to hurt any people, what if they were damaging some*thing*?" I suggest.

"They want to get in the way of the plans to move," Win says. "Could we give them access to one of the storage bays? Tell them there are supplies for planet life–building there that they could destroy? We can pick a place that has the least essential materials possible, things that have nothing to do with moving—I doubt they'll know the difference."

"I know how the programming on the storage bays works, from when we gave ourselves access before," Britta says. "We can have Jule pass on the instructions." She looks down at Isis on her stool, touching her shoulder. "There, are you satisfied?"

Isis is frowning, but she reaches to put her hand over Britta's.

"It does seem to cover every concern," she says. "I suppose the only question left is who will go. We only have the three time cloths."

"Three is all we need," Win says. "I wouldn't want to risk more of us after last time. I've already memorized the fastest routes to the Project Nuwa rooms. I'll take Markhal again since he's familiar with the Health division's file system. And—"

"I'm still going," I break in. When he looks at me, a fear he can't quite hide flickering through his eyes, I think of Kurra charging at us in the tunnel, Celette's ruined arm. I swallow. "I have to. I'm the only one here who saw people actually collecting data for the project. I might be able to make connections no one else can."

He inhales, and I brace myself for an argument. But all he says is, "There. We have our three."

22.

Win

Markhal and I are waiting by the shuttle stop when Skylar joins us, holding two steaming cups. Despite the knot in my gut, my mouth starts to water the instant the rich aroma hits my nose. "Is that . . . ?"

"It is." She grins and hands me one of the cups. "I thought a little boost before we head off might be welcome."

"Where did you get it?" I make myself ask. We've kept a policy of not interfering with people's private property, as evidence that we're only taking a stand, not taking advantage of our fellow citizens. I might let this one thing slide, though.

"Let's just say it's legit," she says.

I bring the cup to my mouth, close my eyes, and sip. The pleasantly bitter liquid races over my tongue. It's been months since I tasted coffee—sitting in a cafe with Skylar as she told me about the odd feelings she had and I became more and more certain she was the key to completing our mission. It's strange to think there was a time when that's all I saw her as. Now, after what happened less than twenty-five hours ago, every inch of my body is alert to her presence. I want to kiss her, but not with Markhal standing right here.

Instead, I focus on my drink. Coffee seems a frivolous thing to miss, but I'm going to savor this cup as long as it keeps its heat.

Skylar turns to Markhal with the other. "I didn't know if you'd want . . ."

"You should have it," he says.

She makes a face. "No, really, that's all right. Caffeine and I don't get along."

"If you insist." Markhal takes the cup, raises it as if to make an Earthling toast, and glances at me with a glint in his eye. "I compliment your taste in women."

I choke on the mouthful I was just swallowing, and Skylar pats my back, her grin returning. I hadn't said anything to Markhal . . . Well. According to Celette, it isn't hard to tell.

The thought of Celette makes my stomach clench. I checked in on her when I went to get Markhal from the medic center. She's still on and off of the chair where he and the other medic are trying to restore more nerve function around the stump of her shoulder. She wouldn't even let me apologize.

"I knew something like this could happen, Win," she said. "I knew speaking up for Earthlings was going to put me in danger from the first time I did it. It could have been worse."

It could have. She could be dead. The fact is, though, that it won't be much of a life if they can't get an artificial limb working well enough for her to continue a regular career. Even for scroungers, the Industry division has certain performance standards.

Skylar gestures to the public view screen across the hall from the shuttle stop. "Here they go."

Someone from the tech crew has just patched in the surveillance feed from outside the storage bay we directed Vishnu to. A few dozen followers crowd around his skinny form as he taps at the entry panel.

This was my plan. All the same, an urge grips me to shout to Britta to cut off access before he gets in. From the moment I let the idea come out of my mouth earlier today, I've been feeling ill about it. None of the others looked too worried about using Vishnu's group, but I'm uncertain how well they know him.

The door slides open, and the anti-movers pile inside. We don't have a view in the bay itself, but I can easily imagine them falling on the supplies and equipment in gleeful destruction. Nothing we keep on the station is totally useless, but Britta identified a space that holds mostly jet-pods and ship parts that exist in reasonable numbers elsewhere. Vishnu's people won't ruin anything completely essential.

We've considered all the variables. There's no reason this shouldn't work without causing lasting harm.

The coffee no longer tastes quite as satisfying, but I finish the cup as we stand in silence. The screen flashes, and then darkens to black: Isis's signal that enough Enforcers have left their tunnel patrols that we're safe to go.

We clamber onto our gliders, the backs of the bars now carrying a fat disc for additional power, and hover down through the shuttle stop entrance. When we land on the spiral seal, I bring up the control panel. Entering the command manually should prevent Security from noticing our activity here.

The spiral begins its steady unfurling in the glimmer of light emitted by the panel. When it's large enough, Markhal activates his glider and drops through first. Skylar darts after him. I instruct the seal to shut before I follow.

We stay close together as we descend along the tunnel wall, so we can alert each other through touch if necessary. The hum of the gliders' enhanced power source sounds thunderous in the dark, but Zanet assured us it won't be audible from more than a short distance away.

At the fifth level, when my glider is just starting to shudder, I tap the others' arms. We stop there and pull our time cloths over us while the gliders recharge so no unexpected patrol will see us. My glider's display creeps back to full power. As we prepare to go on, Skylar finds my hand in the darkness, intertwining her fingers with mine for a second. Then we're off again.

Sweat chills on my skin in the unheated air. We've just passed the fourth level when a faint vibration tickles over me. I throw out my arms to push my companions toward the wall. An instant later, an inner-shuttle rushes past, the windowless car little more than a surge of moving air before it's gone. My clothes settle back against me. I swipe my hair from my eyes as my heartbeat returns to its normal pace, and then motion us downward.

On the second level we have to stop to recharge again. Though the glider is doing most of the work, my wrists are aching from the awkward angle I have to hold them at to keep my balance. Another shuttle approaches, and the others pick up on the shift in the air at the same time I do. Then, gliders ready, we fly on.

At the first level, we head left. I count the stops we pass, and press the control panel to open the set of doors Britta indicated. We hang back long enough to confirm there's no one waiting in the alcove and then scramble out, leaving our gliders on a maintenance ledge inside the tunnel. Skylar stretches her arms, rubbing her own wrists. Markhal looks worse off, his brown skin cast with a green-ish tinge, his lips pressed tight. I'm not certain if it's fear or physical discomfort.

The narrow hall before us has the dull lighting and gray-toned walls of all the station's industrial sectors. I drape the time cloth over me and stride to the doorway to this secret group of rooms. The cloth's camouflaging function doesn't work perfectly when the user is in motion—it's mainly meant for concealing the tentlike form the cloth takes for Traveling—but it'll be enough to keep the surveillance system from registering our identities. I suspect all our faces have an alert assigned to them now.

The door reveals nothing. I part the flaps of the time cloth to press the lock-breaker chip to the panel next to it. Isis said it should be able to handle any level of security with direct contact, but that it would take time to process.

As we wait within our individual time cloths, the Enforcers will be subduing Vishnu and his group. When they're finished, those who were called from their posts will return. We don't know how much time we have.

Finally the panel flashes, and the door whispers open. I let out my breath. Britta's scans led her to believe these rooms are only used at select times, and that they should be empty now, but I'm still relieved to see the inner hall is dark in the moment before the lights flash on at our entry. We keep our cloths over us like hooded capes as we head down it, Skylar and Markhal vague rippled figures on either side of me.

This could be the turning point in our civil war . . . or it could be the most disappointing of dead ends. I scan the line of doors, the back of my neck prickling.

Skylar pushes into the nearest workroom. "Come on, we have to start collecting the data."

The space we enter looks like a meeting room, filled by a table surrounded by stools. A half-size console stands against one wall. Markhal sits down at it. After a few gestures, he smiles.

"I've got this," he says. "I'll be able to start loading the archives onto the data drive in a moment. There are *thousands* of records and reports in here."

"Let's see what else they have," I say to Skylar.

Across the hall we find a tiny room with five consoles crammed together and nothing else. Then we come to what looks like a laboratory: two consoles at one end and an isolation chamber set against the far wall, attached to a bulky tech fixture that's taller than I am.

"What's that?" Skylar asks, easing back the flaps of her time cloth to study it.

"I don't know." I edge closer, but I'm not experienced enough with tech work to identify the functions of the bubble-like protrusions or the twists of circuitry dappling its boxy body. "I've never seen anything like this in a medical center . . . or anywhere else."

Skylar is rubbing her wrist again. "Are you all right?" I ask her.

"Yeah," she says. "It's just tricky staying on those gliders, with the bar so narrow. Apparently I need to get a little more upper-body exercise in."

"I'd like to note that I think all parts of your body are excellent as they are," I remark with a grin. Skylar gives me a startled glance before smothering a giggle. Some of the anxiety leaves her face.

She shoulders me to the side as she heads to one of the consoles. "Maybe this can tell us something useful."

I join her as she flicks up the floating display. "Open that," I suggest, pointing to an icon I recognize. It's a program we use in Earth Travel for analyzing experimental results.

A flood of figures fills the display. "I don't know a lot of those characters," Skylar says, her forehead furrowing.

I lean in, reading the words between the numbers and calculations. "They've been working on something with . . . *vorth* energy. That's what the station core generates, by processing starlight and siphoned gases, to power the station."

She sidles over to give me easier access to the display. I flip through more of the data before closing that program and venturing deeper into the interface. Most of the files I come across are diagrams and log notes, but the picture they're forming doesn't make sense to me.

"I think that machine produces *vorth* energy," I say, nodding to the tech fixture. "At a level much more concentrated than the current levels for normal usage. They've been comparing that production to readings on various chemicals and biological compounds . . . and there are some hypotheses about 'reversals,' but it's hard to tell what that's referring to. It sounds as if there's another lab where they're running related processes."

"Reversals?" Skylar says. "Maybe they really have found a way to undo the time shifts' damage. Does it say anything about Earth in there?"

"Not that I've found so far, but the subjects are all referred to only by number. Let's look for that other lab."

There are two doors left, one across from the room we've left and one at the end of the hall. I'm drawn to the latter, perhaps because of the sense of a larger space on the other side: more to be revealed. The door refuses to admit us until I've pressed the lock-breaker chip to its control panel and let another minute slip by us.

The door whispers to the side. We step past it into darkness. Then the low lights blink on, throwing a bluish pallor over the dozen or so clear cylinders before us that stretch from the floor to just below the ceiling. It takes a second for my eyes to adjust, and another two for what I'm seeing to sink in. My grip on the time cloth loosens. It almost slips from my head. A tiny pained sound escapes Skylar's lips.

Each of the cylinders holds a suspended slack, naked body. They're human bodies. Their clouded eyes are open, their mouths agape, like the dangling trout I saw in a market on one of my first training Travels on Earth.

They aren't normal bodies, though, I realize as my stomach rolls. Spindly pink lines claw across the skin of the one in the cylinder closest to us. The next shows a similar pattern, and all its fingers end abruptly at what should only be the third knuckles. My gaze passes over a third with a yawning, over-wide jaw and a nose that ends just past the upper cartilage. I can barely make out the one beyond other than the filmy layers of sloughed-off skin hovering around it.

Skylar has turned, her free hand pressed against her mouth. Footsteps patter down the hall toward us. "I've loaded all the archives," Markhal says in Kemyate, so wrapped up in his excitement he's forgotten Skylar's not one of us. "I skimmed through it while it was transmitting to the drive—most of the records have to do with vorth emanations and the deterioration of matter, but the ones I glanced at were sketchy about exactly what they think will be affected . . ."

He trails off as he gets close enough to see our expressions within the blurring of our time cloths. Three steps farther, he peers past us into the larger room. His lips part, but no words come out.

"Are they Earthling or Kemyate?" Skylar asks, her voice muffled by her hand. She hasn't turned to look again.

I edge forward, swallowing another surge of nausea. A series of characters imprints the nearest body's ankle. "Not exactly either," I say. "They're experimental bodies—lab grown." That means they'll have no more brain than an insect. At least this isn't a display of conscious suffering.

My mind whirls through the information we've gleaned: the deterioration of matter, chemicals, and biological compounds, vorth emissions. The question running through the data: Can it be reversed? Every attempt recorded was a failure.

I force myself to walk to the console beside the door and bring up the display there. I know what I'm looking for now. A few swipes and the data starts to come together into a pattern so undeniable it squeezes the breath from my lungs.

"They've been testing the effects of exposure to *vorth* energy on human cells," I say. "The effects of *accelerated* exposure." Regular exposure is, of course, what every person on Kemya experiences simply by living on the station.

Markhal comes up beside me. He tweaks the screen and pulls up a chart that I hadn't noticed. His hand falls. "Minute escalating mutations across multiple units within the DNA," he murmurs.

We've been so arrogant. We watched Earthlings struggle with pollutants and radiation, and no one I know has ever questioned whether our own source of energy is truly consequence free. Why wouldn't it be? We're Kemyates. All of our tech is so clearly, vastly superior.

I remember the way Skylar looked at me when I told her the shifts we'd been making on Earth across the millennia had degraded the atomic bonds of all the matter on the planet. I suspect my face has formed a similar expression of horror. Was this how she felt then: this creeping, shuddering dread that burrows right down through me, already too deep to dig it out?

This is why the secrecy. This is what the Council has been hiding. The station we've all considered home, that we've based our sense of security on for thousands of years, has bit by bit been deforming our genetic code.

A frantic impulse rises up, to spin and run away, but the knowledge will still be there.

"It's us," I hear myself say. "What they think—what they *know* has been affected. It's all of us."

• • •

"But there's nothing wrong with us," Zanet says, so loud Markhal winces beside me. "We're fine. You said they were using stronger emissions for the experiments—it's not the same."

Markhal has a better grasp of the science than I do. "It is," he says grimly to the cluster of our fellow Kemyates—the first small group after Isis, Britta, and Tabzi we've shared the information we found in the Nuwa labs with—standing around us in the workroom we've taken for this impromptu meeting. "They increased the emissions to duplicate the effects of millennia of built-up exposure. It isn't exactly the same, but the physical issue with our genes has increased as they were passed on through the generations. The errors are duplicated and carried on and continue to grow. Some of the reports we've found are quite clear."

"Then why haven't we seen any problems after so long?" a woman whose name I don't know demands. "The effect must be so small . . ."

Even I can answer that. "There *have* been problems," I say. "The Council has tried to pretend there's nothing odd about it, but haven't you heard of people whose thinking has become confused, and the medics can't bring them back to health? The first of those cases occurred only two hundred years ago. Last year there were fifteen new instances. In another few centuries, the mutation could be so pervasive that everyone suffers from that condition once they reach a certain age. If we don't get off this station, away from the vorth energy."

On K2-8, where we can rely on wind and water as well as sunlight and our habitations won't require anywhere near as much power as the station, we'll have other options.

Zanet and a couple of the others shake their heads in denial. I grit my teeth, but I know how hard this is to hear.

"Just look at what we found," I tell them. "There are logs, images, video files. You'll see."

They have to. If we can't convince even them, how will the rest of Kemya react if we attempt to reveal our leaders' duplicity?

Skylar and Britta have been sifting through those files at one of the consoles across the room. Markhal and I go to join them as the others head into the hall, muttering among themselves.

"Have you found out why the Health division was testing the Earthlings?" I ask.

"As far as we can tell, they thought we'd make good subjects because we'd never been exposed to that kind of energy before," Skylar says. "A clean slate." She conceals a yawn. It's late, but none of us has slept since we returned.

"What about the reversal procedures?" Markhal says. "Is there any mention of progress at all?"

Skylar's mouth flattens at the question as Britta answers with a shake of her head. "As far as I can tell, there were already so many tiny defects in any given person's genes by the time the Health division realized what was going on, none of their therapies can correct them," she says, her voice unusually subdued. "And fixing a few flaws here and there sometimes set off a reaction that sped up the decay of the other affected areas. They experimented with shielding, to see if they could prevent further harm by blocking off the core, or the energy channels, but . . . With the output we need to keep the station running and in orbit, it's impossible."

"The Council knew," Skylar puts in. "There are references to per-missions from Council members and mayors all the way back to the first discovery. It looks like it was just them and a restricted num-ber of Health workers who were aware of the problem. Studying the medical cases. Running those experiments to see how bad the effects could become."

I grimace at the thought of the mutated experimental bodies, their genetic flaws revealed in grotesque clarity in their bodies.

"Knowing how our people think, the first researchers who found out likely assumed the problem couldn't be too immense for them to find a solution, and they didn't want to tell everyone without that solution in hand," I say. "Then they left each new Council with a big-ger problem compounded by the secrecy. Kemya forbid any of them admit to a rotted mistake."

"I know," Britta mutters. "Even if they didn't want to tell us, they could at least have initiated the move earlier."

"It would have been difficult to convince everyone it was time without revealing the reason, I suppose," Markhal says. "For some of that time they might have believed they were making progress. It could be only recently they were certain the problem was unsolvable."

I remember the calm on Nakalya's face that day by the VR room. "Nakalya and the others haven't exactly seemed upset about having an obvious incentive to move on. Before, almost everyone at Earth Travel would have fought it. In a way, by taking down the time field, we *helped* them."

"Do you think Ibtep knew the whole time?" Skylar says. "There's no mention of her in the records, and she always acted as if she believed we had to hide our intentions from the Council."

Back then I would have said I didn't think Ibtep could have known something that horrible and hidden it from us. Now . . . "It's possible," I say. "I suppose it doesn't really matter either way. Have you come across anything else significant in the records?"

"There was one thing . . ." She gestures at the screen. "It looks like not everyone's affected equally. Any families who used gene engineering on their kids have higher rates of mutation. How common is that?"

"Most of us consider 'customization' an unnecessary extravagance," Britta says. "You have to contribute a lot of credits to the Health division. It'll mostly be rich families."

"Oh," Skylar says. "Jule said his grandfather had gone kind of 'senile.' I wonder . . ."

She flicks up a database of patient files. I follow the names flying past until a familiar one snags my attention.

"Wait!" I say. "Go back a little."

Skylar eases up through the list, and I point, my eyes widening.

"They have a file on Kurra."

23.

Skylar

Win rests his hands on my shoulders as I open Kurra's file. Britta peers over and makes a clucking sound with her tongue.

"Look at that. Early intensive testing conducted due to the extent of her genetic shaping. Two definite high-level mutations identified at age twelve. Likelihood of early onset of outward effects almost certain." Her voice drops. "The Health staff advised her parents to limit her responsibilities. That's why they supported her younger brother as a politician and not her."

I overheard someone make a remark along that line once—saying Kurra had been set aside because of some "mistake." "But they wouldn't have told her parents why, would they?"

"They couldn't have kept this so hushed up if they were doing that," Britta remarks.

Kurra must have no idea the real reason her parents withdrew their trust. Although I have to say that giving her a blaster and sending her off to maintain law and order doesn't seem much like restricting responsibilities to me.

"She was acting a little odd, when she came to search my family's apartment," Win says. "I never would have thought . . ."

His fingers have tensed. Something about that and his tone sends an uncomfortable twinge through me. Another echo of what I felt seeing the disbelief on his and Markhal's faces when they finally understood what the Nuwa lab meant. My thoughts have been churning since we started the slow hover back to the upper levels, but there's been too much commotion since we returned for me to sort them out.

"Ignoring orders to go off on her own to patrol for us—that is pretty . . . obsessed," Britta says.

"She blames us," Win says. "The way she spoke—she believes we and the Earthlings are responsible for making her look incompetent. I think she may have been demoted after she failed to prevent us from carrying out the mission to disable the time field generator."

"Well, she'll know the truth about her situation soon enough, won't she?" Markhal says. "We have to get this information out there. Maybe if everyone knew and more minds were working on the problem, we *could* find a solution."

Another uncomfortable twinge runs through me at the thread of desperation in his voice.

"I don't know," Britta says quietly. "It's not my area of expertise, but they've brought in the most skilled people available. I think if there were a fix, they'd have it by now." She shudders, and glances at me. "Wouldn't it have been nice if you *had* found some secret to healing Earthlings instead?"

It would, but all at once the little prickles of unease converge into a flare of irritation. "Look," I blurt out, "I'm not happy that we found this, and I wouldn't have wished it on anyone, but— It shouldn't matter. If you honestly believe that I and all the other Earthlings are full, capable human beings even with the kind of degradation we've experienced, why should this really change anything?"

The three of them stare at me. "Skylar—" Win starts.

"Don't tell me it's not the same." I drag in a breath, fighting for patience through a haze of fatigue. "We wanted proof our Earthling degradation doesn't mean we're less. We *got* that. Not in the most pleasant way, but . . . You Kemyates are still human. So you have some new flaws in your DNA? They're affecting hardly anyone in a noticeable way. When you get off the station, they won't get any worse. My *atoms* are defective. You've still accomplished all the things you've accomplished, that Kemyates have been so proud of. We're all still the same human beings we were before we knew about this."

Win squeezes my shoulder. "I wasn't going to tell you it wasn't the same," he says. "I was going to say you're right."

"Oh." My face flushes. I should have realized I knew him better than that. I look to Markhal and then Britta. "Do you see? This *proves* that whatever flaws we have, they don't make a difference. If the rest of Kemya can accept that they could still do great things in spite of this"—I wave at my display—"then they have to accept that being degraded doesn't necessarily make Earthlings less smart or strong either."

Britta tugs at a stray lock of her hair. "I know what you're saying, Skylar. I'm just not sure I can see it that way yet, even if I want to."

"I get it," I say. I didn't exactly feel great when I first heard Win explain how his people had damaged Earth. "I'm sorry for going off on you all."

"Skylar!" Zanet calls from the other side of the room. "People here for you."

What? I turn to see Jai and Mr. Patterson standing by the doorway.

As I hurry over, worried something has gone wrong in our sector, I realize it's not just the two of them. The middle-aged Inuit woman, Iqaluk, one of the Japanese monks—Nobu, I think his name is—with the Kemyate guy who's been speaking to them, and a tall lean woman I don't know are standing behind them in the hallway.

"This is Shuanda," Jai says as the woman bows her dark head. "She's one of the pets who has completely recovered. She and the others here expressed that they would like to offer their help to the rest of us. I thought you would have the best idea where they could be of use."

"There have to be more ways we can contribute," Mr. Patterson says.

I hesitate. "This isn't exactly the best time," I say. "We found something that the Kemyates need to discuss among themselves." I turn to Iqaluk. "You really don't need to leave your family," I tell her as Jai translates. "We can look after everything."

She makes a darting motion and a hasty comment. "*This* is looking after her family," Jai says.

Win has come up beside me. "We can figure out places they could help, even with all this going on," he says. "If they want to be involved, why shouldn't they?"

Because I didn't mean to drag them right into the fight? Because . . .

A blaring trumpet sound reverberates through the room. I flinch and the Earthlings outside draw back.

Britta scrambles to her feet. "That's our evacuation signal. Someone's broken through to the eighth level." She touches the console's controls. "Where do you need us, Isis?"

"*She's busy,*" a frantic male voice answers. "*They've managed to cut off part of our power—we can't keep the deflection fields up everywhere they're hitting us."* He rattles off a series of sector numbers. *"We've lost the eighth level already. Get whoever you can down to the ninth to defend those points."*

One of the number sets sticks in my head. It's just a couple sectors over from our Earthling enclave. "I'll go to 93-5," I say.

"I'll come with you," Win says, but I shake my head.

"You should handle one of the other spots. There are too many."

The lights in the hall have dimmed further. *They've managed to cut off part of our power.* My pulse thuds as Britta ducks into the room we've been using for tech storage and thrusts stun-only blasters, earpiece communicators, and rolls of that sealant material out to the rest of us. Then Jai, Nobu's translator, and the Earthlings who came with them run with me through the hallways. Our home sector isn't far.

Most of my group of Earthlings is out of their apartments, murmuring in nervous clusters. "What's going on?" Angela asks, rushing over the moment she sees me. "The Kemyates who were around took off without saying anything."

"The Enforcers have broken through to the eighth level," I say. "We're sealing off the ninth to make sure they don't get any farther. I'm going to need help."

Angela's mother grabs her arm, wide-eyed, and says something to her in Filipino. Angela's expression pinches. I wouldn't blame her for a second if she opted out of this particular undertaking. I head for the service stairs, gripping the strap of my sack of equipment so tightly my fingers ache. I've just reached the doorway when Angela catches up with me, Evan beside her. His face is drawn, but they both look more determined than I've ever seen them.

"We're not giving up," Angela says.

We charge down the stairs. Two of the Kemyates who've been assisting with the Earth Studies evacuees are braced on the landing below, watching the solid surface of the breach shield where the opening to the next set of stairs used to be. The tech crew has already managed to seal off this level, then. Maybe we're all right.

Before I can feel even a fraction of relief, the guy there says, "They're trying to cut through the seal. They keep stopping—the deflection fields are rotating—headquarters can't keep them everywhere continuously. As soon as it moves on they'll be at it again."

"Here," I say, handing him a blaster and a roll of sealant material from my sack.

As he starts tearing off hunks of sealant, the woman with him says in Kemyate, "*It's not just here. They're down the hall, a couple of different places . . .*" Her voice wobbles. She glances at my earpiece. "*Are they making progress with the power?*"

"*I don't know,*" I have to admit. The communicator has been silent. "*We'll help.*"

She glances at the group that's gathered behind me, mostly Earthlings, with undisguised skepticism, but I don't have the energy to be offended. I duck out of the stairwell. Solma and a few Kemyates I don't know are staked out around three spots along the length of the sector hall. "Spread out," I say to my companions. My parents, Daniel, Jeffrey, Cintia, and Ms. Cavoy have joined the rest of us. I hand out the blasters, which I hope are intuitive enough that they can figure out how to use them, and toss one of my two remaining rolls of sealant down the hall so the people there can share it.

Evan, Mr. Patterson, Jai, and Iqaluk join Solma at her spot in the middle, Iqaluk immediately bending to start tearing the sealant into strips as I'm doing. When she has a pile of several, she passes the roll on to the last group. Then she catches me staring at her, and gives me a flash of a smile. I guess she *was* ready to help, whatever we threw at her.

A hum passes through the floor. I freeze. "Field is down," the Kemyate woman we joined murmurs with a heavy accent. Below us, the Enforcers will be digging their way through again.

"*Is there anything in the apartments that might help?*" I ask, nodding to the open doors around us.

Her eyebrows lift. "*The medic kits,*" she says. "*The . . . discs pick up heat and electrical signals. They'd help us judge how close.*"

"Get the medical kits out of the apartments!" I call out, thankful that I showed everyone where to find them in their own apartments when we first moved in.

Across the hall, the Earthlings who speak English fan out. Mom and Angela return to my spot with a couple of kits each. We pop them open and dig out the discs. The Kemyates with us decide where to place them on the floor. All six of the discs flicker and flash, a couple brighter than the others. We form a loose circle around those two.

"What exactly are the people down there doing?" Dad asks, his hand clenched around a strip of sealant.

"Cutting their way up from the ceiling below," Nobu's translator says. "Even without the deflection field, they can't do it quickly. There are several layers of dense material between each level, as well as the breach seal, and they'll have to be careful of the tech lines, but—"

Someone gives a cry down the hall from us. A crackle of energy leaps from the floor, sparking in one of the Kemyates' faces. He stumbles back, cursing, and Ms. Cavoy whips a healing pad from her medic kit. The other Kemyate who was guarding that spot slams a strip of sealant over the just-formed hole, and Daniel slaps another on top of it. I tense as the strips bubble, but they hold just long enough for the vibration in the floor to fade away.

"*Field is back,*" the woman with us says, wiping sweat from her forehead despite the chill that's crept into the air. The tech crew must be siphoning energy from the heating systems too.

The Enforcers have to be close to breaking through all over now. "You need anything over there?" I shout to Ms. Cavoy's group.

"We're all right," the man who was burned says, pressing the pad to his jaw. His eyes twitch to an apartment doorway. "The tabletops detach," he says to the Earthlings with him. "See if you can grab one. That will slow them down."

Jeffrey and Daniel run into the nearest apartment. Solma gestures to Evan, and they dash into another. The vibration starts up again. I clutch my blaster. The disc on the floor is flashing even brighter now.

"Here they come," the Kemyate woman says.

I startle as a jet of sparks jumps from the floor to the left of the disc. Dad stomps a hunk of sealant over the spot and yelps as a second plume leaps up right beside his leg.

"Dad!" I cry. Mom yanks him to the side. The woman waits a split second until the sparks die away, and aims a quick stunning blast down the fist-size opening. There's a thump below, but whoever she caught wasn't alone. An answering shot twangs out, striking the woman in the wrist. She manages to toss her blaster to Angela as her arm goes slack.

I try to take a shot, but mine bounces against the edge of the hole. Nobu and his translator, who I hadn't even registered leaving us, race back carrying an apartment table: a slab of thin but dense metallic stuff. They drop it over the hole just as a fresh spurt of sparks shoots up. Mom and I throw ourselves beside it to smack sealant around the edges, melding it to the floor.

Dad is holding his leg, the fabric of his pants still smoking. Another bolt of sparks sears through the floor just a few feet from the table. I toss a strip of sealant down as Nobu and his translator run to grab another table.

"Isis!" I shout, tapping my communicator to confirm it's on. "Whoever's in headquarters, we need that field back in sector 93-5."

"*Trying,*" a voice too breathless for me to identify responds. "*Almost . . .*"

"Can you get all of them?" I hear Solma yelling.

"I don't know," Evan answers, his voice strained. At a shriek, my head jerks around.

A whole chunk of floor is flying up. It strikes Solma in the stomach so hard she topples backward, groaning. Mr. Patterson and Iqaluk dash for the tabletop they left leaning against the wall. Jai rushes to the edge of the hole, firing his blaster. In the heartbeat after the shot rings out, an Enforcer lunges through the hole, braced against something beneath. He shoots his own blaster right into Jai's face.

A shriek of my own catches in my throat. Jai's body teeters and slumps, his head crackled and blackened. The Enforcer pushes himself farther out, aiming at Solma, who's just squirming out from under the chunk of flooring. I shoot, but the bolt of light streaks past his shoulder.

Nobu's translator is already sprinting, halfway there, but Evan moves faster.

Angela makes a choked sound as our friend hurls himself at the Enforcer. The shot glances off the wall an inch from Solma's head. As the Enforcer stumbles down, Evan falling partway through the hole after him, another twang cuts through the air. Evan's body spasms.

"No!" Solma says. She shoves the chunk of flooring aside as the translator yanks at Evan. I can see the seared mark stretching from his chest up to his neck as his limp form lolls to the side. His eyes are blank.

Mr. Patterson and Iqaluk slam the tabletop over the hole. It's barely big enough to cover the gap. More sparks are flying near my feet. My eyes are full of tears. I can barely breathe.

My voice rips out of my throat. "Isis, please, *do something!*"

A Kemyate curse carries through my earpiece. "Hit it!" Isis's voice hollers, and the floor shudders with the boom of a thunderclap. Then it goes still. The sparks fade. There's no sound from below.

"*All Enforcers down,*" another voice says in my ear.

Mom grabs me, pulling me into her arms. Her breath is ragged. I cling to her, squeezing my eyes shut. I can't stand to look at the scene in the hallway, the bodies lying there.

"Is he . . ." Angela says distantly.

"The head or the heart," Solma says softly, "there is no recovery."

A ping sounds on the public screen on the wall. I pull back from Mom in a daze. It takes several moments, blinking away tears and pulling my scrambled thoughts together, before I can process the message that's appeared. A general Security alert requesting all Kemyates stay clear of one of the first level wards. Is something happening with the Nuwa labs?

"Isis," I say raggedly. "Anyone at headquarters—what's this Security alert about? Do we need to be worried?"

No one answers. My chest clenches tighter, the ache inside spreading through my whole body. I thought we were done, but maybe we're not.

My gaze slides over my companions, stuttering when it hits Evan's body. A fresh wave of tears wells up, but I *can't*, everyone else here still needs me, I have to—

"I'm going to check with headquarters and make sure we're all right now," I say. I sway on my feet as I turn around, and Solma catches my arm.

"I will go with you," she says fiercely. "Security will answer for this."

It's a short jog up the stairs and through the halls. The alert has popped up on all the screens we pass. Each time I see it, I push myself faster. The familiar rhythm of my strides, like cross-country practice oh so long ago, forces back the shock and grief as long as I'm in motion.

We burst into headquarters just behind Win, who looks equally concerned. The tech crew is flicking through their displays and calling information to each other, a blur of readings and terms I only have a basic grasp of. Isis and Britta are leaning together, staring at her display, which is divided to show footage of a series of angles of a large room. Figures dwarfed by the hulking apparatus they're scrambling over are smacking and prying at its knobbed surface.

"What's going on?" Win demands before I can ask.

Britta answers, her voice hoarse. "Some of the anti-movers got out of the storage bay before they could be arrested. They've managed to break into the station engine rooms while Security was launching its attack on us. It looks like they're trying to destroy the engines. They've already disabled one, at least temporarily."

As I step closer, I can see a chunk torn out of one of those hulking shapes' sides. A fizzle of sparks flickers amid greenish flames. A woman tosses some sort of chemical from a packet into the midst of the fire, and it flares brighter.

"Why haven't the Enforcers gone to stop *them*?" I say.

Isis threads her fingers through her red-streaked curls. She closes her eyes, and opens them again. "To get them to back off—the

Enforcers, while we finished recovering power—I sent out a shock pulse. I didn't have time to calculate the appropriate intensity across all that distance. Security sent everyone they had after us. They could be knocked out for hours."

The thunderclap. *All Enforcers down.*

Win's face has gone gray. "We gave Vishnu the idea," he says. "We gave him the idea that he could interfere with the moving plans by destroying equipment. Of course he'd think to go for the engines themselves."

"Security's summoning any off-duty Enforcers they can reach," Isis says. "It'll just take time. Maybe I can . . ." Her hand hovers vaguely in front of the display.

"No," Britta says, hands on her hips. "*You* need to go get some sleep. You're running yourself into the ground, Ice, and you can't handle anything like that."

"I can manage a little longer."

Britta pauses. Then she says, in a low voice, "You might have made a mistake with the shock pulse. And did Security really manage to launch this attack completely under the radar, or did you miss something that would have tipped us off?"

Isis's jaw works. She locks gazes with her girlfriend, but she's the first to look away. "There might have— I saw it just before they hit us."

"So go and come back fresh, and you will catch the next thing," Britta says. "Trust our team. Trust me. I haven't had a dizzy spell in days. We'll deal with the anti-movers."

Isis rubs her face, and stands up.

"All right," she says. "You're on lead for the next four hours. Then switch off with Zanet, all right?" She touches Britta's cheek. "I do trust you."

"Then get going," Britta says, but she kisses her quickly before giving her a gentle shove away.

"*Still no Enforcer presence at the engine rooms*," one of the crew says. "*And . . . they've attacked the maintenance workers who were on duty.*"

The display at the console Isis left zooms in on three figures crumpled on the floor. They look not just stunned but wounded, three dark red marks across one's face and another's arm.

"We have to stop Vishnu," Win says. "If Security can't, we have to go down there and stop him ourselves."

"Win," Britta says, but he doesn't let her get any further.

"It's our fault," he says, motioning to the screen, his expression so anguished I want to pull him to me, away from the streams of smoke and flickers of firelight. "It's probably our fault he thought to attack the engines. It's *definitely* our fault that most of Security's forces are disabled."

"What will happen if we don't stop them?" I make myself ask. Those engines are the key to moving the station, to reaching K2-8—to everything we now know we need more than ever.

Britta's mouth tightens. "Nothing good," she says after a moment. "All right. We have those enhanced gliders. When I was looking at the station schematics before, I saw there's a maintenance passage along the ceiling of the second room, with a hatch. We bring the stun guns, shoot down all the anti-movers we can, and then we get out of there as soon as Security gets their act together. I'd better be one to go—I've put in some target practice, and I know engines. Maybe I can reduce the damage they've started. Zanet, you're on lead now."

"I'm going," Win says immediately. "I have practice getting through the tunnels on the glider, and I know Vishnu."

Panic flashes through me, with an image of Win sprawled out like those injured workers—or blackened and blank, like Evan. I wobble, and hear myself saying, "I'll come." I can't let him go alone. I have to make sure he gets back.

Win stares at me, the determination in his eyes softening. He takes my hand. "No," he says. "Vishnu and his group, they hate Earth. They'll recognize you from the feeds—they'd target you ahead of anyone else. It'd be twice as dangerous for you."

I don't care. I'm not losing him too. But before I can speak, Solma is saying in her thick voice, "Not meaning an insult, Skylar, but your shot is not . . . ideal. If we are going to be taking them down while hovering, it should be people with good aim." She raises her chin. "I will join you."

I remember the shot I missed just minutes ago, the one that could have saved Evan his desperate leap, and my protest dies in my throat.

"Then we're set," Britta says. "There are only the three fully enhanced gliders. Let's move before things get any worse down there."

Win turns to leave, and my heart shudders. Fear swells inside it, through all the places I thought were broken edges, as if it's a whole thing after all.

Maybe it is. Maybe it always was. I can feel the echo of another fear within it—the possibility of caring too much, of hurting so badly all over again. Maybe the pieces I thought I'd lost have been there all along, and I let myself believe my heart was more than just cracked and bruised out of self-preservation. But I hurt now at the thought that I might never see Win again, and the pain is like a breath released after being held too long. A reminder that I'm alive.

That I do care, and there is no such thing as too much.

I catch Win's arm. The only words I can produce amid the whirl of my emotions are, "Come back."

"I will," he says. "I promise."

I tug him to me, kissing him quick and hard. I know there isn't time for more. I can only hope he understands how much it means to me that he keeps that promise.

24.

Win

As we squeeze around a bend and come to the hatch Britta antic-
ipated, sounds penetrate the maintenance passage walls from
below: hisses and crackles and triumphant whoops. I've been listening for Enforcer fire, but it hasn't come. Zanet reported to us over the
communicators that a couple of Enforcers reached the engine rooms
a few minutes ago only to be caught by a makeshift laser weapon
someone in Vishnu's group has constructed.

I'm trying not to wonder how long it will take before they do
irreversible damage. If I wonder that, then I have to wonder if they
already have. It will be because of us if Wyeth and everyone else on
the station never experiences the real blue sky and bright sunlight,
moist breeze and warm soil, of the planet he cautiously accepted in
the VR room.

We're dragging our gliders with us, and Britta has a carry-sack
slung over her shoulder. She reaches the hatch first and eases it open.
Gusts of green-tinted smoke cloud the air below. I make out a couple of figures near the main entrance, Vishnu hollering orders, and

flickers of green flame. The harsh smell prickles in my nose. A minute ago I was starting to feel my exhaustion leaching at my bones, but the thump of my pulse washes it temporarily away. I grip my gun.

We will fix this.

"Stay as high as you can until you're ready to shoot," Britta says to Solma and me. "I'm going right down—I have to try to put out those fires. They're doing most of the damage."

We drop out one by one. We're only twenty feet above the floor—the gliders should hold their power longer than they did in the shuttle tunnels. Whether they'll give us enough time, we can't be certain. From the glimpses I caught on the display in headquarters, Vishnu still has some fifteen people with him who either escaped arrest during the storage bay incident or hadn't participated in that assault.

The smell seeps down my throat, coating my tongue with a bitter flavor. My mouth has already gone dry. Adjusting the controls with my heel, I skirt a billow of smoke and head toward Vishnu. If we can knock him out, it's possible the others will scatter of their own accord. Britta dips down, and Solma veers away from me toward the other of the two engine covers in this room.

I'm just coming up over my former classmate's position at the head of the room when a woman glances upward and notices me. She yells out, pointing. The man beside her spins, and I finally see this weapon they've been using. He whips a wand-like object in his hand and a three-tongued laser sweeps out into the air. It soars higher than I expected. I jerk to the side, my skin stinging with heat as the forked laser hisses past me.

The man pulls back his arm for another attack. I thrust my gun toward him, shooting four times in succession. My arm is shaking, so the first two go wild, but the third hits the man's foot and the fourth his chest. He lurches and slumps onto the broken engine cover.

The woman snatches the laser weapon from him. I kick the glider's controls, risking a sudden plunge. My stomach jolts, but I catch her in the head with a stun shot just as she swings around.

My descent has brought me into the view of the other anti-movers in the room. A boy who can't be much older than Wyeth springs at me. As I push the glider higher, Vishnu himself turns to glare at me. He's holding another one of those wands.

"Vishnu!" I call out. "You have to stop this. This isn't how we—"

Isn't how we Kemyates solve our problems? How can I say that when I led a takeover that displaced a third of our people from their homes? How can I say that when our Council solved their problems with Earth by wiping out all life on the planet?

Before I come up with the right words to reason with him, Vishnu lashes out with his laser. The forked tail sizzles toward me. I press a burst of speed from the controls, shooting forward, but I'm not quite fast enough. The third fork sears across the extra power source on the back of the bar. It sputters, and the glider bucks. I point it downward, using my momentum to fly close to the other engine case before the hover function cuts out completely. The glider drops, and I jump onto the cover's knobbed surface.

My right ankle twists under me as I hit the engine. Pain spikes up my leg. I stumble on the slippery curve. My gun—I've lost hold of my gun. I spot it lying next to a gouge in the case and scramble toward it.

A girl who was cutting at one of the knobs with a more standard laser tool lunges at me. As I fumble for my gun, a shot catches her from the side. She topples, and Britta hurries over.

"Quick," she says. "Help me with this . . . Oh." She stiffens.

I glance over my shoulder. Five Enforcers have just entered the room. The crinkling of the air in front of them tells me they're wearing deflector shields. It's wise of them, because as I catch sight of them, Vishnu does too, and casts his laser weapon toward them. It sputters off the fields with a shower of sparks. One of the Enforcers takes a step closer. It's Kurra.

"I didn't expect to see her," Britta says. "The records showed Security removed her from duty after that stunt in the tunnels. They really are desperate." She shakes her head, ponytail swishing as she spins around. "Come on, we have a little time while they're distracted."

I limp after her over the arc of the engine cover. On the other side, a line of flame dips and wavers along the tubes and revealed tech panels where the cover has been torn away. Britta unfurls a glinting sheet from her sack and shoves one end into my hands. We heave the sheet over the flames. It ripples as they hiss out.

A twang slices past us to strike a man who was clambering up the cover toward us. Solma dives to us through the smoke. "Let's get out of here!" she yells.

Britta clutches another sheet, looking to a burning patch at the back end of the cover. "Just a minute," she says. "If we can stop more of the fire . . ."

I check the doorway. The Enforcers are spreading out to surround Vishnu. They can't shoot through their deflector shields, but once they have him from all sides, one of them can drop the shield to take him down. Vishnu is screaming something I can't make out, flailing the whip around him.

As I take that in, Kurra swivels and our gazes meet. My fingers clench around my gun. Her eyes narrow, and she starts to move toward us instead of Vishnu.

"We're trying to *help*!" I shout, waving my arm at Britta's fire-dampening sheet as I sway backward on my sprained ankle.

Kurra hesitates, gun raised, glancing from me to Vishnu. I suppose the two of us don't look so different right now.

We are different, though. The burn of smoke in my throat and the flicker of flame all around us sear that certainty into me. I've done everything I can to avoid doing harm; he's doing everything he can to cause it. I may have nudged him in this direction, but that screaming, flailing figure is not my creation. Even as another prickle of guilt runs through me, I can see there's nothing that can stop him now except a blast to the head, and this devastation confirms just how much he needs to be stopped.

"It's *him*," I say, jabbing my hand his way. At the same moment, one of Kurra's colleagues calls out. A couple of Vishnu's followers are pelting the ring of Enforcers with flaming tech scraps. Kurra turns, her gun hand swinging toward them, and that may be all the opening we get.

"Go!" I holler to Britta and Solma. "Now, or they'll have us too!"

Britta has just flung down her other sheet. Solma takes off on her glider toward the hatch in the ceiling. I don't even know where my glider is, though by all evidence it wouldn't do me much good if I did. I rotate on my feet, searching for another way out. A hand grabs my shoulder. Britta is hovering on her glider just a few feet off the ground.

"Hold on," she says, pressing the front of the bar into my hands. The second I catch on, she fiddles with the controls, and we lurch upward. My elbows jar. My legs dangle as the glider rises, my arms straining, fingers already aching with the effort. A shot flickers past us and disappears into the smoke. Britta urges the glider on into the cloud. I cough, curling my fingers tighter.

"Almost there," Britta mutters. "You can do it." I'm not certain whether she's talking to the glider or to me. The bar jolts, and I almost lose my grip. Then my head bumps against the hatch.

Britta hops out into the passage and grasps my arm, giving me a heft so I can pull myself up after her. Solma yanks my other arm, and I'm in. With Britta's heave of the hatch door, the chaos below disappears from sight.

. . .

The footage on the display gives only a distant impression of what I experienced firsthand: the green flames eating across the wrenched-open engine cases, the smoke mingling with slashes of laser light and bolts of blaster fire. Even at that distance, it's enough to make my throat sting in memory as I sit on the stool at this workroom's single console. Skylar's hand clenches my shoulder where she's standing beside me. We were sorting through devices from a tech disposal bin, looking for parts to enhance more of the gliders, when Isis called over that the Council was sharing its official report on the fight in the engine rooms.

Alongside the video footage, the written report flows by. The facts are laid out plainly: Of the six station engines, four suffered substantial damage. Traveling with only two operational engines would extend the journey to K2-8 from twelve years to nearly fifty. Experts in the Tech division are studying the original engine schematics and will deliver an additional report on repair strategies within the next few days, but the public should be advised that recovery will not be easy.

The Council assures the public that the individuals directly responsible for the attack have been subdued and regrets to say that the group's leader was behaving in such a destructive manner that Security had no choice but to execute him on the spot to prevent further harm. They hope the Earthling sympathizers will consider how their misguided concerns allowed this horrible incident to take place and turn themselves in as a show of the loyalty they owe Kemya.

I wave my hand at the display, and it blinks out. My gaze lingers on the spot where it was. A lump has risen in my throat. Everything beneath feels empty.

I need . . .

I tug Skylar to me and she sinks onto my lap. A hitch of breath escapes me as I wrap my arms around her. She hugs me back, kissing the side of my head.

I'm aware of the doorway we left open in our rush, and the sound of voices and movement down the dim hall outside. It would be easy for someone to walk by and see this embrace. I find I don't care. Let my fellow Kemyates think and say whatever they want. Skylar makes me stronger. Holding her, I feel a little more able to face the implications of the Council's message.

The journey will be fifty years if the Tech workers can't fix those ancient engines. We'll be getting old, if we even survive this. My parents may have passed on by then, my grandparents almost certainly. The same could be said of most of the people currently living on the station. And all the while the hum of energy flowing through the walls will continue its slow and steady decay of our genetic code.

"Do you want—" Skylar says softly, and I shake my head before she can finish. There's only one thing I want from her right now.

"Just stay," I say, and then amend, afraid that may have come out too emphatically, "for now."

She hugs me tighter, and I adjust her against me so we're more closely entwined. She tips her head to mine like a caress. Then a shadow crosses the doorway. Skylar tenses. I look over her shoulder, and my grip on her automatically loosens.

Her mother is standing on the threshold. Her gaze twitches. "I'm sorry," she says, sounding embarrassed, "but Skylar, we need you."

25.

Skylar

I hop off Win's lap, my face flushing, and Win stands up beside me to face my mom. "Is it a problem I should notify headquarters about, Mrs. Ross?" he asks politely.

She gives him a faint smile. "No," she says. "Just a small disagreement we were hoping Skylar can help sort out."

It sounds like she doesn't want to explain in more detail in front of Win. "I'll find you later," I tell him, intertwining my fingers with his for one last moment. He bobs his head to both of us, but his eyes still look haunted by the report we just read.

I ache to fix this for him, to patch up the guilt and grief the way Markhal patched his sprained ankle, his burns. All I could do is be here. Part of me is just glad he made it out with only those minor injuries. He came back, like he promised.

I grope for words as Mom and I head down the hall. She saw me kiss Win when we first broke out of the zoo, but what she just walked in on feels a lot more intimate. I'm not sure whether it looked that way too until, after a few awkward seconds, she says, "What's going on with you and him . . . is it serious?"

"I don't know," I say automatically, and then reconsider. I might have trouble imagining what my life will look like even a few days from now, but I can't imagine Win not being there, one way or another.

"Yeah," I correct myself. "I think it is." I look at the floor. "Is that a problem? I wasn't trying to hide it from you and Dad, there's just been so little time to talk . . ."

It's hard to picture them setting rules now—curfews or other dating restrictions—if we could even call this "dating." But I remember how upset she was about me keeping things from her before.

Mom pauses. "It's strange, isn't it?" she says, reaching to tuck a strand of hair behind my ear, a gesture so familiar it pulls up all my memories of home and so gentle I stop bracing for a rebuke. "So much has happened, you've been through so much without us, I'm starting to feel as though we're the kids and you're the parent."

"Yeah," I say with a choked-up laugh. "I don't really *like* it feeling that way. You know that, right? And I still *need* you. I don't know— yesterday, after Evan—if you weren't here—"

A rush of my own grief, and maybe some guilt too, washes over me. His body was already gone when I returned to the scene of the attack. He was only there because he followed me. Maybe I should have told him to stay back. I knew how much he was struggling.

I stop, and Mom draws me to her. My eyes have welled up. She wipes a tear from my cheek.

"We'll sort things out," she says. "When things are okay again, I'm not going to tell you what to do—I can see you can handle a lot on your own. I just don't want you to forget that we *are* still your parents, and you don't ever have to be on your own."

"I know," I say. "I always know that." I exhale shakily. "So what's this disagreement I need to sort out?"

"I think I'd better let Angela explain," Mom says. "I was only there for the end of it."

When we reach our sector, the meal cart is hovering at the other end of the hall, loaded with bowls—but the Kemyates who help distribute the food are nowhere to be seen. Several people from our group of Earthlings are clustered nearby. Their voices drop to a hush when they notice my arrival. Angela hurries over.

"What's up?" I say.

Her mouth twists. "It might be my fault," she says. "I was just—Solma saw the memorial we made for Evan." She nods to his apartment door. All of us took turns etching commemorating words into its surface earlier today, before I stumbled off for a few hours of uneasy sleep. "She said something about how he shouldn't have gotten involved—that the Kemyates should be the ones dealing with their own Enforcers. I told her . . . that maybe he thought this was the best way he could be generous, the way we were talking about before? And maybe he was hoping he'd be back with his family and Lisa and everyone, after." She closes her eyes with a wince. "He was really hurting."

"Yeah," I say quietly. I force myself to think back to the moment when Evan threw himself on the Enforcer. I couldn't see his expression. One thing I do know: "He saved someone. That was important to him."

Angela nods. "I just thought it might help her to realize he could have been thinking something good would come out of it for him, that dying wasn't the end. But she got all upset and said it didn't make sense for people to make decisions based on superstitions, and Mrs. Green and Jeffrey and some of the others jumped in, and the other Kemyates too, and . . ." She tosses her hands in the air. "It ended up with the Sinclairs telling all the Kemyates to get out of the sector, so they went."

As if we don't have enough things to worry about—as if there aren't enough real reasons to be upset about Evan's death. We're in the middle of a station-wide catastrophe, and we're going to break our alliance over someone's religious belief? I stride over to the group near the meal cart. At the pale tension on the faces that glance back at me, more anxious than angry, some of my irritation dampens. Okay, maybe people are squabbling *because* we're in the middle of a station-wide catastrophe, and most of us can't do anything other than wait for more news.

But we're never going to get through this catastrophe if we can't stay united with even the few Kemyates willing to support us.

"Come with me," I say, squeezing through the cluster to lead them down the hall. I'm relieved to find Solma and a few of the other Kemyates are standing just beyond the archway, in the midst of what sounds like another argument.

"*. . . letting your feelings get in the way of—*" one guy is saying. He cuts himself off as we join them.

"All right," I say. "This is how it is. Our friend is dead. We're upset about that. We wish he wasn't. I wish Jai and everyone else the Enforcers hurt was okay too. But turning that into a debate about whose beliefs make more 'sense' or who should have done what in the middle of a fight is the *least* sensible thing I can think of."

Solma's jaw twitches. "I apologize," she says, lowering her head. "It was an error in judgment. I only . . . We did not know each other long, but I liked Evan. It is hard not to think that if the Earthlings—other than you, of course, Skylar—had left the work to those of us more prepared, as before, he might still be alive."

Queasiness pools in my gut. *As before.*

Of course Solma is thinking that. I've dissuaded the others from getting involved, acted as if they needed extra protection—and in doing so I've encouraged the Kemyates to assume we Earthlings can't handle as much as they can. I look back at my companions and spot Iqaluk and Nobu peering at us from farther down the hall, and my stomach clenches tighter. Not just that. I let *myself* believe the other Earthlings couldn't handle as much, just because they were born in another place, another time. But they were right there with us during the attack, picking up the skills they needed as they went. We might have lost more people without them there. We might have lost the whole war.

"This is my mistake too," I say, turning to Solma. I meet her eyes, and those of the other Kemyates. "We Earthlings should have been doing *more* before, not less now. Everyone here is just as capable as me. They can all help just as much as I have . . . if they decide to." I swallow hard. That's what I forgot. Evan made his own decision. He deserved to have it. Just like every other human being here. "I've had my own worries," I go on. "I let myself get in their way, thinking it would keep them safer, but that was wrong of me."

My voice has started to waver. I draw in a breath. "*I'm* sorry," I add to the Earthlings behind me. "Whoever wants to get involved from here on, you should. We don't all have to believe the exact same things as long as we're willing to stand and fight together. Right? That's the whole reason we're fighting here in the first place."

"But they—" Mr. Sinclair starts.

"Did they hurt you?" I interrupt. "Did they make it more difficult for you to stay alive? Or did they just say things you didn't like hearing?"

His lips press into a flat line.

"So we won't talk about how much sense anyone's beliefs make unless those beliefs are about what we're going to do to get out of this mess," I say. "There'll be lots of time to have philosophical arguments later." *I hope.* "Also, I think lunch is getting cold."

We congregate around the cart, and Solma starts handing out the bowls. Mrs. Green wrinkles her nose.

"Is it . . . supposed to smell like this?"

I lean close and catch a whiff—a funky sour stink like cheese gone rancid. I may not love Kemyate food, but I've never come across any that was outright repulsive.

Solma frowns. She opens a second bowl, and a third, and makes a face. "*It shouldn't be . . .*" she murmurs. "It was fine when we prepared it," she tells us. "It is not right that they should be ruined already."

• • •

By the end of the day, it's become clear that our ruined cart of meals was more than a freak occurrence. Reports come in from the other cafeteria volunteers, and the fresh batch Solma brings produces the same stench on arrival. We have no choice but to dig into our stash of packet foods, which suddenly looks a lot smaller.

Isis calls our core group into headquarters a few hours later. "We've identified the issue," she says. Despite the break Britta insisted she take, she already looks exhausted. "One of the people with us is from the food processing plants. He says there's a microbe they use there, that they can program so it interacts with a chemical element in the food to produce certain flavors and textures . . . From what he can tell with the equipment we have, Security released one of those microbes into the air up here, likely during that attack. This one has been programmed to produce a toxin."

"A toxin?" I repeat. "They're trying to poison us?"

"As if we're stupid enough to eat anything that smells like that," Britta remarks, rolling her eyes.

"They may be just attempting to reduce our provisions," Isis says. "All of our food contains that chemical element. As soon as it's unsealed, the microbe is attracted to it, and begins affecting it and multiplying in it. There's a small window before the food is ruined."

"So we'll have to eat as soon as the food is prepared," Tabzi says. "Go to the cafeteria . . . in shifts?"

Isis shakes her head. "It's not that easy. For now, eating quickly will work. But the more food spoils, the more the microbe multiplies, and the spoiling will happen faster and faster."

"Can't we do anything to get rid of it?" Win says. "They must have options in the processing plants in case there's an accident."

"The tech for that is kept in the plants," Isis says. "And there aren't any on these levels. It doesn't sound as if the deactivation machine is light enough that we could haul it up here on a glider either." She sighs. "I've set the air filters to the highest intensity we can afford the energy for. That should slow things down, but it sounds as if it's already multiplied too much for us to remove it completely."

"They couldn't shoot us down, so they're trying to starve us out," I say. We didn't have much more than a week's worth of food left as it is. How long can we last now? We could break our policy of stealing from the private apartments, but that won't help if the microbe reproduces enough to ruin food within a few seconds of it being opened.

I turn to Isis. "Can't we send the Nuwa information out there? Show everyone that they can't trust the Council's version of events? If we can make them understand that they've been full human beings even with some errors in their genetics, they'll have to start accepting

Earthlings are just as . . . as valid. Won't they? And then we can end this."

"We've tried," Britta says. "Four times now, in different ways. It looks as if Security has finally found a method to cut off transmissions from our levels. I can't even send out a post about footwear without it being deleted almost instantaneously. It's possible, if we had enough time . . ." She rubs her temple.

My heart sinks. "So we can't reach the rest of Kemya at all?"

"We can still contact Jule," Isis says. "The connection I set up isn't through the network. But I can only talk to him, not send him files. Even if he could get the word out, I don't think we have any hope of people believing this without definite proof. It's hard enough to take in *with* the proof."

"What about—" Win starts, and a chorus of pings sounds through the room.

Isis swivels to her console. "The Council has issued an updated statement about the engines," she says.

"Already!" Britta leans closer. "Maybe the damage isn't as bad as they . . ." She trails off as her gaze darts over the display, her face falling.

"What?" I peer over Isis's shoulder, but she's flicking through the report so quickly it's hard for me to process the characters. She murmurs a Kemyate curse. Her hand drops. Then she lifts it again to tell the console to translate the words into English.

The Council has determined that it would be unsafe to attempt moving Kemya to the planet K2-8 with only two engines functioning. The risks of those engines malfunctioning or failing during the fifty-year journey are too great. The Technology division is committed to repairing the other four following the original schematics to ensure proper functioning, and once this work is completed, plans for the move will resume. Mayor Nakalya assures everyone that Kemya will only leave orbit when the success of the journey is certain. Two days from now, he and the rest of the Council will be holding assemblies to address the concerns they expect the public will have.

"*When the success of the journey is certain,*" Britta quotes with a scoff. "The success of even a zip around the solar system is never completely 'certain.'"

I wish I could think that wording is an exaggeration, but it's waiting for some magical "certainty" that's kept the Kemyates stuck here for so long already.

"Do you think the Council believes the repairs won't take very long?" I ask. "It sounds like they've already started."

"I've studied those engines," Britta says. "The original . . . boosting conductors were made out of . . ." She says a Kemyate word I don't know. "That mineral was common on our planet before the detonation, but after, the heat and the chemicals in the air broke it down, and we've never been able to artificially generate it in a stable form. The little bit we still use we've mined from sparse deposits on asteroids. I don't know exactly how much they need to repair the engines, but having seen the damage . . . I doubt we could gather enough in less than a hundred years, and that's being hopeful."

"So they're making the same mistake as before," Win says with a frustrated gesture. "They thought they could fix the problem with the *vorth* energy quickly, and it's been, what, seventy years since Project Nuwa was formed? This Council will be replaced over time, Ibtep will lose the spotlight, everyone will get complacent again—we could end up here forever, until some future generation of Kemyates turns out like those . . . *things* in the lab."

Nothing we've done will matter. Nothing anyone else has done either. Earth's destruction won't have saved even one group of human beings.

"*This* Council knows about Nuwa," I say. "How can they act as if we're all safe here, as if staying on the station isn't a problem?"

"They obviously care more about not taking the blame," Britta says. "Keeping everyone calm and under control and ignorant." She bites out the last word.

"All this time Nakalya's been talking about loyalty to our fellow Kemyates and staying united, while he and the rest of the Council put themselves above everyone else," Win says bitterly. "They're supposed to be *serving* Kemya."

"Won't anyone question their decision?" I say.

"Not enough for them to listen," Isis says. "You didn't see . . . Well, you lived here for a time, you may be able to imagine. People accepted the idea of moving because the Council said it was the right course, but most of them were still nervous. Many might even be relieved to have it delayed, to give them more time to get used to the idea."

"There have to be other options," I say. "Other ways to repair the engines, or design new ones. Maybe more risky ways—but if everyone knew about Nuwa, then maybe they'd be okay with those risks."

"The Council won't admit to it," Tabzi points out, "and they won't give us the chance to."

"Maybe they don't all think this is the right way," I say. Hope sparks inside me. "What about— Ibtep risked her career, maybe even her life, following through with Jeanant's mission. She wouldn't just give up now. We have to talk to *her*."

26.

Win

Skylar and I meet Zanet above the seal on the ninth level, stopping our gliders as we wait for final confirmation from headquarters. After a few long minutes, Zanet opens the seal. Skylar touches my face in the dark, drawing me close for a kiss. It lasts just long enough for me to wish we were somewhere else, safe and alone. Knowing what Ibtep thinks of her, I wish she weren't coming at all, but I had to agree with the arguments she made. She can speak for the Earthlings to prove they'll stand behind any deal we make, and, as the last person who talked with Jeanant, she may be able to use that connection to push Ibtep to hold on to his dream.

The seal's motion halts, and we pull apart. It's time to move.

"Isis or I will signal you the moment we get any sign of Security movement," Zanet says. Jule was only supposed to pass on the go-ahead message if the Council agreed to let our supposed "negotiation of surrender" happen without interruption, but we don't have much faith in their sincerity at this point.

I don't trust *Ibtep* either, but by all evidence, we can at least trust that she wants to see Kemya reach K2-8 in her lifetime. Every shift in allegiance she's made has been to serve that goal.

The glide from the seal to the shuttle stop is brief, one level down and half a sector over. The hall we step out into is vacant. Security hasn't moved anyone back here yet.

The apartment we're using is right next to the stop, to make for an easy escape if necessary. We're first to arrive. Skylar taps down the benches in the table area, and we sit where we can watch the entrance.

I've barely had time to catch my breath when Ibtep and Jule walk in. Skylar's fingers brush mine as we stand to greet them.

Ibtep strides to the edge of the table area and stops, folding her arms in front of her. "I'm here," she says, her cool voice more clipped than usual. Her eyes slide from me to Skylar and back again. "What do you have to say?"

She obviously realizes this isn't about surrender, so I get straight to the point.

"We've seen the Council's plan to delay the move," I say. "Britta says it'll take at least a hundred years before the engines can be repaired by the original methods. We know you can't approve of that long a wait."

"You believe you know what I think that well?"

"I believe you couldn't be happy spending half your life working to bring Kemya to a new home only to lose that chance, maybe forever," Skylar says. "I believe you're smart enough to have already come up with a dozen other options that would get people to K2-8 faster."

"We're offering you our backing," I add when Ibtep ignores her. "You couldn't have disabled the time field without help. If you can't challenge the Council's decision without help either, we can increase the pressure on them for you."

Ibtep gives me a thin smile. "I was under the impression that you soon won't be in the position to offer much but your actual surrender."

"I didn't say we'd help without compensation," I say. "You provide the means for us to continue this standoff, and we'll use the time gained to wear down the Council and sway the public's opinion."

"And if I stand by the Council's decision?"

I stare at her. She sounds serious.

"Why would you?" Skylar says, looking as startled as I feel. "After everything . . ."

"We haven't needed to consider such large-scale propulsion in a very long time," Ibtep says evenly. "No one has been studying methods or developing new ones. It is safest to follow the original guidelines."

She can't really be saying this. We expected resistance to working with *us*, not resistance to the idea that we have something to work toward.

"You led illegal expeditions to Earth, plotted against the Council, and now you're worried about trying anything slightly beyond the existing guidelines?" I say. "Why do any of it if you're going to give up now?"

"What did those efforts result in?" Ibtep says, her shoulders tensing. "Yes, I took risks—I risked everything I had—and here we are with the station in disarray, the engines we need nearly destroyed, chaos among our people. Kemya knows what would come of giving you more time to damage the rest of us. I'm not a fool. I might have overstepped once, but I won't be that careless again."

"Your problem isn't that you risked too much," Skylar says. "It's that you kept too much of that Kemyate thinking. None of this would have happened if you and the Council had treated us like people and not . . . pets, or lab rats, when we first got here."

Ibtep's voice is starting to rise. "Those of us who are elected do what we think is best to protect those who understand less. Consorting with shadows only weakens us. We'll set down on our planet eventually, we *Kemyates*. If it takes a hundred years, or two hundred, at least your kind will be gone by then. There's no place for *you* there. You've proven what you stand for."

There's such disgust in those last words that Jule, who has hung back by the door, takes a step toward us with a frown.

"What she stands for?" I echo, my shock transforming into anger. "You mean seeing the Earthlings treated like the human beings they are? Standing up to a government that's spreading lies? Being *willing* to face a little danger for what we believe in? How can you accuse the Earthlings, when it's our own refusal to act that's weakened us in ways we may never recover from?"

"Caution and endurance are not weaknesses," Ibtep says.

"That's not what I meant," I say. "I meant the labs, the project—"

I hesitate. A look of what appears to be honest puzzlement has come over her face. Did she really think I was only criticizing Kemyate philosophy?

We assumed she knew about Nuwa now, if not before. She was the one who delivered the threat to Skylar after our supporters started searching for information after all. It could be, though, that the Council was using her much as she once used us.

"You don't know," I say.

Something of the weight and the truth of the situation must come across in my tone. A hint of fear flickers behind Ibtep's careful composure. Then it's gone.

"Know what?" she says dismissively.

I glance at Skylar, whose mouth has tightened. We've brought no proof with us. Is there any chance she'll take our word for it?

"The Council has lied to you too," Skylar says. "They've been lying to everyone, all the Councils have, for—"

"Enough!" Ibtep snaps. "I have no interest in rot. If you've said all you intended to, you have my answer. You can surrender or you can starve."

I reach for the last tool we have. "Didn't you learn anything from Jeanant?" I say. "You saw Skylar's memory re-creations—you know it was that fear of taking risks and changing his plan, even when the situation changed, that *killed* him."

Ibtep's eyes narrow. She raises her hand. "Respected Ibtep!" Jule says, striding forward, but she waves him off. He stops a few feet away, poised.

Ibtep points a finger at Skylar. "It was *Earth* that killed Jeanant, *Earth* that inspired your little rebellion, *Earth* that's caused every failure we're facing now. For too much of Kemya's history we've been distracted from our goals by that rotted planet, playing with it, trying to save it. I wish I could have gone back in the time field and destroyed your pathetic world before it had barely begun."

"I tried to save Jeanant," Skylar says quietly. "I did everything I could. He wouldn't let me."

Ibtep snatches at her, catching her arm in a grip so firm Skylar winces. "Hey!" I say, springing forward, but Jule is already there, grabbing Ibtep's wrist and maneuvering between them. I touch Skylar's shoulder, letting her know I'm here if she needs me.

"Let her go," Jule says, his voice radiating anger. I'm not certain I've ever seen him this furious. It convinces me finally, completely, whose side he's on.

Skylar yanks her arm sharply enough to break Ibtep's hold. Ibtep jerks away from us, brushing her hands together as if it were merely a slip. The same thought about Jule has clearly come to her.

"So," she says to him in Kemyate, "who are you really here for?"

Skylar reaches for my hand. "I think we should go," she says. The hopelessness in her eyes echoes inside me. Ibtep's mind is too set. Giving her a wide berth, we head for the door.

"Not for someone so blinded by bigotry and fear she puts her own concerns above the people she claims to serve," Jule retorts behind us. His feet scrape the floor as he strides to catch up.

"If you go, your family goes too!" Ibtep says.

Jule doesn't look back. "You should know how little that matters to me now," he says, and then, to me and Skylar, "I can't keep on with this. If you have any use for me up there, let me come with you."

Skylar doesn't speak, but she gives her acquiescence with a squeeze of my hand.

"All right," I say, "but you're going to have to climb."

• • •

"We can't hold these levels much longer," Markhal's medic colleague says. "Already we can barely keep anything edible for more than five minutes before it spoils."

"We know our time is limited," Isis says from where the five of us stand at the head of the long meeting table, where we've gathered a few dozen others from different areas of our miniature community.

"That's why we're holding this meeting. We need to put our minds together if we're going to make it out of this unharmed."

"How is *that* going to happen now?" a woman calls from off to the side. I spot Jule lurking behind her, his gaze distant—but I can't blame him if he's distracted. Britta shared the Project Nuwa records with him just a couple of hours ago.

"We need to accomplish two things," I say, raising my voice so it carries through the room. "We need to find a way to present the Nuwa information to the rest of Kemya so people see they can't trust the Council to treat us fairly. Then we need to propose a solid alternate plan for getting everyone to K2-8, to replace the Council's, offer hope of escaping the *vorth* problem, and show we really are focused on Kemya's best interests."

"Just that?" one of Celette's friends says with an edge of sarcasm. Celette, standing next to him with her new, barely mobile prosthetic arm, nudges him but says nothing.

"The second part shouldn't be that hard," Skylar says. "The Council hasn't considered any other options. Maybe we can reconstruct the engines with different materials that are easier to find. Maybe we can enhance the remaining engines so they'll move the station faster. You've had thousands of years to develop new technology—some of it must be useful."

"It isn't tech for propelling an entire space station," the woman near Jule says. "If the Council hasn't presented any other options, it could mean there aren't any. You don't know the station."

"We know the Council has had no issue with hiding information from us," I point out, "and we all know our history, don't we? Humans on Earth were able to spread across an entire planet with nothing but boats made of *wood*. We're resourceful enough to find a solution that won't take a century or more."

Skylar's eyes light up. "You *got* those people to Earth without moving the whole station. The smaller ships travel so much faster. Why can't we use those?"

There's a moment of silence. I find myself suddenly breathless. Of course. *I* should have thought of that.

This is why we need Skylar and the other Earthlings. We Kemyates have gotten so used to staying within the lines we've drawn around ourselves we can't see what's right in front of us.

"That was only a few hundred people," Zanet says, though he looks thoughtful. "And Earth is—was—closer."

"How much closer?" Celette asks eagerly. "How many ships do we have that could cross the distance?"

Britta taps her lips. "Our fastest ships could reach K2-8 in a ten-day or so, barring difficulties. Cargo ships and that sort, likely a month. The real difficulty will be fuel capacity. I don't think we have *any* vessels that could carry enough fuel to travel that far and then back to the station. We'd be stranded on the planet without any way of returning here for supplies or other help."

"Don't we need the station tech to get us settled?" Solma says. "How much could we carry on those ships?"

"Not a lot, if we want to make sure there's room for all of *us*," Britta says. "We'd have to make do mostly with the resources on the planet. But that's not impossible, only harder."

Skylar arranged for some of her fellow Earthlings—the tall, Zambian-looking man she's said was a teacher at her school; a woman from the Inuit Earth Studies exhibit; a man from the Japanese exhibit; and a former pet originally from Sumer—to join her here so they could provide their perspectives, with the help of a tablet translator program. At this last comment, the former pet murmurs to her tablet and hands it to the Kemyate guy who's been helping them.

"Shuanda wants to say that her people crossed a desert every year with only what they could carry in their hands and on their backs," he says as he reads from it. "She is not afraid to leave behind the"—he pauses and glances at her with a twist of his mouth—"the 'cold, stone-type things' here she sees no point in worshipping."

"All of us Earthlings are used to living on a planet," Skylar says. "The groups from Earth Studies have done some farming and even hunting. And we've all dealt with land and water transportation, and protecting ourselves from the weather—"

The Japanese monk speaks up, and she pauses. "There are others who have the skills to make clothing, and . . . tools," the Kemyate guy translates for him. "They would all rather help than be put back in that pretend home."

"That's all fine to say," Zanet puts in, "but we've only studied K2-8 from a huge distance. We won't know everything we'll need until we can analyze it closer up—and then it'll be too late if we've left behind something essential. None of us Kemyates are prepared with planet survival skills. We expected to have twelve years to learn beforehand."

"You won't need twelve years for the basics," Skylar says. "And we wouldn't have to leave immediately."

"But even the trip *there* might be dangerous in a smaller ship," another voice pipes up.

"So *what*?" I find myself saying in frustration. "We *know* it's dangerous to stay here on the station. I've seen how much data Ibtep has collected on K2-8. We'll have a good idea what to expect—better than the original settlers on Earth had."

The crowd has fallen into a hum of conversations among themselves. "It doesn't matter," a defeated voice says above the others. "No one will listen to us. No one trusts us now. Why should they? If we hadn't started this fight, we'd still have the engines and this wouldn't even be a problem."

The same thought gnawed at me as I watched Vishnu raging in the engine room, but the murmur of agreement that follows makes my gut clench.

"No, we wouldn't," I say. "Before any of us did anything, Vishnu and his group had decided to do whatever they could to keep us with our old planet. What could be more obvious than destroying the engines? Do you really think it would never have occurred to them? Look at the weapons they'd made. They didn't care who or what they hurt. They didn't get that idea from us either. If the Enforcers hadn't been focused on us, Vishnu would have created his own distraction, and likely hurt even more people along the way. Then the engines would still be destroyed, but, without us, the Council would have found an excuse to 'dispose' of the Earthlings, and we wouldn't have them here to help us when we need them more than ever."

"That doesn't change the facts," the medic says. "The moving plans assumed we'd have the support of the whole station. How could an attempt with a tiny portion of the resources we expected to have possibly succeed?"

That doubt is familiar to me too, a gnawing voice in the back of my head, conditioned by every Kemyate teaching I've been exposed to since birth. What if we can't? What if we forget caution and charge forward—and make a horrible mistake that ruins everything all over again?

That's the most horrible mistake. It's not the disaster that destroyed our planet, or our failure to foresee the problems the station's energy source would cause. What's *really* wrong with us is that we've let fear of failure become our defining characteristic.

All at once, I'm furious at all the mayors, the Councilors, the teachers, and everyone else who's encouraged that fear. The Earthlings standing in our midst have been ripped from their homes and are still willing to face the unknown with uncertain companions and unfamiliar tech, while we, despite all our pride in Kemyate competency, cower at the thought. This isn't who our people should be.

I'm furious enough that when a wild idea pops into my head, I don't dismiss it but follow it. I follow it onto the stool at the head of the table, onto the table itself, feet planted, staring down over the sea of heads. The murmurs die down as everyone stares.

Blast proper Kemyate decorum. I don't care if they think I'm ridiculous or overwrought. This could be the most important decision we make in our lives.

"When the first Kemyates landed on Earth," I say, "they were given nothing. They had no tech, no guidance, only their own minds and bodies. *Human* minds and bodies. The same as everyone on this station has. They and their world were worn down by shifts in time as the rest of us used them, but think about how much they were able to accomplish."

Words aren't enough. Tabzi is holding a coiled tablet. Before I've even asked, she sees my extended hand and tosses it to me, her eyes wide.

With a few jabs, I connect it to the large screen on the wall behind me. Images flash by as I flick through the Earth archives in the network. Feats of construction: massive bridges and dams, skyscrapers and towers. Works of art: da Vinci, Kaizhi, Yathentuk. Scientific leaps: compasses, steam engines, computers, spacecraft.

"That's what human beings are capable of, starting from nothing," I say, pointing to the screen. "We've spent thousands of years developing our tech, our resilience, and our efficiency. Our DNA may be flawed, but that doesn't have to stop us from accomplishing everything we want to. Humans are *stronger* than that. We could be capable of so much more if we stopped being afraid to reach for it. None of the people who created those things were perfectly prepared for their futures, and we don't need to be either."

"You can't be," Skylar says into the hush when I let my voice drop. "You can never be prepared for everything. There's too much in the universe that's beyond our control. So you use what you have and keep going after what you want. That's what we do. That's what being human should mean."

The gazes fix on her: the girl who unexpectedly lost her entire planet just weeks ago. We all know she and the Earthlings next to her will face a far harsher punishment than anyone else in this room if we fail, and they're ready to push on all the same.

"Just a couple months ago, a group of ten Kemyates managed to work secretly to bring down the time field around Earth with only a fraction of the resources they should have needed," Jule speaks up from the corner. He's talking to the crowd, but he looks at me, with no hint of the derision I might have expected before. "Four Kemyates organized you all to take over an entire third of this station with barely anything. You've followed Darwin's crazy ideas this far—and even I have to admit he's pulled them off. What's so different about this?"

The people around the table start to murmur again. Then Zanet says, "All right. So how would we convince the *rest* of Kemya to follow?"

Do we need the rest of Kemya? For a second, I'm tempted to say the bunch of us should hop on a couple of jetters and take off on our own. Of course, we need *some* supplies, and most of them are in the lower-level storage bays. There is also the small matter of Security being fully able to shoot us down before we make it out of station range.

Even if we could make it, my parents are still down there somewhere. Wyeth is still down there, counting on me. All of the people around me have friends and family they shouldn't have to leave to the Council's lies. I didn't take all those risks for myself. I took them for a better life for all of Kemya—for all human beings.

"The Council is holding their assemblies tomorrow," I say. "We can't communicate with everyone over the network, but we could reach a huge number of people face-to-face there. As long as there's a way we can . . . crash one of those meetings."

I glance back at my colleagues. Britta raises an eyebrow at me, and then hops onto the table herself.

"They'd arrest us before we can say anything," the medic says.

"Only if we don't plan it right," Britta says. "We have twenty-four hours to come up with a strategy: how to get ourselves in there, how to keep the Enforcers off us, and how to share what the Council has hidden, our alternate plan, and the value of the Earthlings' cooperation in a way that everyone will believe." She shrugs. "We've done more with less time before."

"If we could force the Council to admit to everything in front of all those people," Skylar says. "Bring the message, have them confirm it—it'd be nearly impossible for them to deny it later. And the blame will stay on them."

"That's a starting point," Isis says. "Talk about this, everyone. Think, research, do whatever you need to, and bring us any ideas you come up with—as soon as you can."

27.

Skylar

I zoom in and out, adjusting the angles of the 3-D assembly hall representation on my bedroom's computer terminal. Measurements and tech specifications blink around the edges as I explore. Getting in there is more Isis and Britta's area of expertise—I'm looking for inspiration for what we can do once we're in. How can we gain the stage? Convince the Council to corroborate what we say?

"Take a break sometime," Angela told me before she headed out to help escort half our sector's inhabitants to the cafeteria. "It's not all on you, you know."

It's not. But *someone* has to figure this out by tomorrow, or we're all screwed.

The doorbell sounds. I get up, glancing at the main room's screen out of habit as I go to the door, but the tech crew has the identification systems turned off. So I'm not remotely prepared to see Jule on the other side.

He's standing a step back from the doorway, his shoulders slightly hunched as if he's trying to compensate for how intimidating his height could be. Neither of those gestures stops my stomach from knotting.

"Hi," I say. I will not think about all the other times I've looked into those dark brown eyes, all the tiny joys that didn't mean half what I thought they did. I said everything I needed to before. He has helped us. I can be civil.

"Hi," he says. "I—" His gaze flicks up and down the hall. "Can I come in?"

I back up automatically, allowing him space to walk past. It's only once he's inside and the door has slid shut that it hits me: this is the first time I've been alone with him since the morning I drugged his coffee and forced him to confess to his betrayal. In a room nearly identical to this one. I cross my arms in front of me, wondering if he's remembering that too.

Jule is taking his time getting to whatever he needed to see me about. He meanders into the dining area, absently opening one of the cabinets. The one that still holds a few of the packets I took from his apartment. He glances at them, and then at me.

"You went?"

I shrug. "It was the only place on these levels I really knew." Civility. "Thank you."

He tips his head in acknowledgment. The silence stretches, itching at me. "What Ibtep said," I say, "about your family—do you think she meant it?"

"Maybe," he says. "It'd be difficult for her to bring them any lower than they've already brought themselves. I've told my father I'm not going to support him anymore. I shouldn't have for so long." His mouth twists. "Do you know, *he* never said so much as a thank-you when I bailed him out, all those times. It was throwing credits down a hole. I should have figured that out before I started."

"Yes," I say, unable to stop a bit of acid from creeping into my voice. "That would have been nice."

"I never saw it as choosing my family over the group," he says. "I thought I could serve both. It was stupid. I admit that."

"And your grandfather . . . ?" The one family member he spoke of with affection.

Jule waves his hand dismissively. "It's not as if he's all that clear on what's going on around him these days anyway. As far as he's concerned, the family's already disgraced, so if we're actually disgraced, it'll mean he's back in line with reality. His collections and his deluxe apartment aren't going to cure him."

He says it matter-of-factly, but then he lowers his gaze. "You've looked through the records. You didn't see any progress toward a treatment?"

I don't need to ask which records he means. "No," I say. "I'm sorry. You know—just because he's that badly off, it doesn't mean he passed those genes on to you."

"Everyone's been affected to some extent," Jule says. "And the effects are only increasing as long as we're on the station, aren't they?"

The comment reminds me of what I've been doing for the last few hours—the brainstorming I should be getting back to if we're going to be able to leave. I shift from one foot to the other. "Why are you here, Jule?"

"To talk to you," he says.

"About the genetic stuff? Because I'm really not the expert on that."

"No," he says. "I . . ." He stops, frowning, and I realize he doesn't have an urgent reason. This is all about *him*, again, waiting for some response from me he should know I'm not going to give. My patience snaps.

"I have things to do, Jule. If you just wanted to chat, this isn't a good time."

His eyes flash. "It's not—" he starts, voice raised, and cuts himself off with a muttered curse. He turns, bracing a hand against the wall. After a moment, he seems to have gathered himself. But he doesn't look up.

"Are you ever going to forgive me?" he asks quietly.

There's no impatience or accusation in the question, only raw pain. I swallow, my annoyance draining away. He's hurting. Because of his own actions, and, yeah, there might have been a time when I'd have *wanted* to know he was hurting after the way he hurt me, but now all I can think is there's too much pain in this place already. So I answer him honestly.

"Never is a long time."

He glances over at me. "Not any time soon, then."

"Jule . . ." I exhale. "I mean I don't know. Does it make any difference? I can work with you if I need to. If you just want your conscience clear for when you go after the next girl—"

"I don't *want* anyone else," he interrupts, and steps toward me.

"Well, you can't have me," I say, scooting backward. At my retreat, he stops advancing. He mutters another curse, a string of Kemyate I can't make out other than to catch the name *Darwin*.

"It's not about Win," I say, annoyed again. "Listen. You could be the only guy left on the station, and I *still* wouldn't be with you."

He hesitates. "You hate me that much?"

"It's not about hate either," I say. I reach inside me, feeling around the spots that are still tender, searching for the words to make him understand. "I don't hate you. It's just—you broke my trust in a huge way, and something like that leaves scars. Every time I look at you, I feel those scars first, before anything else. Even if I forgive you, they'll still be there. I couldn't just forget. And I don't know if that's ever going to change. It's not something I can control. Okay?"

He breathes in and out with a bob of his throat. "Okay," he says, and then, "I'm sorry."

It's the first time he's actually apologized. I don't know what to say.

"If that did change," he adds cautiously, "then you and Win . . ."

"I have no idea," I say. "It's kind of hard to look very far into the future right now. Maybe I'll want things to stay like this with Win as long as he wants that too, for however long that is. I guess it's possible something could happen again with you. Or we could all end up falling for some other people. Who knows? I'm not making any decisions about forever. I'd just like to get through the next few days *alive*."

"That sounds good to me," he says with a flicker of a smile. He heads toward the door, but when he reaches the threshold he faces me once more.

"I want you to know there was a while, with you, when I felt I could be someone else," he says. "Someone who wouldn't have sold his friends' secrets. Someone who didn't care what level his family lived on or what people said about them if it were true. But it's easy to feel you can be different and a lot harder to actually *be* that . . . I'm trying. Even if we can never go back to what it was like then, I'm going to keep trying. I'd rather be that guy."

I find I can smile at him and mean it. "I think I could at least be friends with that guy."

He smiles back, more fully this time. The scars inside sting less than they did a few minutes ago. Then he goes out, and I return to my work.

I sit there staring at the diagram of the assembly hall for several minutes, not quite there. Or maybe more *there* than I was before. I can remember, in vivid detail, gazing up at that enormous domed ceiling, squeezing through the crowd on the ramp between the tiers, standing by a dividing wall with Jule's arm warm against my back as we watched the Joining Day celebration. The spicy scent in the air, the trumpet calls, the impassioned speeches, the dance with its whirling ribbons.

And thousands of Kemyates glued to the spectacle.

I pause, considering the memory. I've been focusing on practicalities: how to maneuver the Council, how to present our message as clear facts our audience will have to accept. But Kemyates aren't all about facts, are they? They have human emotions, human imagination. They can still get caught up in a story. What if we drew out the theme in all this that we already know will hit them close to the heart?

Joining. Coming together as one people. It's already there, woven into their history. We can offer them a chance to recreate the moment when disparate groups of humans joined in cooperation—a unity exponentially more real than the type Nakalya and the Council have talked about, that's excluded so many.

Excitement bubbles up inside me, but the base problem remains. Even with a spectacle, we need time to present it, time the Council's not going to allow us.

Although it's not the Council members who'll stop us, is it? Their power isn't in what they do but what they order others to do. If no one listens to those orders . . .

Ibtep brought down the time field and set her world on a new course simply by appealing to a few people who happened to have the skills and positioning she needed to get the job done. Compared to that, what we need is so much smaller.

We just need to appeal to the right people.

I dismiss the diagram and hurry out to talk to Isis.

• • •

"She's on her way," Isis says through the communicator lodged in my ear. "Five minutes or less."

"Alone?" I confirm.

"It looks as though you got in unnoticed. Just keep it brief."

I glance around the seventh-level apartment, catching Solma's eye. Her answering grin would probably be more reassuring if she didn't look nearly as tense as I feel.

Being here wasn't part of my original plan. Someone on the tech crew pulled up the list of Enforcers assigned to tomorrow's assemblies, and I cross-referenced their families with the Nuwa records, finding two whose relatives have been afflicted with the same incurable "senility" as Jule's grandfather. Tabzi and Britta reached out to them. But of course there was the Enforcer who is herself afflicted, or soon will be. We all agreed that considering her particular animosity toward us, Kurra would be more likely to listen if we show how important this is by meeting her in person. And once we agreed on that, it became immediately obvious that the biggest impact would come from seeing *me*. The Earthling she's chased so long.

I clasp my hands in front of me to stop them from fidgeting. Enforcers leave their blasters in the Security offices when they're off duty. Solma is the best shot among the rebels, and she's got her stun blaster ready in her hand. The inner-shuttle stop that'll let us glide back to safety is just twenty feet down the hall. As long as nothing goes horribly wrong, I'll be fine.

I'd just rather not find out what horribly wrong would look like.

We're standing in the far corner, so Kurra doesn't see us when she opens the door. She stalks inside, white-blond hair swaying in its tight braid, and the door has closed behind her before she turns and her icy eyes stutter over us. Her pale face clenches. She reaches for the panel beside the door without a second's hesitation.

"*Wait!*" I say, my heart thudding, spreading my arms in a gesture of good faith. "*Give me a minute to say what I came to. I've brought something you need. Something that proves you're owed more consideration than you've been given.*"

I hope that's the right angle to take. My success here depends on her caring more about recovering her standing than about pure revenge.

Kurra pauses. Her hand leaves the panel, but she stays poised beside it as she studies us. Calculating how she might disarm Solma, disable us both, I suspect. I don't know if my words have caught her interest at all, or if she's simply thinking it will look more impressive if she presents the Council with the leader of the Earthling dissenters single-handed.

I toss the rolled tablet I was holding to her, and she catches it easily. "*You need to see what's on there,*" I say. "*The Council has kept secrets from everyone on Kemya.*"

"*More secrets about Earth?*" Kurra sneers. She edges closer.

"*No,*" I say. "*Secrets about all of you. Secrets like the reason they told your parents not to support your goals.*"

That draws her up short. Then her lip curls defiantly. "*More tricks. I learned that lesson about you before.*"

I nod to the tablet. "*It's all there. Don't you want to know why they forced you away from the life you wanted? Why your superiors are so quick to demote you? It isn't your fault.*"

She looks down at the tablet, her slim fingers tightening around it, and I risk pushing a little further. I want her to remember this too.

"*We're not so different,*" I tell her. "*Both of us were damaged without our knowledge. I think we both want the chance to prove that doesn't define us, and to stop the same thing from happening to others.*"

Her head has jerked up. "*I am nothing like you,*" she snaps, and then she lunges.

I flinch backward. Solma's arm twitches. The numbing bolt of light crackles into Kurra's hip. She stumbles, a hand's breadth from grabbing my arm. Solma shoots Kurra's other leg, and the pale woman collapses on the floor.

"Time to go," Solma says with a rasp.

Unwilling to give up, Kurra snatches at us as we dart around her. "*The next time,*" she snarls. In that moment, seeing her sprawled, limp limbed and near helpless, I'm not so terrified. I'm almost sad for her.

I pick up the tablet she dropped. "*Look at it,*" I say, throwing it to her again. "*I'm sorry we're leaving you like this. I don't blame you for striking out. You don't know. But when you do, you can help fix this, if you want to. You'll know the right time.*"

I can feel the fury in her eyes burning me even after we've stepped out the door.

. . .

By the time Solma and I reach the tenth level, I'm shaking, as if the full terror of facing Kurra has sunk in only after the fact.

Or not so after. She'll be there tomorrow. She'll have her blaster then—a blaster she's pointed at me before. The blaster that could turn me into a blackened mess like Evan, like Jai, like the boy she killed in Vietnam. Maybe she'll consider what I've said, what's on that tablet, or maybe she'll just be even more furious with us.

Win's waiting outside the shuttle stop. "Did she hurt you?" he demands when he seems me stagger off the glider.

"I'm fine," I say, dragging in a breath, but the shivers won't subside.

"She was great," Solma says.

Win touches my cheek. "Sky," he says, gentle enough to send another sort of shiver through me.

"I'm *fine*," I insist.

"All right," he says. "I believe you. Come here."

He doesn't really believe me, clearly, because where he leads me on my trembling legs is his apartment. But the truth is *I* don't totally believe me either, so I let him gather me against him on the bed. I burrow into his embrace, pressing my face against his chest, taking in his warm sand smell. We lie there, tangled and silent, as the tremors racing through me gradually subside.

Win strokes my hair. I ease away to look at him, and then I can't help kissing him. As he kisses me back, a flutter of desire races through me. But a stronger longing overwhelms it. I know better than to take the easy way again, to count on kisses and caresses to say everything that needs to be said.

Tomorrow our lives hang on the will of the Kemyate public. I've dodged these words, shied away every time I thought he might say them, but today I have to hear them.

I pull back and catch his gaze, falling into those deep blue eyes. It seems like too simple a question to be this hard to ask. Maybe I'm afraid he'll say no after all.

"You love me?" I whisper.

Win gives a breathless laugh and kisses me, hard, until I'm breathless too. He tips his head just enough for our lips to part. "I love you. *By my heart, by Kemya.* By Earth too. I love you, Skylar, more than anything."

I find myself laughing too. "More than coffee?" I inquire.

With a grin, he presses his lips to my jaw. "You taste even better."

"More than sunlight? More than fresh air?"

"I'd rather look at you. I'd rather feel you here."

My amusement dims as it occurs to me how close he's come to making that exact choice. "We could be asking too much, tomorrow," I say, serious now. "If we keep fighting . . . maybe they'll reject the whole thing. The move. Your new planet." The real home he's already fought so hard for.

Win's arms tighten around me. "It wouldn't be worth getting that," he says, "not if I knew somewhere else you were miserable, or . . ."

Or dead, he doesn't need to say.

I lean into him, following the tug of my heart. There's still so much I don't know about my future, or ours together. So much I can't predict. But this much I know for sure.

"I love you too," I say.

I hear him swallow, a quiver running through his body against mine. But when he speaks, his tone is light. "More than coffee?"

I really laugh then. "I should hope so."

He doesn't continue the questions, just holds me close. Maybe he recognizes that I can't say the same as he did. *More than anything.* I still don't know if I could say that to anyone, ever, but in a way that's an amazing thing. The way my scarred and battered but not broken heart has expanded, to hold everything and everyone I love. My parents and Angela, for joining me in this fight without doubting me or backing down in fear. Evan, who gave everything he had. Everyone in our little Earthling community, holding together, working to build a new home out of the scraps of Earth we have left with us and within us. Isis and Britta and Tabzi, and all the Kemyates risking so much to stand beside us. Maybe a little for Jule, still, under the scars. Maybe even for Ibtep, and Nakalya, and the Council, for the part of them that wants to protect their people, to offer safety and certainty. Human beings, stupid and scared and smart and strong all mixed together. Capable of so many sorts of love.

Even if I can't say "more than anything," I know what sort matters most to me right now, in this rare moment that belongs to just the two of us. I wind my arms behind Win's head, and bring his mouth to mine as the words linger on.

28.

Win

I tap on the hover function on my newly enhanced glider and step to the narrow opening in the breach seal. Isis's tech crew has manually edged up one of the overlapping plates that cover the assembly hall's dome where it peaks in the center of the ninth level. The glare of the dome's lights radiates up at me, obscuring any glimpse of the audience below. By all evidence, they can't see us either, but my heart is already thumping.

Security obviously had concerns about the dome reaching into our territory, because beneath the shell of the ceiling lies a vast deflection field, so powerful that, even with Isis's best efforts, she only expects to dampen it for a few seconds. Once we've dropped through it, we won't be able to escape back up. We have no other options, though. We need to be inside the dome to broadcast our data and enact the "spectacle" we've devised.

Tabzi had the idea that we should strengthen the association with Joining Day by wearing the holiday's traditional colors. The metallic gray outfit she found for me clings to my skin, sweat beading under it. Soon that crowd of nearly twenty-five thousand Kemyates below us *will* see me—in the flesh, not just as a recording on a screen.

If what we're attempting today fails, I'm not certain we'll even leave the hall alive.

The assembly has just started. As soon as everyone's in place—

"Go!" Isis says through the communicator link. I don't think, just leap. The six of us—Britta, Tabzi, Markhal, Solma, Celette, and me—plummet toward the dome's lights with a speed that lurches my stomach to the bottom of my throat. It's almost like Traveling, the jerking jump from one place and time to another. The lights blaze around me, and then I'm through, kicking the controls to hold my elevation. A hum so faint I feel more than hear it snaps back into place above me.

I blink the brilliance of the lights from my eyes, my head reeling. More than a hundred feet below lies the central platform where the distant figures of Nakalya, Ibtep, and the Council members stand. The mass of the audience stretches around them, divided by ten narrow ramps like the spokes on an old-fashioned wheel. It's too high for me to identify faces. In that first instant I can't do much more than catch my breath.

The one person who is identifiable even from this distance is Kurra, her pale hair glimmering where she's stationed near the edge of the platform. The two other Enforcers we contacted should be nearby.

"Start the footage," Britta says over the link, hovering at my right. In unison, all six of us flick on the tablets strapped to our sides, spreading out across the ceiling as we do.

The hall's projector display shimmers on around the platform, a translucent cylinder that rises to half the height of the enormous room. The Council members flinch, Nakalya halting his opening speech. Most of the Enforcers in the hall look up, Kurra among them. They knew where to expect us if we came.

My glider is already starting to tremble. We can only hold the safer positions up here for so long. I bring my amplifier to my mouth.

"Kemyates," I say, hearing my voice resonate out into the air, "before you decide whether to continue putting your trust in this Council and their plans, there's something you need to see. They've kept vital information from you to selfishly protect their own standing, but *we* are committed to letting everyone on this station make their choices with full knowledge."

The sea of faces ripples upward and then toward the display as the video archives Tabzi and Angela edited appear there. A melody swells through the room, washing over me. My heart thumps harder. "A spectacle needs music," I said when we were making our plans, and Skylar gave me a little smile, and I found myself not just admitting to my fellow Kemyates that I indulge in a "frittering" pastime but volunteering to create a song for this.

Now tens of thousands of people are hearing my creation. The Kemyate keys designed to provoke compassion and understanding blend with the rhythms of Earth that speak to me of harmony and community into one sweeping orchestration that carries away any lingering embarrassment I might feel. It may not be genius, but it's good. There's nothing frittering about creating a sound that could reach into people's hearts and open them.

"The Health division has been conducting these experiments in secret," Markhal is saying, the amplifier raising his voice above the music as the recording jumps to the deformed bodies suspended in their tanks. A collective gasp passes through the crowd. "Decades ago," he goes on, "they discovered that the vorth energy that powers our station alters human genes. The effects of the energy we've all been exposed to across the generations are adding up inside us, and will be compounded in our children, and our children's children."

"That is what Kemya will descend to, if we stay here," Celette says. "This is what the Council would have you live with, unknowing, so they can escape responsibility."

I seek her out where she's hovering across the hall from me, blue hair stark in the bright lights, head held high. When she volunteered to take part in this, I tried to argue, but she looked at me with that shrewd gaze she's had as long as I've known her, held up her prosthetic arm, and said, *This thing works well enough for me to hold on to a glider. I'm not letting some fault in my body hold me back.* There wasn't anything I could say after that. We're asking all of Kemya to think the same way.

When I glance down, my pulse skips. Several of the Enforcers are lifting off the ramps where they were stationed, legs braced in a *V*, arms up with guns ready. I give a shout of warning. We were counting on being out of firing range for the first, most essential part of our message. They must be wearing the propulsion vests that are normally only used outside the station, for hands-on maintenance work. Those will be slower but steadier than our revamped toys.

The Enforcers rise straight up, which gives us room to dart away toward the walls. One fires a shot my way, shattering a light fixture with a shower of plastiglass shards. I grip my glider, which is now outright shuddering.

Two Enforcers have veered toward Solma from opposite directions. I dip down and swing by to distract them, and the one that fired at me closes in. Her next shot splits the air just over my head, close enough that my breath stutters. Even if they're only using the stunning function, which is doubtful, a fall from this height would kill me.

The glider's almost ready to fall as it is. I study Kurra's form below. She's staring upward, gun in hand. We don't know if she even looked at the tablet Skylar gave her, which held her own medical history and all it portends.

We can't stay up here any longer, regardless. "Down, to the platform, before the gliders give out," I say through my communicator. "Keep talking!"

The display has flashed to archived interviews with patients with perpetually confused expressions. "Do you recognize relatives?" Tabzi says as we dive faster than the Enforcers can follow. "Friends? Former colleagues? We're already seeing minds that were once clear failing in ways the medical centers can't cure. The Council has known what was truly afflicting them, but let the medics tell us that the condition had no known—"

An Enforcer's shot catches the front of her glider, throwing her to the side. Britta zips in to steady her as we drop the last several feet toward the platform, the hover function sputtering out. Pirfi, the head of Security, has motioned the Enforcers around the platform onto it, waiting for us. The images on the display blur around us. I don't think it's been enough. My hands clench around the glider's bar.

Then Kurra springs through the display onto the platform, grabbing Nakalya by the collar. She jams the tip of her gun against his temple.

"Hold your fire!" her crisp voice rings out. Nakalya's lips part, his stance gone limp with shock.

The Enforcers hesitate as the six of us hit the platform. My feet jar against the flexible surface, and I swing the glider around as if I can use it as a shield. Pirfi takes a step toward Kurra and Nakalya, and one of the other Enforcers lunges to block him. A third—*our* third—aims her gun at her colleagues hovering above. All around us, the projected images of slack-jawed faces play on, dappling blue-and-yellow light across us.

"I want to hear this," the man who's facing Pirfi says. "I think we should all hear this."

"We're going to hear it," Kurra says, "or Nakalya dies. The rest of the Council too, if that's what it takes. You know I'm the fastest shot of any of you."

The remaining Enforcers look uncertain. Pirfi starts to speak, likely to give them an order, and the Enforcer in front of him slaps a hand over his mouth.

The audience looks even more immense down here, the sea of faces like a tidal wave flowing toward the platform from all sides. "We're not here to hurt anyone," I say to them all. "We don't *want* anyone hurt. We just want you to see what's true, and how we can help ourselves."

The Enforcers seem to decide they'd rather not risk the mayor's death. They retreat, but their attention is still trained on us, their guns ready.

The interview clips on the display give way to a series of reports. I draw myself up as tall as I can.

"Look at the dates," I say, picking up the thread of our script. "Look at the orders that were given. 'Deflect questions and focus on palliative care.'"

"If we'd all known about this as soon as those few who kept it secret did," Britta says, "we could have decided to move on, get off this station, all that time ago. We could have decided it without Earth's destruction pushing us this way. The Council has talked of loyalty, but they've been loyal only to each other. They, and the Councils before them, stole our choices from us."

When Skylar first explained her idea, part of me balked at dressing up the truth in dramatics. The rapt attention of our audience proves she was right. Barely a body stirs in the crowd. Most of the expressions I can make out look horrified. Now we need to ensure they direct that horror at the right source: not inward to the flaws inside them, but outward.

The Council members and Ibtep are seeing the same images as the crowd, in reverse from the inside of the display. The heads of the Education and Industry divisions look as horrified as the audience, whether because their shame has been made public or because they were ignorant, I can't tell. Enhom, the head of Health, has developed a sickly cast under her beige skin. Pirfi merely looks angry. Our mayor, with Kurra's gun tight against his temple, stands stiffly, his lips a pale line on his russet face.

When I swivel, I find Ibtep staring at me. Then her eyes flick upward again. Her jaw works. She's trying to maintain her composure, but I don't doubt at all now that *she* didn't know.

The footage on the display has zoomed in on the reports, highlighting the permissions given across the last several years.

"Your name is all through those files," I say, turning back to Nakalya. He led the Health division for ten years before he was mayor; he's been aware of the problem perhaps longer than anyone on this platform; he owes us more than any. "Will you deny it? Or will you finally give our people the honesty they deserve?"

Those words are a cue for the tech crew. With a snap, spotlights beam down from above, highlighting the Council members through the fading display.

Kurra jams her gun harder against Nakalya's head. He flinches, but his mouth stays firmly shut.

"This is preposterous—" Pirfi starts to shout, and the Enforcer guarding him pushes the muzzle of his gun closer.

"I've seen your name in those files too," he says. "My mother . . ."

"It's true!" the head of Education blurts out, his amplified voice echoing through the hall. "From the moment I learned of this, I've said you all deserve to know. It isn't right for Kemyates to keep such essential knowledge from each other."

"Easy to argue against the majority to clear your conscience, knowing you'd never have to face the consequences of what you argued for," Pirfi rasps, trying to shove past the Enforcer. With a jerk, the man throws him to the floor, where he pins Pirfi's hands behind his back.

The spotlight has sallowed Enhom's face. She opens her mouth and closes it again, looking as though she might vomit.

"Enhom," I say, taking a careful step toward her. "That is your division's lab. It was your people working there. Are you going to look at so many Kemyates and refuse to answer us?"

A cry I hadn't expected ripples across the tiers around the platform. The voices jumble together, but a few phrases rain down clearly: "Yes! An answer!" "Enough silence!" People are starting to spill onto the ramps, heading toward us. I watch them, tensing. We need their support, not a riot.

Enhom looks not at them, but to Nakalya, the man who handed off leadership of the Health division to her. I wonder if she had any idea when she campaigned for that role of the impossible dilemma that would come with it. Nakalya glances back at her. Just as she's opening her mouth, his square jaw twitches.

"I'll admit it," he says, and to his credit his voice doesn't falter. "What you have been shown is real."

Another cry carries through the hall, an almost wordless expression of the horror I saw on those faces. "If I could have changed it, I would have," Nakalya goes on hastily. He moves as if to stride to the edge of the platform, halted by Kurra's grip on his shirt. "When I was handed this problem, I didn't want to believe it was hopeless. I've spent the last twelve years working to find a solution."

"And getting no further than anyone before you," Solma says, brandishing her glider at him. "We deserved to know. You weren't thinking of us—you were thinking of your career, how people might turn on you if you took responsibility."

"It wasn't just *our* responsibility!" Enhom protests. "All of the Councils before—"

Nakalya raises his hand, and she quiets. "None of that matters now," he says. "I intended to put us on a new course toward a better home as soon as I became mayor. We would be on that course right now if some of our fellow Kemyates hadn't interfered."

Oh no. We are not going to allow him to turn this around on us. The words of his that have pricked at me for so long spring to my mouth.

"You've liked to talk about unity, mayor," I say. "True unity would have included *all* of our people, including those who have lived so long under our control on Earth. There was no unity in destroying so many of them and their world, or in trying to medicate the few who survived into numbness. That was fear."

I turn to the audience again. "Our mayor and our Council are afraid even now to trust in Kemya's capabilities. They've let themselves believe that the errors written into our genetic code make us so weak that any risk is too much. But the fact is, what you've just seen only proves how *strong* we are. Think of everything we've accomplished over the centuries: the tech we've invented, the vehicles we've constructed, the resources we've gathered throughout the galaxy. Think of the harmony we've kept among ourselves for so long. We've been able to do all that *despite* the damage the station has done to us."

"We can leave this station and reach our new home without relying on long outdated means," Celette says, stepping up beside me. "It will not be perfectly safe, but there is no perfect way. Nothing is perfect. Not one of us is perfect." She raises her prosthetic arm. "That has always been true. It's never stopped us before."

"We can move forward, to somewhere better, working with what we have, which is still so much," Britta speaks up at my other side. "We can show that the Council is wrong, that we *are* strong enough to survive."

"And that we have not forgotten the lessons of our ancestors," I finish, "who thousands of years ago recognized the strengths in other people so different from them, and instead of destroying each other, joined together to become even stronger. Among us right now are a people who would help us if we let them, who are strong despite their own degradation, and who have built hundreds of civilizations with nothing but what one planet provided them."

I ease over to the side of the platform, my gaze lifting to the ceiling as I brace for the pinnacle of our spectacle.

29.

Skylar

Y ou're sure you're ready?" I say to the people clustered around me. It's too late to call off this entire production, but if any one of them has changed their mind, I want them to know I won't force them to go forward.

Mom and Dad, Ms. Cavoy and Mr. Patterson, Cintia and Shuanda, Iqaluk and Nobu, and Angela next to me all nod. So do the ten Kemyates standing with us. We've lent them some of our Earthling clothes so each of us can wear a combination of Kemyate and Earthling styles. My Kemyate shirt feels strangely airy above my well-worn jeans.

Isis is monitoring the surveillance feeds from a tablet, sitting with her legs stretched out on the hall floor. Her graceful fingers dance above the thin surface. She rubs her chin and motions to two of her colleagues down the hall.

"Win is finishing up," she tells me. "Time to get out there." She pauses, and adds with a tense smile, "Good luck."

I raise my hand to her, all too aware this could be a permanent good-bye. There are so many people down there who might prefer that my fellow Earthlings and I no longer existed. But my companions are brave enough to face that, and I have to trust that the human beings below us can be brave enough to make the right choice.

Clambering through the opening to the assembly hall's dome, I stop just above the hum of the deflection field that stretches between us and the web of lights below. There, I flick on my glider and cast off. The tech crew worked through the night enhancing all the gliders we have, but they had to prioritize those Win's group would be using, since they'd need to stay out of reach longer. When Isis disrupts the field below us, ours will simply drop—just more slowly than if we had nothing at all.

I count the vertexes where the lines of light intersect until I reach the spot Isis told me to wait at. Angela pulls up beside me. She wobbles a little and steadies herself. We both clutch our gliders as we watch the others form a line across the center of the dome.

I find myself looking for a face I know I won't see. I close my eyes for a second, swallowing thickly.

"Evan would have been here," Angela says quietly.

"Yeah," I say.

He still is, in my mind and hers. He threw himself into danger so the rest of us could keep fighting.

"Ready!" a voice calls from the end of the line. I brace myself. The blue signal light blinks above us, and the surface beneath us falls away.

I can't help flinching as the glider falls with it. We plunge through the web of lights and on, down toward the circle of the platform below us. The cylindrical display that surrounds it flickers as the recorders Win and the others are carrying pick up our images and project them, larger than life, for the entire crowd to see.

The gliders slow as we near the platform, just enough that I feel safe unhooking my ankles and straightening my legs so I can land on my feet. As I catch my balance, I register the figures around us: Pirfi, the head of Security, pinned under a male Enforcer; Kurra standing with her blaster to Nakalya's head; the other Council members and Ibtep staring at us from the edges of the platform where Win's group ushered them to make room.

My companions touch down in their row beside me. Dad stumbles, but the Kemyate woman next to him reaches to help. I drop my glider and grasp Angela's hand, and she grasps her neighbor's. All down the line, our hands link in one long chain.

In front of me, Kurra jerks Nakalya around so she can face us, her gaze sharpening when it settles on me. Nakalya's broad forehead shines with sweat, the ruddy brown skin of his neck reddening darker against Kurra's wrenching of his shirt collar. I find I don't have much sympathy for his discomfort. At any time he could have used his authority to free us, to break the standoff, to speak up for Earth. And he never did.

I look toward the blurred mass of the audience spilling from the tiers onto the ramps, the lights from above dazzling me, and draw in my breath. My mind is whirling, but I know my lines by heart.

"*Hello Kemyates,*" I say, the amplification booming my voice away from me. "*Many of you have thought of yourselves and people like me as two different types of beings: Kemyates and Earthlings. One better and the other lesser, because of how your experiments degraded us and our planet.*

"*You've now seen that none of us is unflawed. But all of the things you did that you felt were great, you still did. I ask that you consider what Earthlings have accomplished the same way. We have crossed oceans and deserts, built cities and formed countries, survived and thrived in every climate from the harshest cold to the scorching heat. We have done all this starting with nothing but the raw materials on the planet where you left us. And all the while we have cared for one another as deeply as you can imagine."* My left hand tightens around Angela's.

"I challenge you to look at the people beside me," I go on. *"Ten of us are Earthling, ten of us Kemyate. Can you tell which is which? Can you see the slightest difference between us?"*

I pause, giving them a chance to look. And to think.

"I see only people," I say. *"Twenty human beings. I know you must be shocked and uncertain. I can give you one certainty. If Earthlings accomplished so much despite our flaws, if Kemyates accomplished so much despite theirs, then those flaws cannot take away our strength or our will. We have survived disasters and we can keep surviving. Thriving."*

As my last word echoes out into the air, a hiss sounds above us. The ribbons of light that accompany the Joining Day celebrations spiral down around us, swirling and licking over each other until they meld into one intertwined circle and dissipate over the audience. Enough of the spectators suck in their breaths that I hear the gasps from where I stand.

"You built your first ideal world, the first Kemya, by joining with the nations around you to make a larger, stronger whole," I say. *"You can do that again. We want to join you. Together, we can leave this station and the harm it's doing. All of us Earthlings are prepared to take the risks necessary. And if you let us join you, we pledge to help you in every way we can."*

"I studied chemistry on Earth," Mr. Patterson says on cue, the translator device the tech crew rigged projecting his words in Kemyate. "I can identify plants that could provide food or medicine; I can help create medicines for new illnesses we may face."

"I trained people in physical fitness on Earth," Mom says. "I can help you adjust to the new gravity and build endurance you'll need for planet life."

"*I hunted with nothing more than rock and bone on Earth,*" Iqaluk says in her own language, translated in turn. "*I can find food and materials for tools and clothing even if every tool we bring breaks.*"

"*I kept my people safe from sandstorms and floods on Earth,*" Shuanda says. "*I can read the weather and teach how to defend against it.*"

"*Each of us can offer something valuable,*" I say, "*And if you welcome us, we can all find that new life in far less time than the Council suggests. The original settlers on Earth didn't need a space station to protect them, and neither do we. You have ships: jetters, cargo haulers, scroungers. We can reach K2-8 in groups, with the most essential supplies, and make the rest with what the planet provides. If you will offer the ships and supplies you own, we will make that journey together.*

"*So we need to know: Do you mean what you say when you celebrate your Joining Day every year? Or would you dishonor everything your ancestors stood for by turning us away?*"

"*As a Kemyate, I welcome the Earthlings,*" Win calls out. "*Join us!*"

"*As a Kemyate, I welcome the Earthlings,*" Britta echoes. "*Join us!*"

One by one, our allies repeat the line. By the time Solma has spoken, the echo is carrying through the crowd.

"*Join us!*" A swell of voices rings out the same way the waves of praise swept through the audience that Joining Day when I stood among them. "*Join us!*"

A grin splits my face. We're not safe yet. Our victory could be temporary. But it still tastes sweet.

"*The more of us who join together, the easier the journey will be,*" I say. "*Think over what you've learned and what we've offered, and when you're ready, reach out to us. Show the Council where you stand. We will welcome all of you.*"

The display disintegrates, clearing the haze from my view. Thousands of Kemyates are crowded between us and the exits. People are shuffling back and forth across the ramps, trickling down toward us for a closer view. And the other Enforcers, the ones not assisting us, are poised around the platform, watching.

"*We've said what we needed to,*" I say. "*Will you let us go unharmed?*"

Win and Britta linger on the platform as Tabzi, Celette, Markhal, and Solma hop down and motion for the spectators at the base of the nearest ramp to move to the side. The people there are still watching avidly, but they all sidle over, clearing a path.

At the same time, four of the Enforcers who've been hovering near the first tier rush forward, raising their blasters. My stomach flips over.

"*Leave them alone!*" someone in the audience yells. Several Kemyates spring up amid the crowd, managing to grab the Enforcers' feet and yank them off course. The Enforcers wheel, aiming their blasters downward now, and several others lift higher before veering toward us.

"*Halt!*" Kurra shoves Nakalya forward, rapping the end of her blaster against his head. The Enforcers racing toward us slow, but two on the platform are edging forward now.

"*Stand down,*" Nakalya says, his voice strained. "*I order it. Let them pass.*"

"*Thank you,*" Kurra says. "*For your compliance, I'll make your death less painful.*"

Nakalya's eyes widen. His gaze darts to Win. "*No,*" he says. "*Please. I supported you—I held the Council back while you made your plans for the time field generator—I wanted you to succeed in disabling it.*"

Win raises his eyebrows. "*I have very clear memories of Enforcers hunting us down, many times. The one holding you in particular. That's what you call 'support'?*"

"*It would have been worse if I hadn't intervened,*" Nakalya says. "*We knew who was involved. We could have had Ibtep and the rest of you arrested, interrogated. We couldn't tell the entire Security division—we had to appear to be exerting discipline—it was the only way to release Earth while the public's opinion was so—*"

"*You knew?*" Ibtep breaks in. She swivels, eyeing each of the Council members in turn. Her olive-toned face has drained of color. "*How long? Who revealed it to you?*"

Silmeru, her superior as the head of Earth Travel, raises her chin haughtily. "*Did you really believe you could reach so far without being noticed? Security began keeping notes on you after your colleague Jeanant disappeared. Your actions following that first illegal expedition Earth-side convinced us.*"

My jaw has slackened. Then the entire time I was on the station, our secret meetings, Ibtep's political maneuvering . . . They knew. Maybe not the details, maybe not about me specifically, but enough.

They knew, they agreed with our cause, and they stayed silent. Did they intend all along that it would end not just with Earth's release but its destruction?

"*You blasted rotted lax-acts,*" Ibtep grates out. "*I fought for Kemya, for our people. I trusted that the Council wanted what was best for us and was only too conservative to realize what that was—but it was cowardice. You knew we needed to move on even better than I did, and you let me and my people take all the risks to protect your reputations."*

The wave of her arm at "my people" takes in Win and Britta but I think stops shy of me, even now. A murmur passes through the hall. Our voices are still projected. Everyone is hearing this discussion.

Most of the ramp has cleared. As disturbed as I am by Nakalya's confession, I realize I'm not all that surprised. Cowardice is the right word for it—and we've seen plenty of that from him and his Council already. I don't need to hear more. I need to get *my* people out of here before those Enforcers decide to take matters into their own hands.

I raise my arm to catch Markhal's attention where he's standing near the base of the ramp. He gives a brisk nod. "Go," I murmur to Angela, nudging her ahead of me. I'm not leaving until every other Earthling is out of here safely.

Tabzi and Solma reach to help Angela down from the platform, and Tabzi accompanies her and my parents up the ramp. A few of the Kemyates reach out as they pass, and I stiffen, but they seem to want only to brush their fingers over Angela's hair, everyone's arms, as if touching us will make them more a part of this moment.

Win comes up beside me, resting his hand against my back in that familiar steadying way. I long to lean into him, but I can't relax, not yet. As the rest of the line hurries up the ramp, with Solma, Celette, and finally Markhal escorting them, the Council members and Ibtep squabble on.

"*. . . our place to make these sorts of decisions . . .*"

"*. . . a duty to inform Kemya of the facts . . .*"

Outside the hall, Isis will have opened the seal on one of the shuttle tunnels, and our Kemyate allies will help us back to the relative security of the upper levels. Iqaluk is the last Earthling to climb down from the platform. I hesitate on the verge of following her, glancing back at the stage. At Kurra, still clinging to Nakalya, gun ready to deliver that fatal shot.

That's not how I want our spectacle to end.

"*Kurra,*" I say, "*there should not be any death here today.*"

At my voice, she yanks Nakalya around. He staggers but manages to stay on his feet. The other Council members fall silent.

"*He deserves to die,*" Kurra says, a manic light in her pale gray eyes. I can't tell if she's speaking to me or the audience beyond me. "*I ought to kill him for everything he's hidden, for all the ways he's allowed us to suffer.*"

"*No,*" I say. "*He . . . We're all flawed. We're all human. And we all deserve a chance to prove we're more than our flaws. He'll face the consequences. He has everyone here to answer to.*"

A hum of approval passes through the restless crowd. Kurra's jaw clenches. With a chill, it occurs to me that, while she might be angrier at Nakalya right now, that doesn't mean she hates *me* any less than before. If she shoots him, who'll be next?

"*How many chances has he already had?*" she demands. "*How many has he taken away from others?*"

"*Please,*" Nakalya says, his voice pained but steady. "*I was wrong, but I meant to help everyone. I swear I'll make up for my mistakes. By my heart, by Kemya.*"

The oath sends a tremor through Kurra. But she doesn't let him go.

"*This is a chance right now,*" Win says beside me. "*Your chance to prove who you really are, Kurra. Do you want to be shot down like Vishnu, too out of control to be saved? Is that how you want to be remembered—as the mayor killer?*"

Like Vishnu. I wonder if Win feels some guilt for how we pulled Kurra into this, not so differently from how we used his former classmate in our plans. But in this, at least, we only told her the truth and let her make her choice based on that. Even if her genetics are working against her, even if at times she's seemed unstable, I believe she's capable of more, I realize. When her blaster twitches, despite the hiccup of my pulse at the thought that she might kill us too, I hold still.

"*It's your choice,*" I say. "*You can decide what's right. They were wrong when they made you feel you deserved less than your brother, than the other Enforcers. You can prove it.*"

Kurra's hand trembles. Then her lips part with a gasp, and she shoves Nakalya away from her. She flings out her arms, dropping her blaster with a clatter as if she finds it distasteful.

"*I expect you to keep that promise,*" she tells Nakalya, and spins to take in the gathered Council. "*I expect you all to make this right.*"

The audience cheers like I haven't heard since Joining Day.

30.

Win

The day after the assemblies, I come out of my apartment and see Britta and a couple others hauling a sleek, bowl-shaped device with a dimpled interior down the hall. Britta shoots me a grin.

"I had a talk with the Industry head before I left the assembly hall," she says, "and a few of her people have delivered. That blasted microbe is about to be—what's the word?—kaput!"

The idea of a meal I don't have to race through makes my stomach pang. "How long will it take to clear out the level?" I ask.

"We need to set up a bunch of these," she calls to me as they hurry on. "But we should be good by the end of the day. Oh, and we've got our network posting access back!"

"Already? Who—"

They're gone through the archway to the next sector. I gaze after them, and my mouth stretches with a slow smile.

Our spectacle worked. There's no other possible explanation.

I'm lightheaded when I reach headquarters, but I don't think it's due to hunger. Isis directs me next door, where Tabzi, Markhal,

Celette, and Solma have already gathered. Skylar and the other Earthlings who've been speaking for their contingent arrive a few minutes later.

"What's going on?" Skylar says, linking arms with me. "Has something official happened?"

"I don't know," I say. I was so focused on putting our presentation together and getting through it alive that I never imagined what the best outcome might look like. No, more accurately, I was *afraid* to imagine and then be disappointed. Now hope is humming in the air. I interlace my fingers with hers, smiling again, and she smiles back before tipping her head against my shoulder.

She straightens up when Isis hustles in with a few members of the tech crew. We join Isis and Tabzi at the head of the table.

"I'm pleased to say that public opinion has swayed in our favor," Isis announces. She still looks tired, but joy shines through her fatigue. "A massive call has gone out for the current Council to be disassembled and new Council members elected. People have already begun evaluating our inventory of spacecraft and other resources to follow our alternate plan for reaching K2-8. And several key public figures, including the heads of Education and Industry and members of the secondary Councils, have spoken up encouraging the acceptance of the Earthlings into Kemyate society."

Celette lets out a little cheer, and the rest of us echo it amid relieved laughter. "What does that mean for us logistically?" I ask Isis. "Do we need to hold our position here?"

"Are we actually *safe* if we leave?" Skylar adds, glancing at her Earthling companions.

"It's too early to tell how stable this change is," Isis says. "And there are still many Kemyates who disagree, who think we should be incarcerated or worse. I think it's wisest to see how the next few days play out before making any decisions."

"Britta said we can post to the network again?" I say, and she nods. "We could present our own recommendations, then, to show how reasonable our intentions are. When we're secure enough, we could give most of the upper levels back to the original residents, but why don't we ask to keep this ward for the Earthlings and whatever other work we need to do? It was unoccupied before as it is. That would give us some protection from any militant anti-Earthers."

"Yes," Isis says. "I think the majority would accept that. Though it looks as though none of us will need to be here for very much longer. I've seen enough people volunteering their private ships and stores for the colonization attempt that I think those of us who wish to take the journey soon will be able to."

"The Earthlings should travel on the first set of ships," I say. "That way they can contribute from the beginning."

"And be out of reach if people here start going back to the old ways of thinking," Skylar puts in.

"Some of us Kemyates will need to stay here to oversee the rest of the move, won't we?" Tabzi says.

"Britta and I discussed that," Isis says. "Neither of us is so impatient to leave Kemya that we'd object to staying behind for the ten or more years it may take to move, if most decide to go. And our skills are best suited for planning flight patterns and load distributions. If anyone should be leading the way with the planet living, it's you two Earth lovers." She arches her eyebrows at Tabzi and me, her light tone stripping the teasing words of any insult.

"How soon do you think the first ships might leave?" Skylar says eagerly.

"Depending on how the first rounds of training go, and how supportive the new Council proves . . . It's likely we could be ready in a few months," Isis says.

I grip Skylar's hand as excitement steals my breath. Just a few months from now we could be setting foot on our new home. A real home.

. . .

As soon as we've adjourned the meeting, I slip into the closest private workroom. The records indicated that Security had released Dad and Mom, but during the few seconds it takes for my contact request to be answered and Wyeth's curious gaze to appear, I'm afraid Pirfi and the Enforcers still loyal to him might have dragged them in again.

"Win!" Wyeth shouts, breaking into a grin, and my parents appear at the screen behind him. They look weary, but well enough.

"I'm sorry," I say at once. "I know Security was holding you—are you okay?"

"The interrogations weren't . . . enjoyable," Dad says dryly, and rubs the back of his neck. "But we made it through. They found nothing to accuse us of."

"Nothing but two parents who believed the best of their child and so didn't press him for details about his activities," Mom puts in. She manages to sound almost amused. I exhale, my eyes suddenly damp. They really are okay.

"I stayed with Uncle Kenn and Uncle Ruul and Petra," Wyeth pipes up. "They basically interrogated me too, but I didn't tell them anything. I mean, I didn't know anything important, I don't think, because you didn't tell *me* anything." His look turns mock accusing. "Everyone's asking me about you now, Win. Are you coming home?"

From my parents' expressions, I think they already suspect my answer. "I can't," I say. "I'm sorry about that too. I have to keep working with everyone else up here to ensure the Earthlings stay safe and the move goes forward . . . You'll join in, won't you? You shouldn't stay here. I promise, we're going to make sure we have a good home on K2-8."

Mom hesitates. "We've talked about it," she says. "I think we'll wait until the reports from the first groups make it back, to confirm they've settled without trouble. Then we'll come."

"If Earthlings can do it, I don't see why we can't," Dad says.

There'll be a year or more when I'm beyond the reach of even making a call like this to them, then. Even as that regret ripples through me, I'm grateful to think Wyeth will be spared the harsher conditions of the first landings. "That makes sense," I say. "We may restrict the first voyages to adults without children besides."

"I'm in upper school now—that's not really a *child*," Wyeth says. "I could handle it."

"I'm sure you could," I tell him, overwhelmed by the urge to try to hug them through the display. "I'll come down and visit once we have our situation here better sorted out."

Just before we end the call, Mom reaches toward the screen as if she's had the same thought. "Thank you, Win," she says, beaming, and I don't know why I ever worried they wouldn't understand why I was doing this.

• • •

I'm in headquarters discussing the training modules with some of the tech crew when the first of two notable calls comes in.

"It's Nakalya," Isis says with a startled dip in her voice.

Our mayor, likely soon to be *former* mayor, hasn't been allowed back into the Council offices since deliberations began on whether to replace him, but he's still been the ultimate voice of authority for the past two years. It's hard not to stiffen when his russet face appears on the display. He's back to looking harried.

"I wanted to extend my hand," he tells us. "Whatever happens next, you should know I don't resent you for what you've done."

"How generous of him," Britta mutters, not quite quietly enough.

Nakalya's mouth slants. "I understand you have many reasons to resent *me*. You should know I— It was never my preference to restrict ourselves to repairing the station engines by the original specifications. I was eager to search for other methods, but I had to listen to my Council, and my Council, for the most part, felt a delayed response while we considered the alternatives would create further chaos. If I'd had more time, I would have—"

"You could have gotten the public's approval to pursue alternate methods by telling them about the vorth problem," I interrupt. "Don't pretend you weren't protecting your own interests first."

He's silent for a moment. "It's easy to accuse when you've never been in the same position," he says.

"Is there anything you wanted to offer us other than your lack of resentment?" Isis asks briskly.

"I'll encourage the Health division to contribute all the medical equipment they can spare for the flights to K2-8," he says. "I still have friends there. If this is what the people want, I'll support it however I can."

"All right," I say. "Then the people will thank you."

I suspect we're all thinking that we'll believe in his support when we see it in action.

Two days later, a call arrives from Ibtep. This time Skylar and I are the only ones on hand. I find myself bracing as I accept the request in the workroom next to headquarters. When Ibtep appears on the screen, she looks as though she's bracing for the conversation too. Her jaw is firm, her shoulders rigid.

"Ah," she says, peering at us as if she expected more.

"Sorry," Skylar says. "You just get us." The edge in her voice reminds me of our last private encounter with Ibtep, when she blamed Earth and Earthlings for everything that's gone wrong with Kemya.

"Why are you contacting us, Ibtep?" I ask, not feeling the need to bother with the usual honorific.

Ibtep's lips purse. For a second I think she might simply end the call. Then she says, "I wanted to ask you to reconsider this plan you're setting in motion."

I'm so startled I laugh. "And you think we'll listen to you?"

"I'm not suggesting that there is no merit to this approach, now that I'm aware of all the factors in play," she says evenly. "Only, in the fervor of the moment, what I'm seeing— I fear people may veer too far in the opposite direction. You can rein them in. Ensure they don't move too hastily."

"We're still going to be careful," Skylar says. "We're just not going to let everyone continue being so careful they never get anywhere. I think you might call that efficiency."

My mouth twitches, holding back a smirk, as Ibtep glowers at her. Watching this woman now, it's difficult to imagine I once respected her above everyone else on Kemya. She used to have dreams she was willing to take risks for. Is any of that person still there under the defensive mask she's giving us?

Just as I'm wondering that, she startles me again by sighing and saying, "Perhaps you are right."

"Really?" Skylar says, one eyebrow lifting.

"I'm not yet convinced . . ." Ibtep frowns. "There's a lot that I need to think through. I'll believe there is no cause for concern when I see that carefulness within the plans you're making. But clearly the course Kemya has been on was unsound in far more ways than I realized. Jeanant said, more than once, that Kemyates have as many flaws as Earthlings do, only different ones. At the time I saw that as poetic exaggeration." She stops, and inclines her head. "Perhaps he was right too. We shall see. I'll at least attempt to look with my mind properly open."

Her admission provokes a pang of sympathy in me, more than I'd thought I could still feel for her. "We aren't going to shut anyone out," I say. "There's room for everyone on K2-8. There'll be a place for you, if you still want to be a part of it."

"Even I'd agree to that," Skylar says quietly.

"I'll keep that in mind," Ibtep says. Then she cuts off the connection.

. . .

Somehow the days slip away from me as we throw ourselves into negotiations, organization, and training. Before it's quite sunk in, I find myself at my last night on the station. My last night on Kemya. Tomorrow I'll step onto a ship and sail for our new world, and I can't picture myself ever coming back. Yet at the same time it's difficult to picture *not* ever being here again—never returning to be hemmed in by the interlocking halls and tiny rooms, surrounded by filtered air and muted colors, as every other trip I've taken has ended.

When I leave the ship and see the planet all around me, that's when it'll be real.

The only thing I'll miss about this place—other than, temporarily, my family—is Skylar nestled here next to me on my bed. Our first group of colonists has plans for constructing living spaces as soon as we set down, of course, but we'll be starting simple so we can adapt as we discover what works most effectively. It'll be some time before we have this much privacy, this easily.

Skylar presses a kiss to my neck and shifts in my arms to gaze up at the ceiling. I just look at her. I could memorize the details of her face, this close: the pattern of her freckles and the faintly pink skin underneath, the curve of her forehead, lips, and chin. It's hard to imagine, too, that not so long ago we were completely unknown to each other, millions of miles apart. We're here, all this has happened, because I took a chance and reached out to her, and she was brave enough to take my hand.

"What do you think it'll be like?" she says. "Living there? I can't let myself assume it'll be a brand-new Earth."

"I don't know," I say, thinking back to the VR room and its limited impressions. "I can say I'm almost certain it'll be more like Earth than this station is. I suppose we'll find out the rest as we go."

She laughs. "True. Like everything, really."

That's true too. For all we Kemyates have tried, we've never been able to predict our own future or truly prepare for it, not with any accuracy, have we? I probe the edges of that idea, expecting it to provoke anxiety, but what comes is relief.

I don't want to know what's waiting on K2-8. I don't want the future to be a walled-in path. I enjoy being in this moment, where anything could lie before us. You could call it uncertainty—but you could also call it freedom.

31.

Skylar

We get one last glimpse of K2-8 from above as we file into the loading hall. In just a few minutes, we'll be dropping through those pearly clouds toward the green and blue of the planet's surface. Like Earth, but not. Someplace totally new.

"How long will it take to get down there?" Angela asks beside me, bobbing up on her toes to sneak a final look at the wall screen before we pass through the doors to the landing carrier, her eyes bright with nervous excitement. My nerves are jittering too.

"If all goes well, approximately an hour," Win says in front of me. "Possibly even sooner."

Jule, ahead of him, turns to arch his eyebrows. "Here eleven and a half years ahead of schedule and still in a hurry," he says mildly. "Do you ever slow down, Darwin?"

"Someone has to make up for the coasters like you," Win replies, but with a quirk of a smile. A small smile of my own touches my lips. The words are the same, but in the last few months their usual snarking has lost most of its bile. I could call it friendly banter now.

It's mainly because of those little steps forward that I gave my okay when Win told me Jule had requested to be on this first ship out.

Seats pack the carrier's passenger bay from wall to window-less wall. The whole space is a dull brown, but the dreary ambiance doesn't dampen my spirits one bit. I let Win and Jule and the other Kemyates with us take spots near the front while I hang back with my fellow Earthlings. It seems appropriate for me to be sitting among them, Angela at one side and Mom at my other, the rest settling down around us, this last fraction of Earth's people.

The planet below can't replace the one we lost or all the people we lost with it. It can't give us back all the choices the Kemyates stole from us over those thousands of years. But the decisions we make about the lives we live down there will belong only to us. No shifts. No panic attacks freezing me up. A world that's *right* and real and truly ours.

A part of me hopes that in that new world, we might all start to heal—Earthlings from the damage of the shifts, Kemyates from the damage of the station's energy emissions. But a bigger part of me knows it's okay if we don't. All of us, Earthlings and Kemyates, flawed in our various ways, are in this together. Once we're living and working and surviving together, I think we'll start to forget we ever saw any differences between us. That's what matters. We were never going to be perfect anyway.

"*All clear for transport*," the pilot's voice says through the communication system, which automatically follows with a translation in the many languages of the people around me. "*Prepare for disengagement.*" A hum rises through the room. Angela grips my arm.

After a few minutes, the seats we're strapped into begin to tremble. The blank walls offer no hint of what's happening outside, but I imagine the carrier descending through the layers of the planet's atmosphere. The trembling intensifies. I lean my shoulder against Angela's. My heart rises to my throat as the pilot's voice counts down to landing.

There's a jolt, and the hum and the trembling fade away. The crowd of us in the passenger bay lets out a collective breath. The pilot chats briefly with his colleagues, confirming the air quality, rechecking for environmental dangers in the landing zone. A restless itch tickles over my skin. Finally, the call carries back to us: *"You're cleared to disembark!"*

With a hiss, the seal on the outer door unlocks. We release the straps and scramble to our feet. My pulse is thudding, my chest tight. Jule, who was sitting close to the door, glances back. His gaze finds me.

"Skylar should go first," he says. "We wouldn't have made it here without her."

It wasn't just me. It took everyone here, and many more back on Kemya still waiting to make this voyage. But a murmur of agreement ripples around me, and Win motions me forward with a grin. I squeeze up the aisle to join him, grasping his outstretched hand. He nudges me half a step ahead of him, toward the door. Jule eases back at my other side to let me take the lead.

I inhale, exhale. Touch the control panel. Enter the command.

The door whispers open, half of the curved surface sliding up into the hull and the other folding down into a ramp. Sunlight streams through the expanding opening. Real, brilliant, beautiful sunlight, with a rush of cool air. Sharp green scents prickle into my nose. None I recognize, but the blue of the sky unfolding above us sends a pang straight through me.

Home.

From this moment on, an infinite spiral of possibilities stretches out in front of us. I raise my head, and step out into it.

ACKNOWLEDGMENTS

As I bring the Earth & Sky series to a close, I offer my immense gratitude to:

The Toronto Speculative Fiction Writers Group and my critique partners Amanda Coppedge, Deva Fagan, and Gale Merrick, for helping me clarify my vision in the early stages.

My agent, Josh Adams, for finding this series its home and taking care of all the details I'd forget.

My editors, Lynne Missen and Miriam Juskowicz, for pushing me to make this series as good as it could be.

The teams at Amazon Skyscape and Razorbill Canada, for everything they've done to make the finished books beautiful and get them into the hands of readers.

My family and friends, for always being there when I needed them.

And everyone who has followed Skylar and Win this far, for your excitement and support—I hope the conclusion to their story is everything you hoped for!

About the Author

Like many authors, Megan Crewe finds writing about herself much more difficult than making things up. A few definite facts: she lives with her husband, son, and three cats in Toronto, Canada (and does on occasion say "eh"); she tutors children and teens with special needs; and she can't look at the night sky without speculating about who else might be out there. Along with the Earth & Sky trilogy, she is the author of the paranormal novel *Give Up the Ghost* and the postapocalyptic Fallen World trilogy. She can be found online at www.megancrewe.com.